HER Guarded HEART

A NOVEL BY SHARLENE MACLAREN

HER *Guarded* HEART

WHITAKER
HOUSE

Her Guarded Heart

Sharlene MacLaren
www.sharlenemaclaren.com
sharlenemaclaren@yahoo.com

ISBN: 978-1-64123-799-4
eBook ISBN: 978-1-64123-800-7
Printed in the United States of America
© 2022 by Sharlene MacLaren

Whitaker House
1030 Hunt Valley Circle
New Kensington, PA 15068
www.whitakerhouse.com

Library of Congress Cataloging-in-Publication Data
Names: MacLaren, Sharlene, 1948- author. | Whitaker House (New Kensington, Pennsylvania), other.
Title: Her guarded heart / Sharlene MacLaren.
Description: New Kensington, PA : Whitaker House, [2022] | Summary: "Romance novel set after the assassination of President Lincoln centering on a young woman trying to hang on to her family farm, a neighboring farmer, and a land baron who will stop at nothing to get what he wants"-- Provided by publisher.
Identifiers: LCCN 2021054513 (print) | LCCN 2021054514 (ebook) | ISBN 9781641237994 (trade paperback) | ISBN 9781641238007 (ebook)
Subjects: BISAC: FICTION / Christian / Romance / Historical | FICTION / Romance / Action & Adventure | GSAFD: Christian fiction.
Classification: LCC PS3613.A27356 H46 2022 (print) | LCC PS3613.A27356 (ebook) | DDC 813/.6--dc23
LC record available at https://lccn.loc.gov/2021054513
LC ebook record available at https://lccn.loc.gov/2021054514

1 2 3 4 5 6 7 8 9 10 11 ⅏ 29 28 27 26 25 24 23 22

DEDICATION

To Marcia, my forever friend,
the one with whom I share grandjoys and giggles,
but also a special bond that makes us sisters.
"Marcia! Marcia! Marcia!"

⌒

When I wrote the above dedication to my dear friend Marcia Tisdel, I had no idea that on May 17, 2021, Jesus would take her home. My heart tore in two that day. I didn't see it coming. None of us did. But looking back, I do see that God had a perfect plan. He always does.

You left too soon, my wonderful friend, but this one thing I know...I will see you again.

I love you and miss you.

Northwest Plot
Clue #1
Warm Waters Creek
Corn Field
Garden
Grazing Land
Drake Road
Soy Field
Clue #2
Southwest Plot

↑ *Fuller Land*

Northeast Plot

Grazing Land

Grazing Land

N
↑

Warm Waters Creek

✗ *Clue #4*

Tree Stump

Corn Fields

↗ *Fuller Land*

Hansen Farm
50 Acres

If thee uses thee eyes and searches thee mind,
a jeweled treasure thee will find.

Wheat Fields

Clue #5
✗ Large Boulder

↗ *Wish Bone Tree*
✗ *Clue #3*

Stone Boulders

↓ *Fuller Land*

Southeast Plot

1

June 1865 · Lebanon, Ohio

Jesse Fuller wiped his sweat-soaked brow with his sleeve, then lifted the jar of water to his mouth and gulped a few swigs, twisting his face into a frown at its lukewarm temperature. At least it was wet, he told himself. Briefly staring up at a hazy sky, he absently screwed the lid back down on the jar and set it on the wagon seat next to him, then took up the reins. He didn't coax the horses into moving quite yet though. No, instead, he cast his gaze out over the acres and acres of Fuller land—as far as the eye could see—with the exception of one portion of their property that butted up to the Hansen farm. Knee-high fields of corn bent to the hot, dry winds as he lowered the brim of his hat to ward off the worst of the sun's burning rays and looked off in the direction of the farm.

Newell Hansen had collapsed in his barn a couple of months ago—eerily, one day before the assassination of Abraham Lincoln, a tragedy that made mourning his neighbor and family friend more complicated, as emotions of every kind swirled with a punishing vengeance. Even now, a rock-like heaviness settled at the center of Jesse's chest, a combination of worry and guilt. Newell had left behind his daughter and son, Anna and Billy Ray, and while Jesse and his brothers had done their best to help the two stay afloat, it was clear Anna couldn't hang onto that farm much longer. Some months before his untimely death, Newell had mentioned that the bank had started foreclosure proceedings. According to the county coroner, Newell's death came as a result of having consumed some poisonous substance—arsenic had been the doctor's best guess—but it was unclear whether Newell, in his distress, had consumed it intentionally...or whether something more sinister had occurred. The coroner knew the cause of death, but the circumstances surrounding it lay in question, a fact that left the citizens of Lebanon a bit on edge.

Sheriff Charles Berry and his deputies had interviewed multitudes of people, including Jesse and his brothers, seeking any clues that might shed light on the mysterious death. Some speculated Newell may have taken his own life; it was no secret he was experiencing a financial crisis ever since his hired bookkeeper had robbed him last year and then run off to gamble away the stolen money. But Jesse couldn't imagine Newell Hansen, a godly man in his eyes, ever ending his own life. He was young enough, fifty something, to start over. Besides, he had a daughter and young son who depended on him. No, impossible. But neither could he fathom anyone wishing him bodily harm. He'd never known anyone to dislike the fellow, and if he did have any enemies, Newell had never mentioned them to him or his brothers.

"You ought to marry that Hansen woman," Jack had said a couple days ago while they were in the barn brushing down horses after a long day in the fields.

Jesse had stopped and gawked at his older brother. "What? Where did that come from?"

"Why not? Your marrying her would ensure we got our hands on that property before someone else snags it up. Rumor has it Anna and her kid brother will be forced out of their home, and who knows if they even have a place to go. Think of it—adding Newell's fifty some acres to our own farm could mean expanding our business into an even bigger, more successful operation."

"Yeah, and you could stop being a mama's boy," Joey had added, grinning from behind his horse. As if *he* should be giving advice after advertising for a bride, fer cryin' out loud!

Jesse had snorted and went back to brushing his horse. "Don't be crazy. Just because I live with Ma don't make me her favorite, even though it's clear I am. As for Anna Hansen, I did take her out a couple of times before Newell passed, but it didn't go all that well."

"What was the problem?" Joey had asked.

"I don't think she much liked me."

Jack had shrugged. "Well, you do lack charm."

"Yeah, maybe Jack and me ought to teach you a few things," Joey had added with a laugh.

"Yeah, because both of you are dripping with charm. Uh-huh."

"What'd you do on your first date, bring her down here to the barn and show her your prized heifer?"

"No! Not that it's any of your business, but I took her to one of those traveling shows. There was a magician, some dancers, and a guy who played some instruments and tried to sing. It was in early spring, maybe late March, and still pretty cold out. She didn't dress warm enough."

"Did you give her your coat?"

"Huh?" He'd looked at both brothers as if they'd lost all their teeth. "No, I didn't think to."

"Well, there's your first mistake," Joey had told him. "A woman likes to know she's being cared for. Your coat over her shoulders would have been a nice gesture."

"Oh." Jesse hadn't thought of that. "Well, when we got back in the wagon, she did pick up the blanket in the back, and I helped throw it over her lap."

"*She* picked it up? Jesse, what's wrong with you?"

"Okay, so I lack experience!"

"You shouldn't. It's not like she's the only girl you've ever dated. Did you ever try to redeem yourself with her?"

"I did take her out one more time, but I wound up doing all the talking. That time, we walked around town and looked in the windows. I think she was bored to tears, even though we did stop at Dinah's Bake Shop and get a pastry to share."

Joey had rolled his eyes. "Man, you're romantic."

"Lebanon isn't overflowing with things to do. Anyway, a couple of dates was enough. Besides, she's too young for me, probably still a teenager."

"She's at least nineteen, maybe twenty," Joey had said. "And she's as pretty as a poppy."

"And I'm twenty-seven. So, like I said, too young."

"That's not too young. Lots of women marry older fellas," Jack had chimed in.

"Why you bringin' up marriage? I don't have time for a woman in my life, much less one with a little brother."

"You like kids. Our own young sprouts are all over you," Joey had argued.

"They're my nieces and nephews. That's different. I don't have to feed them."

"You're not gettin' any younger, little brother. Most twenty-seven-year-olds already have a passel of kids."

"Whatever happened with Martha Weaver?" Jack had wondered. "You took her out a few times last winter. I thought maybe something would come from that."

"Yeah, I took her out a few times, but she was way too eager for my liking."

Jack's eyebrows had shot up. "Eager? How so?"

"That woman is bent on getting married. She brought up the subject herself. Scared the leaping lizards right out of me. I let her off at her door one night and told her I didn't think things were going to work out for us. I heard just a couple of weeks ago she's engaged to marry Frederick Upton, the barber."

"Whoa! She doesn't waste time," Jack had said with a chortle.

A bit of silence had come between them as they finished brushing down their horses, putting the tack away, and filling hay nets and grain bins.

"I say you ought to give dating Anna Hansen one more try," Joey had said. And of course, Jack had agreed. But Jesse hadn't favored them with a reply.

Now, staring out over the vast property, he mulled over that discussion. It wasn't that he didn't like women. They were fine, he supposed, and Jack and Joey had solid marriages. He just wasn't convinced marriage was for him, never mind that even Newell himself had encouraged Jesse to give his daughter a second look. "Come on over for supper some night soon," he'd mentioned only days before he'd died. "I'll have Anna fix us a good supper, and you'll find out what a fine cook she is." Of course, the supper had never transpired, and now with Newell gone, he was certain things would be all the more strained between him and Anna. Besides, he'd convinced himself she didn't like him. Just this morning he'd taken a rare look at himself in the mirror and determined he wasn't much to brag about, so was it any wonder?

He didn't wish for Anna Hansen to lose her father's farm, but why should saving it become his responsibility? Sweat dripped off his four-day-old beard. About once a week, he shaved. If he were really looking for a woman, he'd care a bit more about his appearance, although Martha Weaver never had complained. Great Scott! She would've married him if he'd been missing an eye and half his teeth! He found himself staring off in the direction of Newell's farm again. He still had a difficult time believing he was gone. Who had poisoned him? Or had he accidentally consumed it in something? One of these days soon, he'd pay a visit to the sheriff's office and do a little snooping. Hopefully, the case hadn't gone cold already.

He unscrewed the jar of warm water and took a couple more gulps, then threw the rest of it on the ground and set the jar back on the seat beside him, mulling things over as he perused the land around him. He supposed marrying Anna did make a hair's breadth of sense, but only a *hair*. The extra land *would* be useful for grazing and planting additional crops, not to mention getting out from under Ma's clutches. For the teeniest moment, he wondered if he ought to go knocking on Anna's door just one more time to see if he caught the slightest glint of interest in her sky-blue eyes. He shook his head several times and scowled, his brow going taut. What was he thinking? Had today's scorching sun started frying his brain?

His stomach growled, reminding him of the supper hour. Without any further ado, he gave the reins a little flick and put his two-horse team into action. Ma would have supper on the table, and she wouldn't want it getting cold. As he made for the big house on the other side of Fuller land, the wagonload of chicken wire and fence-mending tools rattled behind him.

$\mathscr{B}$ut, Anna, you know I hate asparagus," the boy whined.

"Hush, Billy Ray, you know better than to complain about what I fix. We don't have much, but what we do have, we eat, and we give thanks for it."

"Sorry." The ten-year-old forked another short spear, stuffed it into his mouth, then winced and followed that up with a quick gulp of water.

She might have smiled if she'd seen any humor in it, but her own plate of lettuce leaves, cucumber slivers, a small portion of fried potatoes, and a slice of dried meat did little for her appetite either. She was scraping the bottom of the barrel, being that every extra cent she'd earned from selling eggs in town and doing odd sewing jobs for folks went straight to the bank. "I did make rice pudding. How about we eat what's left on our plates and then have our dessert?"

Billy Ray shoved his food around a bit and nodded, then made a valiant effort to eat another cucumber slice before digging into his potatoes.

"Did you finish your barn chores before supper?"

"'Course I did. Don't I always?"

"Yes, you do, and I appreciate it."

"Who'd you sell Harold to? I miss taking the slops out to him."

Harold had been their fattened hog. Anna's heart ached just a bit at the mention of the critter. As many times as she told herself not to get attached to the farm animals, it never seemed to fail. "Mr. Bartlett from up the road bought him. I gave most of the earnings to the bank, keeping out just enough to get us by until—well, until Mr. Daly tells us we have to vacate the premises." Another wave of sadness came over her.

"Yeah, I saw him come up the drive the other day. Did he come to beg more money off of you?"

"No, he just came out to check on us—and to remind me of our impending deadline. What money I give him doesn't make much of a dent in our debt. I've whittled it down some, but that's only because I forced myself to sell most of Papa's farm machinery and a lot of our livestock."

"And Mr. Daly ain't willing to work with us?"

"I'm afraid it's a rather dire situation. I hate to be the bearer of all this bad news, but it happens to be our present reality."

Glum-faced, he poked at his food, staring down. She knew the feeling. It was hard to cook a tasty enough meal when you lacked the ingredients. She needed to find a job in town that would earn her enough money to rent a little house and support them. It sounded like an impossible task, but with God, all things were possible. Even now, she said a quick prayer for guidance and provision. Lately though, little doubts about whether God truly cared had been pressing in on her. They needed a miracle, but so far, none had come.

Her mother had died just one year after Billy's birth, and her father had passed two months ago. It had been a great shock to find him lying flat out in the middle of the barn floor, a shovel still clutched in his hand. Her heart ached now at the memory, especially if she allowed herself to ponder the cause of his death—heart attack, yes, but by natural causes or something sinister? Doctor Roossien said the county coroner had detected a poisonous substance in his blood, but he told her not to worry too much about it. He said if there was any investigating to be done, the sheriff would see to it. She knew now Doc Roossien had only said that to appease her. If poison had entered his bloodstream, how had it gotten there? Folks didn't discuss it in her presence, but she knew full well tongues wagged. Did someone purposely poison Papa, or had he intentionally swallowed it? Had his sorry financial state driven him to take his own life? She couldn't even bear such a dreadful thought, and so she rarely dwelt on it. By now though, everyone about town knew the farm was in foreclosure proceedings, so she supposed it was natural that folks would wonder. The whole thing plain rattled her, making her question everything about her life.

"We wouldn't be in this mess if that Mr. Carlisle hadn't stolen from him."

"Yes, that is true, and now he'll be sitting in prison for ten years. Not that that helps us any. I didn't realize till after Papa died just how much that bad egg set Papa back financially. I knew he cheated Papa out of hundreds of dollars, but Papa always led me to believe that we still had plenty to get by on."

"But we didn't?"

Anna gave her head a sad shake and stared down at her wilting lettuce. "I wish I could protect you the way Papa tried to protect us, but—"

"I don't need protectin', Sis. I'm growin' up." This he said with a sternness she'd never heard before, and it was difficult to accept that perhaps it was true—he was growing up. Since her mother's death, she'd taken over the primary care of him while their father and his hired hands worked the fields, and it occurred to her that she'd not been much older than Billy Ray was now when she'd taken on that responsibility. Grief and loss had stolen her childhood, and now the same thing was happening to her brother. Sadness tried to force tears, but she wouldn't have it. She had to stay strong, and by gum, she would!

She pulled herself straight in her chair, cleared her throat, and lifted her chin. "Yes, you are growing up. I won't argue with you on that. We are going to get through this one way or the other, Billy Ray."

"And keep the farm, you mean?"

"No, not that, I'm afraid, but whatever comes our way, we'll get through it together. God will make a way for us."

"Do you really believe that—about God?"

"I should say so, and you must as well. I know we haven't been back to church in a while, but perhaps we will one of these Sundays."

"I don't want to go back without Papa."

"I know. Since Papa's passing, everything has been a bit harder for us, but as time goes by, we'll adjust." She tried to don a smile, but it wasn't easy. "I know it's sometimes difficult to believe God has a purpose in all things, but He does. We must cling to that truth. Doubting His goodness only brings discouragement, but clinging to Him in faith brings hope. Just yesterday I read in my Bible about His deep, unfathomable love for us, especially in times of sorrow and great need."

"Hmm," he mumbled, obviously not too interested in hearing another of her sermons. "When did Mr. Daly say we have to move out of our house?"

She took a sip of water before answering. "We have until June thirtieth."

"Do you think Papa knew the bank was going to take back our farm?"

She thought on that for a moment. "Yes, I'm afraid he did."

"I wonder if that made Papa sick. Maybe his heart gave out because he was over-worried."

She stared at the ten-year-old, and for a moment she felt as if she were gazing at a little old man. He had too much wisdom for one so young. "The thought has occurred to me, but...I don't know the answer." She had never mentioned to Billy Ray about the coroner's findings, nor did she intend to. There were some things a young'un was just better off not knowing.

"I hate Mr. Daly!" Billy said out of the blue.

"Don't say such a thing! There is no room for hate in this house."

He hung his head. "Sorry."

"Never mind. You're entitled to your feelings, but, really, it isn't Mr. Daly's fault. He's just doing his job. Let's finish our supper, shall we—and talk about something else?"

They each resumed picking at their food, pushing it around on their plates as they mused their own separate thoughts.

Outside, Rex, their black and white farm collie, barked—as he was prone to do at the least little movement. He made it his responsibility to let everyone know if so much as a squirrel had the nerve to scamper across their property. She had learned to ignore his barks.

"I wonder who's gonna buy our farm—if we can't keep it."

She gave a sigh. "I don't know. I know Mr. Blackthorn has expressed interest. Mr. Daly told me he's quite determined."

"I know that guy. He used to come out to see Papa off and on. There was a few times when I was out in the barn doing chores when he stopped by. Sometimes, they raised their voices at each other, but I never paid much attention to what they talked about. I always had the feeling Papa didn't like him much though. Don't know as he'd like it if he knew Mr. Blackthorn was gonna buy the farm."

"I have to agree, Billy Ray. Papa once told me that bad blood flowed between him and Mr. Blackthorn, but he refused to elaborate on it, saying it was pure foolishness. He said he'd tried various times over the years to clear up any misunderstandings, but that Mr. Blackthorn wouldn't listen. I don't know anything beyond that. And now I fear I've told you more than you need to know."

"No you haven't. I ain't any smarter now than I was ten minutes ago."

She looked at him across the table and giggled. "Well, I guess that's true. I've told you exactly what I know, which is nothing." They both took another nibble from their plates before Anna added, "I do agree there was something about Mr. Blackthorn's visits that put Papa on edge, but he always told us to be kind and love our neighbors, so if he did have any harsh feelings for the man, he likely would not have admitted it.

"Anyway, let's not talk about it anymore. I've been looking realistically at our future and realize I must get a job in town, something that pays enough for us to have a little place of our own while also putting food on our table. I could work as a seamstress, or a baker, or a restaurant cook."

"You don't got much experience in any of those."

"What do you mean? Are you questioning my abilities?"

He gave a shy grin. "No, I just mean you haven't never had a real payin' job. I don't know if you can do anything good enough to get paid for it."

"I beg your pardon. I have taken on a number of tailoring jobs, and folks seem very satisfied with my work. Maybe I'll open my own little shop."

He stared at the wall over her shoulder. "I s'pose you could do that." His light blue eyes brightened. "Maybe you could open a restaurant. You're a fair cook."

"Only fair?"

He lifted his upper lip in a dour way and cast his eyes at the pathetic fare on his plate.

She snickered. "I'm not a magician. I can't make a delicious meal if I don't have the required ingredients."

"I know, I'm just joshin' you, and to prove my point, watch this." He forked up another portion of asparagus and practically swallowed it whole. Just as quickly, he snatched up his water glass and took a big gulp. "There, how's that?"

"My goodness! I'm proud of you. I guess."

They shared a bit of laughter before he grew serious again. "You seen any 'Help Wanted' signs in town?"

"No, but every time we drive into town, I do look for them. I'm not too worried. Something will work out. Perhaps tomorrow I'll go pick up a copy of the *Lebanon Western Star* and look for postings there. The main thing for both of us is to remain positive and not forget that God is in control, and He will provide for us."

The boy just nodded, and she said a silent prayer that her words would ring true.

3

"This is good, Ma." Jesse shoveled another spoonful of thick beef stew onto his spoon, then blew at the steam coming off it before putting it in his mouth and enjoying its rich flavor.

"I can tell by your slurping that you're enjoying it." She gently patted her chin with her cloth napkin.

He instinctively sat up a bit straighter, knowing if he didn't, she'd remind him he was slouching. And now he was slurping, so he had to correct that behavior as well. He didn't resent her, not in the least. She was a good, strong woman who expected the best from her sons. She washed his clothes, prepared his meals, and even straightened his bedding. Good grief, he had it made! Still, he did at times wish he had his own place so he could kick back and put his feet on the sofa table if he felt like it. He chewed a few more bites, drank some water, and thought about Anna and her little brother a mile up the road. Strange that he could not stop thinking about her. He blamed his brothers for that, them and their cockamamie idea about him marrying her. Ever since Newell had had to let go of his hired hands, Jesse and his brothers had been lending him a helping hand in the fields, but since his passing, they'd stepped up their help. There was no way Anna and her little brother could manage all the work, much less pay off the mortgage. How were she and the boy faring?

"You're awfully quiet tonight—other than that slurping," Laura Fuller said. "Anything on your mind?"

He gave a slight grin in spite of himself. His mother knew him well. Couldn't fool her any more than he could his brothers. Did he have to be so transparent? "Not much," he said. "Just thinking about Newell Hansen's passing."

"Ah, that was a tragedy—and on the day before the dreadful assassination. In some ways, the president's death put a cloud over our town, and perhaps even made some folks forget about Newell's passing. I think often about his dear daughter and son. I'm glad you boys are doing what you can to help her with the plowing and planting."

"We can't do it forever. The Hansen farm's in foreclosure."

"Yes, Jack mentioned that the other day."

They each took another sip of stew. Laura touched her mouth with her napkin. "I ought to put together a care basket and have you deliver it to her and her brother tomorrow."

"What? I'm not delivering anything to her."

"That's nonsense. I'm sure they could use a little cheering."

"It's not my job to cheer her up, Ma."

"For goodness sake, Jesse. One would think I just asked you to feed an egg to a rattlesnake. I know you took her out a couple of times a few months ago, but you've never mentioned a word about how it went with her."

"Because I didn't want to talk about it."

"Well, she's a fine young woman. I think you should—"

"Ma, don't be like my brothers and try to tell me what to do. Please."

She gave a little sniff. "Goodness, you're touchy tonight."

"Sorry, but I can't help it. First, my brothers are telling me to marry her, and now, you're putting together a basket you want me to deliver. Are you in cahoots with them?"

She gave a good-hearted chuckle. "My suggestion to deliver her a basket of food is not some ploy to get you to marry the girl, although it's not a bad idea. So far, you haven't succeeded in finding a wife on your own. Perhaps you do need a little nudge."

Ire rose in him. "I do not require anyone's assistance."

"All right, all right, calm down. I'm merely asking you to take a basket of food to her tomorrow. If you don't wish to converse with her, you can set it on her doorstep and leave. I'll attach a little note."

Jesse calmed a bit, took another spoonful of stew, and begrudgingly nodded. "I guess it wouldn't kill me to do that much."

"Exactly. I fear I've neglected my neighborly duty by not acting earlier. With all that's happening in Washington, the death of Mr. Lincoln and the trial of those conspirators, I've forgotten about the needs that are right under my nose."

"That's understandable."

"Gracious! It seems every time I pick up the *Western Star*, there's another article about those wicked people responsible for Mr. Lincoln's death."

Jesse didn't really care to discuss the trial or the people involved. It was about the only thing anyone ever talked about in town anymore. "You shouldn't let yourself get so absorbed in it, Ma."

"Whyever not? I like to keep abreast of things. They say that woman, Mrs. Surratt, will hang for the part she played in the assassination. Can't remember when the courts have ever hanged a woman."

"I'm sure it's happened somewhere."

"I don't know. If she's guilty, I s'pose they'll give her the same punishment as those awful men."

"They're all guilty, Ma. It was a conspiracy."

"Do you think that Doctor Mudd fellow is guilty?"

"That'll be up to the courts to decide. I'm just glad I'm not sitting on that jury."

"It's not your typical jury trial, but a military commission."

"I understand that. Still wouldn't want to be involved."

"I heard Mudd was Booth's acquaintance, but how could he have been in on the conspiracy? It wasn't like Booth planned to break his leg that night in the theater. I don't believe Dr. Mudd knew he was treating the president's murderer, do you?"

"No telling what Booth told the doctor when he knocked on his door that night. You're asking all the same questions everyone else wants answers to, Ma. Like I said, we'll have to leave it up to the people in charge. I hear the trial will most likely go on at least a few more weeks."

Laura moved her head from side to side. "It's a shame, that's what it is. Our country is in a sad state no matter how you look at it. Why, I wouldn't be surprised but what God comes back real soon. The country's split in half. How much longer will God allow such hatred?"

"You never can tell what God has in mind, Ma. He's got His plans. We just have to be ready to obey them."

"Why, listen to you, sounding all preacher-like."

"Ha! A preacher I am not, but I do enjoy reading God's Word and following His precepts."

She stretched a hand across the table and touched his arm. "You know I'm proud of you, Son. You've always been a good boy."

That made his cheeks go warm. He slipped his arm out from under her light grasp. "I'm a grown man, Mother. You seem to forget that."

She sat back. "Well, blessed stars, I know that, but between you and me, I like to remember you as my little boy."

"Ma!"

She flicked her wrist and gave a light laugh. "Oh, for pity's sake, I'm just teasing you."

"Well, don't ever say stuff like that in front of Jack and Joey. They already consider me your favorite."

She gave a little cackle. "Well, none of you is my favorite, but that doesn't mean the baby of the family isn't looked upon with a little more tenderness."

"Ma…"

"As long as you choose to live here, you should expect a little coddling."

He heaved a good long sigh, then finished his stew in a few more swallows. He pushed his chair back and its legs squealed against the hardwood floor. "If you'll excuse me, Ma. I have to go out and tend to chores. It's near milking time."

"But there's dessert, custard pie. Your favorite."

He patted his belly. "Can you put aside a piece for me? I'll eat it later."

She looked only slightly put out. "I s'pose. Take your dishes to the kitchen—"

"I always do, Ma."

He couldn't help the tiny bit of resentment welling up. He was twenty-seven years old, for pity's sake, and his mother was still telling him to take his dishes to the kitchen. Why tonight should be any different from all the nights before, he couldn't actually say. Maybe it *was* time he moved out. "If you want to put something together for Anna Hansen and her brother tomorrow, I'll run it over after lunch."

"I'm glad to hear it. I'll pack something extra tasty."

4

You got the final figures ready for me? I'd like to seal this deal up as soon as possible." From his chair situated on the other side of the bank president's desk, Horace Blackthorn took a long puff on the stogie Cyrus Daly had given him, then blew out a grey cloud that filled the office. Daly waved his arm around to ward off the pungent odor. Although he'd opened his office window, no air moved outside, so the room was hot from the noonday sun.

"I gave her till June thirtieth to pay off the debt. I'll have to wait to see if she can come up with the funds."

"I don't want to take any chances on losing that land, and don't forget about that tidy little bonus I promised you if you tie it together right quick."

"Yes, yes, I know, but I have to follow the law."

"Ha!" A gruff laugh came out of him. "Since when do you follow the law? Ain't accepting a bribe against the law?"

"Shut up. These walls aren't that thick."

Horace laughed again. "You're a little skittish, ain't ya?"

"I'm cautious is all."

"Well, call it what you want. I'm impatient, that's what I am. I told you six weeks ago I'd take the property."

Cyrus Daly rolled his shoulders around in a nervous gesture, then he gave a sniff and a sneer and straightened his bowtie. "Things will work out, you'll see." He was a rather small man with spectacles that rested on a jutting nose. Nothing to look at, that was for sure, but he was pretty cunning, which was the one trait Horace liked in him. He knew when a foreclosure was about to come into play, and he let Horace know about it in advance so he could determine if he wanted to jump on it before anyone else got the chance. In this case, he definitely wanted the Hansen property. It should've been his from the very start, dating back to when his grandfather, Wilbur Blackthorn, owned the parcel.

"Don't see why it's so blue-fired important to you to buy the Hansen farm," Cyrus said.

"It's good farm land, that's why." But there was another reason far more important of which Cyrus had no inkling. A treasure lay buried on that land, gems and jewels from what he'd been told, the result of a stagecoach holdup his great-grandfather, Nolan Blackthorn, had participated in in the early 1800s. As the story went, from his jail cell, Nolan Blackthorn, confessed in a letter to his son Herbert, Horace's grandfather, that he had buried a box of valuable jewels, diamonds, rubies, emeralds, and such, on Blackthorn property. He advised him where to find the first of four clues, but told him he'd have to go in search of the remaining clues in order to find the buried treasure. Nolan Blackthorn and two other robbers had been caught and sentenced to life behind bars, and a good deal of the stolen fortune had been confiscated by the law—except for what remained on Blackthorn property, of which the law had no knowledge.

Grandfather Herbert had spent years looking for the alleged clues and was able to find the first two, but that is where his search ended. As a boy, Horace recalled incessant arguing between his father, Wilbur Blackthorn, and Grandfather Herbert regarding the supposed treasure, Horace's father casting doubts and his grandfather being adamant about its existence. Over time, Grandfather Herbert became an incessant drinker and gambler, neglecting his farm and eventually going bankrupt. To pay off his gambling debt, he reluctantly sold his farm to Charles Hansen, Newell Hansen's father. Horace's father hated to see the land go to the Hansens, but seeing as he himself held little interest in farming, he wasn't keen on buying it for himself, treasure or not. Instead, he enjoyed his work in blacksmithing, and had built a fine reputation in Lebanon. He tried to interest Horace in learning the trade, but Horace much preferred gentleman farming, so as a young man in his early twenties, he bought a piece of land in north Lebanon and began accruing a small profit which grew over time, providing him enough money to begin buying more and more parcels. Grandfather Herbert lived out the remainder of his days with his son and grandson, Wilbur and Horace, in the house on South Broadway, Horace's mother having passed when Horace was a boy of seven or eight. Grandfather Herbert's drinking became excessive to the point that it ate away at his liver, precipitating his death at the age of sixty-seven. On his deathbed, he had dragged Horace down close to him and whispered with a weak and scratchy voice, "Do your best to get back that Hansen property, boy. It belongs to the Blackthorns. And—and—find that fortune."

Those words had burned a permanent mark on his mind and fed him with a fiery need, an obsession he couldn't contain. Yes, he would reclaim that land all right, and he would find the remaining clues, the first two of which he kept safely stored, along with a poorly scribbled map, on the third shelf up in his library, under Nathanial Hawthorn's *The Scarlet Letter*. Every so often he'd take them out and reread them, but he needn't have bothered. They were so ingrained in his head from memory, he could recite them backwards and forwards.

Horace sucked a deep puff of tobacco smoke into his lungs, then slowly blew it back out, making a fancy ring that drifted above his head. "This is a no-brainer, Daly. Anna Hansen is young, single, and entirely unable to pay off that property. Can't you up the date of the foreclosure?"

"No, it's already been filed. In fact, by all rights, it should go to public auction, giving others a chance to bid on it."

Horace slid forward and slammed a flat palm down on Daly's desk, making the frail man jump back in his seat. He cursed. "You get that land for me, Daly," he said in a loud scolding tone, "or I'll drag your name through mud and grime. One by one, your clients will move to the bank across the street, you hear?"

Cyrus Daly's face went red. "Yes, yes, I hear you, and—and it shouldn't be a problem. C-calm down before my assistant comes bursting through that door."

Horace heaved a few smoky breaths and seethed inside. "Just see to it you do your best to make this deal work out in my favor—and yours. And if you can possibly speed up the process, do it."

"I'm doing everything I can, but Anna Hansen is no dummy, and she is well aware of the deadline date of June thirtieth. I can't pull anything over on her."

"Does she know I'm the one who wants her property?"

Daly nodded. "Yes, I told her, but she's pretty determined to stick this thing out in hopes of finding the money. The poor thing has given me just about every penny she earns, thinking it will make a dent in her loan."

"Well, tell her to stop wasting her money. She isn't going to be able to make up the difference no matter how hard she tries. I want her off that land by the last day of June."

"What's the big hurry? She'll need to find a job and a place to live."

"She's not your worry, Cyrus. Get that through your head."

"Newell was a good man."

"Yeah, well, in the end, he couldn't provide for her and her kid brother, could he? Fool ended his own life."

"There's no proof of that. I doubt Newell would've done such a thing. More than likely he consumed it accidentally—or…"

Daly screwed up his face in a most unpleasant way and stared across his desk at Horace through his somewhat crooked spectacles, his hands clasped on his desk, thumbs twiddling. "Why you lookin' at me like that?" Horace asked, perturbed.

The man jolted and straightened his squirrelly shoulders. "I'm—I'm not looking at you in any particular way."

"You sure were. Your eyes got all beady-like, as if you were accusing me of something."

"I wasn't accusing you of anything. I was just thinking, that's all."

"About what?"

"I told you. I was pondering the matter of Newell Hansen's untimely passing."

"Well, stop thinking about it, would ya? It ain't your worry—just like that girl and her brother ain't your business. Your business is to sew up this deal for me so we can both get on with our lives."

"All right, all right, just settle down."

"Stop telling me what to do. You're getting on my nerves, Daly."

Daly gave his throat a good clearing, then whisked his fingers through his thin gray hair. "I'll hand off the necessary paperwork to my assistant and hopefully get this matter put to bed within the next few days."

"Good." Horace slowly rose, then snuffed out his cigar and set it on the tray on Daly's desk. Daly pushed himself up, and when he stretched to his full height, he was still a whole head shorter than Horace. Horace sniffed and forced a smile and a calming tone. "As always, nice doing business with you, Daly."

The fellow gave a short-lived grin. "We'll be in touch," was his clipped reply.

"You bet we will. Wouldn't want you forgetting about me."

Daly nodded. "I seriously doubt that could happen."

Horace chuckled, then turned and walked out.

Back in his wagon, he maneuvered his horse down Broadway, passing the Town Hall, Jake's Tavern, the Livery, and The Golden Lamb restaurant and hotel. He crossed Main Street and proceeded south in the direction of his land out on South West Street where he would meet up with his foreman to talk some business. Just as soon as this deal with the Hansen property went through, he planned to put his foreman in charge of the whole of his properties, overseeing the work of his hired men, so he could devote as much time as needed to dig up that beloved treasure of which he would soon have clear ownership.

On the drive, he thought again about Newell Hansen's demise. Naturally, Sheriff Berry was doing his due diligence in investigating Newell's death. He'd questioned everyone in town—everyone who had any connection to Newell Hansen. Shoot, he and one of his deputies had even paid him a call one evening, asking him where he'd been on the night of April 15. Naturally, he gave them an alibi. He'd gone to the saloon. And it checked out. Humph. The timing may have been a bit off, but it didn't matter. They'd never pin anything on him. Impossible. He gave a low chortle as he rode along. Newell had known about the buried treasure for as long as Horace had, thanks to Wilbur, Horace's father, handing off the clues to Charles, Newell's father.

That had made Horace livid. "But my grandfather told me that treasure was mine!" he'd shrieked.

"It's not Blackthorn land anymore, Son," his father had said, reserved and unemotional. "It belongs to the Hansens. It was only right that I should pass the clues down to Charles. You have a copy of them if you and Newell should decide to set out on a search together, but as for Charles and me, we think it's pure nonsense."

Although Horace had suggested he and Newell work together to dig for the treasure on a couple of occasions, he was never interested. "If such a fortune exists—and it's highly unlikely—we'd have to turn it in to authorities anyway since it's stolen goods," Newell had said the last time Horace had broached the subject.

"No, we wouldn't. The authorities would never have to know. Besides, if you find something on your property, it's yours."

"Not if it's stolen, Horace," Newell had argued. "As a Christian, I wouldn't be able to sleep well knowing I'd kept property that wasn't rightfully mine. Now, what I don't know won't hurt me, so if there's buried treasure somewhere on my land, it can stay there. But purposely digging all over the place for something that likely doesn't exist is pure foolishness. Your Grandfather Herbert wasted a good share of his life searching. Sure, he got two clues for all his hard effort, but he never did locate the third, and in the end it drove him to drink. That's why Wilbur had little interest in pursuing it. He saw what it did to your grandfather. You ought to follow your father's example."

"Don't lecture me like I'm some fool kid."

"I'm not, Horace. I'm just speaking truth."

He'd sworn at the fellow, making him cringe. "You ever tell your daughter about the buried jewels?"

"No, haven't told her or Billy Ray. I don't want it eating away at them for the rest of their lives. You would do well to let it rest as well."

"I told you not to lecture me."

Newell had just ignored that comment, shook his head, and walked to his tack room at the back of the barn. Horace had followed.

"So, what did you do with the two clues your father gave you?"

"I put them away."

"Where'd you put 'em?"

"Not that it should matter to you, but they're stored away on a high shelf where my son won't get at them."

"Can I see them?"

"What? Why? You've got the same clues."

"How do I know that? I never saw what Wilbur passed down to your father. Maybe I want to see if they match up. What could it hurt? It's not like I'm going to tell anyone about them, seeing as I keep mine hidden under a book in my library."

Newell had given Horace an eye roll and a deep sigh. "Have it your way." He had walked to the other side of the tack room, grabbed a step stool, climbed to the top step, and brought down a small metal box, brown and dusty. "I haven't opened the lid on this thing in years."

Horace's mouth had gone dry at the sight of it. His father had never provided him with any sort of special box. Jealousy raged within. Newell had lifted the hinged lid, allowing Horace to peer inside. Three pieces of folded paper lay at the bottom, along with something else Horace had never seen before: a key. He had swallowed a dry lump, but tried not to show any sort of emotion. "Are you going to open them papers and show me what they say?"

Another long sigh from Newell. "I'm sure you've got the same clues in your possession."

"Yeah, but yours might be a little different. I'm just curious."

The first piece of paper Newell had unfolded was a map. At close inspection, it seemed to resemble the one Horace possessed, except this one marked certain areas of the map with Xs and had a number beside each X, no doubt marking the correct order of clues. It was clear that Newell had the original map, whereas he only possessed a poorly scribbled copy made by his father. Why had his father given Newell's father the original? Anger soared up within him at the utter unfairness. Newell had folded the map back up, returned it to the box, and then opened another paper and read from it.

"Clue number one says, 'On the north creek bank, where warm waters flow, four feet deep, in a jar below.'" He'd given Horace a blank stare. "That's it." Refolding the paper and returning it to the box, Newell had then unfolded the last one. "And clue number two says, 'Center of the south piece, twenty paces west. Buried in a vase at the bottom of the crest.'" He had looked up after reading it. "And there you have it, Horace. Same as yours, I'm sure. I've never even considered digging around for the third clue because I think it's a waste of time, and I don't want to allow it to dominate my mind. It dominated your grandfather's and drove him to drink. It's not worth it." He had folded the final paper, put it back in the box, clamped down the lid, and returned the box to the upper shelf.

Now, weeks later, cold fury still burned inside Horace when he thought of that conversation, Newell's better map, and the key that might unlock the treasure chest. "So, why do you hang onto the clues if you're never going to do anything with them?" he had asked Newell.

Newell had shrugged. "Perchance the day will come when I'll feel compelled to turn them in to the sheriff."

Horace had sizzled inside, but he held his temper. "Why in Sam Hill would you do that? If the treasure's found, mayhap it could save your farm."

That statement had blindsided Newell. He had stood still as a boulder, his jaw twitching and his eyes turning a steel gray. "What do ya mean?"

He had smiled at Newell and arched a brow. "Oh, was your farm going into foreclosure a secret?"

Newell had scowled. "I'm doing my best to work out a deal with Cyrus. If he's been sayin' I'm in foreclosure, he's a bit premature."

"Isn't it a little late for working out a deal? We all know how Carlisle drained your bank dry with his gambling habit. How you going to come up with the money?"

"That's my worry, not yours. I'm working on it."

He'd chuckled. "You're somethin', Newell. You always thought you was better than me growing up."

"Where in the world did you come up with that notion, Horace? I've never thought any such thing. I always tried befriending you, but you'd have nothing to do with me."

"'Cause you thought you were better than me."

Newell had shaken his head and given him a pathetic look. "That's ridiculous, Horace, and you know it. Look, I got work to do. Do you mind?"

"No, not at all." He had turned, then started for the door. "You have a good day, Newell."

"I plan to, Horace, and you as well."

Over his shoulder, he called. "I'll be thinking about buying your farm when ol' Cyrus takes it back."

Newell had given a gravelly chortle and called back, "Over my dead body, Horace."

Horace had kept walking. "Might be," he mumbled to himself. "Might be."

He had let three days pass before going back out to Newell's farm, this time, bearing a peace offering in the form of a small plate of cookies. He'd found Newell out in a cornfield, not far from the north side of the barn, sowing seed, so he'd left his horse at the edge of the field and walked out to him, glad that Newell's son wasn't with him. It would've been hard to tell the kid he couldn't have a cookie, since the two he intended for Newell were laced with a good amount of arsenic. He'd hauled down a cookbook from a kitchen shelf to figure out how to make a batch of cookies, then separated a small amount from the rest of the dough, added a loaded teaspoon of colorless, flavorless arsenic he'd acquired from the druggist to the mixture, then spooned them onto a baking stone and baked them. He'd also baked a couple for himself, not laced, of course, so that they could partake together and Newell would be none the wiser.

At first, Newell had put up his guard. "What brings you out here again?"

Horace put on his pleasantest face. "It was the least I could do after the way I behaved the other day. I was rude, so I'd like to apologize. Decided I'd bring some cookies."

"Oh?" Newell had grinned.

"My housekeeper made them," he had lied.

Fine Christian that he was, Newell accepted a cookie, commented on how good it tasted, and said between bites, "Apology accepted." They'd talked about the weather and the possibility of a drenching spring rain and what that would do to the crops. While munching on the second cookie, Newell had talked about what good friends their fathers had been and how nice it would be if the two of them could put their differences aside and be close like that. After a bit, Newell had sat down on an old stump and wiped his soaked brow, while Horace had taken a seat on the ground, his eyes trained on Newell, waiting for some evidence that the arsenic was doing its job.

"You and me ought to be friendlier to each other," Horace had said. *Another lie, obviously.*

"Yeah, I don't know why we weren't friends in school. You always seemed to hang with a rougher crowd than me." About that time, Newell's face had turned a putrid shade of gray. Rising from the old stump, a bit wobbly, his wrinkled face betraying his confusion, he'd said faintly, "I think I'll go back to the barn, if you don't mind."

"You all right? You don't look so good."

"I don't know. I think the sun is getting to me." Newell had put a hand to his gut. "I think I'll go back to the barn where it's cooler. I got a few things to do inside anyway." He'd taken off his hat and fanned his face.

They had walked off the field, Newell heading to his barn, his steps a bit staggered, and Horace climbing back on his horse and riding off, glad not a soul had spotted him. Out on the road, he had given Newell one last glance, but Newell didn't acknowledge him, just disappeared into his barn. He'd had no idea how long before the arsenic would take full effect, but the next day he'd overheard some fellows jawing on a street corner about Anna Hansen finding her father's dead body on the barn floor last night around suppertime. Apparently, it wasn't like him to miss supper, so she'd gone out looking for him. They talked about what a shame it was and how much the community would miss him. "He was a fine citizen," one of them said. Horace had slowed his gait just enough to hear what he wanted, then moved on down the street undetected, doing his best to cover his gratified grin. The day after that, all talk of Newell Hansen's death ceased when conversations about the assassination of Abraham Lincoln dominated every street corner, storefront, and front porch.

It was not until two days later that Horace realized he had left the plate that had held the cookies out in Newell's cornfield. Later that very night, once full darkness settled in, he took a ride out to Newell's property, carrying a lit lantern to search the area where they'd sat. He found the old stump, but no plate. What the livin' devil had happened to it? He couldn't think of a single reason why anyone would've walked out there, not when Newell's body had been found in the barn. He could only surmise a raccoon or some other varmint had hauled it away, having smelled the cookie crumbs on it. That was his hope anyway. Not that anyone would trace the plate back to him. To be on the safe side, though, he'd boxed up all his dishes that matched the plate that very night and put them out in his backyard shed. Then he'd gone to the general store the next day and bought a new set, telling Gus, the clerk, that many of his dishes had broken, and he needed new ones.

His horse whinnied, dragging him back to the present. He gave a little sniff and swabbed his brow with his sleeve. Hansen's land was as good as his now. Along with the buried fortune.

5

Anna hefted up the basket of wet clothes she'd just washed, and headed out the back door to the clothesline. She was glad for the warm sunshine, as they would dry quicker. If this morning's cloudless sky were an indication, they were in for another scorching summer day. Fine by her. The hot weather didn't bother her. Rex rose from the hole he'd dug next to the porch and gave a good, long stretch upon seeing her. Then he approached to sniff out her apron pocket where she almost always carried some sort of treat for him. She withdrew the end piece of bread she'd saved for him and he gladly took it, sauntering over to a tree where he plopped down to enjoy the gift.

Out in the field, their two horses grazed in one field, Carlotta their cow in another. Since she'd had to sell off much of her livestock, the fields appeared so empty and forlorn. Last night, after Billy Ray went to bed, she had hauled out Papa's big account book again in hopes of finding something, anything, she'd missed, but it was all for naught. Dad blast that John Carlisle who'd stolen all of Papa's profits the year that Papa had handed over the books to him, thinking him trustworthy. After all, he'd worked ten years for Papa and had never once given him reason to believe otherwise. He was a good worker and dependable, as far as Papa knew, but he had a gambling problem that Papa didn't know about. Over a period of time, he started taking money from the profits but never let on. One day, he skipped town, simply failing to show up for work. That's when Papa discovered his thievery. It took the law ten long days to finally catch Carlisle, and when they did, they found him drunker than a skunk, lying in a dark alley outside a saloon in Cincinnati, an empty purse clutched in his hand. In ten days, he'd squandered thousands of dollars, almost all of Papa's hard-earned money, forcing Papa to lay off his three remaining hired hands. Sadly, Papa had kept the full truth from Anna, leading her to believe he still had enough money in the bank for them to get by. It wasn't until later that she learned what money did remain was only enough to make a few more measly payments to the bank. After that, Papa started falling further and further behind on his bills. She'd known he met often with Mr. Daly at his office, but she assumed it was to discuss the hardship Carlisle had brought upon him, not that Mr. Daly was planning to foreclose on him.

Billy Ray sauntered out of the barn carrying a pail. He walked to the pump, gave the handle several thrusts until water gushed out, then filled the pail and headed back toward the barn. He'd already done that several times during the course of the morning while she washed clothes. He was a good boy who rarely complained, but since their father's death, he'd become sullen. These were all chores he used to do with Papa close by, but now he did them alone. On his way back inside the barn, he glanced at her and gave a tiny smile and wave to acknowledge he'd seen her. Her heart dipped with sadness for all he'd endured in his mere ten years of living.

She pulled a clothespin out of her apron pocket and placed it on the last corner of the shirt she'd hung, picked up the straw basket, and made her way back toward the house. At the sound of an approaching wagon, she stopped and turned, the basket hoisted on her hip, and lifted the rim of her sunhat so she could make out the driver. Of all people, it was Jesse Fuller. He sat high on the buckboard, bigger than life in her eyes, and she instantly wished she could sink into oblivion. She knew she must look horrid, what with her torn dress, soiled apron, and disheveled light brown hair coming untucked. Surely she looked like the pathetic, homeless waif that she would soon become.

She straightened and put on as pleasant a face as possible. "Hello, Jesse. What brings you out here?"

"Afternoon to you, Anna." He touched the brim of his hat and looked down at her, studying her for a second longer than she thought appropriate. She shifted her weight while awaiting his answer. She hadn't seen him since just before Papa's passing—and that had been fine with her.

"Ma sent me on an errand." He picked up a wooden box covered by a piece of colorful cloth and held it up for her viewing. "She put together a couple of meals for you and Billy, along with some other delicacies, and ordered me to deliver it." He issued her a nice smile, set the box down on the edge of the seat, and jumped down to the ground. She was certain his six-foot-plus frame must surely have shaken the earth. At least, he'd sent a lot of dust flying. Putting his back to her, he reached both arms up and took down the box...and Anna couldn't help noticing the ripple of muscle. 'Course they'd known each other since childhood, but she'd gone out with him exactly twice, and that was it. She didn't blame him for not calling on her again. Clearly, they were in two different social classes; he and his entire family were held in high regard about town, and she was a mere orphaned peon. Good granny, why had he even invited her out in the first place? To her way of thinking, there was nothing appealing about her looks.

In haste, she gathered her wits. "Goodness sake, she needn't have done that, nor put you to the trouble of delivering it."

His one-sided grin came off almost impish. "No worries. When Laura Fuller puts her mind to something, you don't argue. You just do as y'r told."

"I see. Well, it was awfully kind of her—and you." She had yet to give him a full-on smile, too afraid of putting him off with that one slanted tooth in the top front. That's no doubt why he hadn't invited her out a third time. Papa used to say that slanted tooth gave her smile a certain charm, but whenever she smiled at herself in a mirror, all she saw were faults. The freckles on her cheeks and nose only added to her list of imperfections. She adjusted the basket of clothes resting on her hip.

"How 'bout I carry this into the house for you since your hands are full?"

"Oh! All right—if you don't mind." Perspiration beaded on her forehead, and she knew there was a large sweaty spot on her back that would surely show when he followed her to the house. Good granny, why must she look such a sight? And, worse, why must it matter?

Just as she reached the back stoop, Jesse's footfall tromping behind her, Billy Ray came running up from the barn. "Hi, Mr. Fuller. What y' doin' here?"

Anna pivoted on the bottom step. "His mother put together a basket of food for us. Wasn't that nice of her?"

Billy's face blossomed. "Seriously? What kinda food?"

Jesse grinned down at the boy. "I have no idea, but you can have the first look if your sister doesn't mind."

"I don't mind." They climbed the two steps and entered the house. She glanced around at the clutter—a pile of dirty clothes here, breakfast dishes that still needed washing there, and a stack of folded clothes she had yet to put away on the pine table. She wondered what Jesse thought about her plain little farmhouse compared to his big house, which was practically a mansion. But then she quickly scolded herself for caring. Besides, her father had always spoken highly of the Fuller brothers. "They are good neighbors," he'd say. And wasn't it true that just as soon as they heard about her father having to let go of his hired help, they all showed up to help him plow the fields? Truth be told, they would likely be glad to hear that Horace Blackthorn would be buying her farm. The responsibility would then fall to him, and not the Fullers, to see about the fields.

She hurried across the room and cleared a space on the table for the crate of food. Jesse followed after her and set it down, after which Billy Ray eagerly tore off the cloth and quickly perused the contents. "Yum!

There's fresh bread in here, Sis, and some dried meats and strawberries and, oh! Some cookies! And a pie! Sis!"

"There's some soup sealed up tight in a couple of those jars too. You might put them in your cellar to keep them cool for later."

"Indeed. Thank you so much, Jesse. I don't even know how to thank you."

"No need. Ma said she felt bad for not doing it sooner." His kind tone forced a smile from her, and he smiled back. She quickly put a hand to her mouth. "Please tell your mother we are ever so grateful."

"I'll do that." When he might have made his way toward the door, he stayed planted and glanced around her house, as if to give it a once-over. She sucked in a deep, awkward breath and wondered if she oughtn't to walk to the door herself and open it for him. "This is a nice little place, Anna. You've done well to keep it up since Newell's passing."

She didn't wish to talk about her father's death, nor her house, for it brought up thoughts of the foreclosure. "Thank you," was all she said.

"Before Newell died, he told me I ought to come over for supper some night. 'Course, his death put a hold on that notion. He did brag on your cooking, though."

Her cheeks went instantly hot. It was true. Papa had mentioned she ought to make up a nice supper and then invite Jesse Fuller to come as their guest. She had completely balked at the idea, telling him, "That's a terrible idea, Papa. I don't think he much cares for me. We went out on a couple of dates and had very little to talk about." But Papa had thrown her a mischievous grin, then said, "Perhaps you didn't give him a fair chance."

"Well, just the same, I have no interest in entertaining Jesse Fuller for supper, much less considering him a prospective beau. He is not at all my—my—sort!"

"Your sort?" He'd tipped his head and squinted. "What *sort* do you think he is?"

"He's much—well, far higher on the social scale than I—than *we*. Their family is very well regarded in the community."

"Yes, but that don't make them uppity. Shoot-fire! Jesse's a fine Christian man, as are his brothers. He's the type o' fella you ought to be seekin' for a husband."

"Papa, I'm not seeking a husband."

"Well, you ought to be. Y'r almost twenty-one, ain't you?"

"That makes no matter to me. I'd rather stay single and take care of you and Billy Ray."

"Well, for cryin' in a pail, I don't need takin' care of, an' Billy Ray's gettin' to the age of knowin' how to get by."

"No, he's not, Papa." She recalled having sighed in exasperation. They ended the discussion after she'd made him promise not to invite Jesse to supper, and the subject had not come up again—until now. Apparently, her father had mentioned the possible invitation before bringing up the matter with her. Now she was purely mortified. Glancing briefly at Jesse, she nervously took a strand of hair and stuck it behind her ear, then shifted her weight. "I—I'm sorry it didn't pan out."

He still wore that crooked grin, as if he carried some secret. "No problem. Perhaps we can—work something out for the future?"

Her eyes went wide. Was he serious? "I—I'm not the cook that Papa made me out to be."

"Yeah, she ain't the best," offered Billy without looking up from the crate of food he was still pawing through. That made her blush all the more.

Jesse chuckled. "How 'bout we bypass the home-cooked meal for now in favor of going to a restaurant?"

"A rest—?" She couldn't even finish the word, let alone the sentence.

"Do you enjoy the Golden Lamb restaurant?" he quickly inquired.

"The Golden Lamb?" Her brain went fuzzy, and she was certain her eyes had doubled in size. Was he inviting her on another date? And if so, why? She'd thought they had little in common.

"Yes, have you been there?"

Too stunned to answer, she merely gaped at him.

"Can I go too?" Billy Ray blurted.

That seemed to have stopped Jesse in his tracks, for he removed his dusty hat, scratched his head, then set to turning it in his hands. "Well, I was thinking—um, yes, yes, you can come if you like."

Anna tried to think what to say, but the words got all tangled in her head. "That's really nice of you to offer, Jesse, but—I don't think—I mean, it's not necessary." She felt her cheeks flush. Gooseberries! Was he aiming to be something other than a good neighbor?

"I know it's not necessary, but I'm still inviting you." He stared her down for all of five seconds. "And Billy Ray too."

How could she turn him down? Nothing came to mind. This offer of a full-fledged restaurant meal, the Golden Lamb of all places, floored her. A *real* restaurant meal? She would have to thank Billy Ray later for inviting himself, even though it had been rude on his part. If she were going to accompany Jesse to a restaurant, she would most heartily want her little brother to tag along. He was sure to keep the conversation lively.

"Well? What do you say?" Jesse asked, his honey brown eyes dancing.

"I—"

"Sure, we'll go. Right, Sis?" Billy Ray cut in.

"I suppose that would be just fine. When did you have in mind?"

"How about tomorrow night?"

"Tomorrow? So soon?" Now her head filled with cobwebs. What had possessed Jesse Fuller to ask her out again—especially after those first couple of failed dates?

"Tomorrow sounds good," said Billy Ray.

"Great, then I'll pick you both up at five o'clock sharp, how's that?"

Her answer came out in the form of a couple slow nods since no reasonable response came to mind. Were she and Billy Ray really going to a restaurant? She couldn't remember the last time she'd walked through the doors of one. It seemed so lavish, so extravagant. Something gnawed at her. Surely, he had ulterior motives for inviting her because there certainly wasn't anything attractive about her—unless it was the simple fact that she wasn't as big as a barn.

He plopped his hat back in place, then tipped its brim at her. "Tomorrow it is." He put that crooked grin back on, swiveled on the heel of his boot, and made for the door. When he closed it behind him, she suddenly realized she hadn't sufficiently thanked him for the crate of food, so she ran to the door and opened it. He was just preparing to climb up to his wagon seat.

"Thank you again for the basket of food. Please give your mother my best."

He gave a nod and a friendly wave, climbed aboard his wagon, then turned the horses in the opposite direction, and headed down the long driveway, his rig rocking and rolling along the bumpy two-track. She watched until he turned the corner and disappeared behind the cusp of trees.

6

Jesse readied himself for his three-person "date" in his upstairs bedroom, his stomach a tumble of nerves. What in the world was he thinking by asking Anna—and then her brother—to accompany him to the Golden Lamb for supper? Their first two dates hadn't gone well, and he could tell when he'd invited her this time that she wasn't overly enthused about the idea. He wasn't much of a gentleman, he knew, so he'd have to work on that. The town was sure to wag their tongues about it. Sheesh! He hadn't even told his mother, as he'd wanted to do this thing in private. He gave his head a couple of fast shakes, as if to get his dizzying thoughts to settle down, but it didn't help. On his visit yesterday, he'd tried to gauge whether she might be interested in courting again, but with her brother underfoot, he hadn't had the chance. Shoot, he'd only eked a tiny smile from her, one she'd covered with her hand. For all he knew, she wasn't the least bit interested, but she didn't know how to turn him down in front of her brother. Suffering saints, there was a strong likelihood he was about to make a big fool of himself.

He took one final look at himself in the mirror, tried to get a stubborn piece of hair to lay flat, then whispered to himself, "Oh, chicken feathers! What do I care?" and left his room, closing the door behind him.

He found his mother in the kitchen lifting the lid off a kettle on the hearth. At the sound of his steps, she turned. "Are you leaving?"

"Yes, Mother."

"Mother? Why so formal? And"—she carefully looked him over—"I thought you said you were going to meet someone on business."

"I did. I—am."

She sniffed the air. "I am smelling something other than my chicken stew." She set the lid back in place, wiped her hands on her apron, and approached. *Great.* He feared his secret was out. "Why are you wearing your Caswell-Massey Number Six Cologne? And did you douse yourself? It's too much." She'd bought the expensive, musky fragrance for him three Christmases ago, and he had never once used it—until now. Bullfoot! He knew nothing about how much or how little to use.

She frowned and tilted her head at him as if to peruse him from a different angle. Then she lifted her hand and tried to get that same pesky cowlick to lay flat. "Ma, stop." He shifted away from her.

She lowered her hand and narrowed her gaze, her hazel eyes glinting. "You didn't mention who you were meeting for supper. Was that intentional?"

He released a sigh and shook his head. "It's just—just…aww, what's the use? I'm taking Anna Hansen and her little brother to the Golden Lamb."

Rather than react in the way he thought she would, she simply lifted one eyebrow and cleared her throat. He was certain she was trying to cover her surprise. "I see. Well, you could have told me. I'm not opposed to your taking her on a date. Maybe this time you'll make a better impression."

"Thanks, Ma. I appreciate your confidence in me," he said with a note of sarcasm. "Billy Ray is going too, so it's not like a real date."

"And whose idea was that?"

"The boy—invited himself."

She snickered. "How do you feel about that?"

"I'm perfectly fine. I don't think he's ever eaten at a restaurant before."

"Hm. The Golden Lamb." She brushed at something on the front of his shirt, then turned up her nose. "We have to get some of that cologne off you."

"It's that bad?"

She frowned. "I can't believe you don't smell it yourself."

"I do, but I thought a person was supposed to smell nice."

"You are, but there is a limit to *how* nice."

"Pfff. I don't know about any of this. Why am I even going to the trouble?"

At the sink, she reached into the water and brought out a clean rag, then wrung it between her hands. "Here. Rub this over some of the places you applied the cologne. Not all, just some. That should take care of it."

He did as told, feeling like a child. Good heavens. Here he was a twenty-seven-year-old man, and his mother was still taking charge of him!

"All right then, that's much better." She gave a great sniff and then looked him over one last time. She opened her mouth to say more, but he put a hand up to stop her.

"Please, Ma, I don't need your womanly input."

She clamped her lips shut and stood straight, but a tiny grin still made it to her mouth.

He walked to the door, put his hand to the knob, then turned and pointed a finger. "And don't wait up for me as if I were some teenager."

"Oh, silly, I wouldn't do that."

"Right." He gave her a slight nod and walked out, situating the hat on his head that he'd snagged from the hook by the door. At the top step, he stood for a second and took in the scents of the warm, muggy air. Dark clouds off to the west warned of possible rain. He whispered a little prayer that the night might go well, and set off toward his waiting, covered buggy, his stomach aflutter, confident that, at least, he smelled better!

∽

"When's he gettin' here?" Billy Ray asked.

For the past thirty minutes, the boy had been prancing back and forth from the kitchen window overlooking the two-track trail in the field to the front window facing the road, not knowing which route Jesse would take. His excitement and beeline movements were making Anna increasingly nervous. As much as she hated to admit it, she rather looked forward to this date. But—was this even a date considering Billy Ray was accompanying them? "He said he would be here at five o'clock, and it's not quite five. I have a feeling he'll be prompt."

"Okay, well, I'm gettin' anxious."

"I never would have guessed."

The minutes ticked away, and she busied herself in the kitchen with things that didn't need doing when Billy Ray squealed, "He's comin'! He's comin', Sis. I see him comin' 'cross the field."

"I hear you. Please calm yourself."

But he paid no attention to her plea, just ran to the door and scrambled outside. "Hi, Mr. Fuller. Y'r right on time!"

Anna draped the cloth with which she'd wiped her worktable across the rim of her wash pail, took a hasty peek around her tidy kitchen, put a hand to her chest to settle her heart, and walked to the door that Billy had left wide open. She stepped out onto the back stoop. Jesse brought his two-horse team to a halt, jumped down, and looped the rope over the hitching post by her kitchen door. Despite Billy's high-pitched chatter, he at last made eye contact with her. He smiled, and her heart jumped a little. Glory goodness, but he was fine looking, anything but ordinary. In fact, he was even better looking than yesterday, dressed up as he was in his tan trousers and tucked-in pale blue cambric shirt with sleeves rolled up to the elbows. What must he think of her? She had no fine clothes, save for the dress she wore now, which she'd stitched four years ago for a cousin's wedding in Sandusky. It had a low, square neckline, gathered waist, and full skirt, minus the hoop. She never had been one for hoops, as she considered them completely unsuitable for the farm. In fact, she usually donned her papa's coveralls when working out in the barn, no matter that they were big enough to swim in. No one ever came to call anyway—until now.

"Hello, Jesse. Billy Ray's been watching at the window for the past thirty minutes. I guess you can tell he's a bit excited."

"I see that." He ruffled her brother's longish hair. Goodness, she should have insisted on cutting it today. The way his wavy brown hair fell across his eyes made him look like some unkempt scamp. At least he'd taken care to wash his face and hands at the well earlier.

"Well." Anna brushed her sweaty palms together. "Would you— like to come inside for a bit before we leave, or—did you wish to go right away? I could offer you a cool drink."

"That would be nice." With his hand on Billy Ray's shoulder, he directed the boy to the door, then motioned for her to go ahead of them. Inside, she walked straightaway to the tall cupboard that held her tin mugs and glasses and brought down three mugs. "I made some straw-berry punch if that suits you."

"That sounds mighty refreshing."

While she prepared their drinks, Billy Ray started talking, and she worried he might monopolize their entire evening, but then she thought how convenient that could be, not having to come up with fresh topics of conversation. She handed the cups of punch to Jesse and Billy, then returned for her own, grasping it between both hands and tasting of its natural sweetness. "Hm, delicious," Jesse said. "Don't know when I've had anything more refreshing."

Well, that was an exaggeration, she knew, but she gave a timid smile nonetheless. "I'm glad you enjoy it." They stood there sipping before it dawned on her that she hadn't offered him a seat. "Would you care to sit? My furnishings are very plain, but I'll offer you our most comfortable chair if you—"

"No, that's fine. Perhaps we should start out for town so we can beat the supper crowd. The Golden Lamb is a busy place this time of day what with all the travelers using Lebanon as a stopping off place."

"Yes, yes, I'm sure you're right."

They all finished their drinks, set their cups on the sink board, and made for the door. "I'll take the front and steer the team, and you two can sit in the back," Jesse said. "Billy Ray, how about you jump up first, then give your sister a hand?"

"Sure thing," Billy said, leaping up to the back seat like a grasshopper. As instructed, he turned and put out his hand to his sister. There was no feminine way to board a rig, but Anna set about giving it her best try. However, she needn't have worried, for as soon as she took Billy Ray's hand, two strong hands encircled her waist from behind and easily lifted her to the step so that she could climb aboard without incident. The way he lifted her made her feel as light as a duck feather. Good gracious she must instruct her soaring heart to behave itself.

Billy Ray's happy chatter started up as soon as Jesse set his horses in motion and the wagon wheels squeaked into action. Jesse gave patient responses; whereas she sat quietly, worried that Billy might never stop talking. Somehow, she had to take her brother aside and tell him not to talk so much. Yes, he was a ball of excited energy at the prospect of going to a restaurant, but he needed to learn his place among adults. When there was a slight lull, she leaned forward and whispered, "Be sure to allow Mr. Fuller to say a few words."

His eyebrows shot up, as if his overenthusiasm just dawned upon him. He formed a round circle with his mouth and nodded, then happily grinned. "You can say somethin' too," he whispered back.

She smiled and mouthed, "I know," but when given the opportunity, she couldn't think of a thing to say.

Finally, Jesse filled in the gap. "Your crops are looking good."

She gazed out over the corn and the plot of beans Jesse and his brothers had sowed. "Yes, they're looking lovely. I must thank you for the help you and your brothers have been since before Papa passed and up till now. It's meant a great deal to us."

Without turning his head, he answered, "It's been our pleasure. We'll help come harvest too."

"If we're even here," Billy put in. "There's a man who wants to buy everything out from under us."

Now Jesse jerked his head around to make eye contact with Anna. "Is that right? Who might that be if I may ask?" He turned back around to steer his team onto Drake Road.

She scowled at Billy, who sat in the seat across from her, his back to Jesse. "I'm afraid we may be forced to sell if I can't make payment on our farm, but we needn't discuss that now."

"I'm sorry if I come off as nosy. Just curious who's interested is all."

"It's Mr. Blackthorn," Billy blurted.

"Billy Ray Hansen, button your lips."

He hung his head and looked at his dangling feet. "Sorry, Sis," he muttered.

Jesse gave another backward glance. "Didn't mean to get you into trouble, friend," Jesse said, glancing back at the boy. "Blackthorn, huh? He's known about town for buying up parcels when they go into foreclosure. I consider him a shyster if you want the truth. Maybe someone else will come up with the funds before he snatches it up."

She tried not to let the worry slip out in her voice. "To my knowledge, no one else has expressed any interest."

"I see. Well, maybe someone else will come forward."

Anna had no response to his wishful thinking, and besides, she really didn't wish to discuss the sad subject of her foreclosure. "Did you tell your mother how much we appreciated the basket of food?"

"I did, and she said it was her pleasure putting it together."

Overhead, a few gray clouds had started stealing the sunlight; she hoped it didn't mean they'd be coming home in the rain. "The sky is looking gray," she said to make conversation.

"Yes, I noticed that. We should be okay though. It looks pretty clear in the west."

She had nothing further to say, so they drove along in silence save for one squeaky wheel and the sound of some squawking crows flying about. Now she wished she hadn't shushed Billy Ray, who sat sulking across from her.

In town, Jesse found a spot to park his rig in front of the Golden Lamb. A livery fellow met them, immediately reaching up a hand to assist Anna down to the ground. Billy came to life and landed on the ground, then took Anna's other hand so she could climb down from the rig with some semblance of dignity. Once on the ground, she brushed the wrinkles from her skirt, and the livery fellow turned to Jesse and handed him a livery ticket, took his team of horses, and promised to fetch them back once they finished their dinner.

Jesse looped his arm for Anna's taking, and together they climbed the steps and walked through the main door. Upon entering, an immediate rush of awe came over her, the very notion of eating food prepared by someone other than herself seeming an outright luxury. Add to that the wonderful cooking aromas, and her senses were awash with wonder. A quick glance at Billy Ray told her she wasn't alone in her feelings. She only hoped he could control his excitement when it came time to seat themselves.

⌒

The place was busy, but Jesse managed to locate a table for them in the center of the room. He didn't miss all the sets of eyes that followed him as he took Anna's arm and escorted her and her brother there, Billy Ray lagging and gawking.

"This place smells way better than a garden full o' roses, don't it, Sis? Can you smell them pies?"

Jesse chuckled at the boy's unreserved enthusiasm.

"Shhhhh, Billy, not so loud," Anna said, looking a tad bit rosy in the cheeks as they passed other diners. Jesse recognized a few acquaintances, but the rest were most likely travelers just passing through town. He tipped his hat at one fellow sitting at a corner table whose name escaped him.

When they reached the table, Jesse pulled back a chair to seat Anna, then nodded at Billy Ray to sit in the one across from him as he sat down beside her. He smiled at her brother. "I'm sure the food will taste even better than it smells."

The boy's dancing blue eyes trailed around the room. "Who's that a picture of?" He pointed to a painted portrait on the wall adjacent to their table.

Jesse studied it for a moment. "I believe that's a picture of William Henry Harrison."

"Who's that?"

"He was our country's president several years ago. Actually, he only served a total of thirty-one days before his untimely death."

"Oh yeah, now I remember ar' teacher Mr. Nordland tellin' us about that guy. How come his picture is up there?"

"Because he visited our town. In fact, he stopped in Lebanon and stood on this restaurant's very steps to make a speech when he was on the presidential campaign trail. Lots of dignitaries have passed through Lebanon. Folks find it a convenient and popular stopping-off point for rest and food."

"Well, don't that beat all! Did you know all that, Sis?"

"Yes, I've heard similar talk. Never have seen any of 'em cross through town though."

A middle-aged waitress approached their table, several gray hairs falling from the bun at the nape of her neck. Jesse didn't recognize her. "Evenin' folks," she said, issuing a pleasant smile. "Welcome to the Golden Lamb. We got three specials tonight." She rattled off three different choices—a beef stew with biscuits; chicken and mashed potatoes; and pork roast with fried potatoes. "Which one suits you and yer wife's likin'?"

Jesse didn't miss Anna's little gasp or Billy's giggle. "Oh! We're not—mister and missis."

The waitress put a hand to her mouth, her eyes wide. "Beggin' y'r pardon. I just moved to Lebanon a few months ago. I'm still tryin' t' get t' know folks."

"That's no problem. And welcome to Lebanon. Now then, we'll have the—" He gave Anna a hurried glance. "You like the stew option?"

The rosy hue in her cheeks had blossomed further. "That's fine."

"What's fer dessert?" Billy asked.

"Billy, mind your manners," Anna said. When she meant to give her little brother a kick in the shin, she accidentally booted *him* instead. Jesse withdrew his leg. "Oh, excuse me, Jesse, I meant—"

"That's okay. Billy, we'll talk about dessert after we've had our stew," he told the boy. Then to the waitress, "We'll take the stew."

Flustered herself, the woman nodded, made a quick turnabout, and headed toward the kitchen.

Billy took a few gulps from the glass of water in front of him. When he set it down, he gave a chuckle. "That was funny, her thinkin' you two was married. I wonder if she thought I was your son, 'cause that would really be funny."

Jesse saw the humor in the boy's words, but apparently, Anna did not, for she fumbled nervously with her napkin, folding and unfolding one corner of it before dragging it to her lap. "What—a nice restaurant," she mumbled. "I wonder if they're hiring. That woman said she's new in town."

"Hm. Could be." He tried to picture Anna Hansen cooped up in a hot restaurant but couldn't quite get the vision. He knew she was an outdoor girl, and her tanned, freckled cheeks confirmed it.

"Have you never eaten here?"

"Papa brought us here once or twice when Billy was much younger."

"I been here?" Billy asked. "I don't remember."

She cleared her throat. "As I said, you were much younger."

"Oh."

The remainder of the meal consisted of start and stop conversations, Jesse coming up with a topic and Billy Ray asking something that had nothing to do with it, or Anna and Jesse both speaking at the same time when a quiet lull came between them. To say things felt strained was an understatement. Perhaps this whole notion of getting to know Anna Hansen was for naught even though he couldn't shake the fact that something about her intrigued him. He liked her shy manner and that slightly crooked front tooth that he got only a glimpse of on the rare occasions when she smiled. Add to that her pert nose and her shiny, light brown hair with the flecks of gold in it. She had pulled it back in a loose bun, but her bonnet, which now hung down her back with a ribbon fastened under her chin, had caused a bunch of springy locks to frame her oval face. She was small-framed, but she possessed a certain strength about her that gave Jesse the feeling she would fight to the death for her little brother, no matter that he frustrated her with his boyish outbursts. He couldn't help but admire her for taking over where her mother had left off those many years ago. She'd grown up with no choice but to be strong.

He wanted to continue the discussion about her farm and the foreclosure issue, but he couldn't do that now, not in front of the boy. Perhaps he'd find the opportunity later. After all, wasn't that the reason behind this date? That…and trying to decide whether or not she might make a suitable wife?

Jumpin' butter beans! What kind of crazy thoughts had sneaked into his muddled head? Was he losing his mind?

7

When the farm came into view, Anna gave a deep, yet quiet, sigh of relief. The night was almost over. The meal had been delicious; in fact, she'd had to restrain herself to keep from gobbling it down. She was a lady after all, never mind that she wasn't one bit accustomed to being treated like one. Good gracious, in all her twenty-one years, she'd never even been on any dates, save for those couple times last spring when Jesse took her to the traveling show and then another time when all they'd done was take a walk in Lebanon while trying to think of interesting things to talk about. She was a failure when it came to men, especially ones of Jesse's caliber. And tonight was no different with her little brother tagging along—and fairly dominating the conversation. Of course, Papa had always told her she was pretty, but that didn't count. All told, it plain baffled her why Jesse Fuller would invite her to the Golden Lamb. One day he just showed up at her house with food from his mother, and the next thing she knew, he was inviting her out to dinner. Perchance he thought there was something more to her than what he'd seen last March and April. Wouldn't he be disappointed when he discovered otherwise!

When Jesse turned the horses down the two-track drive leading to her little farmhouse, the tail end of another wagon came into view. It was parked out between the house and the barn, and Rex, her dog, had seemed to be perfectly fine with the whole idea, his wagging tail moving his whole body back and forth. Normally a watchdog, he didn't even take note of Jesse's wagon rounding the curve.

"Well, what're they doing here?" Jesse said under his breath when the mystery wagon came into full view and they saw a man and two boys standing on the ground, making their way over to Rex.

"Isn't that your brother Joseph?" she asked with sudden realization.

"Yes, yes it's Joey, and his sons Isaac and Frankie."

"Oh." Confusion whistled through her veins.

"Hey, we got company!" Billy Ray announced with excitement. "Hi!" He waved and jumped from the wagon before Jesse even reined the horses to a halt, making the dust fly every which direction. "Whatcha' doin'?" he called, running over to them.

"We came t' see if you want to go fishin' with us," said the older boy.

"Me? Sure," he answered without so much as turning to consult Anna.

"Now?" she hastened, looking down on the threesome, four, now that Billy Ray had joined them. Rex flitted with excitement between all of them, his bushy tail still wildly flapping.

"Howdy," Joseph said. "Hope we're not imposing. We were heading down to the creek to catch us a late supper, and I"—he hemmed a bit—"thought we'd check to see if Billy Ray might want to join us." He let his eyes rove from Anna to Jesse then back to her. "Do you mind?"

"I—" she gave a little shrug. "I—guess that's fine. He should be back before dark though."

"I'll see to it." He gave Jesse a curious eye and a slanted half grin. "We should only be gone an hour or so."

Jesse urged his horses forward until they arrived at the hitching post. His arm brushed against Anna's as he tossed the reins down to his brother. Joseph took the reins and looped them around the post, glancing at Jesse as he did so. Some kind of undisclosed message passed between them by way of eye contact, but Anna had no idea what it meant. Jesse jumped down and hurried around to her side to give her a hand down. Again, there was no lady-like way of disembarking, so she was glad for his steadying hand.

"I didn't expect to see you," Jesse said to his brother, slowly turning away from Anna to approach his brother.

"No, I know you didn't." The brothers spoke in quieter tones now while the three boys chattered and laughed, so she decided to give them privacy while she did some weeding among her marigolds and lilies blooming at the front of the house. What a strange set of circumstances, Jesse's brother and nephews seemingly waiting for them to arrive home. And she couldn't remember the last time the boys had invited Billy to go fishing, not that she wasn't happy they had. Heaven knew her brother needed the companionship of other children and the chance to do things boys enjoy rather than spending every waking hour in the barn or out in the fields with her trying to keep things running as best they could. At times, she felt guilty for the way things had turned out, no matter that it was out of her control. Her father had not enlightened her about their household finances, but then neither had she pressed him for details. Had she known he was going to drop dead at the early age of fifty-one, she would most surely have insisted on becoming more informed. Perhaps then, she could have been in on the decision-making, been able to come up with some workable solutions for keeping the farm operational, regardless that most of their earnings had been stolen out from under them.

She bent down to pull a few weeds and ponder her present circumstance, wondering what the brothers were discussing and just what her place was in all of this. Should she simply bid Jesse goodnight and thank him for the meal, or must she invite him inside for another glass of fruit punch? She had no notion how to behave around men, and her pitiful naivety pained her.

She pulled out a few more weeds and tossed them to the side until a quiet throat-clearing sound prompted her to turn around. "Sorry about that," said Jesse with an embarrassed grin. He removed his hat and pushed his fingers through his hair then set the hat back in place. "Joey is—uh, leaving now. He reassured me he'd return Billy Ray before dark."

"All right." She stood then and brushed her soiled hands together. "I was—surprised to see them. It was as if they were waiting for our return."

"Yes. Looks that way. Actually"—Jesse cleared his throat again— "er, apparently, my mother told him I had taken you and Billy to the Golden Lamb—and—"

"Yes?"

He shook his head and frowned. "I guess Joey had some wild kind of notion that"—he gave a nervous chuckle—"you and I might, you know, want to talk—or something."

"Oh!" In the far-off distance, a quiet rumble of thunder interrupted her thoughts. "I—suppose that—would be nice."

"Yeah? Good." His tone lightened. "Why don't we sit on your porch then?"

"All right."

Anna's stomach fluttered with a new set of nerves. What in the world was there to talk about? "Would you like some more strawberry punch?"

"Uh, I think just a drink of water from the well would be refreshing. The air is kind of heavy. Looks like it could rain."

"Yes, I was thinking the same earlier, but then the sun came back out." She giggled for no reason. "Never can tell what sort of trick this Ohio weather is going to play on us."

"That's the truth."

They stepped up to the porch, where a large maple tree provided ample shade. Not that they needed it at the moment. "Have a seat in one of the rockers, and I'll be right back with a couple of tin mugs."

He did as told, so she hurried inside, upset with herself when she let the door flap loudly behind her. Wasn't she always telling Billy to hold the door while he closed it? The blamed thing needed a new spring. She snatched two cups from the shelf then checked to make sure they were clean. Upon a quick inspection, she returned to the door, giving a silent prayer that she might have enough wits about her to carry on a decent conversation.

As soon as Jesse saw her, he jumped up and took the cups from her. "I'll go fill these up. You go ahead and have a seat."

Now *she* did as told, and took a seat. She watched until he disappeared around the side of the house. While she waited, she made some quick sweeps across the faded fabric of her skirt to straighten out the wrinkles. In short order, he returned, and she pulled back her shoulders and put on a smile. He climbed the two rickety steps, handed her a cup, which she gladly took, then seated himself next to her. "Nice chairs," he said. "Did your father make them?"

"Yes, two years ago. I think about him every time I sit in one of them."

"I can see why. They're comfortable and well built." He took a few seconds to look them over, then leaned against the high back, took a big swig of water, and released a loud breath. "That's refreshing."

She took a swallow herself. "Yes, there's nothing like a cool glass of water in the summertime."

A lull followed, which was exactly what she feared, and the only sound that broke the silence was another distant rumble of thunder, punctuated by the back and forth chatter of birds in the overhead maple.

"So..."

"Well," she said in unison. "You go first."

"All right. I was going to ask you how you're managing—without your father, that is."

"We're managing just fine, although we both miss him terribly. His passing was so sudden that sometimes I have a difficult time accepting that he's really gone."

"And the cause of his death—it's still a mystery. Does that trouble you?"

"It does, yes. I hate all the unanswered questions. The sheriff visited me shortly after Papa's passing and asked a few questions, but I haven't heard a word from him since. I have no idea if they're still investigating—or if they've decided to drop the whole matter."

Jesse studied his boots for a few seconds, then looked up at her, the corners of his warm brown eyes crinkled. Serious. "I doubt they've dropped it, but as is the case in most investigations, they don't often let the public know what kind of progress they're making. I bet if you paid the sheriff a visit, he'd answer any questions you might have. At least it might give you a little peace of mind."

"Yes, I suppose you're right. At the moment, I'm a bit distracted trying to figure out my next steps though. I need to find a job." As soon as Anna confessed this, she regretted it. She didn't want Jesse Fuller feeling sorry for her.

"I can imagine you're a bit concerned. Your pa would feel bad about that. He was a good man. I used to enjoy jawing with him whenever we crossed paths. I remember feeling lost when my own father died. He was such a strong presence in our family. Even today, I wrestle with his absence. Ma has filled in nicely, though, just as you have done for Billy Ray."

She relaxed a little. "I've had to play the part of parent and sister, and that's not easy. He can be a handful."

"He's a pretty typical boy, but I bet it's difficult raising him on your own, young as you are. What are you, nineteen?"

Now she bristled a bit and looked him square on. "I'm twenty-one, thank you very much."

His head jerked back and eyebrows raised. "No kidding. I had you figured for younger."

A bit of her former shyness went out of her. "I may seem immature and incapable, Jesse, but I assure you I can handle myself. I have had to grow up quite quickly."

"I never thought of you as immature or incapable. In fact, I admire you a lot."

She smiled in spite of herself. "Well, that's something, coming from someone who's—what? Thirty-five?"

His eyebrows shot up. "I'm twenty-seven and—are you toying with me?"

"I might be," she shot back.

At that, he gave off a hearty chuckle. "I didn't mean to ruffle your feathers."

She giggled. "All right, we've established our ages. I'm older than you thought, and you're younger than I thought."

"You didn't honestly think I was thirty-five."

She gave him a sideways glance and pushed a strand of hair out of her eye. "I never thought about it. I know all your family by name, of course, and Papa always said you were good neighbors, but that's the extent of it. We were only in school together for a couple of years before you started farming full-time." Even as the words left her mouth, Anna wondered if she'd said too much. She certainly didn't want Jesse thinking she spent a second of time swooning over him, thinking of their school days—or recalling those two outings they'd gone on last spring.

"I don't know why we—you know, haven't gotten to know each other better," Jesse said.

"I suppose there was no reason."

Nervously, she brushed a fallen leaf off her skirt and set her rocker in motion. It squeaked with each back and forth rock. Looking up, she noted a few more graying clouds moving in. "It's definitely looking more like rain."

"Yes, it is." They sat there in more moments of awkward silence. "I've never been much for talkin' to women. I s'pose I'm a trifle shy."

This gave her pause. Was he just as insecure as she? It couldn't be. She dared take a hurried peek at him before she cast her eyes at the sky again. "Are you making that up?"

"No, not at all. I've only dated one girl steadily—and that was in early winter. Her name was Martha Weaver."

"I know her. Not well, mind you. She's a few years older than I. Why did you stop courting her?"

Jesse shrugged. "We went out for a few months, but she wasn't really my type. She's more a city girl, and she was, hm, sort of pushy."

"Pushy?"

"Well, I mean she brought up the idea of marriage several times. She sort of scared me off."

"I can imagine. That was rather forward of her."

"That's what I thought."

She would've liked to ask him what his "type" was, but she knew her limits.

"What about you? Have you ever had a beau?"

"Heavens no. I'm accustomed to my singleness."

"Accustomed to your singleness at the ripe old age of twenty-one, eh?" he said, bumping playfully against her and causing her water to spill over. "Oh, sorry."

"No worries," she said with a little giggle, wiping the trickle of water off her skirt. He rattled her in more ways than one.

"You're not opposed to marrying someday, right?"

"What? I mean—no, I guess not. But only if the right man came along, which I don't foresee happening anytime soon. Papa used to tease me about becoming an old maid."

"No. Really?" He started fidgeting with a loose thread on his shirt-sleeve, pulling it and twirling it around his finger, as if he were nervous. Where exactly was this conversation headed?

"I never did tell you that I—rather enjoyed those two dates you and I had in the spring."

Her head shot up. "You did?"

"I was sort of a bumblehead though. I realize that now. I should have offered you my coat for warmth on the night we went to see that traveling troupe."

"Well, that never crossed my mind. It was my own fault for not dressing warmer. I guess I assumed it'd be indoors. And for what it's worth, I never thought of you as a bumblehead."

"You didn't? I had a strong feeling you didn't like me."

"And I thought you didn't like *me*."

At this, they both laughed, and things got a bit more relaxed between them.

Rex came around the side of the house and lapped from the water bowl she always kept in the shade next to the porch. Once satisfied, he sauntered over to the tree and plopped himself down in a shady spot. She gave her chair another push and sipped some water, then rocked, sipped, and rocked some more. In the distance, another rumble of thunder sounded, affirming once again that a storm was moving in.

"I was just thinking…" Jesse began.

"Well, that's a wonder," she teased.

He chuckled. "Yeah, it happens once in a while."

There was an awkward pause before he continued. "I'd like to talk some more about your farm being in foreclosure."

Her stomach lurched, and she stopped rocking. "I don't know why. But I suppose that's all right. What do you want to know?"

"What sort of timeline are you looking at?"

"Mr. Daly said I have until June thirtieth to pay off my debt, but I won't have the means to do it, so I'm guessing Mr. Blackthorn will step in and buy it." Two frustrating tears formed in the corners of her eyes, but she quickly blinked them back and resumed rocking. She didn't think Jesse noticed them. She hoped not.

"Hm. Like I said earlier, I think he's a shyster, hardly worth his weight in feathers. He's trying to buy up every spare inch of Lebanon.

Every time a farm goes up for sale, and especially one going into foreclosure, he's right there, first in line."

"Why do you suppose that is?"

"Power. He wants primary ownership of Lebanon. You familiar with sharecropping?"

"Not especially. I've only read a little about it."

"Sharecropping is something that's growing in popularity in the southern states because the former slaves need jobs and places to live. Businessmen buy up land, then lease out small plots and take a share of the crops at the end of each year. Blackthorn is trying to do something similar here, not because of the issue of slavery, but because the war has caused a lot of folks to fall on hard times. Families are trying to rebuild, but many can't make it financially. Husbands and fathers didn't come home, and those who did can't find work. Long-standing businesses are struggling, stores are closing, and so on. The assassination of our president made for an even more unsteady economy, and in my opinion, Horace Blackthorn is lapping up every opportunity to take advantage of our sad state of affairs. I hear he's not the kindest landlord either."

"How do you mean?"

"It's my understanding he overcharges his renters, then takes more than his share of the crops. I don't think the government has had time to properly regulate the institution of sharecropping. Until it does, Blackthorn will keep doing what he's doing. In some parts of the south, sharecropping is just slavery by another name."

"But that's terrible."

Jesse gave a quiet nod then took a couple more swallows of water. She ruminated over his words while she rocked. "I hate to think he'd use my farm for purposes of cheating folks."

"I can't guarantee he will. It's just a hunch on my part. If it comes down to you vacating your house, where will you go?"

"I don't know. Billy Ray and I have just started discussing it, although it's been on my mind for a couple of months. I've even started packing some boxes, not from Papa's room, mind you, but I know I need to start preparing. I just keep telling myself that God will provide."

"That's a good attitude."

"I know I have to take action though. God gives us two hands and two feet for a reason."

"True. Nothing is impossible where God is concerned."

"Exactly," she said. "It's the only way to think in matters like this."

Jesse stared off into the fields across the road, he too gently rocking. A light breeze had kicked up, cooling her cheeks and rustling through her sleeves. She held her cup with both hands, setting it atop her lap.

"It's quite possible someone other than Blackthorn could intervene." His words were so soft she barely heard them.

"I don't know who would," she replied in an equally quiet tone.

"Hm." He rested against the back of the chair. He gave his head a slow turn till their eyes met. "Might be the Fuller brothers could buy it."

Had she heard right? "W-what?" Her voice cracked when it went up a notch.

He flicked both dark eyebrows at her and gave a small grin. "It might be a possibility."

She still didn't trust her ears. "Are you talking about *my* farm?"

"What other farm is there?"

She shrugged. "I don't know, I just thought I misunderstood. I don't see why—"

"My brothers and I spoke briefly about it the other day. Buying your farm would expand our own property. Jack heard talk about the foreclosure at the hardware the other day. Some fellows were talking about who might take it over, and one of them said he wouldn't be surprised if Horace Blackthorn already had his feelers out. Then when Billy Ray actually verbalized it in the wagon tonight, it affirmed what's already been rumored. The fellow at the hardware said he didn't think Newell would be too happy about Blackthorn buying it."

A long moment of silence followed, and she felt at a helpless loss for words. When she didn't speak, he proceeded. "They suggested I should marry you." This he said as casually as if he were talking about the weather.

Her body gave a sudden jolt, and she stopped rocking. If she were at a loss for words before, she was dumbstruck now. Her mouth opened, and then her jaw dropped. Had she even heard right? She tried to form a word of response, but nothing came out, so she sat there staring at him, leaving his statement dangling there between them. His honey brown eyes were earnest, however, not joking.

He laughed. "I know. It's crazy, isn't it?" He tried to make light of it, but she didn't take the bait. "I mean, the way you're reacting now—that's how I was when Jack suggested it. I even told him it was a ridiculous thing to say." He chuckled, but she remained mute while gawking at him. "Right?"

They had a regular staring match, and soon his smile disappeared. "You should—maybe close your mouth—before you catch a fly," he said.

She still didn't see an ounce of humor, but she did clamp shut her mouth, not having the wits about her to form a decent sentence.

He cleared his throat and rubbed his hands on his pant legs. "Here's the thing. It's not an entirely foolish notion now that I've taken a few days to think about it. I mean, a legal union between us would make the property *my* problem. You could turn it over to me, and my family would assume the debt. The house would still be yours, or *ours*, and…" He shrugged. "You'd have no more worries. You wouldn't even have to look for work. You could just keep maintaining your garden, seeing to Billy Ray's needs, doing your regular household chores, like the laundry and dishes and making meals, and, I don't know, whatever it is that women—er, *housewives*, do."

Now she shook her head and started forming some words in her mind, but the only two that came out of her mouth were: "You're crazy."

There went those dark brows again, lifting in two rather mischievous arches. "I've been called far worse."

"I can't even believe you suggested such a thing."

"I didn't suggest it. It was my brothers' idea."

"All the more reason you shouldn't have mentioned it to me."

"I mean—like I said, I thought it was a crazy notion to begin with, just like you, but I'm starting to wonder if it might make sense."

"Make sense? How could it possibly make sense?"

"Um. For starters, you could stay in your house."

She would secretly admit that part did sound appealing, but the rest of it? Ridiculous! "I see no need to get married. If you want to buy the property, go ahead, but why get married?"

"Good question. I was thinking a marriage license would cement the deal for you. You would still have your house. In fact, it would remain legally yours."

"But..." She put both hands to her head and pressed hard, as if doing so might squeeze out a bit of understanding from her confused mind. Unfortunately, it did not. She shook her head at him and pursed her brow. "What an absolutely crazy notion." She stood up, spilling a bit of water on herself. "I think it's past time for you to leave."

He jumped up next to her and tossed his empty cup on the chair. "Now? But don't you think it makes sense to discuss the possibility of—of—this idea? Didn't you just say a few moments ago that you would marry if the right person came along?"

He dumbfounded her, and any shyness she'd earlier had in his presence, drained out of her like water from a leaky pail. She stood her full height, but still paled next to him. Didn't matter. He didn't frighten her, not one little bit. "Indeed. Need I clarify that I said the *right* person? Clearly, I have not yet found him."

"But—how do you know I'm not it?"

Frustration mixed with anger rumbled out of her. She extended her arm straight out and pointed her index finger at his wagon. "You need to leave."

"But—we didn't talk about..."

"Yes, we did. Just now. It is a harebrained idea. Discussion over." She stepped off the porch, and he quickly followed, hurrying to keep up. She walked with purpose to his wagon, then stopped in front of it and waved her arm in a welcoming gesture for him to climb aboard. "Thank you for the supper, Mr. Fuller. It was quite delicious."

"Aw, Anna. Don't be like that."

"Good night!" she huffed.

She turned on her heel and felt her skirts flare wide. Lightning streaked across the eastern skies. A clap of thunder, closer than before, seemed to accentuate her farewell. She reached her back door and opened it, then turned, surprised to find him still on the ground, holding the reins loosely in one hand and gaping at her, his broad shoulders slightly slumped. Behind him, a dark cloud loomed.

They stood there and stared at one another. "Good night!" she repeated.

"We'll talk soon."

"I think not."

"We'll see." He waved a hand, gave a slanted smile, and climbed up to his buckboard.

"I do not want to see you on my property again, Mr. Fuller."

"Not even in your fields?"

"No! Goodbye."

She walked inside, let the door slam behind her, and then ran to the window to watch him drive away. Her heart had taken to racing so fast, she thought it might just jump right out of her chest. Imagine him asking, no, not asking, *suggesting*, that they marry—all so that he could own her land. He wasn't thinking of her. He was thinking of himself—and his brothers. What in the world would make him think she would fall for such a preposterous notion? A low growl came out of her as she set her half cup of water down on the window sill then snatched up the broom leaning against the wall and set to sweeping vigorous strokes across the uneven wooden planks of her already clean floor.

8

*J*esse allowed a few days to pass for some quiet contemplation. Thankfully, mending fences and working side by side with his hired hands in the milking barn kept him good and occupied. He avoided his brothers at all costs, hadn't even spoken to them in church the other morning for fear they'd want to know how his supposed "date" with Anna Hansen and her brother had gone. There was no way he was going to discuss it. Clearly, she didn't view his pathetic proposal as a solution. He should be glad, he supposed, and yet there remained the predicament of Horace Blackthorn wanting to purchase the Hansen land. The last person he wanted butting up to Fuller property was that brute. Next thing he knew, the fellow would be stealing their water supply or erecting fences where they didn't belong. He'd always had a good relationship with Newell, but he didn't see that happening with Blackthorn. He didn't trust him any more than he trusted a snake in a chicken coop. Perhaps he'd pay a visit to Cyrus Daly in the next day or so and see just where Blackthorn stood on the foreclosure situation.

"Yoo-hoo! Is that you under there, Jesse?"

Lying underneath his wagon to grease an axle, Jesse lifted his head and promptly bumped it on a steel rod. He winced in pain, then angled his head to see his mother's garden boots and tattered work skirt. He'd seen her outside earlier, carrying the watering can to her flowers in the backyard. With a bit of effort, he slid his way out from under the wagon on his back.

"Sorry to bother you, dear. Were you busy?"

He sat up and shook his head. "Uh, no, what gave you that idea?" he grunted as he stood up and brushed himself off. He eyed the basket that she held dangling from the crook of her right arm, a clean towel draped over it. "What do you have there?"

She lifted one corner of the towel. "Oh, just some blueberry muffins. Fresh from the oven."

He reached for one, but she quickly snatched the basket out of his reach. "This isn't for you, dear."

"Who's it for?"

"I thought you could take it over to Anna."

"Anna? Oh, no you don't."

"Well, you told me things didn't go too well, so I thought you could perhaps use these as a sort of peace offering. By the way, you never did tell me exactly what you meant by your comment."

"Because I didn't feel like talking about it then. And I still don't."

"Well, I don't know what could possibly have gone so wrong. Was it because her brother tagged along?"

"No, Ma, that had nothing to do with it. Can we just drop it?" He got a whiff of the muffins. "And now may I have one of those? My stomach is growling."

She took a step back prevent him from snatching one. He gave a low snarl.

"All right, but before I give you one, I have a confession."

"What is it?"

"Joey told me you boys are interested in purchasing the Hansen property."

"He didn't need to tell you about that."

"Whyever not? I am the primary owner of this farm, you know. I should have some say in the decisions made around here."

"Fair enough. So what's your confession?"

"I told him you had taken Anna out to supper the other night, so that's how he happened to show up at her house with Isaac and Franklin. I guess he thought taking her brother off your hands would give you a chance to discuss matters with her—about the property."

He let out a long breath and shook his head. "Ma, you needn't have confessed to something I already knew. Joey told me over at Anna's house that you were the one who informed him I was with her."

She blinked sheepish hazel eyes at him. "You're not mad at me, are you? I've noticed you've been awfully quiet around the house, and you've been coming in extra late. Seems as if you're avoiding me."

He combed his soiled fingers through his dirty hair and felt a glob of sand fall on his shoulders. He needed a bath. Perchance he'd go down to the creek at dusk and bathe there. He could use a refreshing dip in the water after another scorching day. "No, Ma, I'm not mad at you, and even if I were, I couldn't stay that way. Now, may I have a muffin?" He started to reach for one.

"Not yet." she stepped back, blocking his efforts. "Do you plan to marry Anna Hansen?"

"What? Ma! Where did that come from?" he shrieked.

"Well, Joey, you know…"

"He told you that?" He gave his head several fast shakes. "Marrying her was not my idea. My not-so-intelligent brothers hatched it up. And, no, I don't plan to marry her—or anybody for that matter."

"Don't you want to ensure the property lands in Fuller hands?"

"It would be nice, but it appears someone else already has dibs."

Her brow etched three deep lines, and she frowned. "Who?"

He rolled his eyes skyward. If he didn't tell her now, she'd wheedle it out of him sooner or later.

"Aargh," he groused, tossing back his head. "Horace Blackthorn."

"Horace Blackthorn," she repeated, staring off for a moment, then putting a finger to her chin. "Hasn't he already purchased a fair amount of land around Lebanon?"

"Yep. Ma, I gotta get back to work."

"Now, just a minute." She set a firm hand on his arm before he turned, keeping the basket of muffins out of reach just as he thought about making another grab for one. "I remember him now. I overheard him discussing something on the street with a group of old cronies— well, they may have been my age, but never mind that. Anyway, they were talking about the war ending and how jobs in Lebanon were becoming fewer. Mr. Blackthorn mentioned his growing interest in sharecropping, and one of the fellows joked that one day, the whole of Lebanon would belong to him. In return, he said something like, 'That's my goal. Maybe one day, I'll own the whole town.' What sort of man do you take him for, Jesse? Is he the type of person you want running Lebanon? Does he have any sort of power?"

"Not as far as I'm concerned he doesn't. A man only has as much power as people allow him to have." His gut wrenched a little.

"But what if he starts owning more property than most? Won't that give him a lot of undue influence over the citizens of Lebanon?"

"You worry too much. Now, Ma, please, I'm truly famished. Can't I have one of those muffins?"

She rolled back the cloth, and wonder of wonders, held the basket out to him. He took one and enjoyed the first delicious, moist bite— until he realized her scrutinizing eyes were not about to turn away from him.

"What?" he asked between bites.

"So you must have asked Anna to marry you, and you got a flat no in response. That would explain your sour mood over the past few days."

He swallowed the last remaining bites of the muffin and blinked three times at his clever mother. Who was this mind-reading woman? Was there nothing sacred about his life?

As if sensing his frustration, she set her hand on his arm again. "Dear, I can tell when something's bothering you. You may be a grown man, but you're still my—"

"Little boy," he filled in. "I wish you'd stop saying that."

"Well, am I right? Did you ask her?"

"Oh, all right! I brought up the idea of marriage. Are you happy now?"

"Not necessarily, but I think it's interesting. What was this, your third date? Your father asked me on our fourth date, you know. I thought that was early, but I said yes anyway. We talked for hours and hours." She smiled and gazed up at the fast-moving clouds, her eyes suddenly turning a greenish shade and looking all dreamy. "We were so in love, your father and me..."

"Ma." He shifted.

"Oh, I know, I've gone off topic. Well, so you asked her and she said no. Did you give her a reason to say yes?"

"I—told her it would be one way to ensure she stays in her house. I told her she wouldn't have to look for a job in town, that she could continue to stay home and take care of her brother and—and work in her garden—and—and cook and do laundry—and all those other things that wives do."

"What? You didn't tell her *that*!"

"Yes, I did. What's wrong with what I said?"

"Everything. Have you no common sense about women?"

"Apparently not."

She gave a frustrated sigh. "Jesse, a woman wants to be wooed. Courted."

He pursed his lips in exasperation. "Ma, there's no time for courting. In a matter of days, the bank will force her out of her house."

She shoved the basket of muffins at him. "Here, take these. And go up to the house and wash up, then put on some clean clothes and a little bit of that cologne. You heard me—just a little. Then jump on your horse and go over there."

"No. She told me to never step foot on her property again."

"Well, of *course* she did. I'd have done the same. All you have to do is apologize to her. No need for much more than that. Just tell her you're sorry and come back home."

"That's it?"

"Well, don't forget to hand her the muffins."

"Hand her the muffins."

"Hand her the muffins," she repeated.

It sounded easy enough.

9

That one fishing excursion with the Fuller boys had been all it took for the three boys to become fast friends. Oh, they'd known each other from school, so it wasn't as if they weren't already acquainted, but apparently, their time together had been fun despite the fact it had rained and Joey Fuller had brought Billy Ray home earlier than expected. "Sis, we had the best time," Billy had said, running into the house a sopping mess and dripping rainwater all over her clean floor. "We're gonna go out again tomorrow—if you don't mind, that is."

"No, I don't mind as long as you do your chores. I'm glad you had a good time."

And so he had, and then today, he'd finished his chores in fast order and met the boys again. She had watched out the window as they met at the halfway point, the middle of one of the Fullers' cornfields, all carrying their fishing poles, a fourth boy joining them this time, perhaps Jack and Cristina Fuller's son, or maybe even a friend from school. At any rate, he'd found some summertime friends, and she couldn't be happier for him—just in time, unfortunately, for them to move into town.

She'd been down in the dumps of late. Yesterday and today, she'd spent time in Lebanon going from one business to another seeking work. Unfortunately, not a single place was hiring, with the exception of the livery and the Ed Wood Saloon, where she saw "Help Wanted" signs nailed to the doors. She drew the line on those establishments, however. She'd even walked into the Golden Lamb and spoke to the manager, but the kind lady there had told her they had no plans to hire anyone. At least, she'd apologized profusely, more than likely having heard about her plight. What was she to do if no job turned up for her? She had no relatives to whom she could turn and not even any friends who were close enough to ask for a helping hand. She thought about seeking help from the church, but seeing as she hadn't returned since her father's passing, she felt strange now asking for assistance. For the briefest moment, she considered Jesse Fuller's proposal, but just as quickly dismissed it. She could not—would not!—marry some man out of desperation. Besides, he didn't want to help her as much as he wanted her land. That was all he and his brothers cared about, forget that they'd been kind enough to help her during planting season, tilling the land with their big plows and work horses before sowing the seed. Had it been a ploy to win her favor? She had almost reached the point of being glad to move, but then the question rose again—where would she go if she couldn't find work?

It was Tuesday, pie and bread-baking day, and normally her day to shake the rugs and dust the shelves as well. Having slid two loaves into the hot oven, she took a corner of her apron, and mopped her damp forehead. She grabbed a cup from the counter and walked outside to the pump for a cool drink of water. After filling it to the brim and taking her first few gulps, she turned around at the sound of an approaching horse. At the sight of Jesse Fuller coming across the field, a twinge of annoyance coupled with unexpected pleasure shot through her veins. What was he doing here, especially since she'd said she didn't want to see him again? If he planned to bring up that daft notion again about getting married, she just might have to throw the remainder of her water in his face. On the other hand, it might be in her favor to accept. Her mind was an absolute clutter of thoughts and emotions.

As he drew closer, she raised her chin and put on her most solemn face. "Mr. Fuller."

"Miss Hansen," he returned, but not with the same manner of staunchness. If anything, she detected a hint of a smile under his whiskery upper lip. He always seemed to have a shadow of a beard, which she found attractive—much to her dismay. She didn't *want* to like anything about Jesse Fuller, especially after what had happened the other night. He reined his horse to a stop, dismounted, and removed a basket that had been hanging from the saddle horn. He took a few steps forward until he came within a couple feet of her. She eyed the basket. "My mother wanted to share some muffins with you and Billy Ray."

Muffins. It couldn't be helped. Her mouth watered at the mere word. "That's very kind of her. If you'll wait here, I'll take these inside and put them on a plate so you can take the basket back."

"Oh, you don't need—"

But without giving him a chance to finish his sentence, she took the basket, turned, and walked inside the house, taking care not to invite him in. She carefully transferred the muffins to a large serving platter, one by one, and then walked back outside. "Please tell her what a fine neighbor she is." They stared at each other for a brief moment. She absentmindedly swung the basket a little, not sure what to say next.

"Well, the main reason I rode over here was simply to apologize."

"Apologize?" She hadn't expected that.

"Yes, I just wanted to say I was sorry for the way I fumbled up things the other night—by suggesting we marry. That was rude and thoughtless of me."

"Oh. Well." All the anger she had stored up in her heart in case she needed to expel it seemed to drain right out of her. "I appreciate that."

As Anna handed the basket to Jesse, their hands brushed, and she couldn't deny the little tingle that ran through her. Holding the reins in one hand, he hung the basket over the saddle horn, and in less time than it would take a squirrel to scamper up a tree, he was back on his horse. He looked down at her. "How's the job search going?"

She squinted up at him. "Not well, I'm afraid. I drove into town again today, but no one seemed interested in hiring me."

"Hm. Sorry to hear that. Jobs are hard to come by now." He lingered a moment, and for some reason, she wished he'd stay a few minutes, no matter that a few days ago she'd told him never to come on her property again. He tipped his hat at her. "Well, I'm sure something will work out for you." He turned his horse around. "Again, sorry for the other night. I did enjoy taking you and Billy Ray out though."

"You did? He's quite the talker."

He chuckled. "He's a lively one."

She smiled at that. "Indeed. There's been little reason for laughter in our house since Papa's passing, so your invitation came at a good time. Thank you again."

"You're welcome. I'm glad you had a good time." He wiped his brow with his sleeve. "You enjoy those muffins now."

She took a tiny step forward. "Oh, we will, and thank your mother."

"I will."

"And one more thing." Plainly, she just wasn't quite ready for him to go. "I'd like to apologize myself, Jesse—for—the way I showed my temper. I'm not normally given to such outbursts."

"Well, it was a perfectly normal reaction."

"I'm sure I overreacted."

She noted his eyes crinkle with something like amusement under the rim of his hat. "Don't worry about it. What say we start with a clean slate? I mean, as friends?"

"Really?" Unexpected hope stirred up in her, no matter that she tried to tamp it down.

"Sure. I could stop by again—maybe tonight—if you wouldn't mind. Or tomorrow," he added. "Or the next day."

She didn't take over-long to think about it. "That would be fine. I mean—any time."

"Good." He paused only a couple of seconds. "I'll be going then." This time she took a step back and gave him a little wave. He tipped his hat one last time, nudged his horse in the sides, and headed off down the long drive. She watched until he turned onto Drake Road.

10

"I need to see Mr. Daly, please."

The gentleman sitting behind the front desk in the bank lobby looked up, his spectacles falling down his nose. "Mr. Fuller?"

Jesse acknowledged the middle-aged man by removing his hat and nodding at him. "Mr. Grayson, isn't it?"

"Yes, sir, Donald Grayson. I'm Mr. Daly's assistant. What can I do for you?"

"Is Mr. Daly in?"

"He is, but he's currently with a client."

"I'll wait then."

"Oh. It could be awhile, but if you don't mind, you can have a seat over there."

"Thanks, I'll do that."

Grayson pushed his chair back and rose. "I'll just tell him you're waiting."

"No need. I don't want to rush him."

"Very well then." The fellow slowly sat back down, setting his spectacles back in place and resuming his paperwork.

Jesse situated himself in a comfortable chair and looked around the building before setting his eyes on the *Lebanon Western Star* newspaper on a table next to him. He picked it up and read the front page headline: "Trial Continues for Eight Conspirators in the Assassination of President Lincoln!" Jesse's gut twisted at the words. What an evil world it was, folks conspiring to kill the president of the United States—and succeeding! And to what gain? He proceeded to read the article, though decided to mostly skim it. He'd already heard and read enough about the infamous tragedy to last him a lifetime. Besides, his mother kept him well enough informed, as she read every scrap of information she laid eyes on and involved herself in conversations on the street whenever she made trips into town. Jesse didn't hold the same fascination for it as many did, but he also didn't blame folks for wanting to know every detail.

Jesse absently turned the pages of the newspaper, glancing at headlines and speed-reading through some of the articles, interested mostly in local news—until the sound of voices directed his attention away from the newspaper. Of all people, Horace Blackthorn exited the bank president's office and stopped at the desk of Mr. Grayson. "You're to prepare the appropriate papers for the Hansen farm. Cyrus will inform you."

"Yes, sir. As soon as Mr. Daly speaks with me about the sale, I'll prepare the necessary documents."

"Good. I assume you'll get right on it."

Grayson nodded. "Just as soon as Mr. Daly gives me the final figures."

"Fine." Blackthorn turned to leave. In that moment, he made eye contact with Jesse. Jesse didn't readily stand until it was clear Blackthorn intended to approach him. They shook hands, and despite how hot a day it was, something in the handshake gave him a chill. Maybe the fellow's cold eyes contributed to it. "Well, Fuller, looks like you and me are goin' to be neighbors."

Jesse tried not to react, just raised his brow. "That so?"

"You bet. I'm purchasing the Hansen property. Maybe you might want to negotiate the sale of a section of your land that butts up to my line."

"Aren't you a little premature in assuming it's your property? I was under the assumption Miss Hansen had until the end of June to pay off the debt."

The bearded fellow with the graying side whiskers and mustache huffed a little laugh. "Yeah, well, I'm speeding up the process, you see. Now, about that piece of property. I'd give you a fair price."

"Sorry, we're not interested."

"No? You speak for your brothers too?"

"We work as a team and are all likeminded."

He nodded. "I see. Well…"

"Mr. Fuller, Mr. Daly will see you now." This from Donald Grayson.

Blackthorn stilled and looked from Grayson to Jesse. "You got an appointment with Daly, eh?"

"Sure do. Nice seeing you again, Horace. I'm sure we'll be running into each other again. You have a nice day now." He smiled and nodded at the fellow, then left him standing there, knowing full well his visit to the bank had filled the fellow with curiosity, if not a touch of angst.

He found Cyrus Daly sitting behind his large mahogany desk, glancing through some papers. Upon Jesse's entrance, he quickly set the papers aside and rose, extending a hand and a smile. "Well, Jesse Fuller, what brings you here this fine day? You interested in a loan?"

"No sir, not today." Jesse shook Daly's extended hand.

"Why don't you sit down then and tell me what I can do for you?" The banker pointed at the chair on the other side of his desk, so Jesse helped himself to the leather-seated chair. Mr. Daly opened his cigar box and offered Jesse a stogie.

Jesse raised a hand. "No thanks."

"Oh, that's right. You Fuller men don't partake. Now then, what can I do for you?"

"Well, I came to inquire about the Hansen property foreclosure."

The man didn't flinch. "The property has been sold. All that remains is for the paperwork to be drawn up so that I can obtain a signature."

Jesse took great care not to flinch as well. "Horace Blackthorn. I talked to him a minute ago, but see, here's the thing. I consulted with Johnson & Johnson Law Firm before coming here. Anna Hansen has a legal right to reinstatement."

"*If* she can come up with the money by June thirtieth, which she cannot. She's had plenty of chances, and I've given her more than enough time."

"Ah, but I happen to know she *can* come up with the money."

Daly's face wrinkled into a sour frown. "How do you figure?"

"I'll be marrying her in a few days, at which time the title to the property will be in my hands and will become my legal problem. It won't be a problem for long though, as I'll be paying off the remainder of the mortgage."

Daly's high forehead furrowed into several rugged lines. "You're marrying that girl?"

"She's a grown woman, fully capable of making her own decisions." Jesse felt hot around the collar, almost shrinking at his own daring words. Not only that, what would Anna say when he told her what he'd done? *God, what am I doing? Lead me, Lord.* Trusting that things would work out according to the Lord's plan, he charged ahead. "So, you best start drawing up those papers for me, Mr. Daly, not Blackthorn. You're not dealing with Anna Hansen anymore."

The fellow sat speechless, merely gaping, jaw fallen. "What—what did you say?"

"You heard right."

"But, I—I..."

"How about I return in the morning? We can discuss matters more fully then."

"Tomorrow, you say?" Daly's voice quivered. "I don't think—"

Jesse stood then and extended his hand across the table, but Daly didn't take it. Instead, he continued gawking, face gone pale.

"Don't look so worried, Cyrus. It's not like this deal is a life or death matter for you. You ought to be glad Miss Hansen will be paying off the debt. I should think you'd be smiling."

"Uhh, yes, it's just that Horace Blackthorn…"

"Mr. Blackthorn will just have to back off. The property rightfully belongs to Anna Hansen, soon to be, um, Mrs. Fuller." Just saying the words made his stomach churn, and he almost took back everything he'd just said to Daly, but he stood his ground and even managed to put on a smile. Jesse swiveled on his heel. At the door, he turned and tipped his hat at the pale-faced banker. "I'll be back tomorrow, hopefully with Miss Hansen. We'll settle matters then."

Outside, Jesse mounted his horse, turned him around, and then made for his farm. He needed to find his brothers, and the sooner the better. As he rode, the wind cooling the sweat on his brow, he prayed that God would slam the door on this whole crazy notion if it wasn't meant to be.

11

Anna had supper on the table by the time Billy Ray reentered the house after washing up at the pump. Upon his return from his fishing excursion, he'd wreaked of fish odor, having caught and cleaned a couple medium-sized rock bass before coming home. She was grateful for the fish, which she cooked up in a pan with some small potatoes and a few carrots. The smells radiating from the pan made her mouth water.

"So, you had a fine time, did you?"

"Sure did."

They seated themselves, then bowed their heads so Anna could offer a quick prayer of thanks. When she was done, Billy started in with his chatter, talking about his fishing, how one of the boys had fallen into the creek, then lost his fishing pole along with the one and only fish he'd caught. After he fell in, they'd all jumped in and swam for a while, then let themselves air-dry while taking up their poles again. She barely got in a word edgewise until he thought to ask her how her job hunt had gone that day.

She'd not wanted to talk about it, but then recalled how he'd insisted he was growing up and deserved to know about the future of their family farm. She pushed her food around a bit while considering her reply.

"Nothing yet, but I'm not discouraged. I have a few more places I can check tomorrow."

"Where did you go?"

Anna hated to admit that she'd literally walked through the door of just about every place of business in Lebanon, even though it was the truth. "Oh, a number of places. Folks aren't hiring so much right now."

"Well, maybe tomorrow you'll find something."

"Yes! Perhaps tomorrow. I'll ride into town again first thing—while you're out doing chores."

"What if you can't find a job?"

She attempted a reassuring smile. "That is not for you to worry about. Something will turn up. The Lord will take care of us. In fact, He is working out our future even as we talk."

"How do you know that?"

"Because I was just reading in the Bible this morning from the book of Jeremiah about God working out His plans for us. We must trust Him though."

The neigh of an approaching horse had Billy jumping from his chair to go investigate at the window. "It's Jesse Fuller. Was you expectin' him again?"

She laid her cloth napkin down and stood, then instinctively touched her hair, pushing a few wild wisps behind her ears. Goodness, he'd mentioned the possibility of coming for another visit as early as tonight, but she hadn't taken him seriously. Why must he always show up when she looked a sight? She joined Billy at the window. "I don't know what he could possibly want."

"Maybe his mother is sending more food."

"He already brought muffins over. You ate one, remember?"

"Oh yeah…I'll go ask him what—" Billy headed for the door.

"No! You'll do no such thing." He stopped, his hand gripping the steel pull. "Come back to the table, and I'll go outside to talk to him."

"But I…"

"No," she repeated in her sternest voice. "Sit down and finish your supper. I'll return in a minute."

"You're not going to invite him inside?"

"No, not this time." She glanced in the small face mirror that hung by the door. "Good gracious. I look like something the cat dragged home."

He gave her a two-second perusal. "You don't look *that* bad."

She sighed, then pointed at the table. "Go."

"Oh, all right." He slouched and walked back to the table.

Pulling herself to her full height, she took a deep breath for good measure and walked outside, closing the door behind her. "Good afternoon, Jesse," she called from the front porch. "Back so soon?"

He didn't have a full-out smile for her, but rather a more tentative expression, as he urged his horse up the driveway, having taken the road this time rather than cut across the field. He reined his horse to a stop at the hitching post and climbed down. "I couldn't stay away," he said in an attempt to humor her, offering the slightest crooked grin while looping the reins over the post. He was a fine looking man in his rugged attire. She inwardly scolded herself for even taking a second to assess his appearance—and for caring what he might think of hers.

Rather than step down to greet him, she set her hand on the railing and stayed put. "What brings you back?"

He hemmed a bit as he switched his weight from one foot to the other. "Um, sorry about interrupting your supper hour, but I wonder if we might take a few minutes to discuss something."

"My property, you mean?"

"Uh, yes, would you mind if I joined you on one of your father's rockers?"

She recalled what had happened a few days ago when they'd sat on the rockers and he'd brought up that half-baked notion about getting married. She vowed not to overreact this time—if she had it in her. She said a silent prayer, hoping the Lord's ears were inclined to hear.

"I suppose." She knew she ought to offer him a drink of cold water before she sat. She'd been strangely happy to see him this morning, but tonight a wave of uncertainty crashed over her again. If she could figure out her own emotions, she'd be further ahead.

He climbed the two steps and sat down next to her, then removed his hat, giving her a chance to check out his thick, dark brown head of hair and the line that appeared where his hat had been. He pushed his fingers through it, and she couldn't help but notice the ripple of muscle in his forearm. Not wishing to appear interested, she set her eyes on her soiled apron. She quickly folded her hands and placed them over the largest stain.

"Well, I'll get right to the point then."

"I'm listening."

"I paid a visit to Cyrus Daly, the bank president, shortly after leaving your place this morning."

Her ears perked. "Oh?"

"He tells me Horace Blackthorn has but to sign the paperwork, and your property will be his."

Her stomach did a strange, sickly drop. "I'm not surprised by that. It was just a matter of time, and the thirtieth day of June is closing in."

"Yes, it is, and you have every right to stay right where you are until that date. He doesn't have the right to force you to give up the fight."

"Yes, but I—"

He raised a finger along with one dark eyebrow. "I visited Quinn Johnson at Johnson and Johnson Law Office before going to see Daly and learned your rights. If you can come up with the money, then you are entitled to reinstatement."

"Well, I can't."

"Ah, but you can."

Now her stomach took to fluttering. "If you are going to suggest we marry, then the answer is no. I don't wish to be beholden to you, nor do

I wish to be your pawn in the center of a business deal. I am not that desperate."

"I see. Did you find a job then?"

This stopped her. "No."

"How about another place to live?"

She rolled her eyes. "If I don't have a job yet, it would stand to reason I don't have anywhere to go."

"Then I'd say you've reached the desperate stage."

How could she argue with that? She closed her mouth.

"After I visited Daly, I hunted down my brothers, and we came up with a plan of sorts. Would you like to hear it?"

"I'm not sure. Do I have a choice?"

He grinned. "Naturally, you have a choice, but it might be smart to hear me out."

She sat a little straighter and turned to look at him. "All right then. I'm listening."

He squinted at her as if the sun were blinding him. "Promise not to kick me off your land before we've had time to discuss it?"

"Nope." She accompanied her one-word response with a wisp of a smile.

"I guess I'll take my chances." He stretched out his long legs before him, the toes of his boots reaching the porch railing. "Here's the short of it. My family wants to purchase your property. We do not want Blackthorn buying it out from under you and punishing you further by kicking you out of your house. If you and I marry…" She opened her mouth to argue, but he made a halting gesture with his hand. "Hear me out now. I'm aware we've only dated a few times, and we have much to learn about each other, but a legal, binding marriage will give me better leverage for taking over the title to your farm. This would allow you to stay in your house and continue working your farm and gardens as much as you like. You will still maintain ownership, but it would be more a partnership between you and my family. If that makes sense."

Her heart took to beating like a drum, the pulse of which she heard in her head. "But we'd be married?"

"Yes."

"Would you—still live at your mother's house?"

"Those are things we can discuss."

"I—I don't—want, um, *need* a husband, least of all one I hardly know. I mean, not really well."

"You do know my brother Joey married someone he didn't know."

"I heard about that. He needed someone to take care of his four youngsters. Our situation is entirely different."

"Granted, but you need a house to live in, right? And you're somewhat desperate, right? If you look at it that way, our situation is not all that different from Joey's and Faith's."

They sat on the porch for a full minute, each digesting the idea on their own. The only sounds were the whistling and cawing of overhead birds flitting from tree to tree. And that wretched pulse pounding in her ears.

"I don't know what my papa would think about such an idea," she finally said. Her breaths were coming out all jagged, as her nerves jangled and jumped.

Jesse chuckled. "Your dad would be as happy as a kid with a new toy. Might be he's listening from somewhere up there even now and urging you to take a chance on me." He slid his boot back and kicked a stray stick off the porch. "I know I'm nothing special, but I do love and serve the Lord, and I'd treat you fair and square."

She tipped her head at him and tried not to smile. "Fair and square, eh? That sounds more like a business proposition than a marriage proposal."

"Would you like me to get down on one knee?"

She laughed in spite of the situation. "Hardly." She let the idea of marriage tumble around in her mind. Did she dare do something so out of character for her? She batted at a bee that had started buzzing around her head. "I've always prided myself on my level of common sense and responsibility. Marrying you seems so careless."

"But what if it winds up being the most responsible decision you've ever made?"

"I don't see how that could be possible."

"Think about it. You won't have to move, you don't have to go looking for a job, Billy Ray can stay put, you can lay aside your financial worries, and your future would be secure."

She considered his words, all of which held a certain level of appeal. But still, something nagged at her. "I don't see why you'd do this. What do you get out of it? And what happens if some day, you meet up with a pretty girl in town—and maybe even fall in love with her? You'd kick yourself in your own behind for acting so rashly by marrying me."

He tossed back his head in a full-out chuckle. "First, marriage has never been tops on my list of priorities. Would I like to have a family sometime? Sure, but it's not something I *have* to have. Second, I don't remember the last time I came across a pretty single lady in Lebanon, and even if I did, I'd never break my marriage vows. When I make a vow to my wife, it will be for life. Finally, marrying you automatically gives me the deed to your property because that would be a condition should we choose to marry. In the end, though, the decision rests with you. I don't want to force you into something you don't want."

"I—I appreciate that. I suppose I—well, I'll think about it for a day or two."

"Actually, I told Mr. Daly I'd be back in the morning to start the paperwork. Would you like to come with me?"

"You want me to come with you?"

"It *is* your property. Also, if we both show up, Daly will get the idea that we're serious."

"But I haven't given you my final decision. Why must we be in such a hurry?"

"Because I saw Blackthorn at the bank today. Daly is already drawing up papers for him to pay off the mortgage."

"But I still have a few days."

"Not according to Blackthorn. For some reason, he is determined to take over your farm."

A knot of worry balled up in her chest. "This is all so much to take in. I know a few days ago, I took your suggestion rather poorly. Today, I'm not entirely opposed to the idea, but there are things we must discuss beforehand."

"Such as?"

"Well, for starters, I—I don't know if I want to live with you."

He grinned. "I don't know if I want to live with *you* either."

A little sigh whistled out of her. "At least we agree on that."

He gave her arm a very tentative touch. "Tell you what. For the time being, I'll remain at my mother's house. I'm a grown man still living with his mother, but it's not been too bad, save for all the teasing I take from my brothers."

"Really? They tease you?"

"Yeah, they chide me for living at home. They think Ma spoils me silly."

"I'm sure she does. By the way, what would she think of you marrying?"

"Take my word for it, she would love another daughter-in-law."

She relaxed a little—until the front door opened and Billy Ray peeked outside. He wore a mischievous expression. "Sorry, but I—I sort of listened in—not on purpose, but the windows are open."

"Ah," Jesse said. "I guess you heard my proposal then."

"Are you gonna do it, Sis? Are you gonna marry Mr. Fuller?"

Anna lightly pinched the skin at her throat, which she was prone to do when contemplating a decision. "Perhaps."

Billy Ray cut loose a loud squeal then darted past them, down the steps and out into the yard, kicking up dirt with his bare feet, and waving his hands back and forth as if he were leading a parade. Rex jumped up from the shady spot where he'd parked himself and set off after him, bushy tail raised high and wagging! "Yay! We don't have to move! We don't have to move!" he repeatedly hollered, as he ran circles around the big tree. "Wheee! Thank you, Mr. Fuller!"

Jesse winked at Anna then tilted his head at her. "Looks like there's no turning back now."

With slight trepidation, she nodded her answer. "Afraid you're right."

"There's just one thing remaining," he said.

"What is it?"

"Please don't call me Mr. Fuller ever again, even if you're mad at me. Promise?"

She gave a slight smile. "Okay, Jesse."

"What should I call you?" Billy asked, running up to the porch.

"Call me by my first name. We're friends, after all."

"All right! I ain't been this happy since—since we got Rex!" The dog barked at the sound of his name, and the two trailed off to run more circles around the tree.

12

Horace forked another bite of beef from his dinner plate, then took another swig of ale from his mug before setting it back down with a clunk. He picked up the folded newspaper his housekeeper Florence Hardy had placed next to his plate and opened it.

"You needin' anything else before I go, Mr. Blackthorn?" the pudgy, round-faced maid asked.

"No, feel free to leave." He didn't bother looking at her, just gave his paper a little snap. The woman didn't advance to the door. Instead, she stood in place and cleared her throat. He lowered the *Lebanon Western Star* and eyeballed her. "You want somethin'?"

"Um, yes, sir. My wage?"

"Oh, your wage. Yes, I forgot about that." He reached into his pocket and withdrew his coin purse, then handed her a half-dollar. "This should tide you over."

She stared at the coin. "But—this is only half of what you promised, and you still haven't paid in full from last month's work. If you can't pay me what you owe me, I won't be back tomorrow."

"That's a pity. I'll have to hire someone else then."

She stared at him, eyes bulging with desperation. "Please, sir, I need the money."

"Yes, you do. That's why I suspect you'll be back tomorrow." He picked up his newspaper and continued to read when someone started to knock on the front door. "Why don't you answer that on your way out?"

He heard her rasping breath and retreating footfall moving toward the door and a creaking as it swung open. "He's in the living room. Help yourself," she said, apparently leaving after that, as he heard nothing more from her.

"Who's there?" he called out, laying his paper down.

"Blackthorn?" came the voice.

Cyrus Daly. Horace pushed his chair back and stood, then moved from the dining room into the parlor, where he found the banker standing in the open doorway. "She told me to come in."

"I heard. What brings you here?"

"I got some not so great news."

"Can't be that bad. Come in and sit a spell. You want something to drink?"

The banker waved him off. "No, I have to get home. I wanted to tell you that Jesse Fuller stopped in to see me today."

"Yeah, I saw him in the bank lobby today. What'd he want?"

"He wants to buy the Hansen property. He's planning to marry Anna Hansen."

Sudden ire rose up in Horace. "She's getting married?"

"That's what he said."

"Well, I hope you told him the farm's already sold."

"I—I told him you're buying it, but apparently he's done his homework. He consulted with Quinn Johnson, who told him Anna Hansen has until June thirtieth to pay off the loan."

"Well then, alter the paperwork. Tell her you made a mistake on the date."

"I can't do that. She has her own copies."

More anger bubbled up. "I want that fifty acres."

"And I want *my* cut of the deal—but I might not be able to pull it off. It would have been easier if Fuller hadn't butted in today."

A curse word floated off his tongue. "Blast them Fuller brothers. What do they need with more land?"

"What do *you* need with it?"

"I already told you. I want a monopoly on Lebanon. Maybe I'll pay a little visit to Miss Hansen later tonight."

"For what purpose?"

"Humph. Might be I can make her listen to reason."

A curious expression washed over Daly's face. "Now listen, Blackthorn, don't let your power-hungry self do something stupid. I want no part of your foul play."

He laughed. "Me? Foul play?" He wiped the sneer off his face with the back of his hand. "Don't worry none. I'll take care of this matter."

"What are you going to do?"

"That's for me to know. Go on now. You're interrupting my supper and my evening news. See yourself out." He waved a hand at the frail little man and returned to the dining room to sit down at his table once more. When he heard the door close, he gave a satisfied smirk, took another bite of beef, and resumed reading.

⌒

"She really agreed to marry you?" Joey asked at the big house, the three brothers sitting in the living room while Laura Fuller stood at the table in the dining room, folding clothes she'd just brought in from outside. She didn't enter into the conversation, but everyone knew she wasn't missing a single word.

"Yep. I'm going to pick her up in the morning to go talk to Cyrus Daly about sealing the deal."

"Old Horace won't be too happy," said Joey.

"That's too bad. He's not getting that property."

"I agree with you. Since I've been managing the books, do you want me to come along, or can you handle it?" Jack asked.

"I only want to get the paperwork started. When it comes time for the actual transaction, I'll let you handle that."

"That's fine. I have a busy morning anyway what with Howard Warner coming in around nine to pick up his regular milk supply to take down to his cheesemaking plant. Then Tom Walford is coming by later to replace some blades on three of our plows."

"I'll be out with Marv and Fred tilling the land on the east side," said Joey.

"When's this wedding taking place?" Laura Fuller asked.

"No idea, Ma. We haven't got that far yet, but I imagine early next week."

"Heavens to Harriet!" Laura set down the towel she was folding and walked to the living room. "That poor girl must be frantic, thinking about what to wear and who to invite to the ceremony and where even to hold it. I must—"

"Mother." Jesse did his best to hush her. "It'll be much like Joey's wedding. We'll go over to the courthouse and…"

"Oh, no you don't. I'm fed up with my sons getting married in the most unconventional ways. At least do me the favor of asking Reverend Fisher to officiate this wedding. And since you are my youngest, I would very much like to be present for your vows."

He rolled his eyes at his brothers, but they were no help.

"She does have a point. You are her baby," Joey said with a chuckle.

"Oh, cut it out."

"Another thing: that's a little farmhouse. You think you'll adjust to living there? You better hope she's as good a cook as Ma," said Jack.

"I—might not be moving in right off."

"Seriously?" said Joey.

"Well, that makes sense," Laura said. "You barely know each other."

"That's what we both said."

"So you're marrying her, but living apart from her?" asked Joey.

"I'll visit her often."

"How considerate of you," Jack said, casting a sarcastic grin his way.

"So, Ma doesn't have to give you up quite yet then," teased Joey. "Ma, it seems you'll still have some time to spoil your youngest."

"Now, shush, both of you. Give your brother some time to think through this matter. It's a big decision. Both of you go on home now. Your wives must surely be waiting on you for supper."

Lazily, the brothers stood. "Keep us updated. And if you need a witness at the wedding, I'm here for you," said Jack.

"What if he wants me?" Joey asked.

"I'm the oldest, so it's fitting that he ask me."

"But you stood witness at *my* wedding. It should be my turn," Joey said.

"Both of you, git!" Laura said, going behind them and pushing them to the door. "Let your brother rest."

"Oh, he's goin' t' need rest all right," said Joey, laughing.

"Yeah, you better get rested up for your big day, little brother," Jack said. "Your new wife may have a long list of chores for you after the wedding day."

Laura pushed them both out the door and closed it in the middle of Jack's next sentence. Jesse put his head in his hands and looked at the floor. "What have I gotten myself into, Ma?" His stomach was a tumble of nerves, his brothers' banter not helping matters any.

She came and sat next to him, but thankfully didn't put a reassuring hand on his arm. "Do you really want to go through with this thing? Why must you marry her to get the land? Can't you just take the money straight to Mr. Daly and claim it? Perhaps offer the bank more than what Mr. Blackthorn is offering?"

Yes, why exactly was he doing this? For starters, he wasn't getting any younger, and it would be nice to have a place of his own, even though

Anna had made it clear she didn't want to live with him—at least not at first. Second, marrying her did give him better leverage. No matter what Blackthorn's reasons were for wanting the property, Jesse wanted to do what he could to stop him. He didn't know the man well, but what he *did* know had never set well with him. Blackthorn was pushy and obnoxious. He usually got what he wanted, but at the expense of someone else's suffering. He had the financial wherewithal to help people in need, but instead, he hoarded things for himself with no thought for charitable causes. Last, he was a conniving buzzard. Jesse had heard one too many stories of how he'd undermined many a sale just by coming in at the last minute with a higher offer. He plain didn't like the guy and sure didn't want him owning property next door to his family, never mind that Blackthorn would most likely continue to live at his nice house in town. There's no way he'd leave that big house and move into Anna's tiny farmhouse. No, he'd just rent Anna's land out to sharecroppers, greedy land baron that he was.

Something just didn't add up. Why was Blackthorn so eager to claim Anna's land when most of his other properties were on the other side of town? Jesse didn't know the man's motives—but he was determined to find out.

⌒

Anna stood in her tiny upstairs room, looking at the packed wooden crates and wondering if she was premature in thinking she could start the process of unpacking tomorrow. If she were indeed going to marry Jesse Fuller and remain in her own little farmhouse, there'd be no need to do any further packing. The very notion of being married made her stomach jittery, but at the same time, a sense of relief also settled in. She'd made it clear she didn't want to live with him—not yet anyway. But if they took their time in getting to know each other, perhaps she'd find him amiable enough to invite him to move in. Might the possibility exist that she could even fall in love? The mere idea set her heart to pounding. She'd never been in love before and didn't have the least idea what it would feel like. She glanced at the big family Bible on her bed. She'd taken it off a high shelf that morning and lay it on her bed, but because she'd had to go downstairs and make breakfast, it had sat there all day. Rarely had she ever opened it, not only because of its sheer size, but also because she had her own pocket Bible. It was from the American Bible Society, which had printed up God's Word for all the soldiers, both Confederate and Union, and then made it available to the public for a small donation.

Anna sat on the edge of her bed and thumbed through the brittle pages of the heavy old family Bible that had been handed down from her grandmother, Mama's mother. Even now, while studying its gilded edges, a few vivid memories washed over her of Mama sitting at the big table downstairs poring over the printed words. She had loved the Lord and diligently read His Word every morning before starting her day. Anna tried to emulate that practice, but often fell far short.

While sitting on the bed, she looked through her doorway at Billy Ray's room across the hall. He had turned down his lamp as soon as the sun went down and quickly fell asleep, no doubt more relaxed now than he'd been since Papa's passing just knowing he didn't have to leave the comforts of his little farmhouse and his very own bedroom, small as it was. Her mouth turned up in a wee smile before she let her gaze fall again to the big family Bible in her lap. She slowly turned pages, reading verses that popped out at her as she flipped through the book until her eyes landed upon a folded piece of paper. Upon close inspection, she recognized it as a yellowed newspaper article. The headline read, "Stagecoach Thieves Still at Large. Jewels and Precious Metals Amounting to Thousands of Dollars Taken from Driver's Safe." Hm. What a strange article to find folded between the pages of the family Bible! She merely skimmed the article then carefully reinserted it and thumbed through a few more pages before closing up the Good Book and setting it back on the shelf. No point in packing any more items if she were going to marry Jesse Fuller.

Anna Fuller. She tested the name in her mind first, then let it roll off her tongue a couple of times. "Anna Fuller...Anna Fuller." She had no idea how to feel about the sound of it and wondered again if marrying

Jesse was truly her only option. "Lord, give me wisdom. If You don't want me marrying him, please provide another way."

Before donning her nightgown, she had to make one last trip to the backyard outhouse. She left her room, peeked in on her sleeping brother, and then slipped down the stairs, walked through the dimly lit kitchen, and out the back door into the starry night.

13

$\mathcal{H}$orace lurked behind a bush awaiting Anna Hansen's return from the outhouse. When she finally emerged, he stepped into her path and startled the living hades right out of her. Her eyes went wide with terror as they met his, and she squeaked out a hoarse whisper. "What are you doing here? What do you want?"

As if she finally regained some semblance of her wits, she tried to march around him, but he stopped her every attempt by sidestepping her and blocking her passage. "Surprised to see me?"

"I asked you what you want."

"And I'll tell you if you'll just settle down."

"So help me, I'll scream, and Billy will come out here with a rifle and shoot you dead."

That made him laugh. "Is that so? Well then, you must not scream because shooting me would not solve a thing. No, not a bloomin' thing." He touched the bottom of her chin and tried to lift it, but she jumped away as if he were a snake—and maybe he was. It didn't matter one iota to him what she thought. He only had one thing to say to her and so he'd get on with it. "You want to know why I'm here, little lady? I'll tell you. And then—well, I'll be out of your hair. Does that make you happy?" He bent his face close to her just to tease her, but when she tried to run away again, he had no choice but to take hold of her arm and draw her up close to him. She tried to hit him with her free hand, so he had to snag tight to that one as well. "Now listen, you feisty little she-buzzard, settle y'rself down so we can talk real normal-like."

"What—do—you—want?" she hissed between fast breaths.

"I came to tell you that if you marry Jesse Fuller, bad things will happen."

At last she stilled. "What?" she whispered, raising her head in slow motion, her breaths coming out all jagged. "Where did you hear—"

"Never mind where I heard. You just listen to me, and listen good. Bad things will happen if you don't drop this notion of marrying Jesse Fuller. Very bad things. Starting with your little brother." He lifted one eyebrow at her, and the moon was just bright enough that he could see her face clearly. "You love your little brother?"

Her eyes glared with fear and fire. "Don't you dare touch him," she said, stretching to her full height, and facing him head on, which only made him chuckle the more. She couldn't be more than five feet and a few inches. She was a mite of a thing, and if she thought she had the remotest chance of worrying him, she could think again.

"Listen to me very carefully, and nothing will happen to your little brother or you. Do not marry Jesse Fuller, and above all, do not hand over your land to him. This land is mine, you got that? And I intend to take over the deed to it. You hear me?"

She gave no indication that she heard, only breathed heavy into the night air without saying a word, pursing her lips and staring red hot bullets at him. He squeezed both of her arms, and she snapped to attention. "I asked you a question."

"I—hear you, but I—I don't understand your interest."

"You don't need to understand. You just need to stay clear of Jesse Fuller. You got that?"

"But—you have no hold on me. What do you care who I associate with?"

"Oh, I care, little girl." He smiled at her, but he intended it to come off as hard and brief. "You stay away from Jesse Fuller, and you follow Cyrus Daly's orders in signing the necessary foreclosure papers. I pay off the remaining debt, you move out with your sweet little brother, and the deal is done. Simple, right? We'll seal it tomorrow. Be ready."

"What?"

"You heard me. I'll pick you up around noon, take you to the bank, and you'll sign on the dotted line." He leaned close. "It couldn't be any easier." Again, she gave him the silent treatment, so he had to squeeze her arms again. "Right?"

She winced in pain and muttered, "Right."

"Good." He let up on his hold. "Now then, don't even think of telling anybody about my little visit—not if you value your brother's life. You already lost Newell. Such a shame." He shook his head while looking down at her. "They say he poisoned himself. What was it, arsenic? You don't want to lose Billy Ray too, do you? I mean, that would be a tragedy." He made his voice sound sugar-like. "No sheriff, and no tattling to Jesse Fuller."

"I—I have no place to go. And no job."

"Now, ain't that somethin'? I just happen to have a job for you. I just fired my housekeeper today. She showed up late for work and I told her not to bother to come back." That wasn't exactly how it went, but that didn't matter. He could tell little Anna Hansen anything he dirty-well pleased. "You can take over where she left off. I even have a vacant upstairs apartment down the street from me. It's above Henry's Hardware. It ain't much, but it's empty at the moment."

"I wouldn't work for you for all the gold in California—or—or—all the jewels in the world!"

He tossed back his head and laughed. Oh, the irony. *All the jewels…* "Yes, you would. You're just that desperate. What say you report to my house on Monday morning? I'll expect you to prepare my breakfast and suppers every day. I buy my lunch in town sometimes, but occasionally you'll have to pack me a noon meal. I'll give you one day off, Sundays, and the rest of the time you work for me. You'll get two dollars a week, which is good, considering I'm giving you the apartment for free. Isn't that a deal? You should be on your knees with folded hands, thanking me. You got yourself in a little mess with this farm—well, I take that back—Newell got you in a fine mess. I'll say it again, poor man, dying at such a young age."

The little wench gathered all the spit she could muster and blew it straight in his face. He drew back his hand to give her a hard swat, then thought the better of it and laughed instead, mopping his cheek with his hand and wiping the glob on her sleeve. She growled low in her throat, putting him in mind of a lioness. "Let me go, you, you big lousy brute."

He loosened his hold then and laughed. "You're free. Go back in your house."

She took off on a run, but he yelled to her back, "Oh, wait, I forgot to show you something. I believe this came out of your brother's pocket last week when you were in town. I'm a pretty good pickpocket. Just one of my many talents."

She stopped in her tracks, and gave a slow turn. "What are you talking about?"

He held up a small wooden toy. "You didn't even see me in that store. I snuck up behind your brother and removed it from his pocket. Just wanted you to know I've been keeping my eye on you." She squinted in the moonlight, trying to make out the object from twenty feet away. "Oh, in case you can't tell, it's a woodcarving of a dog. Wasn't Newell quite the woodcarver? He did a nice job of replicating him." He held the wooden dog a little higher. "It's black and white just like your... humph... where is your dog, by the way?"

She whirled her body in every which direction. "Rex! Come here, Rex." He heard the frantic tone in her voice. "Come here, boy," she called. Then she turned her gaze on him. "So help me—if you did anything to my dog, I'll—"

"You'll what? You can't go to the sheriff, remember? You can't tell Jesse Fuller anything, 'cause you know if you do...it's gonna be bye-bye, Billy Ray."

He set off walking toward his horse, which he'd tied up to a post on the side of the barn. Once he passed by her, he tossed the wooden carving on the ground. "You wouldn't be able to keep a dog in my upstairs apartment anyway. He's happier where he is."

"Where is he?" she called in a desperate, groveling tone. "What did you do with my dog? Please, tell me."

He ignored her questions and kept walking. "I'll pick you up tomorrow to go to the bank, and then again on Saturday afternoon."

"What do you mean Saturday afternoon?"

"You didn't figure it out? Saturday is moving day for you. I'll take you to your new home. You'll find the location most convenient, just a few short blocks to my place. Be there no later than seven o'clock, starting Monday morning. I like my breakfast served hot and on the table by seven-thirty."

"No need to pick me up on Saturday. I have my own rig and horses."

He looked off in the distance. "Hm. That's a problem. See, your rig goes with the sale of the property."

"What? But I'll need transportation."

"For what? Living in town means everything you need is within walking distance. Besides, the apartment I'm providing doesn't have a barn out back, so you'd have to use the livery, which you wouldn't be able to afford." He smiled, but it wasn't sincere. He wanted her to know that he was taking charge from then on.

"Billy Ray will not be happy if he doesn't have a horse."

"Well, ain't that a crying shame? Goodnight, Miss Hansen, and sweet dreams to you."

She made not a sound, just stared across the dark at him, the moon and stars their only light. He turned and walked the rest of the way to his horse, mentally congratulating himself for doing such a fine job of taking the upper hand.

14

If she slept even a wink all night, Anna didn't recall it. After Horace Blackthorn had ridden away last night, she'd gone out to all the outbuildings and searched everywhere for Rex, calling his name and praying he'd show up, but to no avail. What had that hideous man done to their beloved farm dog? No wonder she hadn't been suspicious of a visitor last night. Rex hadn't barked. All night, she'd cried, prayed, fretted, gotten up to read her pocket Bible, then cried, prayed, and fretted some more. What was she to do? Earlier, she had asked the Lord to close the door on this whole idea of marrying Jesse Fuller if it wasn't God's will, but this didn't feel like the way God would answer that particular prayer—not through an evil man such as Horace Blackthorn. No, this wasn't right. And yet she believed every word when he told her he'd hurt Billy Ray if she went to the sheriff or confessed anything to Jesse. No, she had to tell Jesse she'd changed her mind, that she absolutely couldn't marry him. Somehow, she'd find a way to do it that would make sense to him. Billy Ray wouldn't like it. No, sir, he'd be madder than a skunk, but she couldn't let that sway her. She needed to keep him safe, and that was the bottom line. Horace Blackthorn was evil to the bone, and last night he'd revealed the extent of it.

Weary as a haystack sleeper, she dragged herself up and out of bed, wiped dried tears from her cheeks, and walked to her bureau, where she kept a pitcher of water and a wash bowl. She dipped a dry cloth into the bowl, wrung it out, and made a couple of quick swipes across her face. As fatigued and on edge as she was, the cool water did help to soothe her shattered nerves. She pulled in a deep breath, dried off her face and hands, and then put on her usual work dress. She picked up her hairbrush, brushed free a few tangles, then pulled her hair up into a bun, fastening it with the hair comb she kept on the bed stand. She would not be going into town with Jesse today. Matter of fact, she wouldn't be going anywhere with him. Ever.

Before leaving her little room, she glanced around to make sure it was tidy, hurriedly made her bed, as she always did in the morning, and then walked out. A hasty glance across the hall told her Billy had already wakened and gone downstairs, his bedcovers pulled up and over his tick mattress in an unruly fashion. As was usual for her, she glanced at Papa's closed door on her way downstairs. She hadn't gone into his room since his passing, although she knew it was past time that she did. Now that she knew for sure she and Billy were moving out, she had to buck up and finish the task that lay ahead. Gathering a deep breath for courage, she headed down the steep and creaky wooden stairs.

The house was quiet, so she knew Billy Ray had already gone out to the barn to start his chores, which amounted to feeding and watering the chickens, goats, cow, and two horses. Soon, he'd be coming in for breakfast, and then he'd return to the barn to milk Carlotta the cow and then muck out stalls before leading Carlotta out to pasture. They used to have a slew of animals, but one by one, Papa had started selling them, along with pieces of equipment, and then after his passing, she had done the same, keeping only the essentials, the chickens for the eggs and the goats and cow for their milk. The goats wound up being more pets than anything though, and she simply had not been able to part with them. She wondered what Billy Ray would do with himself once they moved away from the farm. He was so used to staying busy. Perhaps she'd take him with her to Blackthorn's house and put him to work there. Her stomach turned over in a sickening swirl at the idea of working for the wicked man. It was the last thing on earth that she wanted to do, and yet he left her with no choice. She would do whatever it took to keep Billy safe because Blackthorn's threats rang true with her. Which begged the question—what had he done with Rex?

With no bounce in her step, she walked to the cookstove, opened the side door, picked up a few small logs from the stacked pile against the wall, and threw them into the firebox and lit the flame. After stoking the fire for a bit, and satisfied it would take hold, she closed the side door, then set about making a breakfast of fried eggs and bacon. Knowing Billy would come in famished, she cut off a few thick slices of bread from the loaf she'd made yesterday.

After setting the table, she went back to the stove to stir up the eggs and bacon. Satisfied they were thoroughly cooked, Anna grasped the handle of the cast iron pan with the end of her apron, moved it to the cooler side of the cooktop, and draped a towel over the pan to keep their breakfast warm. Then she went to the table to sit down for a spell. She withdrew her small Bible from her apron pocket in hopes of reading a chapter or two before Billy came inside. She had no sooner started to read when a familiar bark had her setting the book aside and running to the window. Romping beside Billy on his way to the house from the barn was Rex, tail wagging in its usual fashion. She ran to the door and swung it wide. "Where did you find Rex?" she asked.

The dog ran to the back door for his morning pat on the head.

Billy crinkled his brow. "What do y' mean?"

"I couldn't find him last night. But he's home now, so that's good." She bent over the dog—and that's when she spotted dried blood on the top of his head. She studied it a bit and dabbed at it with the corner of her apron.

"What's that?" Billy asked, drawing closer. "Looks like he ran into a tree or something. I didn't notice that before."

"I don't know." But a sickening sensation that twisted around in her gut told her she *did* know. That disgusting excuse of a man, Horace

Blackthorn, had hit her poor pooch on the top of the head. "What happened to you, boy?" She nuzzled him with her chin then kissed his long snout. "Well, he looks fine now." She tried to push aside her concern.

"Come in the house now. I have your breakfast ready."

They stepped inside, and uncharacteristic of Rex, he scooted past them when she opened the door and went to the braided rug next to the fireplace and plopped down on it. Billy Ray glanced up at her. "Ain't you gonna chase him back outside?"

"No, he can stay in here and rest. It looks like he had a rough night. Come sit down. We have some things to talk about."

"Like what, you marrying Jesse Fuller?"

She snagged a breath and pulled out a chair. "Sit down, Billy."

A worried look washed over him. "Okay." He sat and she took a seat across the table from him. "I'll dish up our food in a minute. First, we'll talk."

"Okay."

"I don't want you to get upset with me, but—I've made a decision that I think is best for us."

"Oh, great." He stared down at his folded hands, then quickly raised his head, his face twisted into a frown. "I don't think I wanna hear what you're gonna tell me."

⟿

Jesse rounded the curve in the road then urged his team into a faster trot as they approached the Hansen farm. At the long two-track drive, he slowed the horses, then steered them toward the house. Billy Ray sat on a stump in the front yard as if waiting for him, his dog sitting dutifully next to him. Strangely, neither of them jumped up to greet him, which was unusual for both of them. The boy wore a cheerless expression, and as if sensing some kind of unhappy emotion in him, Rex refused to even wag his tail at Jesse.

"Morning, friend," Jesse called, bringing the horses to a halt. "You all right?"

The boy said nothing, just shrugged his shoulders and let them fall back into their lazy slump.

Jesse climbed down. Rather than walk over to greet him with tail wagging, Rex stayed planted next to Billy. Jesse approached. "What's got you down?" he asked.

"Ask my sister," Billy said, fumbling with a wooden toy of some sort.

"What you got in your hand there?"

Billy held up a woodcarving. "My pa carved this for me last year. I lost it last week, but I just found it on the ground. Guess it fell out of my pocket."

"Humph. Your sister in the house?"

"I'm here," came the soft voice.

Jesse swiveled on the heel of his boot. She wasn't exactly dressed for town. Matter of fact, the dress she wore bore a tear in the hem and a few stains on the front. She looked disheveled. And when he cast another glance at Billy, it was clear the boy had been crying. His eyes were puffy and his cheeks red. What was going on?

"Are you—do you want to go into town with me? I thought—we would go to the bank and speak to Mr. Daly."

"No. I—it won't be necessary. I'm—I'm selling the farm. To Horace Blackthorn."

The words crashed against him like a boulder, sounding blunt and rehearsed. Where had they even come from?

"What do you mean?"

"Exactly what I said. Mr. Blackthorn is taking over the farm."

He gave a hurried look at Billy, but the boy remained mute. Had she instructed him not to say anything? He wasn't the usual jovial Billy Ray of yesterday. "What's going on, Anna?"

"Nothing." She used both hands to push several strands of hair out of her eyes that the morning breeze had wrestled from their bun. "I've simply decided not to marry you. It's easier if Mr. Blackthorn takes over the property."

"But I thought you and I had made the decision that the Fullers would buy it so you could remain here. Wait—is Blackthorn offering to let you stay here?"

At that, Billy Ray jumped up and ran to the barn, little sobs coming out of him. In a show of devotion, Rex jumped up and followed after the boy.

"What has happened to change your mind? Billy's crying, you're acting like we never talked yesterday, and now suddenly Blackthorn is buying your farm? Answer my question. Is he letting you stay here?"

"No, I'm moving to town—to an apartment he owns, and I'm going to start working for him."

"Wh-what? When did you decide all this?"

She turned around and headed for her house, her wide skirt blowing up in a gust of wind. She gathered it close to her, and he followed directly on her heels, taking her by the arm when she got close to the house and stopping her before she reached her door. Her eyebrows were set in a tight line and her sky blue eyes looked hard—and desperate. "I don't have to tell you anything," she said grimly.

"No, you don't, but it would be nice if you did, especially since we reached an agreement of sorts just last night."

"We put nothing in writing." She stared down at his hand firmly gripping her arm. "Let me go, please."

He loosened his hold, but didn't let go. Not yet. "Just tell me what happened to change your mind? Did he come here? Did Blackthorn come here after I left?"

She bit her lower lip and shook her head.

"Did he come here?"

"I'm not saying another word."

"Why not?"

"Just—please—let it be."

"I can't just drop everything. There are too many unanswered questions. And I won't go ask Billy Ray. He's already upset enough."

"Thank you," she whispered, staring down at her holey shoes. She needed new shoes. Shoot, she needed a new wardrobe. If she were his wife, he would buy her a new wardrobe. She stepped up onto her front porch. "Now, would you please leave?"

"No. I'm not going anywhere until we talk. Tell me what changed your mind. And how did you come to find this so-called job with Blackthorn?"

She looked like she was about to cry. "I'm sorry, Jesse, I really can't talk about it."

"Why? Did he tell you not to say anything to me?"

A tear dripped out of one eye, and she quickly brushed it away with her palm. "Please just go now. I've already said more than I should."

"What? You haven't told me anything. Instead, you've left me completely confused."

She waved her arm free of him and opened the door. Before she went inside, though, she turned to give him one last look. With her final glance, she said in a tone so quiet he had to lean in closer to hear her, "It was lovely—getting to know you, if only a little bit. Now—go home and tell your brothers things didn't work out. Please."

Before he had a chance to reply, she slipped inside and closed the door with a loud click, as if to emphasize his need to leave.

He turned and looked out over the vast land, then scratched his head. What had Blackthorn said to her? How had he managed to convince her to take a job with him, to move into an apartment in town? She loved this farm. Newell would be upset. Shoot, he should have told her *that*. He should have told her how unhappy her father would be about all this.

He gave his head a couple of fast shakes and walked back to his wagon. After climbing onboard and taking up the reins, he glanced toward the barn and caught a glimpse of Billy Ray standing in the open door, his frame so small against the barn's backdrop. He waved at the boy, but the boy stood mute and still as a marble statue.

15

Later that day, the three Fuller brothers mounted the steps and entered through the doors of Lebanon City Bank, their business faces on, their moods and minds full of purpose.

"I'll do the talking," said Jack.

"As it should be," said Joey.

Jesse said nothing, just nodded and walked into the lobby, he and Joey flanking Jack. He e He felt the eyes of every customer present fall on them. They were well-known in town so it would be normal for folks to throw them a curious glance when they all walked in together.

Daly's assistant, Donald Grayson, went a pale shade of gray when he set eyes on them. "Uh—afternoon, gentlemen. I—uh, assume you wish to see Mr. Daly."

"Indeed we do, Donald," said Jack. "I hope he's in."

"He's in, but—he's…" He hung onto the last word, letting it sizzle a bit.

"Preoccupied?" Jack asked.

"You could say that."

"With Blackthorn, no doubt," said Jesse.

Grayson wasn't sure which fellow to look at, so his eyes darted from one to the other, his nerves obviously spent. "Uh, yes, and…"

Jesse's chest pinched. "Is Anna Hansen in there with him?"

Grayson nodded, and that was all it took for Jesse to head toward Daly's office.

"Jesse," Jack called. "Hold up."

Jesse stopped, standing just outside the door, his hand reaching for the knob.

"You men should wait here," Grayson injected, jumping up and pointing at the chairs on the other side of his desk.

"Let me do the talking," Jack said to Jesse. "That was the agreement, remember?" All three of them ignored Donald Grayson.

Jesse gave a slow nod, and stepped back, allowing Jack to slowly open the door, forget that they weren't invited in. First thing he saw was Blackthorn hovering over Anna while she sat at a visitor's chair across from Daly, pen in hand over a bunch of papers.

Cyrus Daly glanced up from his desk and immediately stood. "Gentlemen, what—"

That made both Blackthorn and Anna turn. Blackthorn's eyes went dark with rage. He quickly turned to Anna. "Finish signing those papers."

Her face was a picture of fear and confusion. She turned and continued her task.

"Stop, Anna," Jesse said, paying no heed to Jack's earlier instructions. He approached Anna, but Blackthorn cast a big arm in front of her in an effort to block Jesse from reaching her. She rose shakily to her feet.

For a brief second, she and Jesse stood eyeing each other. He read the angst in her eyes. "Don't sign anything, not yet. Not till we've talked," he said.

"There's nothing to talk about, Fuller," Blackthorn said. "She's already made up her mind. The property is going to me."

"It's not going to you," Jack said. "Anna has until the thirtieth of June to sign those papers."

"She doesn't want to wait that long, isn't that right, Anna?" Blackthorn said, looking down at her. "Keep writing, missy. You have several more pages to go."

With obvious hesitation, she turned and resumed writing. Jesse's own frustration built. "Jack, do something."

"Cyrus, what is this all about?" Jack asked.

Cyrus Daly shrugged. "Horace has been wanting the property. Apparently, Miss Hansen is willing to sign it off. There's not much I can do to stop the transaction."

"Anna, don't do this," Jesse said.

Her hand paused, and then she lifted the pen and stood, turning to face him. She raised her chin a notch. "I'm handing over the farm to Mr. Blackthorn." The statement came off as practiced.

Something in his gut twisted into a painful knot. "Remember how we talked yesterday? Remember our agreement? What did Blackthorn say to change your mind?" he asked.

She bit her lip, but kept mum.

"Sign the papers, girlie," Blackthorn said in a low, stern tone. Jesse wanted to rip his tongue out.

"Anna?" Jesse said, pleading with his eyes.

"I'm sorry, the decision has been made." Emotionless, she turned back to her task of signing papers.

Jesse directed his next words to Horace, "So help me, Blackthorn, if you threatened her in any way, I'll—"

"You'll what?" Horace cut in, throwing back his shoulders in an all-important manner. "You can't lay a hand on me, you know. The sheriff doesn't look too kindly on assault."

There were so many things Jesse could have said regarding the legalities of Horace's forcible treatment of Anna, but without any proof to go on, without Anna's admission, he felt helpless. While she signed yet another paper, he whispered across the room for all to hear, "Your pa would not be happy."

That gave her great pause. She lifted the pen and gave his words a moment of thought, but rather than acknowledge them, she snatched up one last paper and signed it.

Daly released a loud breath, as if he'd been holding it since the second the Fullers entered the room. "Seems to be a finished deal, boys. You may as well go home now."

"Yes, seems so," said Jack. "I must say, though, Cyrus, my brothers and I are quite disappointed in the manner in which you handled this transaction. We've been your loyal customers for many years."

The man shifted nervously. "Indeed, but, well, Horace here, has expressed interest in the land since, well, since he learned about Newell's hardship."

"Um-hm, and something doesn't smell right about any of it."

Daly pushed his spectacles further up his nose. "Now, see here, I do not partake in shady dealings. If that's what you're implying…"

"Oh, stop talking, Cyrus," Horace blurted. "You don't owe these fellows any explanation. Here's your papers, all signed and legal-like." He shoved them under the banker's nose. "You've got my money, so the property's mine now. Come on, missy. I'll drive you back to the farm. You have some packing to do."

"No need, Horace. I'll see her home," Jesse said.

Blackthorn looked down at Anna. She looked at the floor. "No, thank you," she muttered. "I'll ride with Mr. Blackthorn."

Blackthorn gave a chuckle. "Come on then."

Jesse wanted to go after the thug, but Jack poked him in the side and whispered, "Let 'em go."

Jesse heaved an angry, if not helpless, breath of air as the two exited the office, Blackthorn opening the door and following Anna out of the room. Once the door closed, Jack looked Daly head on. "All right, Cyrus, what gives?"

"Nothing. I told you, she wanted to sell the property to Blackthorn."

"With a bit of persuasion, I'd say."

"I know nothing about any persuasion."

"Is that so?" Joey spoke up then. He stepped closer to Cyrus's desk to better eyeball the man. "Tell me something. Why is it that every time a farm goes into foreclosure, Blackthorn's first in line to buy it up?"

Jesse watched the banker's facial muscles twitch as he tried not to squirm. Daly withdrew a handkerchief and gave his wet forehead a thorough wipe-down. "I suppose he's eager to own more property. I can't fault him for that."

"I've known of others who wanted certain parcels, but somehow Blackthorn beat them to it. Can you explain that?"

"The bank will go with the highest bidder."

"Is that always the case? What about in the matter of Albert Mosley's property?"

"What about that?" Daly asked.

"Well," Joey said, "I happen to know Bradley Poole offered the bank two thousand dollars, but you sold it to Blackthorn for eighteen hundred."

"How would you know that?"

"I did a little research. Visited the register of deeds office, and I spoke directly to Poole. You reaping some kind of benefit from Blackthorn for doing his deals?"

"That's preposterous."

"Is it?"

Jack cleared his throat. "That would be quite unethical, Mr. Daly."

The man moved away from his desk. "Perhaps you should leave now."

"You inviting us to take our business elsewhere?" Jesse asked.

"I would hope you wouldn't. You've been banking with us since long before I arrived."

"Yes," said Jack, "starting with Howard Simmonds, a man our father greatly admired."

Daly clamped his mouth shut, apparently done talking, his face having gone from ashen to red.

"Let's go, fellas," Jack said. "I believe we've finished our business here. For now."

Without another word, they walked out, their boots stomping on the hardwood floor.

Outside, Jesse all but exploded. "Are we just going to let Horace get away with this? He's done or said something to Anna, put some kind of fear in her. I saw it in her eyes."

Jack put a hand on Jesse's arm. "Yes, yes, we all saw it, but now is not the time for emotion. We have to let this thing play out."

"Just like that?" Jesse said.

"Listen to you, little brother. I'd say in a few short days, you've developed some sort of feelings for that young lady," Jack said.

Jesse could not disagree, but he wouldn't admit it either.

Jack chortled. "Don't look so worried. We'll figure this thing out."

"You got something in mind?" Jesse asked.

Jack's deep blue eyes seemed to darken as he raised them to the hazy sky. "The Lord will reveal it in His time," he said softly. "All in His good time."

Jesse knew that in his head, but his heart had some catching up to do.

⌒

Ever since Blackthorn dropped Anna back off at the farm, Billy had been giving her the silent treatment. She knew he was full of questions, but right now, he was too angry to speak to her, and she couldn't blame him. He had no idea why she'd done what she'd done—and she wouldn't tell him either. No point in burdening his ten-year-old shoulders with the knowledge that Blackthorn had intentions of hurting him if she didn't abide by his demands. It would likely give him nightmares. No, she would bear this secret on her own.

After finishing packing up the dishes, pots, and pans, not knowing how equipped this new apartment they were moving into might be, she moved around the little house and started taking little knickknacks and other paraphernalia off shelves and tables, carefully wrapping each one in a towel or clean rag to prevent breakage. They had very few possessions, so this would not be a difficult challenge in terms of labor, but in terms of sentimentality, it would break her heart into a million pieces. Not only had she failed Billy Ray and herself, she'd let down her father. Jesse had taken it upon himself to remind her of that when they were at the bank. Her heart pinched at the memory. She didn't owe Jesse Fuller or his brothers anything. Yes, they wanted the property, but she had to put her own brother ahead of them—and everyone else. An unexpected sob came out of her, and then a couple of tears followed. For a second, she stopped and laid her hand on the fireplace mantle, gripping its edge. "Lord, help me know how to obey Your commands. Lead me in the way that is right. Help me trust You, God, because I feel like I'm drowning in a sea of confusion and misery right now." The words came out in a tiny whisper. A frantic whisper. Anna dabbed her eyes.

The house stood silent, the only sounds coming from outside— twittering birds, the wind kicking up, and some chattering squirrels. Then a robin called out. "Cheer up, cheer up!"

Unexpectedly, the tiniest hint of peace came over her, as light as a feathery cloud. She stopped and closed her eyes. Then she heard God speak to her heart. "*My child, I am with thee. I will not leave. Trust Me to guide thy steps. Trust only Me, and nothing more, for I am enough.*" The words so comforted her that she dropped to her knees, bowed her head, and raised her hands skyward. "Lord, I trust Thee. With all my heart I do."

For several moments, she knelt there, too afraid to move for fear of disturbing the grand sense of peace that washed over her in wave after wave. In time, the door opened, and in walked Billy Ray. When he saw her kneeling, hands raised upward, he stood in the doorway and gaped.

A bit of embarrassment came over her, but she just as quickly brushed it off. No sense in being embarrassed over something the Lord Himself had given her. She merely stood and issued him a timid smile. "Are you hungry?"

He stared for a moment longer, then walked to a chair and sat. "Nope."

"What have you been doing?"

"Nothin'. Finished all my chores. What's goin' to happen with the animals? I'm not goin' with you if Rex can't come along. I'll run away first."

"Rex can come," she said. And she didn't care what Blackthorn had to say about it.

"That monster better not hurt him."

"He won't."

He turned up his lip in a sneer. "I can't stand him."

"Let us try not to be hateful. At least he is giving us a place to live. And a job."

"Pfff. I ain't workin' for him. What's goin' to happen to our goats and chickens and horses? And what about Carlotta? And who's goin' to take care of ar' crops?"

"Mr. Blackthorn has hired men. I am sure he will put them all to work in the fields."

"Why can't I work in the fields with everyone else?"

"Because I want you with me."

"What if I don't want to be with you?"

That drew her up short. He was developing a mind of his own, and she wasn't sure she was ready for it. "Let's not fight anymore, please."

"I better be able to take a horse with me. Is there a stable there?"

"No, I'm—afraid there isn't. I haven't seen the place yet, but I do know there's no barn out back. Mr. Blackthorn informed me of that."

"You don't even know what we're getting into, Sis, and yet you agreed to give up everything? How could you do that when Jesse promised you we wouldn't have to move?"

That wondrous sense of God's peace somehow started to escape her. She looked at her brother and suddenly saw a little man in a very young boy. It shouldn't be this way, and yet his childhood was slowly slipping away from him. "We're going to be fine, Billy Ray. We need to trust the Lord."

"You say that all the time, but Pa died, and now we're losing the one thing he worked so hard to hang onto—and we're moving into a place you haven't even seen yet—and working for a man we can't stand. Is that what God wants for us?"

She held her head with both hands and pressed hard. "I don't know. I only know that we are doing this because—"

"Because why?"

But she didn't know how to answer him.

He stared at her for all of a half minute while she tried to gather her thoughts. Then as quickly as he'd walked inside, he turned and walked back out, slamming the door behind him and making her jump.

16

Horace nibbled at the plate of food he'd thrown together for himself, missing his usual homecooked meal. Since Florence Hardy had quit on him, he'd been fending for himself, and he was none too good at it. He could only hope that little wisp of a Hansen woman knew how to cook to his liking. He berated himself for giving up that two-room dwelling above the hardware. It could have provided him with a few extra dollars every month, but instead he'd given it to her and her brother. She would probably expect something bigger, but he'd tell her to be thankful for what she got. At least she'd have a roof over her head.

He picked up the map again. If he'd studied it once, he'd studied it a thousand times. The thing about this map was that it wasn't an exact copy of the one Newell had showed him. That one had been numbered, whereas his only showed a picture of the land with the trees, the house, the outbuildings, and the creek running through the property. How was he supposed to figure out the exact location of each clue without the proper map? All the more reason he needed to get his hands on that box sitting on a high shelf in Newell's barn. Correction. *His* barn now. Once he got himself on his new property and moved Anna out, he'd be able to give the entire property a thorough search and discover for himself where that treasure lay.

He bit off another chunk of dry meat and growled at its bland flavor. He needed a real piece of hot cooked beef, the kind that fell apart in his mouth, not some dry slice that had been sitting on a shelf in his outside lean-to. He studied the map for the hundredth time until a rap came at his door. He slid his chair back, wiped his chin, and then went through the living room and the parlor to the front door, swinging it wide without even looking through the curtain. "You again?" he said to the banker. "Come in, come in. What is it this time?"

"We might be in a bit of trouble," Daly said.

"What are you talking about? What kind of trouble."

The fellow wrung his hands. "Those Fuller boys might be onto our little game."

"Oh, pfff, you worry worse than a toad in a road. What'll it be next? Someone will find out you wore the same socks two days in a row?"

"I wouldn't do that."

"Cyrus, it was a joke!"

"Oh."

"Stop fidgeting, will you? You make me nervous." He turned and walked back toward the dining room. "You want a drink?"

"No, no—I just wanted to tell you."

"Come in here. I can't hear you,"

The man dillydallied at the door. "Well, I s'pose for a minute, but my wife will start wondering where I am."

"Come, come." He motioned with his hand. He swore the poor man had to be hand-fed. "Now then, what has you so worried?" He turned to the wheeled cart next to the table, made himself a drink, and then turned back toward the banker after taking a sip.

"Well, Joseph Fuller said he noticed you're the one always buying up foreclosed properties."

"So what? It's what I do. I invest in properties."

"Yes, yes, but then he said he's suspicious that I'm somehow benefiting. One of them said it wouldn't be ethical."

He chuckled. "He's right there, but so what? They can't prove anything. Not that there's any law against being unethical. I told you to stop worrying."

"I don't like that they're suspicious."

"Well, I don't like that money don't grow on trees. So just relax, would you?" He raised his glass to the fellow. "You sure I can't make you one of these?"

"No, I'm sure. I gotta get home."

"You always gotta get home to that wife of yours. I s'pose she's the boss in the house, eh? I never could stomach the idea of marriage. Don't need some woman runnin' my life. I am the only boss I'll ever need."

"Yeah, well, I didn't come here to talk about my marriage. I just wanted to tell you to beware of the Fuller brothers. They really wanted that property."

Horace snorted. "Well, bully for them. They didn't get it. But I appreciate the warning. Now, stop y'r fussin' and go home to your little wife."

The banker turned around and started for the door, but then stopped and gave a quick turn. "You best treat Anna Hansen with kindness, 'cause if you don't, I think you'll have a bigger battle on your hands than you bargained for—if you get my drift."

"Yeah, yeah, I get your drift all right. I'm not worried. I'll treat her in whatever way I see fit."

Daly said nothing more, just shook his head at him as if he'd lost his last ounce of sense, then walked out.

When Horace heard the door close, he gritted his teeth. *Blasted Fuller brothers!* He drank the rest of his beverage in two gulps then mixed himself another. Might be a good night to drink himself to sleep.

Friday nights were Fuller family dinners at the big house. Tonight's dinner conversation ran the gamut, everything from the trial of the conspirators in President Lincoln's assassination, to Mary Todd Lincoln's deep sorrow, to the country's economic struggles, and right down to current local gossip. Of utmost interest to everyone in the room but Jesse was the manner in which Jesse and Anna's plans to marry had disintegrated overnight. He'd not wanted to discuss it with the whole family, especially not with all the nieces and nephews present, but no one seemed to care about that. What exactly had Blackthorn said to Anna to strip her of her backbone—or had his offer of a job and a place to live appealed to her as a more desirable solution than marrying him? It had done a number on his self-esteem. Was he really that unattractive? He'd taken another gander at himself in the mirror that morning and ruled he wouldn't want to marry someone with a mug like his either!

"Why ain't ya gettin' married after all, Uncle Jesse?" asked twelve-year-old Elias, Jack and Cristina's son.

"Who's gettin' married?" asked Joey's young daughter Miriam. "Why is it I'm always the last one to find out about these things?"

"'Cause you always got your face in a book," quipped her brother Franklin. Then to Jesse he said, "When's the wedding?"

"There's no wedding," Jesse answered. "It sort of fell apart."

"Did you cry?" asked Miriam.

"No, no, I didn't cry."

"Then good thing you didn't marry her," she said before spooning up her chicken stew. Some of the adults tried to muffle their chuckles.

"Well, it wasn't about love," Jesse said.

"My daddy didn't love Mama Faith when he married her, but it worked out. Sometimes, you just have to do what your heart says to do," said Miriam.

"What is this?" Jesse asked. "When did my six-year-old niece suddenly become the authority on marriage?"

"She is a wise little soul," said Faith.

"Maybe she didn't want to marry you 'cause you don't shave often enough," chimed in Catherina, Cristina and Jack's daughter.

"Yeah, he is a little on the unkempt side," said Joey, smirking.

It took all of Jesse's strength not to push back in his chair and storm out of the room.

"Now, now, everyone," Laura said. "Leave Jesse be. Sometimes things happen that we can't control."

"Thanks, Ma." He glanced around the table at everyone, including the youngsters. "Could y'all stop focusing on me? Let's talk about something else."

"Well, I for one want to know what you boys plan to do about Horace Blackthorn buying up the Hansen property," Laura said. "Was everything hinging on whether or not Jesse married Anna? I mean, did you increase your offer to Cyrus Daly?"

"It was pretty much a done deal when we got to the bank, Ma," said Jack. "She had already signed most of the paperwork."

"Well, surely you could have brought up the matter that Anna had until June thirtieth to sign the papers."

"Jack did, actually. Apparently, she didn't wish to wait," said Joey. "That's what we were led to believe anyway. I still think there's something suspicious going on."

"Maybe he has a different motive for wanting the property," suggested fourteen-year-old Isaac, Joey's oldest. Isaac used to be a real rapscallion, but he'd shown a great deal of maturity in the past year.

"What sort of motive?" Joey asked.

"I don't know. Maybe he knows something no one else knows."

"Such as?" Jesse asked.

The boy shrugged. "I don't have no idea. I'm just sayin' it seems odd that he was so set on buying up our neighbor's land. I mean, didn't Uncle Jesse say most of the land he bought was on the other side of town?"

"Well, the man makes a hobby of buying foreclosed property all around Lebanon," Jack said.

The topic of conversation changed when Laura started talking about the strawberry pies she had made for dessert. The women and older girls started clearing the table, and Joey brought up the topic of one of their wagons needing a new wheel.

Jesse said little, just mulled over the earlier discussion and particularly Isaac's comment about Horace possibly having an ulterior motive. Was it possible? And if so, what could it be? He vowed to find out what he could, even if it meant hounding Anna for answers. Maybe she could shed a bit of light.

17

It was Saturday afternoon, and Anna had finally managed to pack everything up in crates, boxes, and barrels. As for furnishings, she had very little and decided she would wait until she arrived at the apartment to see what she needed.

Billy Ray had been completely uncooperative, leaving all the packing to her. It had been terribly difficult dealing with his stubborn, if not defensive, behavior, but she understood it. In fact, she didn't even blame him for lashing out at her. It was the only home either of them had ever known, and his frustration at the situation came out in the form of angry outbursts. She mostly took them in stride, as much as they hurt. What else could she do?

Papa already had most of his items stored in crates, so she didn't bother going through them. She just heaved them up and carried them down her steep stairs, arriving on the main level in a drenching sweat after each trip. Billy Ray was hiding out somewhere, perchance in the barn with his beloved farm animals and Rex. She envisioned him talking to each one and trying to explain to them why he wouldn't be coming out to greet them every morning. She could only hope that someday he would speak to her again. She couldn't bring herself to tell him what

Blackthorn would do if she went to the authorities. No, she could not risk telling him the truth. It would either create a deep fear in him or somehow make him feel responsible for their having to move. She wouldn't put that on him.

Downstairs, she walked to the window to see if Blackthorn had come yet, but got no glimpse of him. She hoped he hadn't forgotten he'd told her he'd pick them up on Saturday afternoon. Perchance he was simply busy and would come closer to evening. She had already packed away most of her kitchen, and so she couldn't even put together a decent supper for herself and Billy. She glanced around the little farmhouse, devoid now of any keepsakes, and tried to quell the deep ache in her chest. She hadn't shed a single tear today, and she wouldn't either. Somehow, whether from God or her own resolve, she'd built up a wall of defense to keep her emotions at bay. One day, after all this was over, and she managed somehow to adjust to new surroundings, she'd let the wall come crashing down. But not now. No, certainly not now.

With most of her work behind her, she chose to go outside and sit on the front porch to wait. Somehow, she had to find room for Papa's rockers. No way would she leave those behind. Hopefully, Blackthorn would arrive driving a big wagon.

Just as she seated herself, she got a glimpse of a wagon coming up the drive, but it wasn't Blackthorn. Instead, there was Jesse Fuller. Her gut took a big dip. She hadn't seen him since the day at the bank. She figured he was furious with her and had stayed away because of that. Now she was curious what brought him over today. It was too late to buy the property. Blackthorn had already forked over the money. If he was coming to drill her with questions, well, she had nothing to tell him. Good gravy, what would happen if Blackthorn arrived while Jesse was here? He'd given her strict orders not to associate with Jesse Fuller. Her stomach tied itself into a terrible knot. She glanced toward the barn to see if Billy Ray would come running, but he didn't show himself.

She stood up and walked to the edge of the porch. "Afternoon, Jesse."

He didn't reply. Perhaps he hadn't heard her. He halted his horses and climbed down from the rig without a word. As always, there was a ruggedly handsome demeanor about him. He had just a trace of a smile, but she wasn't sure how to take it or what to expect.

"What brings you here?" she asked, a bit of angst stirring up in the pit of her stomach and her pulse pittering like a drumbeat.

He still didn't respond, just climbed the steps and helped himself to the other rocker, seating himself ahead of her. She swallowed hard and sat down next to him. He set to rocking, letting the chirping birds take up the silence between them. When it got to be too much, she spoke again. "I know you're upset with me, but did you come here just to taunt me with your silence?"

He rocked a moment longer then took in a deep breath. "I'm confused is all."

"I know."

"Not about you turning down my proposal of marriage. That makes sense. It was a pretty preposterous notion, and I probably wouldn't have come up with it if my brothers hadn't suggested it. I'm glad they did though because it forced me to approach you. I have enjoyed getting to know you—at least a little bit. In the long run, I suppose a marriage between us didn't make much sense." He rocked a little more then turned his head toward her. "Besides, I took a gander at myself in the mirror and saw right away why you wouldn't want to marry me."

"What? No, no, I think you're fine looking." Now she felt silly—telling him what she thought of his looks. "I've never carried on a conversation with a man—other than my father—and now you, so I don't know how to act. I mean, no man has ever expressed any interest in me."

"No? Well, that's their loss. You're quite beautiful."

"What?" Now it was her turn to laugh. "I suppose I should thank you, but let's just say I too have looked in the mirror, and I am not beautiful."

"Are you kidding?" He stared long and hard at her—so that she had to turn her gaze away and focus on something else. She chose a robin who'd been busy flitting back and forth, carrying bits and pieces of things for building her nest. "You're the prettiest thing I've ever seen," he said in a hushed voice. "I don't know why I waited till last spring to ask you out. I guess I always considered you a young thing—but then, somehow, you grew up."

Her cheeks went hot and not because of the sun. "I suppose I've been forced to do so."

"Yeah, life has a way of doing that to us, doesn't it? I think the war turned a bunch of boys into men."

"Yes, you're right. I'm glad Billy Ray was not of age. It would have shattered me had he gone to war. As it was, Papa had to pay the fee to the government to avoid going. He didn't want to leave us, but he left anyway, though not of his own free will. I hope so anyway."

"What do you mean, you *hope*? You don't think he…"

"No, no, not that, but—it does bother me sometimes, thinking about it and, well, wondering how that poison got into his body."

"Like I said a while back, you ought to go to the sheriff and ask him if he can shed any light on the case. I'd go with you if you wanted me to."

"No, no, I—I wouldn't put that on you."

"Why not? I'm just as curious as you."

She didn't say anything, just shoved off in the rocker and listened to its droning squeak.

After a while, Jesse said, "You miss him."

"Of course I do. I loved Papa."

"A few minutes ago, I told you I was confused."

"Yes."

"And you assumed it was because I couldn't figure out why you changed your mind about marrying me."

"Well, wasn't it?"

"No, not really. My confusion rests more with Blackthorn."

She stopped rocking. "What do you mean?"

"I'm confused why he was so bent on getting your property. Doesn't it strike you as odd? Sure, he's a big bully, intent on buying up land all over Lebanon, but he was especially keen on getting your farm. And I'm curious to know why."

"He was desperate, I'll give you that."

"Do you have any idea why?"

"No."

"He came here, didn't he?"

"Yes, but I can't tell you anything beyond that."

"Because he warned you not to."

She didn't say anything, just nodded her head.

"It's all right. I don't need to know what he said."

She let out a breath of relief. "Thank you."

They rocked on, and for a few minutes, both had their own thoughts.

"Is he coming to pick you up?"

"Yes, I expect him most any time."

"I think I should leave before he gets here."

"It would be best. He doesn't—want me to associate with you."

"What business is that of his?"

"I—don't know exactly, but—please—don't approach him about it. It's—not a good idea. In fact, I shouldn't even be talking to you about any of it."

He laid a hand on her arm. "Slow down, okay? It's all right."

She realized then how fast she'd been talking and how frantic she sounded. She gave a slow nod.

"What sort of job has Blackthorn given you?" His tone was steady, reassuring, and comforting.

"Housework and preparing his meals."

"I see. And where is this apartment he's setting you up in?"

"Over Henry's Hardware."

Jesse nodded. "I'll be able to check on you."

"No, I don't want you to. I mean, you don't need to."

He studied her a little too intensely. "But I'm going to." This he said with great earnestness.

"I'm not sure if Blackthorn…"

"He doesn't own you, Anna. Don't give him the impression that he does."

She swallowed. "I'll do my best."

He didn't look convinced. "That man is a brute. Tell me something. Did your Pa ever have anything to say about him?"

"Not a great deal. Blackthorn came here a few times, but—I wouldn't say they were friends, even though they grew up together. Their fathers were better friends than they were."

Jesse scratched his chin and scrunched his brow in thought. "That's interesting. In all the years I knew your father, he never mentioned anything to me about growing up with Horace Blackthorn. I didn't even know they were acquainted."

"Like I said, it wasn't a friendship."

"Why did he come here then?"

"Papa never told me. I just assumed it was business related. He never seemed to want to talk about him."

"That's the oddest thing. I wonder if they were in discussions about this farm even before he passed."

"I don't think so. It seems like Papa would have told me if that were the case."

"But would he? I don't think Newell wanted you to know how bad off his financial situation really was."

"You're right. I wish he would have disclosed more to me."

"Did Horace stop in to see your pa before he passed away?"

She had to stop and think about that. "I don't know. He may have, but that last week of Papa's life has gone all foggy on me."

"Don't worry about it. I was just curious."

They rocked some more, both mulling over their words. After a time, Jesse raised his head and looked around the yard. "Where's Billy Ray?"

"He and Rex are out in the barn. He's been downright mad at me ever since Blackthorn took over the property. He's worried about the animals after we leave them. Do you think Blackthorn will do well by them?"

Jesse shook his head. "I have no idea what he has in mind. You want me to take the animals to my farm?"

Her mouth opened on its own, and she gawked at him. "You would do that?"

"Sure. My nieces and nephews will fawn over them. I'll wait till after you've left with Blackthorn, then come back and lead them over to my pasture. They'll adapt fine. What about Rex?"

"Oh, he's coming with us." As if the dog had sensed his name coming up in conversation, he appeared around the side of the house. "Billy Ray would never forgive me if we left that dog behind." She gave a pathetic little laugh. "Actually, *I* wouldn't forgive me either." The dog meandered past them and walked to his water bowl for a few refreshing laps then turned a couple of circles before plopping down next to the porch.

"Maybe I will go out and talk to Billy."

"Oh, that would be nice."

He stood and gave a stretch of his long arms, and she couldn't help but admire the ripple of muscle. Embarrassed for noticing, she quickly averted her eyes, casting them toward the road and secretly wishing Blackthorn would forget all about them.

He gazed down at her. "Before I go out to the barn, is there anything you need from me, anything I can do to make this easier for you?"

She couldn't believe his kindness. Here she'd thought he was coming over to voice his anger at her for blowing their chances for buying the property. Instead, it was the opposite. "I appreciate that, Jesse. I—can't think of anything."

He gave a half-smile. "Well, any time you do think of something, I'm at your service." He gave a little bow.

She smiled. "I appreciate that."

He tipped his hat at her and skipped down the steps, then headed out toward the barn.

18

Jesse found Billy Ray sitting on a milking stool next to the goat pen, talking to the goats. The boy hadn't heard him come in so he lingered back and listened.

"I'll be leaving soon," he was saying. "I don't want to go, but I got no choice. My sister says you'll be all right. I done said my goodbyes t' the horses an' chickens and Carlotta. The chickens'll be fine, but I worry about the rest of y'." The goats all banded close together, as if hanging onto his every word. A couple stood on their hind legs trying to nuzzle him over the wooden enclosure. He put his hand up and rubbed their noses. "Nope, I don't like it no more than you, but I can't do nothin' about it. Anna says we got no other choice. I ain't talked to her much, 'cause I'm pretty mad at her."

Jesse stepped forward. "Hey, Billy, how you doing, friend?"

Startled, Billy Ray jumped up and quickly turned. "I didn't hear y' come in, Mr. Fuller."

"You can call me Jesse, remember?"

"Okay. But Anna said she ain't marryin' you after all."

"I know. That's a disappointment, but, hey, that's no reason you and I can't continue our friendship, is it?"

He shrugged. "I don't think I'll see you again."

"What makes you say that?"

"Anna an' me will be busy working for that dumb Mr. Blackthorn. I got no idea what I'll be doin', but I hope it ain't housework. I hate doin' laundry an' such."

"I don't blame you. What say I pick you up sometime and bring you to the Fuller farm to work for me?"

His head jerked up, and his light blue eyes danced with sudden excitement. "Really? That'd be great. Like tomorrow?"

Jesse laughed. "Well, let's give you and your sister some time to get settled in at your new place first."

"I don't wanna go to that dumb new place. What if his hired hands don't take good care o' my animals?"

"I told Anna I'd take them over to my pasture. They'll fare well in our fields and in the big barn. I'll see to it."

His face brightened just a little. "Thanks. Carlotta likes a little extra attention when she gets milked. I usually bring her out an apple in the morning."

"I'll do my best to remember that."

The boy sat there staring at nothing in particular. "I still don't wanna go."

"I know you don't, but it's best you cooperate with Anna because she's doing the best she can for you."

He dipped his head and looked at the barn floor, kicking a stick and watching it fly. "I know. It's just—I don't like Mr. Blackthorn. He's mean."

"Has he ever been mean to you?"

He shrugged. "Not to my face, but there's somethin' I don't like about him."

"Did you ever know him to come over and visit your Pa?"

He narrowed his eyes in thought. "Sure, I seen him here a few times. The last time I saw him was a couple days before Papa had the heart attack. I was back in Carlotta's stall when they were arguing. I never did tell Papa I was back there. Do you think I should have?"

Blackthorn had visited Newell just days before his death? Jesse dragged in a deep breath and let it out slowly. "I'm sure it's fine that you didn't. What were they arguing about if you don't mind telling me?"

"I got no idea. I couldn't hear most of their words very well. I did hear Mr. Blackthorn say something like, 'Where do you keep them clues?' I *think* he said clues."

"Clues?"

"Yeah. Papa went back in the tack room. I made sure to duck down so he wouldn't see me. He must have showed Mr. Blackthorn something. After a little bit, they raised their voices like they were sort of mad, and then I heard Mr. Blackthorn say he was going to buy our farm, and Papa said the words, 'Over my dead body.' I never heard Papa say words like that before. After that, Mr. Blackthorn sort of laughed and then muttered somethin' I couldn't hear. I stayed real quiet in Carlotta's stall while she ate her hay. When Mr. Blackthorn left, and I heard Papa walk around to the other side of the barn, I hurried up to the house without him seein' me 'cause I didn't want to get in trouble."

Again, Jesse tried not to show any emotion. "Hm. And you say this was a few days before your Papa died?"

"Yup. I wish I wouldn't have listened in like that. It wasn't none of my business."

"No, you shouldn't worry about that. You did very well to remember everything and then tell me about it. Is there anything else you can remember about that night?"

The boy put a finger to his chin and screwed up his face in thought. "Umm, I don't think so." But then he brightened. "Oh, wait. After supper that night, I came out to feed the hog. I saw a horse brush on the ground, so I picked it up and took it back to the tack room. That's when I saw something."

"What do you mean? What did you see?"

"I saw a brown metal box. It was on a bench by the door. I figured that must've been what Papa showed Mr. Blackthorn that day."

Jesse's heart jumped. "Really? What sort of box was it?"

"Just a small one with a lid. It wasn't nothin' much. And I never told Anna about it 'cause I didn't want to add more confusion to her head, so if I tell you, then you can't tell her I told you."

His heart thumped a little faster. "What was in the box?"

"Do you promise not to tell her?"

"I guess that depends. If either of you is in danger, then I suppose I'd have to tell her."

The boy thought on that for a few moments. "It's prob'ly nothin' special anyway—what I found."

"Wouldn't hurt to tell me about it."

"I'll do better 'n that. I'll show you. Follow me."

The boy stood up from his perch on the milk stool and walked to the back of the barn. Trying not to appear overly anxious, Jesse followed behind. Once inside, Billy Ray reached up and brought a small metal box with a hinged lid down from a shelf. "Here it is." He held it carefully in his hands.

As much as he wanted to, Jesse did not try to hurry the boy, figuring it was up to him to reveal the contents. He snagged another breath and practiced patience.

The boy went on. "Just as I was looking at what was inside, Papa came out of nowhere and scolded me for snooping," Billy said. "He made me jump and I almost cried. Then I told him I wasn't snooping. He quick apologized for yelling at me, then took the box and set it on a high shelf where I couldn't reach it. He said it was just some little thing his papa had given him and that he'd show it to me later—maybe when I was about twelve. He said it was time to go in the house, so I followed him out of the barn."

"And so he didn't tell you what was in it?" The boy had captured his full attention.

"Nope. He just said it was ar' secret, and I wasn't to talk about it to no one, so I promised I wouldn't. But then—then he died a couple days later." He ended that last sentence on a choking sob, so Jesse put a reassuring hand on the boy's shoulder. "When the sheriff an' the doc was here that day, I thought about the box, but I didn't tell them anything 'cause it didn't seem important. And besides, Pa told me not to tell anybody."

"Well, he's gone now, so I think perhaps the promise you made might be insignificant, especially if it's more important than you realize."

The boy shrugged. "Maybe. I did climb on a couple of stacked crates to get it down after Papa died, but I felt guilty."

Jesse's heart went out to the boy, but his curiosity shot up by several degrees. "And what did you find?"

The boy screwed up his face. "Just some papers that didn't make too much sense to me."

"Are you going to show me?"

Without another word, Billy slowly lifted the lid. Jesse had to lean forward to see inside.

"Let's step out where it's a little brighter," he suggested, so they moved out of the tack room and into the main area of the barn. Splashes of afternoon sunlight from the open doors and a loft window sent lazy swirls of dust about them. An inscription on the inside of the box lid read "From Herbert to Charles." And inside the box lay three folded pieces of paper and an old key. "May I?" Jesse asked the boy before reaching inside.

"Go ahead."

Jesse gingerly reached in and picked up the top paper. Finding it brittle and yellowed with age, he took great care in unfolding it. Once he'd opened it, he merely stared at a drawing that meant nothing to him. It was a map of some type with a squiggly line indicating a stream, a few squares he took to mean buildings, perhaps a house, a barn, and some other structures, and then several circles that, given some imagination, might have passed for trees. On various parts of the map were Xs with numbers one to four next to them and a few neatly printed words, including "Creek," "Barn," and "Wish Bone Tree." There were some other words that had faded over time and would require closer examination in order to decipher them. In one part of the drawing, printed in small letters, were the words:

"*If thee uses thee eyes and searches thee mind, a jeweled treasure thee will find.*"

"What in the world?" Jesse whispered.

"See? It don't make no sense. There's two more papers in here." Billy offered up the box, so Jesse refolded the map, put it back in the box, and then removed the other two folded papers, finding them equally brittle.

Aloud, he read the neatly printed words, "*Clue number one: On the north creek bank, where warm waters flow, four feet deep, in a jar below.*" He squinted at the clue for a moment, giving it some thought, then read the last piece of paper. "*Clue number two: Center of the south piece, 20 paces west. Buried in a vase at the bottom of the crest.*" Jesse could make no sense of either "clue," but his chest had taken to thumping even faster than before.

"Ain't it strange?" asked Billy.

"It's a puzzler all right." He studied the cryptic clues a few moments longer and then the strange little gray metal key for a few seconds, then folded the papers back up, placed them in the box, and closed the lid. "Best keep this close by. I wouldn't keep it in the barn though, as Horace Blackthorn might find it, and since your father was going to explain it to you someday, it's clearly yours. It appears to be something your father considered very important or he wouldn't have kept it hidden for so long."

"You think there's a treasure somewhere?"

Jesse tossed back his head and gave a little chuckle, albeit a nervous one. "You never can tell, friend. If there is, I'd guess it's yours."

"Really? But—there's something else."

"What?"

The boy turned the box over and pointed to some words carved into the bottom of the box that read: "Property of Charles Hansen from Wilbur Blackthorn ~ 1835."

"Hm, that was thirty years ago. Do you know who Charles Hansen is, Billy?"

"I think that was my grandfather. He died sometime last year."

"Yes, I'm aware, and I'm sorry. Charles was your papa's father, and Wilbur Blackthorn was Horace Blackthorn's father."

The boy wrinkled his nose. "I don't get it."

He ruffled the boy's thick brown hair. "I don't get it either, but I guess it meant something important to these men. Obviously, your grandfather passed this box down to your papa. I wonder why Charles Blackthorn didn't want it to remain in Blackthorn hands."

"What do you mean?"

He looked at the boy's puzzled face and gave a little chuckle. "Never mind for now. Maybe someday it'll make sense to you. In the meantime, you best hang on tight to this box."

Outside, Rex barked. Jesse started to move to the doors. "Jesse?"

Jesse stopped and turned. "Yes?"

The boy held the box out at arm's length. "Do you think you could keep it in a safe place for me?"

He paused and thought a moment, then replied, "You bet I can. You can count on me."

"Thanks."

Rex barked again, this time more heartily. Jesse reached the door and peered out. "It's Blackthorn. Looks like he's come to fetch you and Anna."

They paused in the doorway, and Billy said, "I don't wanna go."

"I know you don't, but you'll be fine, and I'll take good care of the horses and Carlotta and your goats."

Jesse put a hand on the boy's shoulder and gave him a little nudge. The boy gave an audible sigh, stood taller, and walked out. Jesse set the box down on the worktable next to the door and followed after, thinking it best to take the box with him when he returned to fetch the animals and whatever other pieces of property Anna might want in her possession.

19

W hat are you doin' here?" Horace asked Jesse, feeling ire rise in his chest. "You're on my property, y' know."

"I'm bidding Miss Hansen and her brother goodbye. I didn't think there was any law against that. Also thought I might help y' load up her possessions."

Hmm. "Well, I guess that'd be all right. You two ain't been talkin', have you?"

"Sure, we've been talkin'. What did you expect? That I was coming over to have a staring match with her? I asked her where she was moving; she told me to an apartment you've so generously offered. I asked her what sort of job she had lined up; she said she'll be doing general house-keeping for you. That sort of thing."

Horace sized the man up from his high perch. He never knew whether to believe Jesse Fuller or figure him for a cheat. He glanced at the girl, who stood staring up at him with anxious eyes. "Humph. General housekeeping and making my meals. She better be a good cook." He kept his eyes trained on her. Then with lifted brows, he turned his gaze on Jesse. "I fired my last maid, you know. The little miss here, she came into the picture at just the right time."

Jesse shifted his weight and looked anxious to say something, but instead he pursed his lips. Good. Let him worry his tiny little brain over his girlfriend—if she even was that. For all he knew, he'd wanted to marry her just to get her land. Well, too late for that, thanks to his own clever ways and little threats. Yes, indeed, he had the little lady right where he wanted her, scared as a trapped gopher and doing his bidding. Jesse Fuller stared at him as if trying to read his mind, and Horace almost laughed. He tossed the reins over a bar, jumped down, and gazed out over the vast land that was now his. He'd come back tomorrow when it was just him, and he'd begin to plan his strategy. The first thing to do would be to take down that box Newell kept stored on a high shelf so he could study its contents in detail, particularly that map with the numbers one to four on it. He wanted to compare it to the one his father had given him and see if there were any major contradictions. Yes, tomorrow was all his, but for now, he had to get this little gal and her pest of a brother to their new place.

"Well, where's your things?" he asked. "Time's a'wastin'."

She jumped to attention. "In the house. I'll—*we'll*—get them. Come on, Billy Ray."

She turned and headed to the house.

"I'll help," Jesse said.

"Not so quick there, Fuller." Horace snagged him by the arm, but the man whipped out of his grip faster than a runaway horse and gave him a red hot glare.

"Don't you ever touch me again, Blackthorn." He ground out each word between his gritted teeth, his tone as cold as ice.

Horace laughed, pretending indifference, but he could sense that Jesse would like nothing more than to choke the air out of him. Suddenly aware that his size didn't quite equal Jesse Fuller's, he raised both palms and took a step back. Jesse used the opportunity to advance on him, looking down on him with fire in his eyes. It enraged Horace—but he knew he wasn't in any position to react just now. Dad blast! He didn't even have his gun on him. If he had, he would shoot the lout and call it self-defense.

"And you best not lay a hand on Anna Hansen either, you scum-sucking pig," Jesse spat. "I ever hear you done so, I'll rattle your bones like they were nothing more than a sack of marbles. You got that?"

"Yeah, yeah," Horace said, pushing on the other man's chest with both palms. It felt rock solid and about as impossible to move as a brick wall. He stepped back, hating that he felt compelled to do so. Then Jesse had the nerve to move in closer. What was he trying to do, back him into a corner? Horace didn't like being made the fool by some young, uppity snit, and by gum, he'd go after him later if he so much as touched him with his filthy hands. "Get away from me!"

One side of Jesse's top lip raised in a sneer as he looked down. "I'm just giving you fair warning, Blackthorn, that's all. Did the message get through to your pea-sized brain?"

Horace scowled. "I wouldn't talk about brain sizes if I were you, Fuller. Now, back off. I'll not be laying a hand on your little lady—if that's what she even is to you. I figured you wanted to marry her for her property, and now that I've bought it fair and square, the idea of marriage has been nixed."

"Fair and square, eh? You call pressuring her into selling it fair and square?"

"Whoever told you I pressured her?" So help him, if that little Hansen wench ran off her mouth to Jesse Fuller, he'd take her little brother away from her tonight and she'd never see him again.

"Nobody told me anything. I'm just surmising. Anna and I had a plan to marry, and then suddenly, overnight, she changed her mind."

"What's that got to do with me? She didn't want to marry you. Swallow your pride and accept it, Fuller. You ain't no kind of prize."

"What's going on out here?" Anna stood on the porch, holding a large crate in her arms—and that mangy mutt was right beside her! Blast it, that thing was still alive? Billy Ray came up behind her, his own arms full.

At last, Jesse stepped back and turned his eyes on Anna. "Nothing much. Your new employer and I were just coming to a little understanding. Isn't that right, Blackthorn?"

With all he had in him, he wished to spit in the man's face, but he supposed now was not the time for retaliation. "Yes, yes, an understanding. Is that all you have right there?"

"No, I—have several more containers inside."

"What? Well, I hope my wagon will hold it all. Your quarters are not nearly the size of your house."

"Well, I'm sure we'll make everything fit just fine. And Rex can follow the wagon."

"Rex?"

"My dog."

As if on cue, the dog gave out a single bark, and then bounded down the porch steps and started making its way toward Horace, growling menacingly. What in tarnation? He should have made sure that mutt was dead when he'd come upon it the other night and whacked it hard over the head with a rock. Horace took a few steps back, wondering how to defend himself against it should the need arise.

"Rex, stop it. Rex, come back here," Anna called. Fortunately for her, the creature obeyed.

"You don't expect to bring that mongrel to your upstairs quarters I hope," Horace said, eyeing the ugly thing.

"We can't leave him behind."

"That building isn't suited for a dog."

"Then I ain't going," piped up Billy Ray.

"Fine, you can stay here for all I care," Horace told the kid.

"Billy is coming with me and so is Rex. That's settled," the Hansen gal said, sticking out her chin in a stubborn fashion.

With Jesse right there, Horace didn't feel like arguing. "Fine, fine, but the first sign of complaints from any other residents, and he's out on the streets."

"What other residents?" Anna asked.

"There's other people living up there."

"At our apartment?"

"You didn't think you were getting the entire second floor to yourself, did you? You got two rooms, and that's it—and they're connected."

Her face turned an ashen color. "I see. Well, I'm sure we'll make do."

"You don't have much choice, missy. Now, let's get your stuff loaded on the back of my wagon." He turned to Jesse, whose stance had not softened. "You can help if you want, but no dallying. I've got a tight schedule."

Jesse scowled at him as if he had plenty more to say but would save it. Good. He wasn't up for any more of his nonsense.

"I don't know where you think you're going to put all this stuff," Horace said after he loaded the last bit of paraphernalia on the back of his weighted-down wagon.

"I'm sure we'll find a place," Anna said.

"And what you don't have room for, I'll take back to my place and store for safekeeping," said the meddlesome Jesse Fuller.

"I appreciate that."

"I'll follow you to the hardware, Horace, and help carry everything upstairs," Jesse said.

Horace wasn't in favor of having the fellow come along, but he didn't much cotton to helping the little miss and her pesky brother haul all their junk up those stairs either. Matter of fact, he might just drop her off and let the three of them tote it up while he went to Ed's Saloon for a drink. Yes, indeed, that's exactly what he'd do!

⌒

Anna's first glimpse of their new quarters turned out to be worse than what Blackthorn had led her to believe. Yes, they had two rooms, and they were adjoined, but it was more like one larger room partitioned off with a thin wall to make it into two rooms. Only one room, which would be hers, had a door that led to the hallway. Each space contained a narrow cot, a small chest of drawers, a tattered braid rug, and oil lamps on the wall above the tiny bedstands. Thankfully, the lamps were lit, so all she'd need to do before going to sleep each night was turn them to a low flicker and then add oil as needed. They each had a small window covered by some old faded curtains. The wooden floors creaked, and the place smelled like musty leaves. As if he knew better than to complain, Billy Ray kept mum, only letting his eyes trail around the place, his mouth sagging open.

"Where am I supposed to cook our meals?" she asked.

"You'll eat them at my house, in the kitchen," Blackthorn said. "I'd appreciate you not eating me out of house and home though."

"Okay." The last thing she wanted to do was eat his food. That would make her more dependent on him. But what could she do about it? Not a single thing—until she found a better paying job that would allow her to get a tiny little house with a real kitchen. It's a good thing she had thought to pack some sandwiches and a couple of jars of strawberry punch for tonight's supper! Her heart already ached for her homey kitchen, the stone fireplace, and the table that Papa had built. And her rockers! How would they fit in this tiny place? Her little farmhouse with its airy windows overlooking the fields seemed like a mansion in comparison. One window here looked out onto a busy street with shoppers moving to and fro. The view from the other window was even sadder— just the side of a building next door and a narrow alleyway down below.

While her spirits were indeed crushed, she had to make every effort not to show it, so she took in a deep breath of stale air and put on a smile. "Well, I'm sure we'll be just fine."

"Good. I'm heading up the street to the saloon. You make yourselves t' home."

"But—I thought—you—"

"Don't worry about it, Anna," Jesse said. "I will help you carry up the rest of your belongings." It was the first she'd even dared to look at him. What must he think of her new "home"? No doubt he was full of self-righteous thoughts such as, "If you'd just married me, you wouldn't be in this predicament" or "You shouldn't have let Blackthorn talk you into this. Just look at this rotten place."

And she wouldn't blame him if he voiced them. All she wanted to do was cry, but she'd have to save that for tonight—after she laid her head on her pillow. Thankfully, she'd thought to bring her bedding and Billy's. Fiddle-faddle, by the look of things, they were lucky to at least have a tick mattress on each cot!

20

It was pushing past seven o'clock by the time they finished setting both tiny rooms to rights, hanging a couple of small paintings on the walls, and setting out familiar trinkets to make them homey, then unpacking clothing items to put into drawers. Anything that did not fit went into a specific corner of Anna's room for Jesse to take back to his place for storage. She kept apologizing, and he had to keep reassuring her she was not inconveniencing him. On the one hand, Jesse was glad Horace had at least offered them a place to live. Her farm had gone into foreclosure, and his offer to give her a job and a place to stay didn't go completely unnoticed. On the other hand, Horace's stubborn determination to obtain the property before Jesse had the chance to marry Anna continued to bother him.

Something had driven Horace's unwarranted desire for the property—but what? Did it have anything to do with the strange contents of that box Billy Ray had shown him? Horace had undoubtedly convinced Anna not to marry Jesse, but why? To keep her from stressing too much, Jesse hadn't pressured her to expound, but even if it took up all his spare time, he would someday figure out what it was that motivated Horace.

While Anna puttered about, situating her belongings in drawers and on top of the chest in neat stacks, he stood in the adjoining doorway and perused both areas. Billy sat on the edge of his yet unmade cot looking glum. Anna, with her back to him, moved about in almost rote fashion, as if staying busy was the only thing that would keep her from facing her current reality. Of course, both were unhappy, and that knowledge put a pang of empathy in Jesse's chest. What was it like to be ripped away from all things familiar? At least Rex seemed to be content, stretched out on the floor and watching Anna. Jesse was glad that at least Horace had given in to allowing the dog to join them. Perhaps he'd realized that arguing would get him nowhere.

Jesse cleared his throat. "I can start taking those extra crates back down to my wagon if you like."

She turned and gave him a blank stare. "Pardon?"

With his chin, Jesse gestured at the pile of possessions she wouldn't be able to fit into the tiny living quarters. "I can take those extra things downstairs if you like. It'll make your room look a little bigger with them out of the way."

"Oh, yes, I suppose. Leave those two big crates closest to the door though. They belonged to Papa, and at some point, I want to sort through them."

"I will do that." He pushed off from the doorframe and walked toward the corner, his arm slightly brushing her as he passed by. She gave a tiny gasp, so he stopped to study her forlorn face. Without considering the consequences, he instinctively moved closer and wrapped her in a warm hug. Her slight frame trembled in his embrace, but she didn't pull away, and he knew without looking that the tears had started dripping down her cheeks. He didn't want Billy Ray to see her like that, so he called out to him, "Billy, your sister and I are stepping out for a minute. Why don't you start putting some bedding on your cot? You'll find it folded right there next to you." In response, he got a quiet, morose-sounding, "'Kay."

He took Anna by the hand and led her out of the room so that they stood in the quiet hallway. Then he closed the door so that Billy wouldn't hear. At once, she let out a tiny sob that literally crushed his heart into a million pieces. He drew her close again, as close as was possible, and then gently kissed the top of her head. If it bothered her, she didn't let on, and in fact, perhaps she hadn't even noticed. "Everything will be all right," he heard himself whisper. "You'll see."

"I should have married you," she said on a choking sob.

A smile formed. He gave a slow nod, and then rested his chin on her head. "Yes, you should have, but perhaps that wasn't God's plan just yet. Besides, Blackthorn got to the bank ahead of us, and you signed those papers, giving him the rights."

She wept quietly into his shirt. "I'm sor-ry," she got out. "I—I had to do it."

Jesse kept holding her, even though he wanted to step back to search her wet face. "Why?" he asked.

"I—I can't say."

"All right, we'll leave it at that, but someday, you may need to tell me."

"I—I just want to go back to my own house, just Billy Ray and me."

"That's not possible, honey." The endearment slipped past his lips without warning, but she didn't seem to notice, or perhaps her quiet weeping drowned it out.

"I—I know, but I can still wish."

Another smile popped out on his lips. "Yes, you can. There is always room for wishing. For now, though, you have to make the best of things—for Billy's sake."

She sniffed, then stepped out of the circle of his arms and dabbed her eyes and cheeks with her apron until they were devoid of tears. Then she pulled back her shoulders, sniffed again, and raised her face to see into his. The whites of her eyes were now bloodshot. "Thank you," she said with new resolve. "I guess I just needed to mourn the loss of my home—and Papa leaving us in this—this dilemma." More sniffing. "I don't blame Papa, mind you. He did what he thought was right—kept me from knowing the full extent of our financial woes. It's just that—"

She stopped mid-sentence, so he pressed her with a gentle, "What?"

She shook her head. "I don't know. I wish he'd trusted me more, that's all."

Now he bent and kissed her forehead, then straightened and, with purpose, held both her shoulders and looked down into her eyes. "He trusted you. He just didn't want to burden you. He loved you and Billy Ray, you know. He wanted only the best for you."

If she'd noticed that little kiss on the forehead, she didn't acknowledge it. He wondered now if she'd react to a kiss on the *lips*, or would that too go unnoticed? She gave a little shrug and let her gaze fall to her soiled work shoes peeking out from underneath her long skirt. He studied her drooping frame. She was a picture of defeat, and he innately knew that wasn't the norm for her. No, she was a strong and stubborn woman by nature, always up for a fight and not one to easily give in. Had Horace stripped her of her dignity with his cutting words? From his observations of her, this giving-up spirit did not mesh with the Anna he knew. Still, he had only considered her a friend and neighbor in the past, so it rather rankled him that he was even thinking about kissing her. Something inside him had started going awry, his protective nature coming to life as he thought about her and Billy Ray fending for themselves in this loathsome, shabby building. But what could he do? He couldn't bring them to the big house, not without a certificate of marriage in his possession. Folks would take it the wrong way, never mind that his mother would hover over the Hansens like there was no tomorrow. Besides, it *was* Ma's house, and he didn't have the right to invite newcomers under her roof. It was bad enough that *he* still lived with her.

He lifted her chin with his pointer finger till their eyes met. "Tell me what's going on in that pretty little head of yours."

She didn't even hesitate. "I couldn't hold onto the only home that Billy Ray's ever known, and for that, I'm ashamed. I keep wondering what I could have done differently to convince Mr. Daly to give us more time. I should have started looking for another job before Papa died."

"Then who would've watched over Billy while your pa worked out in the fields?"

"He worked alongside him most of the time anyway."

"Who would've prepared the noon and evening meals while they were working? Who would've kept your farmhouse neat and tidy? Who would've washed all the clothes, tended the garden, and baked the bread, not to mention all the other things that go along with running a household?" He still kept her chin tilted up, and she didn't object.

"Maybe I could've done all those things while also bringing in some extra income for Papa." She finished her sentence on a hiccupy sigh.

Without thinking, Jesse leaned down and kissed her forehead, then straightened again. "You are a very capable young woman, but that all sounds a bit too overwhelming. Besides, your having a job probably wouldn't have helped your father's financial situation. Had my brothers and I realized just how serious Blackthorn was about obtaining your farm, we would have approached Newell before his passing to see about buying him out. We'd have been fair with him."

Her eyes filled with more moisture. "I know. Papa always thought so highly of your family."

Jesse raised his other hand and wiped both of her cheeks with his fingertips. That simple gesture made her close her eyes and bite down on her lower lip. It seemed only natural that he should kiss her, and so he did—and she kissed him back. To his utter joy, the kiss lingered, even built, as he tasted of her sweetness and indulged in her soft, moist lips, his brain swirling with all sorts of thoughts and his heart crashing against his chest. After an all too brief period, she pulled away and stared up at him, her dark blue eyes wide in shock.

"Oh!" she muttered, bringing her fingertips to her mouth to cover it.

She'd never been kissed! It occurred to Jesse that he should have asked permission first—or perhaps he shouldn't have kissed her at all! It was premature of him, and he had no idea what had gotten into him.

Until that moment, he'd not realized just how deep his romantic feelings for her were. Suddenly, she was all he could think about. What was he going to do? Her eyes were big and round as she stood there staring up at him, her palm still plastered across her mouth. If the kiss hadn't made such a powerful impact on him too, he might have seen a bit of humor in her shocked expression.

"I'm so sorry, Anna. I didn't know until a moment beforehand that I was going to do that."

"You need to go now." She dropped her hand from her mouth. "I don't want Blackthorn coming back and finding you still here."

"It doesn't matter what he thinks, Anna."

"But—it does."

"He already has your property, so what you do with your life now is none of his business."

"But—he's given me this place to live, so I'm—beholden to him."

"No, you're not. He may be your employer, but he doesn't own you."

She straightened her narrow shoulders and took a step back from him, then at last dropped her hands to her side. "I just think it's best you leave now. But thank you for helping me."

"I'll retrieve the things I'm taking back to my place to store. After I put them away, I'll stop back at the farm, and lead your animals to my pasture."

"I—appreciate that. Billy Ray and I will help you take the boxes back downstairs."

She turned to go back into the room, but he reached in front of her and latched onto the doorknob. With his mouth close to her ear, he whispered, "I am doing my utmost best not to pry, but I want to know if Blackthorn has threatened you in any way."

"I don't want to talk about him."

"Please, Anna—tell me if..."

The doorknob turned from inside and the door opened with Billy standing there gawking at them. "What are you two doing?" he asked, as innocent as a baby bird.

"Nothing," was Anna's quick reply. "We were just talking."

"About what?" he asked.

"Jesse was just getting ready to leave," she answered. "You're going to help us carry the things downstairs that we couldn't fit in our rooms. Jesse has been kind enough to offer to store them for us until such time as we are able to get a bigger place."

"So that's what you were talking about?"

She walked past him and entered the room, then walked to the corner and began retrieving odds and ends from the pile and placing them in Billy's arms. In another corner were the two rocking chairs Newell had built.

"Do you want me to carry down those chairs?" Jesse asked.

She gave a forlorn look at her beloved rockers. "I think we'll put one in each of our rooms. It will make things extra crowded, but I can't bear to part with them."

He smiled, but she did her best not to look at him. That kiss must still be lingering in her mind. He could not get it out of his head either.

After several trips up and down the staircase, they finally finished retrieving the items that didn't fit in their little rooms and had them loaded into his wagon. She'd even packed kitchen supplies for a kitchen that didn't exist. A wave of sympathy for what she'd lost swept over him. If she were going to cry again, though, she didn't show any signs of it. Jesse figured she would not allow herself to show weakness in front of Billy Ray.

"Thank you for everything you've done, Jesse," she said, putting an arm around Billy's shoulders and drawing him close to her side. A man and woman Jesse didn't recognize passed by and gave a bit of a curious glance at Jesse's filled wagon. "We appreciate it. Tell Jesse thank you, Billy Ray."

The boy cast him a glum face. "Thanks."

"You are entirely welcome. When is it you begin working for Blackthorn?"

"He told me to report at seven on Monday morning," Anna said. "He wants his breakfast on the table at seven-thirty every morning."

"Humph, and not a second earlier or later, eh?"

"Something like that. He says I can have Sundays off."

"Very generous of him," Jesse quipped. And just like that, an idea started percolating in his head. "What say I pick you up tomorrow morning and bring you two to church with me? We attend Lebanon Community Methodist in case you weren't aware. Afterward, you can join my family for dinner."

Her head jerked up. "Oh, we wouldn't impose like that. Besides, Black—"

"Yes! What time will you be here?" Billy asked.

"Billy Ray!"

"What?" The boy stood tall and stuck out his chin. "We haven't gone to church since Papa died, and he would be disappointed to know that."

If she planned to argue that point, she didn't let on. "I suppose you're right. But it's not necessary for you to pick us up, Jesse. Billy and I can walk over on our own. It's just a few blocks."

"Just the same, I'll stop by, park my rig in the back alley, and we can walk together."

"I'm—not sure that's a good idea. People will talk."

"What will they talk about?" Billy huffed. "A few days ago, you were going to marry Jesse, remember? I bet plenty of folks heard about that. Besides, we went to the Golden Lamb together. And anyway, why should we care if people want to talk?"

Jesse reached across and patted the boy on the shoulder. "You are a brilliant young man, you know that? He makes all kinds of sense, Anna."

Anna took a deep breath. "It will be strange going back to church without Papa."

"But it will do you good to return, and with it being a different church than the one you attended with your father, you won't have thoughts of sitting in the same pew with him. You're strong, but you still need the sort of strength that only God can give you."

"I know you're right. I just hope Blackthorn…doesn't…"

"He don't own us, Sis. He can't tell us what to do."

The boy was more than brilliant. He had insight beyond his years.

Anna smiled at her little brother then reached out and ruffled his already mussed wavy brown hair. "All right then, you win." Then to Jesse. "What time should we expect you?"

"I'll be here at nine-forty-five. Sunday school starts at nine, but we'll skip that and just go to the church service. How does that sound?"

"That sounds fine. Thank you for your help today."

"You are more than welcome." Jesse stood there studying her for a few brief moments, thinking mostly about that kiss and the impact it had made on his heart. Best put that out of his mind for now with Billy Ray standing right there watching them. "All right then, I'll see you in the morning." He climbed aboard his loaded wagon, turned the horses in the right direction, then tipped his hat at the pair and headed out of town.

21

$\mathcal{H}$orace seethed with anger. That morning at almost ten, he'd glanced out his upstairs bedroom window overlooking Broadway and spotted Jesse Fuller strolling up the sidewalk with Anna Hansen and her scruffy little brother. Did the girl have no sense about her? He'd clearly told her to stay away from Fuller, yet there she was blatantly disobeying his order. It was enough that Fuller had helped her move her things in yesterday, but did he have to return the very next day? Did she presume that since he now owned her property, he'd abandoned his requirement that she stay away from Fuller? He didn't trust her with Jesse, not for a minute. What was to keep him from wheedling information out of her regarding Horace's threats toward Billy? His eyes followed the trio until they turned the corner and headed east on Main Street and out of view. They were no doubt heading to church. It was Sunday, after all, not that the day held any importance to him. He knew that most folks ceased work and went to their places of worship, but that never appealed to him.

He dropped the curtain and grumbled under his breath. "I'll have to make myself a little clearer tomorrow when she shows up for work.

Humph, might be I'll even give that boy of hers a little scare. It would serve them both right if I put a little fear in their bones."

He growled and moved away from the window, then walked out of his bedroom, the big poster bed yet unmade. Making his bed daily was a maid's duty, so he'd add that to Anna's list of responsibilities when she arrived in the morning. He would make her list so long she'd have not a second to spare for the likes of Jesse Fuller. Yes, sir, he'd make it plenty long.

⌒

Anna fully enjoyed the service at Community Methodist Church. The pipe organ was quite enthralling and the singing was refreshingly inspiring. She found herself singing at the peak of her lungs during the hymns, yet still not hearing herself for all the melodious voices surrounding her—all on key as far as she could tell. Even Billy Ray joined in, and it turned out Jesse had a fine voice. Just being in the presence of other Christians bolstered Anna's spirits, and attending with Jesse, Billy Ray sitting between them, made the experience all the more pleasant. She decided to fully immerse herself in the beautiful music and block out all thoughts pertaining to folks whispering about their entering the church together. Let them think what they wanted.

The preacher delivered a fine message about love and unity, mentioning how President Lincoln's assassination had created an even worse divide in the country, with some American citizens thinking the president got what he deserved and others mourning the country's grievous loss. Because her father had passed away the day before the president was shot, the terrible tragedy in Washington, D.C., had taken a back seat in her heart and mind. As much as she'd tried to mourn Abraham Lincoln's death, her own personal grief ran far deeper. However, the reverend's message did resonate with her, challenging her to look beyond her own deep sorrow and practice a hospitable, kind spirit with her neighbors. Did that include Horace Blackthorn? Must she be hospitable with him? In her spirit, she knew she must at least try, so when the pastor gave the closing prayer, she asked the Lord to make her able and willing.

It was a lovely day, sunshine lighting up a cloudless sky and a gentle breeze keeping the air at a comfortable temperature. It would have been a perfect day for working in her beloved garden—if only she had one. For the tiniest moment, she let that thought take hold, but then she just as quickly dismissed it. Outside, parishioners gathered in clusters to visit, most of them dressed in their Sunday best, women of all shapes and sizes wearing lovely, flared gowns and floral hats to complement their frocks, and men dressed in fancy suits. She hadn't missed Jesse's dapper looks when he'd stopped to retrieve her and Billy Ray that morning and had hoped not to embarrass him in her own plain gown. It was kind of him to tell her how pretty she looked, but on the inside, she knew he must surely view her as a pathetic farm girl in her outdated dress, never mind that it was one of only about three dresses she owned that didn't bear stains or rips. And it was the same one she'd worn when they dined at the Golden Lamb.

While standing in the shade of a beautiful sugar maple tree, Isaac and Franklin, Jesse's nephews, walked over to Billy Ray and encouraged him to come with them to visit with some of their school friends. He was more than eager to tag along, failing even to glance up at Anna to seek permission before dashing off with the boys, their yelps of glee echoing across the churchyard.

An older gentleman approached. He looked familiar, but Anna couldn't place him. He shook Jesse's hand. "Good to see you, Jess." His eyes drifted to Anna. "And who might this beautiful young lady be?"

"This is Anna Hansen, Newell Hansen's daughter. Anna, meet Ernest Jenner."

The man's wrinkled face went from pleasant to serious. "Oh, Newell, yes, that was tragic. I'm sorry for your loss, Miss Anna. Must have come as a shock. Also sorry to have heard of your farm going up for auction."

"Thank you." Anna extended her hand and he pressed it briefly to his lips. "It didn't actually go up for auction, sir. A fellow named Horace Blackthorn purchased it."

"I might have known. Hear tell Horace is snatching up a good share of Lebanon's foreclosures, so I s'pose it stands to reason that he'd want your property to add to his collection. Just the same, I'm sorry for the loss of your father and your farm. I hope you're managing fine."

"Yes—yes, my brother and I are doing just fine."

"Well, I'm glad to hear it. My wife and I run Jenner's Grocery on East Warren Street, although our two sons have mostly taken it over so the wife and I can enjoy our final years. I believe I've seen you there a time or two. I just didn't put two and two together."

"Yes, I've purchased goods there." Anna realized that's why she had recognized him.

Ernest Jenner's old eyes squinted as he briefly looked toward the sun then back at her. "Your mention of Horace Blackthorn reminded me of an age-old tale about his great-grandfather, old Nolan Blackthorn, taking part in a bank robbery, or maybe it was a stagecoach robbery. Not sure about that detail. As a young lad, I recall my own grandpa talking about Nolan. He was a mean old cuss from what Grandpa said. Of course, the law caught up with him and his cohorts, and they all landed themselves in jail, where they lived out their remaining days."

"Really?" That piqued Anna's interest as she recalled that yellowed newspaper clipping in the old family Bible. Fleetingly, she wondered if Mr. Jenner's story of a robbery might be related to that newspaper story.

"I'm interested to hear more," said Jesse, as if reading her mind.

Mr. Jenner scratched his mostly balding head, where only a few strands of white hair still remained, and pulled on his white beard. "Can't recall much about it, really. His son Herbert was a scamp himself, drinking, carousing, and gambling a good share of his life away. He carried around some sort of chip on his shoulder that made folks want to avoid him. There was a fist fight in the middle of town once that folks still talk about from time to time. My father was the one who ultimately broke it up. Those two were going at it in the dirt in front of Pete's Saloon. I happened to witness my daddy picking them both up by the scruffs of their shirt collars, and pushing them off in opposite directions. I believe the spat was with Edward Hansen, your great-grandfather, Miss Anna."

That bit of information gave Anna a jolt, and her mind filled with all manner of confusion. "Yes, my great-grandfather's name was Edward, but why would he have been fighting with Herbert Blackthorn?"

"I suppose Blackthorn wanted his land back, and Edward wasn't about to sell it to him."

Now her head filled with more confusion. "He wanted *his* land back?"

"Yes," Mr. Jenner said. "He acquired a gambling debt, so he sold his land to your great-grandfather to pay it off, but as the story goes, he wanted to buy it back once he raised the money, but your great-grandfather refused to sell. Something along those lines. I was just a lad at the time and didn't think much about grown-up matters, so don't quote me." He smiled and looked from her to Jesse. "I'm sorry. I believe I've confounded you with all my blather."

Jesse shook his head. "Of course not, Mr. Jenner. And thank you for reminding me of that story." He turned to Anna. "I completely forgot about that. It was before our time, of course, but your farm used to belong to Herb Blackthorn. That at least partially explains why Horace might want it back, even though it hasn't been in his family for many years."

"But Papa inherited the farm from my Grandfather Charles," she said. "I just assumed it had been in our family's hands for many generations."

"Well, it has been a *few* generations," Mr. Jenner said. "Just not as many as you may have thought."

Anna's mind spun with a muddle of thoughts. "I've never heard the full story. I wish I knew more. I do know that there was some sort of a strain between Horace Blackthorn and my father, but Papa never relayed any details to me. Papa was a fine Christian man who always told me the past belonged in the past and that we must live for today, treating our neighbors with love and kindness, and accomplishing as much as we can for God with the time we have."

Mr. Jenner pulled again on his beard. "Well, that's fine advice. I always liked your pa and was mighty sorry to hear of his passing—and the strange circumstances surrounding his death. I hope they can get to the bottom of it someday."

"Yes, I hope the same," said Anna.

He put on a thoughtful face and gazed off. "Hm, I haven't thought about that saloon fight my father broke up for many years, but when you mentioned Blackthorn buying your farm, well, bits and pieces of the old tale came back to me. I hope I haven't caused you undue sadness by mentioning it."

"No, not at all. In fact, I appreciate it," Anna said.

Mr. Jenner grew more serious. "Your Grandfather Charles and I used to be fine friends as lads, but time and life sort of sent us off in different directions. I was sorry to hear about his passing a year or so back. I heard he went to live with his brother down in Tennessee some years ago."

"You heard right, sir. My father visited him a couple of years ago, but I stayed back with Billy Ray to tend the farm. After Grandpa's brother died, he moved in with his nephew, but his health had been declining for some time. The last time I saw him I was a girl of thirteen or fourteen. His health wasn't the best, but he was determined to visit the farm and the town of Lebanon one last time. We had a grand time as I recall. We exchanged letters after that. This will sound harsh, but I'm glad he passed ahead of Papa. I would have hated to relay Papa's death in a letter, especially the suspicious part that goes with it. That would've bothered Grandpa terribly."

"Yes, indeed it would have." Mr. Jenner looked off across the church-yard. "Well, I see the missus is standing next to my rig. I best get along now. It was a pleasure to see you this morning, Miss Anna, and I hope you'll return."

"Thank you."

"You take good care of yourself now. And naturally, it's always good to see you, Jesse."

"The feelings are mutual, sir," Jesse said.

At that, Mr. Jenner turned and headed to the long line of parked rigs, his gait unsteady.

"Well, that was interesting," said Jesse.

"Indeed it was. He's an interesting old fellow."

"Isn't he? By the way, how did you like the church service?"

"Oh, it was divine. I believe I enjoyed it even more than Country Baptist Church where Papa always took us. Thank you for inviting us."

"Next week, same time?"

"Oh, I—I don't know about that. I mean, if we did decide to return, there'd be no need for you to pick us up."

He dipped his head toward her and grinned. "What if I wanted to?"

Her heart instinctively leaped. "I don't—"

"Forget about Blackthorn's supposed authority over you. You have your own life to live."

She couldn't help it. Blackthorn's threats remained primary in her thoughts. She hesitated a bit before answering. "I'll—think about it."

"Good. It's a date then."

"What?"

He laughed. "And now, young lady, let us go to the Fuller farm for a good old-fashioned Laura Fuller Sunday dinner."

He looped his arm for her, so she stuck her hand through it—and found herself enjoying the moment. Phooey! What if Blackthorn *did* spot them together? Jesse was right. He didn't own her! The three boys came bounding over. "Billy's goin' to ride to Grandma's house with us," Franklin announced.

"We'll see you there in a few minutes then," Jesse said.

And off the boys ran.

Oh, my, a carriage ride to the Fuller farm with just Jesse? What would they find to talk about? But how foolish of her to have worried, for they both talked a blue streak all the way there, most of their conversation centering on everything that Mr. Jenner had brought up.

22

Horace had arrived at the farm right around noon, and the first thing he did at the entrance to the long drive was nail a wooden "No Trespassing" sign to the trunk of a big old tree. He didn't want anyone snooping around his property or asking questions about what he planned to do with the farm other than to maintain the crops. For this particular parcel, rather than renting it out for sharecroppers, he would hire a few men to tend the already flourishing crops and harvest them come fall. Then next spring, he'd hire them again to till the land and plant new seed. As for the harvested crops, he'd sell it all and make a good penny. Looking out at it now, it appeared Newell and those Fuller boys had done a fine enough job, and the soaking spring rains had given them a healthy start.

In the barn, it angered him to discover all the animals gone, along with the rig he'd told Anna went with the sale of the property. He had no doubt she'd instructed Jesse Fuller to take them. He could fight the matter in court, but he didn't much cotton to starting any big racket with the Fullers. He'd already experienced Jesse's wrath, and the rig and those blasted animals weren't worth his time and energy anyway.

Blamed things needed to be fed and watered and stalls mucked, and that wasn't why he'd wanted the land anyway.

From the barn, he'd walked to the house to see what, if anything, Anna had left behind. There were a smattering of odd dishes and a couple of tin mugs, a tattered old braid rug, a wash pail and basin, the cookstove, a stack of wood against the wall, an ancient table with two benches on either side, and a chair with a broken leg. The walls were bare save for lanterns, a faded and crookedly hung painting, and the curtains on the windows. He noted empty hooks where it looked like a rifle had once hung, but he had no recollection of her putting one on his wagon yesterday, so Newell had probably hidden it away somewhere so that the boy wouldn't get his hands on it. Just as well. He didn't want that woman having a weapon in her possession. No telling how she might use it against him sometime.

After giving the main level of the house a good looking over, he mounted the steep wooden steps to the upstairs. There, he found three very small rooms, each with bed frames and tick mattresses, but minus any bedding. They all contained small bureaus with mirrors hanging above them. Nothing stood atop the chests, so if she'd had any wash basins and pitchers, clearly she'd taken them. He walked over to each bureau upon entering the small rooms and pulled open all the drawers, only to find them bare. The girl had done a fine job of emptying the place out, but then, she didn't have all that much in the way of possessions. He wasn't sure what he'd expected to find, but there was nothing in the house that hinted of the hidden treasure. Fine. He didn't care. He had his map and the authentic one was hidden in that brownish-colored metal box out in the barn, along with that all-important key.

He walked to the bedroom window that overlooked the backyard. The place was as still as a cemetery, its barn and outbuildings standing like monuments, the wind blowing the door of one of the sheds open and shut, open and shut. Not even a chicken remained, no doubt thanks to that Jesse Fuller. That was fine by him too. He didn't need chickens wandering around the yard and leaving their droppings everywhere.

He took one last gander around the small upstairs, and then walked back down to the main level. He would spend the remainder of his time out in the barn investigating. Might be he'd find some things out there to catch his interest.

~

Sunday dinners at Laura Fuller's house were always chaotic. There was Jesse's oldest brother Jack, his wife Cristina, and their three youngsters, Elias, Catherina, and baby Martin Jack. Then there was Joey, Faith, and their clan: Isaac, Franklin, Beth, and Miriam, with another child on the way. What must Anna think of all the commotion? She had grown up in a quiet home with just her father and her brother. As far as Jesse knew, she never had been one for socializing, with the exception of attending church every Sunday before Newell's passing. And now here she was sitting in the middle seat at Laura's long wooden farm table, no doubt trying to keep up with the conversations coming at her from all sides. He'd tried to warn her before bringing her inside that it might be noisy and hectic—but had she realized just how much?

Isaac and Frankie were bickering about whether they should go fishing after lunch or go riding. Isaac had his own horse, and now Franklin was complaining that he needed a horse of his own, while Joey insisted he had to do a little more growing up to do before taking on the responsibility of owning a horse. Besides, Joey had pointed out, they already had plenty of horses.

"But they ain't mine," Franklin whined.

And while *that* conversation was going on, Beth, Catherina, and Miriam kept throwing girly questions at Anna.

"What's your favorite flower?"

"Do you have any dollies?"

"What Grimm's fairy tale do you think is the scariest?"

"Quiet, all of you," Laura chimed in sternly. "You'll scare our guest away. And this is Sunday anyway, a sacred day of rest. It's not proper that you engage in any loud or raucous play on the Sabbath."

"Fishing ain't play, Grandma. It's quiet stuff. You ain't s'posed to talk when y'r fishing," Isaac put in.

"Well, just the same, you should be content to sit at home, read your Bible, and pray."

"How come you go out and pull weeds on Sunday? Ain't that work?" asked Elias.

Laura picked up her napkin and dabbed at her mouth, then did a little throat clearing. "I pray while I'm pulling."

"Well, I pray while I'm fishing," said Isaac.

"No, you don't," said Franklin. "All you do is talk. I'm always tellin' you to shush up 'cause you make the fish head off f'r another part of the stream."

"All right, all right," Jack put in. "Everyone has made their point. I think we could all do with a little Sabbath rest, and I would agree that weeding the garden and fishing are quiet activities. I doubt very much the Lord would condemn either one. As long as we ponder on His holy Word while we go about our day, that's enough for Him. Now then, let's talk about something else, shall we?" His eyes trailed across the table to Anna and Billy Ray. "It's very nice of you two to join us for dinner." He lifted both eyebrows and smiled. "*Brave* too. I would love to say we're not always this loud, but that would be an untruth. Ma likes to make us think she doesn't appreciate all the chatter, but she wouldn't know what to do if we all sat here quiet as the dawn. Right, Ma?"

Laura gave a friendly grin. "I s'pose you're right." She too turned her eyes on Anna and Billy Ray. "I'm ever so sorry about the loss of your father and then your beloved farm. I shall be praying everything works out for good, just as the Good Book says it will in Romans eight, verse twenty-eight."

"I'm sure it will, Mrs. Fuller, and thank you for this lovely meal. It's rare that Billy Ray and I enjoy a meal this lavish, isn't that right, Billy?" Jesse saw her nudge him with her elbow.

"Yeah, um, yes—I mean. Sis ain't near this good at cookin'." That comment earned some chuckles. "I mean she cooks good an' all—I guess—but we don't get meals like this most times."

His recovery was a bit pathetic. "I think what Billy's trying to say is that his sister is a fine cook, but it's much different preparing a meal for two than for a big clan like ours," said Jesse.

"Yeah, that's what I was tryin' t' say." Billy wiped his mouth with the back of his sleeve, then hastened to pick up his napkin as an afterthought and dabbed again.

"No one cooks as good as Grandma," said Catherina.

"Well, thank you, darling," Laura said, beaming.

More talk ensued until, like clockwork, Faith, Cristina, Catherina, and Beth all stood and began to gather the dishes. They had a routine: Laura made the meals, and the other ladies cleaned up afterward. Although Jesse helped his mother when it was just the two of them, he rather enjoyed the spoiling on Sundays. Anna started to push back in her chair, but Jesse stopped her. "You're our guest, remember?"

"But I—don't mind helping."

"Jesse's right, Anna," offered Faith. "Guests are not permitted to lift a finger. If you come again, though—and I hope you will—we may just rope you in."

"Oh, well, that's very kind of you. The meal was wonderful, Mrs. Fuller."

"Please. Call me Laura."

"All right then…Laura. You are a fine cook."

Jesse slid his arm along the back of Anna's chair, so when she sat back, he cupped his hand over her shoulder. At first, her body gave a little jolt, but then just as quickly settled in. Was he making headway with her…and if he were, what did he hope to gain? Blackthorn already had her farm. Jesse had no reason to woo her—except his heart was urging him on. He'd never felt this way with any other woman, yet for some reason, his attraction to Anna was mounting. And the memory of those kisses they'd shared last night came back to stir about in his rattled head.

As soon as they'd all finished their dessert, the children asked to be excused, and as soon as their parents granted it, they made a fast exit for the door. Jesse used that opportunity to bring up the discussion he and Anna had had with Ernest Jenner after church. "Ma, what do you know about the Blackthorns once owning Newell Hansen's property?"

She tilted her head in thought. "Hm, that's something I haven't thought about in years. It was a few generations back, from what I recall. I do know that when I met and married your pa, though, the Blackthorns held no claim to it. Why do you ask?"

"No particular reason, I suppose. Just curious. We visited with Ernest Jenner after church today, and he brought up the topic of Horace buying Anna's land, saying it was likely Horace wanted to buy back the farm for sentimental reasons."

Jack grunted. "Blackthorn doesn't strike me as particularly sentimental about anything or anyone. He used to call his own father Wilbur. Don't think they ever had much of a relationship. No, there must be some other reason why Blackthorn was so keen to get Anna's farm besides him being a greedy stinker."

Jesse could not help thinking about the mysterious map, the so-called clues, and the key in that hinged metal box that Billy Ray had given him for safekeeping. The box was now tucked away in one of his bureau drawers in his bedroom. Now was not the time to mention it, however, particularly since Anna had no knowledge of it.

23

$\mathcal{I}$saac and Franklin had convinced Anna to allow Billy Ray to spend the afternoon with them on the farm, and Billy was eager to visit the horses, Carlotta, and his beloved goats to see how they were faring.

"I'll drive him into town around suppertime," Jack said. "How does that sound?"

"I suppose that would be fine." He was terribly bored at the apartment anyway, but Anna wouldn't voice that to the Fullers lest they feel sorry for them. She had convinced herself, especially since hearing this morning's sermon, that she must make the best of her circumstances. "No rough play though," she said. "Remember what your grandmother said about it being the Sabbath." While everyone else gathered in the living room, Laura was doing last-minute puttering in the kitchen.

Even so, Isaac must think Laura could hear as well as a jackrabbit, for he leaned in and whispered, "Grandma don't know what Pa lets us do on Sunday. We might even be able to wade in the creek."

"Oh!" Anna stifled a giggle. "My own Papa always honored the Sabbath, but he acknowledged that certain farm chores had to be performed seven days a week, like feeding the animals, milking the cows, and so on. Sometimes we even got to go for a swim in the creek as long as we took soap powder with us. Soap powder equated with taking a bath, and baths were always permissible on Sundays." This drew more chuckles from the men and boys, and it did Anna's heart good to laugh right along with them.

"We do the same thing," said Catherina. "Daddy doesn't like us roughhousing on Sunday Sabbath, but if we take soap down to the riverbank, and then be sure to use it, he says it counts as a bath."

"I always thought that made perfect sense," said Anna to the young girl, reaching down to give a playful tug to her long braid. She was a pretty thing, and for just a brief moment, Anna wondered if the day would ever come when she'd have her own little girl. Just as quickly as that thought came to mind, though, she squashed it. No point in dreaming up such silly notions.

Just as Laura Fuller's grandfather clock struck the half past two hour, Anna declared it time to go back to town. There were things she wanted to do to prepare for her busy week ahead.

After many goodbyes and well-wishes, Jesse was soon helping her board his wagon. She adjusted herself on the high buckboard, and quick as a flash, he climbed aboard and seated himself next to her, taking up the reins. Very little urging was needed to put the two horses in motion. As if they'd taken the route to Lebanon a thousand times before, the team headed up the long drive toward Drake Road.

Anna was the first to speak. "Your family is wonderful. Papa always told me how much he enjoyed the Fuller boys, and now that I've met the whole family, I have to say I agree."

"Well, I'm happy you joined us today, I hope we can do it again soon,"

"I'm sure starting tomorrow, I'll be very busy."

"Not too busy for church I hope. That's where you get your weekly dose of spiritual strength."

She didn't answer immediately, just thought on his statement. She felt his eyes on her.

"I enjoyed spending time with you today," he said.

How to answer him! She'd so enjoyed being with him, was even starting to care for him, especially since those kisses they'd shared, but she couldn't allow herself the luxury of taking their friendship to the next level for fear Blackthorn would increase his threats. Oh, how she despised the hold he had on her. If only she could be honest with Jesse.

"You're awfully quiet," he said, stopping at the end of the long drive.

"Perchance I was just reflecting."

"Reflecting?"

"Yes. Thinking about my farm and Papa, and—just a number of things."

He leaned his frame against hers while they sat there and said in a low voice, "Might you have been thinking about those kisses we shared last night?"

She promptly attempted to put a bit of distance between them. "Oh, that. Well, I'm afraid you caught me in a weak moment. I think it's best we don't let that happen again."

"No?" He gave a little snicker. "How do you expect me to resist trying?"

She didn't see the humor. "I'm serious, Jesse. It would not be a good idea."

"Because—Blackthorn might not like it?"

"I don't wish to talk about him."

"I see." He gave a long sigh. "Somehow, he's convinced you not to feel anything for me."

To that, she remained silent, determined not to indulge him further. Then, rather than turn the horses in the direction of Miller Road, the next intersection, he made a right on Drake. "Where are we going?"

"I thought you might wish to drive past your farm."

"It's not my farm anymore."

"I know, but just for old time's sake. Besides, you said you were thinking about it."

"I'll always think about it." They reached the long drive leading up to her farm. On instinct, Jesse drew the horses to a halt in the middle of the road. "Look at that," he said.

"What?" She fixed her eyes on the empty little farmhouse and yard.

"Look at that sign." He pointed to a "No Trespassing" sign nailed to a tree. "I wonder why he did that."

Her stomach took a little dip. "I—I have no idea. He doesn't want anyone invading his privacy? Do you think he's in the house right now?

"I don't see any sign of him. No horses tied to the post. No wagon tracks."

"I wouldn't want to run into him."

"Don't worry about it."

They remained in the middle of the road. "Did you happen to leave anything behind in the house or in the barn?"

"No, nothing of value. Why?"

"Are you sure? You can't think of a thing?"

She pondered his question until she thought she understood what he was hinting at. "Well, I did leave an old chair with a broken leg."

"Good." He gave a half-smile and clicked at the horses to start trekking up the drive. "That gives us a reason to trespass. You left behind some property."

Horace swatted at some flies swarming around his sweaty brow. He'd combed the entire barn but could not locate that ding-blasted box Newell had told him he kept stored on that high shelf in the tack room. In fact, many of the items he'd seen in Newell's barn from previous visits were missing, no doubt thanks to that Jesse Fuller, who undoubtedly helped himself to whatever he wanted. The no-good stinkweed more than likely took it! Would he now trespass and attempt to find the treasure ahead of him? He could hardly stake out the area twenty-four hours a day unless he hired security, and that could cost a pretty penny.

But how else was he going to keep his land free of prowlers, short of living here?

He growled to himself. "Where is that dad-burned box?" He swept a hand through his grungy gray hair and began to question his sanity. The neigh of a horse coming up the drive stole his attention. Who would dare ignore his sign? Couldn't they read? He snatched up the rifle he'd leaned against the wall and propped the butt of it against his shoulder, then walked out.

"Horace, put the gun down!" Jesse Fuller called out, bringing his horses to a halt.

Blast him—and *her*! "What you want? Didn't you see my sign?"

"We saw it, but Anna needs to pick up something she left in the house."

He lowered the rifle. "I didn't see much of anything in there worth coming back for."

"There's a rickety chair that I'm going to work on repairing for her." He paused. "You don't mind, do you?"

He hesitated. "Go ahead, but don't loiter."

"We wouldn't think of it," Jesse said, his tone lacking all pleasantries.

Horace followed them to the house, where Jesse's rig was parked. "No point in both of you going in. The little miss can stay put," Horace said.

"She might want one last look around." Jesse jumped down and extended a hand to her.

"I'll wait here," she said.

"I'll just be gone a minute." He walked up the steps and into the house.

Horace drew closer to the wagon. She sat straight and rigid, eyes pointed straight ahead.

"What are you doin' runnin' about town with Jesse Fuller? I saw you walkin' up the street this morning, and now here you are again, ridin' high on that seat like you're somebody. Did you forget what I told you? Don't you love your little brother?"

That gave her a good jolt. She whipped her head around and stared down at him, her face gone crimson red. "I have not said a single thing to Jesse about your threats. You had best leave my brother alone, or I'll—"

"You'll what?" he interrupted. "Can't go to the sheriff, can't tell Fuller, can't even tell your bloody dog. I guess I should have clobbered him a little harder. I won't make that same mistake twice."

"You—awful—beast!" She hissed the words through her teeth.

He was about to tell her Billy Ray was next, but the door opened and out came Jesse with that dilapidated chair on his arm. Jesse gave Anna a hurried glance and then hastened a steady look at Horace, walked to the back of his wagon, and hoisted the chair over the railing. On his way back to the front of the wagon, he gave Horace a sideways glance that almost gave him a cold chill.

Horace watched Jesse climb aboard, situate himself on the seat, take up the reins, and start to turn his team around. Horace decided he'd better throw in a little warning. "Next time, don't ignore the sign."

Jesse stared down at him. "Why do you need a 'No Trespassing' sign anyway, Horace? What are you afraid of?"

"I ain't afraid of anything!"

"You think someone's going to steal something?"

"Hardly. You seem to have already stolen everything there was."

"I didn't steal a blamed thing. Everything I took belongs to Anna, and it's all being stored in a safe, secure place."

"Humph. I told her the animals and rig went with the sale of the property."

"Nope. That wasn't in the paperwork. I had my lawyers check."

"You took other items as well."

"Such as?"

Horace's blood boiled. Had Jesse found the metal box? He could hardly tell this troublesome character what he specifically wanted. That would for sure raise suspicion. Still, he needed its contents to proceed with his search. At least, it would help a great deal since the box contained a key. Rather than prolong the slow-witted weasel's stay a minute longer, however, Horace stepped back. He gave a flat smile to the pair. "Never mind," he spat. "Get off my land—and don't bother coming back."

Jesse directed his horses in a big circle, so they were facing the road, then drew them to a halt and looked down at Horace. "You never can tell, Horace. My brothers and I might want to pay you a neighborly call sometime, see how the crops are faring."

"No need. My hired hands will see to the farming. I'm already forecasting a good harvest."

Jesse sniffed and rubbed his shadow of a beard. "Well, you got what you wanted, didn't you, Horace?"

"Indeed I did, Fuller. Indeed I did." But deep down, Horace worried that the treasure might not be as easy to get his hands on as he'd hoped.

24

At morning's first bird calls, Anna's eyes popped open. She'd slept poorly all night, waking off and on to pray and ask the Lord for peace. Rex had sensed her unease and kept a closer than necessary eye on her, often jumping up to nudge her in the side with his long nose, then walking into Billy's room to check on him. Satisfied, he came back to her, sniffed her again, and then turned a few circles before lying on the floor next to her. He was a good dog, keenly aware and as protective as a mama bear. He wasn't much accustomed to staying indoors, but he took to it surprisingly well—almost sensing his need to remain faithful and steadfast. She patted his head then rubbed his velvety ears. He leaned into the affection and gave a tiny whine. "I know, this isn't normal for you, boy. Nothing's normal right now." He rested his head on her chest as if to say he understood.

She had no way of knowing what time it was, and so she gave Rex a gentle push, and crawled out of bed. She padded over to the lantern on the wall and turned up the wick so she could read the hands on the mantel clock that was perched on the chest of drawers. It read five past five. She sighed. No point in getting up quite yet with no chores to do and no breakfast to prepare in her little farm kitchen. She could get up and read her Bible, but the room held a chill, and she wasn't quite ready to get dressed, so she walked back to her bed and climbed back under the covers. On instinct, Rex curled up on the floor beside her again. A new wave of sadness washed over her, as she pondered all that she'd lost, but to keep herself from caving into her raging emotions, she began to count her blessings. She still had her little brother and her loyal dog, they had their health, they were both young and had plenty of time for achieving new goals, she had discovered a friend in Jesse Fuller, and, best, she had the Lord and His faithful Word.

She allowed herself to think about Jesse. He was kind and considerate, and she enjoyed his company—far more than was permissible in Horace Blackthorn's eyes anyway. Oh, how she'd longed to tell Jesse about his threats, but oh, how frightened she was to do so. Horace Blackthorn seemed fully capable of hurting Billy. He had her pinned in a corner from which she couldn't escape. She no more wanted to show up at his house this morning than she wished to encounter a grizzly bear, but show up she must if she wished to keep a roof over her head.

She recalled her conversation with Jesse in his wagon after they'd left the farm. Jesse had asked if Blackthorn had said anything to her in the brief time he'd been inside the house. She'd hemmed a bit because she didn't want to lie. "He said a couple of things, but nothing of great importance."

"Such as?"

"I—would rather not say."

He had frowned down on her and given his head a shake. "Did he threaten you? I swear I'll turn this wagon around and go give him a piece of my mind. What is his problem, and why does he continue to give you a hard time even after he stole your farm right out from under you?"

"He didn't steal my farm, he paid off the debt. But never mind. I don't want to discuss him." She knew he was frustrated. "I'm sorry. I just—don't want to be on Blackthorn's bad side."

"Well, I think you already are," he'd said. "The problem is, I don't know why."

"Can we talk about something else? Please?"

And so, with reluctance, he had changed the subject, and they talked about a number of other things—from his lifelong love of farming to his brothers and their families, and to the passing of his own father some years back—until they reached her apartment. She'd once considered Jesse unapproachable, but now thought of him as friendly and amicable. Of course, she still considered herself out of his social league and told herself they could never be anything but friends. That's why when he'd parked the rig in front of the general store, helped her down to the ground, and asked if he could walk her upstairs, she'd shaken her head no. "I don't—think that would be appropriate. Someone might see."

He had glanced up and down the empty street. "You just may be right. I mean, the town is buzzing today."

In spite of herself, she'd giggled. "Just the same, I think it's best you didn't. Thank you for everything you've done for me, Jesse, but Billy and I will be fine. I don't expect you to do anything more."

He had stared down into her eyes. "I happen to like you quite a lot, did you know that?"

She'd grown uncomfortable with his simple admission because she dared not admit any similar feelings. She let the sentence hang there between them until he broke the awkward lull. "I promised Billy Ray I'd pick him up and bring him to my farm to help with chores. What say I do that a couple of times a week, at least through the summer?"

"I—suppose that would be fine. Not this week though. I want him to get used to our new routine. He'll be coming with me every day and I'll give him odd jobs. I know he'd love to spend every single day with you, but I can't allow that."

"I understand."

"He hates the idea of having to go to Blackthorn's house though. I'm afraid this is going to be a difficult adjustment for him."

"I'm sure you're right, but most kids are pretty resilient. Will you promise to let me know right away if you have any serious problems with Blackthorn? I don't want to hear of him mistreating you or expecting too much from you. You shouldn't have to work for him more than six or seven hours a day."

"I'll keep that in mind."

He had lifted her chin. "I mean it. Contact me."

His touch had sent a little chill up her back. She nodded. "I will."

She could tell he'd wanted to kiss her, but she'd already convinced herself it would be a bad idea, and so before he had the chance, she had turned and headed for the outside staircase that led to the upstairs hall-way. At the bottom step, she gave him one last glance. "Thank you for this lovely day."

He smiled and gave a little wave. "How about we repeat it next Sunday?"

"Oh, I'll—have to think about that."

He didn't make any move to board the wagon, just kept his eyes on her. "Don't think too hard."

She smiled, gave a little wave back, and mounted the stairs without another backward look.

At exactly seven o'clock the next morning, Anna knocked on Blackthorn's front door while Billy moped at her side, staring at the ground. Standing between them, Rex's eyes moved from one to the other, tail wagging slowly. "Stand up straight, Billy," she instructed. "We must make the best of this situation."

Without a word, he squared his shoulder and lifted his chin. "That's better," she said.

The door opened, and there stood Blackthorn, his face as sour as a lemon. "What are you planning to do with that hairy mutt?" he said, pointing at Rex.

"I couldn't leave him alone in the apartment all day. It's hot and stuffy up there."

"Hm. You didn't answer my question. What are you going to do with him?"

"He'll come in the house with us and lie down in a comfortable spot. He won't cause you any trouble."

"Dogs belong outside."

"Well, I don't have a yard anymore, so he has nowhere to go. He won't be a problem; I promise you that."

Anna prayed Rex wouldn't growl. He had a very keen sense about people, and he would react if he sensed trouble brewing. She recalled how Rex had rushed right up to Blackthorn on Saturday and bared his teeth, and how she'd had to scold him for his behavior. The thought crossed her mind that Rex might recall Blackthorn being the one who'd conked him on the head. He stood guard like a soldier, sniffing the air around him and poking his nose inside the house to get a few whiffs.

Blackthorn wrinkled his nose at the dog, but he at least opened the door a little further, then stepped aside to allow their passage. "Just so you know, I'm not a bit happy about this. You should've let Jesse Fuller take him off your hands like you did your farm animals—and everything else you had in that barn. If he makes a mess in my house or leaves hair everywhere, he's out of here."

"He will be the best behaved dog you've ever seen."

"Pfff. No such thing as a well-behaved dog."

She chose to ignore that statement. "Tell me where your kitchen is so Billy Ray and I can get started on your breakfast. After you finish eating, you can tell me about my responsibilities here."

"Fine. From this day forward, no need to come to the front door. Enter through the kitchen door at the back of the house."

"That will be fine. Just show me where everything is."

"Come on then," he grunted. They followed him to the kitchen, Rex staying close beside them.

Anna let out a breath of gladness when Blackthorn left at eight o'clock. At last, she could relax. He was an ornery cuss, with his long list of daily chores and his grousing and grumbling about one thing or another. She doubted he even had a single happy bone in him. In fact, she wondered if his face might crack if he ever dared smile. "What makes him so cranky?" Billy Ray asked when the man closed the door behind him after giving her one last task to add to her already long list.

"I have no idea, but we are going to do our best not to give him one more reason to be so hateful. Now, let's get to work cleaning up the kitchen, and then we'll start on our list of chores."

"I'm not used to doing a woman's work," Billy said.

"Oh, stop it, you'll work just as hard as if you were out in the barn, and I'll not entertain your complaints. At least, we have full stomachs."

He rolled his eyes only a little. "That part is true, except Mr. Blackthorn did tell us not to drain his pantry dry with our overeating."

"Piffle. His pantry has enough dry goods to last a good six months. I'm sure one of my chores will be to keep his pantry well-stocked. He's just a selfish snoot who doesn't like sharing, but you are a growing boy, and as long as we are working here, I'm going to see to it that you get plenty to eat."

She looked at the list of weekly and daily chores Blackthorn had written on a piece of paper, numbering each item. "Upstairs: make the bed, sweep floors, dust the shelves, beat rugs, clean bathroom, organize linen storage shelves in hallway, dust remaining two bedrooms, wash windows. Downstairs: prepare two meals per day, breakfast and dinner, sweep floors, dust all shelves, wash windows, beat rugs, mop floors weekly, wash window sills and floorboards, dust low hanging chandeliers, keep kitchen sink clean at all times, shovel ashes out of cookstove, wash clothes and bedding once a week, keep fireplace hearth clean, wipe all doorknobs." And at the bottom of the list, it read, "I will add more to this list as I think of additional things."

Billy Ray leaned close, scanning the long list of chores. "What does he take us for, his servants?"

"Yes, I suppose he does, but at least he'll be paying us two dollars a week. I would like to start a savings so we can buy you some new shoes.

He glanced down at his shoes, one of which had a hole where the big toe had started to emerge. "What's wrong with my shoes, other than they're starting to get tight on me? These aren't that bad. You're the one who needs new shoes and a couple new dresses."

She smiled and ruffled his thick head of brown hair. "We'll take out some time today to cut your hair. I haven't cut it since Papa's funeral." Just saying the word stirred up memories of their father, but she tamped down all sadness. "And if we finish our chores in a timely fashion, we can take a walk through town."

"Finish that list? I got a feeling that's gonna take us all day long, and then to think we have to do it all again tomorrow."

She tapped his nose. "Now, now, no complaining, remember? Think new shoes."

"Yeah, yeah, I'd rather think new fishing pole. Speaking of—when am I ever going to get to go fishing again?"

"Perhaps you can take some time to do that on the days that Jesse picks you up and takes you to the farm."

"When will that be?"

"Not this week, but maybe next."

"Why not tomorrow?"

"Because I want to give us a few days to adjust to our new environment before you go running off to the Fuller farm."

Over in the corner, next to the brick fireplace, Rex raised his head and made a little whimpering sound.

"Don't you start in with *your* complaining, Mr. Rex. A woman can only handle so much."

At that, the dog put his head back down, but he kept his big almond-shaped eyes trained on her, no doubt missing his farmyard. "I know, I know, everybody's homesick, but it's time we turn the page and start looking forward to a new future." She perused her list again. "What say you go fill a pail with water, Billy Ray, find a cloth, and start the business of washing the windows?"

Rather than groan about his assignment, he called to the dog. "Come on, Rex, help me find what I need."

The dog leaped up, eager to do his bidding.

25

At just past noon, Jesse entered the sheriff's office. A male clerk greeted him right away from behind a counter. He donned a cheery smile. "You're a Fuller, aren't ya? Which one? You all sort of resemble your father."

"I'm Jesse, the youngest."

"Ah, that's right, Jesse. Well, what can I do for you?"

"I'd like to speak to Sheriff Berry if he's in."

"He sure is. He just got back from a three-hour detail guarding some inmates while they dug some draining ditches out on East Orchard Avenue. I'll go fetch him for you,"

"Thanks." The fellow stood, and disappeared down a corridor. Within a minute, he returned. "Sheriff will be right with you. You can have a seat over there if you'd like."

"Thanks." Rather than sit, though, Jesse wandered around the room, casting his eye on a few wanted posters tacked to a board and some other legal notices. About the time he headed for a chair, the lawman arrived, wearing dark gray pants and a blue cotton shirt, his badge pinned to his lapel. He was a middle-aged man with dark hair and a bushy mustache.

He extended his hand. "Jesse Fuller. Good to see you. Come on back to my office."

He followed the lawman into his office and sat in the chair offered to him. Once the sheriff seated himself behind his desk, he asked, "What can I do for you?"

"Well, Sheriff, I was just wondering how the Newell Hansen case is going."

Charles Berry sat a little straighter in his chair. "It's moving along, although not nearly as fast as I'd like. Did you come to shed some light on the case?"

"Sorry, all I have are questions. Nothing concrete."

"Tell me some of your questions."

"For starters, do you think it's odd that Horace Blackthorn was so eager to snatch up Newell's property?"

Intent on Jesse's words, the sheriff steepled his hands, and touched the tips of his index fingers to his chin, his light brown eyes narrowing in thought. "How do you mean?"

"Somehow, he talked Anna Hansen into selling her farm to him. He's provided her an upstairs, two-room apartment in town and has hired her for housekeeping duties. Don't you think that's odd?"

"Hm," the sheriff mused. "I find it interesting."

"My brothers and I wanted to buy that land, but as soon as Blackthorn found out about our interest, he set things in motion and somehow got Anna Hansen to sign all the papers before the deadline. I'm concerned he has something up his sleeve, and yet I have no proof of anything."

"We can't really fault him for buying more property. He's known around town for his real estate investments. Do you have anything more solid on him?"

Jesse didn't feel right about bringing up the matter of the box containing the mysterious clues without discussing it with Billy Ray first, so he decided to table that for now. "Do you happen to know anything about an age-old dispute between the Hansens and the Blackthorns?" he asked instead.

This seemed to pique the sheriff's interest. "Oh, I've done my research. I asked around town and found a few tidbits here and there. Seems one of the Blackthorns was a thief. He got himself involved in a robbery of some sort and lived out his remaining days in prison. I even went to the courthouse to see if they had any records of said robbery, but they said if it didn't happen in their jurisdiction, they'd have no knowledge of it. The elder Blackthorn's son took over his land, but at some point, he got into a heap of debt and wound up having to sell it off to one of the Hansens. I couldn't tell you which one. I hear tell that same Blackthorn wanted to buy it back, but it never transpired. Don't know what Horace's motivation would be for buying back the farm unless he felt somehow entitled."

"Yeah, that's about as much as I know. Does the jail keep records of crimes such as the robbery the elder Blackthorn committed that landed him in prison?"

Sheriff Berry shook his head. "Afraid we don't have any records going back that far. I believe it took place around the turn of the century, somewhere in the Cincinnati area, but that's even unclear. At any rate, our records only cover Lebanon and its environs."

Jesse decided to try another tack. "I read that Newell's cause of death was arsenic poisoning. Are you any closer to determining if he accidentally consumed it or whether someone had a hand in his death?"

The sheriff winced a bit as he rubbed his mustache. "I'm really not at liberty to discuss this case in detail, Jesse, but I will say we did a thorough search of the property, and one of my deputies found something of interest out in Newell's cornfield. It has raised some suspicion on our part, but since we can't identify exactly where it came from, we're at a bit of a crossroads."

"What was it you found?"

"I can't disclose that information. I will say I showed the item to Miss Hansen, but she didn't recognize it."

That was all Jesse needed to know. He would find out from Anna what the sheriff had shown her. He tried to think if he had any further questions.

The sheriff must have read the angst in his face. "I know it's frustrating not to know what really happened to your friend and neighbor, Jesse. I don't want you to think we've given up on exploring this matter. That would be far from true. We get tips here and there, and we follow through on them until we reach a dead end, but we will not quit until we are sufficiently satisfied that we've done all we can."

That didn't make Jesse feel any better. "Newell would not have consumed arsenic on his own, Sheriff. He was a fine Christian man. He loved his children. He wouldn't have purposely left them, no matter what sort of financial stress he found himself under."

Berry nodded. "I appreciate that, Jesse."

"You believe me, right?"

"As I said, this is an ongoing investigation."

Jesse let out a loud, frustrated breath and looked at the ceiling. Then, just as quickly, and without forethought, he fastened his eyes on the sheriff and blurted, "I think somebody killed him, and I'd keep my eye on Horace Blackthorn if I were you!"

The sheriff didn't flinch. Didn't even blink, just sat back in his chair, set both elbows on the chair arms, and clamped one hand over top of his fist, gaze trained on Jesse. "I appreciate your sentiment, Jesse. I hear you, and I can assure you we are keeping our eyes on him—and a number of people."

"A number of people? You have more than one suspect?"

"I didn't mention anything about suspects. We are looking into this matter, and gathering as much information as we can from as many sources as we can. Let me just say this much: Newell Hansen was a fine man, well respected in the community, a devout churchgoer, and a good father. I personally—I'm speaking from a personal point of view now, not a professional one—do not believe he would've purposely ended his life. And now, I'm sorry, but I cannot discuss this any further. However, if you happen to come up with anything else that would help this investigation along, don't hesitate to come to me."

Jesse knew he had to say something. "I can tell you this much," he said slowly. "Anna's brother Billy Ray told me Blackthorn visited Newell a few days before Newell's death."

The sheriff sat up a little straighter. "No one ever told me that. What did the boy have to say about the visit?"

"He said he was hiding in one of the stalls, so his father didn't suspect his presence. He didn't want to come out because there was a bit of arguing going on."

"About what?"

"He couldn't tell. He said most of the words were muffled, but he did overhear Blackthorn say something about buying Newell's farm, and Newell saying, 'Over my dead body.' But that was pretty much the extent of it. I don't think you should question the boy just yet though, as he is only ten and is pretty emotionally distraught right now. Plus he doesn't know that his father died of arsenic poisoning."

"I wouldn't question him unless I had something more concrete. That does add a new dimension to this—but not much of one."

Jesse sighed. "I figured as much, but I didn't think it could hurt to mention it."

"No, no, it's helpful and certainly interesting."

Berry stood then, so Jesse took that as a friendly dismissal. He put his hands on his knees and pushed himself up. Across the sheriff's desk, the two men shook hands again, this time as a farewell gesture. "I appreciate it, Sheriff. You have given me a certain sense of relief to know you're still investigating. Thank you."

"You bet. And thanks for stopping by."

At that, Jesse turned and left, not wholly satisfied, but at least glad to know that Sheriff Berry had not yet closed the file on Newell Hansen's death.

Horace spent the entire day exploring his new property. He'd read and reread those blasted clues, then studied the map his father had given him, growing angrier than the day before that he didn't lay claim to the original one, not to mention that key Newell had shown him. On the chance he ever dug up the treasure and didn't have the key to open it, he would find some sort of practical tool that would assist in prying it open. It was more important now that he find the wretched treasure—and find it he would, even if it took him up to his final breath.

Aloud, he read clue number two for the dozenth time that day: *"Center of the south piece, twenty paces west. Buried in a vase at the bottom of the crest."* He'd studied the scrawled map several times today and worried again now that his father might not have done a good enough job of replicating the original. He looked around. "I'm standing at the center of the south piece—as long as my figuring is right," he mumbled. "Twenty paces…" He walked back to the place from which he'd started walking and went through the paces again, looking at the sun to ensure he was indeed going west, counting each step carefully, guessing as to what was considered an average pace and cursing as he walked. Each time he stopped at the precise location where he'd started digging, he found it not to be at the bottom of a crest, which he presumed to be a hill of some sort. Had the terrain changed that much since his great-grandfather had written the clue? There was a slight incline, but was it enough to call it a crest? Anything was possible after sixty years. The terrain could well have changed. Wearily, he resumed his job, digging deep, throwing dirt over the edge, digging, throwing, digging, throwing, drops of sweat falling off his face with every toss of the dirt. "I will find this treasure if it's the last thing I do," he mumbled.

An hour later, he was no closer to finding the supposed vase and had convinced himself he was digging in the wrong place. He was hungry, thirsty, and grumpy as a wild beast. He didn't even know what time it was, as he'd accidentally left his pocket watch at the house this morning. One more blasted shovelful, he told himself…just one.

And it was that last shovelful that did the trick. He'd hit something. He threw his shovel aside and went down on his knees in the hole, wide and deep enough now to easily fit three or more large-framed bodies. He used his hands to continue digging, frantically throwing dirt every which direction. At last, he spotted the corner of a piece of rounded glass. The vase? Could it be? He kept digging around the form until at last, a bit more of it emerged from the dirt. The object was red with a longish neck. Finally, Horace unearthed what appeared to be a vase—*the* vase. He grasped hold of it and raised it to the sky, then gave a loud whoop in the air. This was it. Success! Ah, how good it felt! His persistence had finally paid off. He lowered the vase to give it a closer look. It was covered with dirt, so with his thumb, he rubbed circles into it until he got a glimpse through the cloudy glass. Pulse pounding in his neck, he brought it close and squinted through the small area. Sure enough, he caught sight of something inside. He took a kerchief from his pocket and began to wipe a bigger area until he got a better look, and indeed, inside the vase was a folded piece of paper. Now to get it out. He stood, elation bubbling up from within, and set the vase on the ground at the top of the hole. Then, grabbing hold of a root, he pulled himself up and out of the giant hole. Tomorrow, his muscles would burn like fire, but he didn't care. He'd dig for the next clue, and the day after that, the next—and on and on until he laid hold of that treasure.

Once back on solid ground, Horace retrieved the vase. Under the lowering sun, he could see it was nothing more than an ordinary vase, so breaking it to get the clue out was his only option. He laid it on the ground, picked up his shovel, and gave it a hard whack! Crack! The vase broke open, and there in the midst of the shattered glass lay a folded piece of paper. He threw down the shovel and snatched up the piece of paper, blew the dirt off of it, unfolded it, and began to read.

"Clue number three: Find the mark on the Wish Bone Tree where blade of knife did carve a B. Walk ten paces north and dig, not far, and find you there a blown glass jar."

His chest heaved with great emotion, if not a sense of deep satisfaction. He was right—had been right all along. There *was* a buried treasure. Somewhere on this land, there was a treasure! His father had been a fool not to have pursued it. A plain old fool. As had been Newell's father, and Newell himself. Lazy fools, that's what they all were, afraid of a little work—not to mention Newell's ridiculous notion that finding any buried treasure would mean having to turn it in to authorities. Hogwash! He'd killed a man for this treasure, and he'd do it again. No regrets.

Only one question remained prominent on his mind now. What in tarnation is a Wish Bone Tree, and where is it located?

26

For the next several days, Blackthorn did not return home before the supper hour, so every day, Anna put his plate of food on the table at 5 p.m., left a note that she would wash his plate in the morning, and left without seeing him. It was fine by her. She would much prefer him to be gone before their arrival every morning as well, but he wanted that hot and hearty breakfast every day. That whole first week, he told her to pack him a lunch too, because he expected to be working on the farm. She assumed he meant *her* farm, but she didn't ask because she didn't want to seem interested—or give him any reason to converse with her. It was her best guess though because the clothes he left on a chair next to his bed were filthy, and he wanted them washed every day.

She didn't mind that his list of chores was long because it kept her mind and body busy, but Billy Ray hated it, so a couple times that week, she allowed him to take his fishing pole down to Turtle Creek. He'd met up with a boy in town he knew from school, and she was happy to have him leave the house for a few hours just to avoid his complaints.

It was Sunday, her one day off, and Anna decided to resume the practice of attending services to set a Christian example for Billy Ray.

They set out for Sunday school at 8:45 a.m., thereby missing the opportunity to ride to church with Jesse. She didn't want to give Blackthorn cause to follow through on his threats if he should happen to spot them going to church together. Billy had been upset with her, saying he didn't particularly want to attend Sunday school and wondering what Jesse would think.

"He will just realize we've already gone on ahead," Anna told him.

"I don't feel like going to Sunday school class," he repeated with a moan.

"That's too bad. We have nothing better to do, so you best put on a happy face. Besides, you may even discover some of your school friends attending class as well." That seemed to perk him up, so off they'd gone.

She had thoroughly enjoyed the ladies' class and found everyone warm, friendly, and welcoming. Most of the women were older than she with the exception of a couple who looked close to her in age but were married and already had a couple of children. Anna had only attended school through fifth grade; her mother's passing had ended her tenure in school, so she'd had little opportunity since then to socialize with people her own age.

After Sunday school, she met Billy Ray in the sanctuary and quickly ushered him to a crowded bench; they situated themselves at the end of the row, thereby making it quite impossible for Jesse to sit with them should he try. At the close of the service, she told Billy that she had brought home some non-perishable items from Blackthorn's pantry that would serve them well for their Sunday fare, but no sooner had she started to tell him that they were going to start walking back right away than he quickly ran outside to the churchyard with some other boys.

A friendly woman who had been in her Sunday school class smiled at her and leaned across the church bench. "Children will be children, won't they? Once they set their minds to something, they seem not to hear a word we say to them."

They struck up a brief conversation, when out of the corner of her eye, she caught sight of Jesse standing just feet away from her speaking to a gentleman. She knew good and well he saw her and was simply waiting for the opportunity to snag her. Sure enough, when she said her farewell to the woman and made for the door, he came up beside her and said in a low tone, "Why are you avoiding me?"

"Oh, did it seem like I was?" she asked, eyes pointed straight ahead.

He took her by the arm and pulled her gently to a quiet corner of the church, out of anyone else's earshot.

"I came by your upstairs room today and knocked on the door."

"I figured you would."

He frowned. "You were afraid Blackthorn would spy on us so you left well in advance of my getting there?"

"I told Billy Ray I wanted us to start attending Sunday school."

"May I pick you up for Sunday school next week then?"

She cleared her throat and leveled her gaze on him. "I'm sorry, but no."

He tilted his face to one side and raised an eyebrow. "Is it Blackthorn, or are you simply trying to tell me you don't like me?"

"I—like you fine, but—Jesse, we aren't suited for each other. Why would you want to be seen with me anyway?"

"You don't think highly enough of yourself, Miss Anna Hansen. I would be proud to be seen with you if you'd give me half a chance. Why don't you come back to the big house for Sunday dinner again? Ma said she'd love to have you join us."

"That's very nice of her, but please give her my regrets. Billy and I are going to spend the day resting. It was a busy week."

"I'm sure Billy's excited about that."

His sarcasm did amuse her, so she managed a smile. "I borrowed several books from Blackthorn's library, so we both have lots of reading material. I've also been allowing him to go down to Turtle Creek to fish with some school friends this week, so that's helped ease his boredom."

"I'm sure he's glad of that. What say I pick him up and bring him to my house a couple of times this next week? My nephews would enjoy his company, and I can put them all to work."

"He would love that. Thank you."

"I'll pick him up at Blackthorn's house tomorrow then, and again on Wednesday. What time should I stop by?"

"Oh, no, don't do that."

"Why? Blackthorn won't be there. I've seen him over at your farm every day. He's up to something, but I don't know what. A couple of my hired hands and I worked out on our south plot all week, and I spotted him riding his horse around, as if he's surveying the land."

That spiked her interest. "He has not come home in the evening till after I go back to our apartment, so I've been leaving his supper on the table."

"Good, you don't have to see him."

She smiled. "Those were my thoughts."

He smiled back, letting it linger there, neither speaking for a moment. She hoped he couldn't read her thoughts. She was coming to care for him but dared not admit it.

"I want to talk to you about something."

"Jesse, I've already told you—"

"No, it's not about my courting you." He pointed at a wooden bench. Most everyone had exited the sanctuary except for a few lingering out in the lobby area. "Let's sit for a minute."

"I—don't know. Billy Ray is outside. He may wonder where I am."

He tipped his chin down. "You really think he will? Can't you hear all those squealing kids running circles around the church?"

"Yes, I hear them. I suppose a couple of minutes couldn't hurt." She was reluctant, but at the same time, she couldn't deny the pleasure she took in Jesse's company. As they sat, she could feel his thigh grazing hers through the fabric of her skirt.

"I went to see the sheriff this week," he said.

That gave her a little jolt, and she lifted her head. "Really? Did you ask about my father's case?"

"I certainly did. Unfortunately, Sheriff Berry wasn't at liberty to speak in much detail because the whole case is under investigation, but I thought you'd like to know they haven't forgotten."

She let out a breathy sigh. "I'm relieved to hear that. I hope they can prove that Papa did not intentionally consume poisoning,"

"Oh, I think they're well on their way to reaching that conclusion. He mentioned something to me that sparked a bit of interest."

"What was it?"

"He said he showed you something one of his deputies had found out in the field and asked you if you recognized it."

"You mean that plate?"

"Was that what it was?"

"Yes, but it wasn't mine. I don't have any idea where it came from, but I had completely forgotten it until you just now mentioned it. Does it play any part in their investigation?"

"It might. Would you recognize it if you saw it again?"

"I absolutely would. It was fine china, white and pretty, certainly lovelier than anything I'd ever own. It had a curvy line around the edging with tiny red and yellow flowers. It looked old. But what's the significance of it? Anybody could have been exploring out there. Maybe someone chose that spot for a picnic and accidentally left it behind. No telling how long it was even out there. Could have been months for all I know."

"Maybe. I was just curious about it."

"Did Sheriff Berry say anything about the investigation? Do they have any leads that you know of—that would indicate anyone else's involvement?"

"He didn't give me any names. I have my hunches though, and I told him."

She felt her eyebrows flick. "What sort of hunches?"

"It's too early to say because I don't have any proof. How has Blackthorn been treating you?"

"I only see him in the mornings, and very briefly, so he's been fine."

"Good. You'll let me know if that changes, right?"

"Jesse, it's not your responsibility to worry about Billy and me."

"Sorry, too late."

She couldn't help the giggle that came out of her. "You're impossible."

He didn't react, just let his eyes roam over her face. She turned her gaze downward. "I should be heading back now."

"How about I simply meet you at church next week? We can sit together, and afterward, you and Billy can come over for Sunday dinner. Sunday is your day off, and Blackthorn need not know you're with me. I'll take special care to make sure he doesn't see us together if that will make you feel better."

She dared study him for a brief time. He really wanted to be with her? The notion gave her pause. "That's so kind of you."

"I'm not trying to be kind. I'm trying to figure out a way to get to know you better."

"I—guess that would be fine then. Next Sunday."

"Phew. Now, don't go changing your mind on me."

She laughed, then covered her mouth. He immediately reached up and took her hand away from her face. "You have a habit of covering your mouth when you laugh or smile."

Her face went instantly warm. "I—have a crooked tooth."

"It's what makes your smile so cute and charming. Don't cover it."

Was he kidding? Her father had told her something similar. "Thank you. I think. As for picking up Billy Ray tomorrow and Wednesday, I was thinking he could walk over to the post office, and you could fetch him there."

"That should work out fine. Tell him to be there at nine o'clock. I'll feed him the noon and evening meals and deliver him to your place at six o'clock. How is that?"

"That will be fine. Drop him back off at the post office earlier in the day and tell him to walk to Blackthorn's if you need to return him earlier."

He nodded. "Yes, ma'am, but I'm pretty sure that won't be necessary."

"No need to bring him upstairs."

"I beg to differ. I'll park my rig in the back alley to ensure Blackthorn doesn't see it should he be driving through town about that time. And then I'll scurry up the staircase, disguised if needs be."

"Oh, you are a sneaky thing, aren't you."

"I can be when the need calls for it."

They shared another brief laugh. "And now I must go outside and tell Billy we're leaving." They stood together, he looking down at her as if longing to kiss her—in the church of all places!

She hurried past him before giving him the chance.

27

*H*orace was completely flummoxed. All last week, he'd tried to locate this so-called "Wish Bone Tree" with the letter B carved into it, but, alas, he'd had not one ounce of luck. If he'd had the numbered map, he could have at least found the vicinity of the tree instead of going to every blasted one on the property. There were hundreds of trees as far as he could tell, especially at the far end where land had never been tilled. Not only that, but a carved letter would be some sixty years old. Was it even visible anymore? To complicate matters, he'd never heard the term "Wish Bone Tree," so it must be a nickname given to a tree because of its shape. Did the limbs perhaps resemble the wish bone found in a turkey? And if so, how was he supposed to find that in a jungle of leafy trees? He figured it acquired its name as a young tree, when its trunk and branches were just starting to take form. Perchance the dadblamed thing didn't even exist anymore.

He climbed down from his horse and perused the land. Off in the distance, he spotted the Fullers' hired men working the land, walking up and down rows of bean plants and apparently inspecting their condition. Pfff. He had no use for those uppity Fuller brothers with their fine, big houses, their expensive farm equipment, and their fertile crops. They'd developed a name for themselves across the state, a reputation for their quality meats, vegetables, and dairy. He'd like to knock them down a notch or two, but he also didn't feel much like tangling with them. That Jesse fellow in particular already had it in for him without his stirring up more trouble. No, it was best he kept his distance and minded his own business. He took his horse by the reins and started leading him through the field, deciding to walk a spell to get the blood circulating in his legs. Where was that so-called wishing tree anyway? Maybe he'd ask Anna if she'd ever heard of it. Trouble was, she was never there by the time he got home. Perchance he'd call it a day and arrive home before supper tonight so he could bring up the subject. He'd bring it up in a nonchalant manner so she wouldn't grow suspicious of him. On the walk to the barn, he pondered how he might put the question to her.

At four o'clock, he entered through his front door. Like every other day for the past several days, he was a soiled, sweaty mess and required a bath. Today was different though in that the gal and her brother were still here. He heard her humming a tune and puttering in the kitchen. Her big old dog came running from the kitchen to greet him, but instead of wagging its tail, it stopped four feet away from him and gave a low growl, then showed its teeth.

"Get away from me, you scraggly mutt."

Rather than retreat, the dog took a step closer and barked. If he'd had his gun on him, he might have conked it on its head again—like that night at the farm when it had tried to take his leg off. Mangy critter! Except that night, he'd had a good-sized rock in his hand. Ever since a dog had taken a chunk out of Horace's arm when he was just a kid, he'd had a deep fear of dogs. Very deep. Terror rose to the surface, and about the time he intended to make a run for it, the Hansen girl emerged from the kitchen.

"Rex! Back!"

The dog immediately retreated and walked to her side.

"I want that dumb animal out of my house. You need to tie him up in the backyard."

"He wouldn't know how to act if I put a rope around his neck and tied him to a tree, Mr. Blackthorn. Don't worry, he won't hurt you."

"Worry? Pfff, I'm not worried. Next time, I'll just have my gun ready."

"What? No, please don't speak such nonsense."

The dog stood attentively at her side, eyes on Horace, as if just waiting for the word "attack" so it could lunge at him and sink in its teeth. He hated to admit his fear of the mongrel, so he tried to relax his shoulders and put on a casual façade. He'd always heard dogs had some kind of sixth sense—and now, he believed it.

"You're home earlier today. I was just starting to gather things together for your supper."

"Yeah," he groused, not taking his eyes off the dog as he walked toward the staircase. Thankfully the dog stayed put. "I'm goin' upstairs to wash up. I don't want that mutt following me."

"He won't. Rex, go back in the kitchen and lie down."

Just like that, the hairy creature turned to do her bidding.

"Humph. He seems to understand you."

"He's been our steady companion for five years now. He's smart as a whip and very protective."

"Yeah, well, he best mind his manners around me, or a whip will be his punishment."

⟳

Upstairs, he washed up, put on some clean clothes, and then lay on his bed for a brief rest. Unfortunately, he fell asleep, and when he awoke, it was ten minutes past five, so he jumped up and scurried down the stairs, hoping the girl and her brother hadn't left yet. He wanted to ask her about that tree. The table was set and his plate of food was waiting for him, the steam still rolling off it, which meant she'd just put it there. Just as he was about to check to see if she was in the kitchen, she appeared with a pitcher of water.

"Where's my ale?" he asked, pulling out his chair.

"I thought you'd do well to have cold water with your meal. If you want something stronger, you can get it after I leave."

"Hmph, you're a stubborn one, ain't y'."

The dog had followed her into the dining room. Anna ignored his statement.

"Does that stinking thing follow you everywhere you go?"

"Not as a rule, but since you arrived home, he won't leave my side. As long as you are friendly to him, he'll be friendly in return."

"I've never been friendly to a dog in my life and I don't intend to start now."

He glanced down at his dinner fare—fried chicken, sliced potatoes, peas, and some applesauce. "I see you're making good use of the items in my pantry, and you must have made a trip to the butcher today for some chicken."

"Yes, indeed I did. I haven't seen you to talk to you, so I don't know what you think of my cooking. Does it suit you?"

"It's fine." He took his first bite of chicken and found it moist, tender, and tasty. "Not bad," he said, not one for doling out compliments.

She stood there watching him eat, her hands behind her, probably clasped if he had to guess. "Are you just going to stand there and watch me eat?"

"Oh! I'm sorry, no. I'll go start cleaning up the kitchen." She started to turn.

"Why don't you make your brother do that?"

"He's not been here today."

He took up another piece of meat and was about to shove it in his mouth, but stopped midway. "Where is he?"

"He's, uh, been working with Jesse Fuller today. He gets awfully bored here seeing as farm life is all he's ever known."

"You let him go to the Fuller farm today? I told you to stay away from that man."

"Perhaps you did, but you never said that applied to Billy Ray too. I don't see what your big worry is about Jesse Fuller anyway. It's not like we're courting or anything."

"You were about to marry him so he could procure your land."

"But I didn't, and the land is yours now, so what does it really matter to you if I choose to associate with him?"

"Because I don't want you blabbing to him about how I forced you into selling your land."

"I already told you, I haven't said a word to him about that."

He reached up and took her by the wrist. "And you best not." Her idiot dog gave a low snarl, so he dropped her wrist. "Get that ugly hound away from me."

"He's not a hound, he's a collie."

"I don't care if he's a cross-eyed rabbit, I don't want him near me!" He waved a hand at the dog, trying to encourage it to go elsewhere.

"You best not be putting your hand out like that, sir." She quickly took Rex by the scruff of the neck and pulled him close to her. "You'll find that Rex will mind his manners perfectly as long as you do the same."

"All right, all right, just—just keep him out of my hair, understand? And leave me now so I can finish my supper in peace."

She turned and headed for the kitchen, the mongrel at her heels. "Oh, by the way," he said. She stopped and whirled to look at him. "You wouldn't happen to know anything about the location of a Wish Bone Tree on your old land, would you?"

The way she crinkled up her face in puzzlement told him all he needed to know. She hadn't a clue.

"Never mind. It was just a foolish question on my part."

"I don't even know what a Wish Bone Tree is."

"Yeah, me neither."

He gave her a flick of his wrist. "On with you now. Clean the kitchen, then go home."

"One more thing," she said. "When can I expect to be paid?"

"I'll pay you tomorrow," he said.

"Fine. From now on, I prefer to be paid on the last day of each work week, which in my case would be every Saturday. You said two dollars if you'll remember."

"Yeah, yeah, two dollars. Don't know as you earned it, but you'll get your first payment tomorrow."

"Very well." She and her dog disappeared into the kitchen.

Feisty little thing. But her cooking wasn't half bad. It was certainly better than his last housekeeper's fare. Within ten minutes, Horace heard the gal and her mutt depart through the back door.

28

As promised, Jesse parked his rig in the alley behind Henry's Hardware, and Billy Ray jumped down before he even brought the rig to a full stop. A typical boy, he supposed, full of energy and always raring to move onto the next thing. He'd worked hard today, mucking stalls, feeding animals, milking Carlotta, and generally sticking pretty close to Jesse's side despite the fact that two of his nephews were there too. No one had even mentioned the desire to go fishing. Jesse had a natural love for kids, which his nieces and nephews seemed to sense by the way they enjoyed hanging onto him whenever he came around. Of course, it helped that every time he took a trip into town, he came back with candy sticks for each of them. Now, he had Billy Ray to add to his list of admirers. He grinned to himself as he watched the boy head for the stairs.

"Did you miss your sister today?"

"Kind of, I guess, but not that much."

He laughed. "Well, that makes a lot of sense."

He followed the lad up the stairs, and then down the hallway to their little bedroom apartment, but after Billy entered, he hung back, awaiting his invitation inside. It was a rather strange arrangement, two rooms that were basically bedrooms with no real living space for guests. He supposed it wasn't appropriate that he even be there without Billy being present.

Within a few seconds, Anna poked her head out and smiled. "Come in."

Upon his entry, Rex rose from his spot under the open window, approached, and then took to sniffing him from his waist down to his shoes. "I guess you smell the farm, eh, boy?" He bent over and patted the dog on his head, then massaged one of his ears. He was a friendly pooch. He stood straight, and the dog walked back to his sleeping spot.

He took a gander at Anna. She looked as pretty as a flower in her long summer gown, the fabric light and airy, the neckline low, and the sleeves puffy. Had she just changed into it, knowing she would see him when he dropped off Billy, or had she worn it all day?

"I haven't seen you in that dress before."

She glanced down as if to recall what she was even wearing. "Oh, this old thing? I've had it for several years, but I didn't usually wear it for outdoor chores. I wore it exactly three times last week to Mr. Blackthorn's house and then again today because I only have three dresses to my name that aren't torn or stained." He didn't want to tell her he'd noticed that little tidbit. Neither did he mention Billy Ray's holey shoes. Glancing down now, all he saw was a pair of bare feet peeking out from the hem of her skirt. My, my, but she was a fetching sight to his sore eyes.

"Well, you look fresh, not like someone who's labored hard all day."

She pointed at the pitcher and bowl on the vanity. "I just washed up. I did look rather horrid when I arrived home. Blackthorn has a long list of chores he wants accomplished every day of the week."

"Yeah, it's more boring over there than watching a row of ants walk across a dirt road," Billy chimed in.

"Well, it wouldn't be if you'd be a little more cooperative about doing the jobs I give you."

"He worked like a young horse at my place today."

She put her hands on her waist and swiveled in Billy's direction. "But you complain if I ask you to carry a stack of folded clothes up to Mr. Blackthorn's bedroom."

The boy twisted his face into a sheepish frown. "What's fun about that?"

"Not all work has to be fun, young man, but I guess you have years ahead of you to figure that out." Anna ruffled the top of Billy's head, but he ducked down to avoid the coddling.

"Thanks for letting me work on the farm with you, Jesse. Can we do it again sometime?"

"How is Wednesday?" he asked, looking from the boy and back to Anna.

She gave a shrug. "It's fine with me as long as he doesn't become a bother."

"He's no bother at all. I enjoy his company."

"Yay! Wednesday it is," squealed Billy. "I'm going to my room to read one of the books I brought back from Mr. Blackthorn's library."

"What book did you borrow?" Anna asked.

"*Moby Dick*," he answered.

"You picked a good one," said Jesse. "Surprised Blackthorn is willing to share."

"Oh, he ain't," said Billy. "Sis says to just take them, and he'll never know the difference. 'Course, we're goin' to return 'em. It's not the same as stealing."

"You don't have to explain anything to me, buddy. Blackthorn's got you working for him. I would expect you to borrow and return them."

"We can't return the food we take though, but Sis says we have to eat on Sunday, so she brings a few things to tide us over since we ain't got paid yet."

"He hasn't given you any money yet?" Jesse asked, directing the question to Anna.

"Not yet, but he promised to pay me tomorrow. We'll see. I told him from here on in, I will expect him to pay me every Saturday."

"And if he doesn't?"

"I'll resume my job hunt."

He wanted to say, "Or you could marry me," but he didn't think that would go over too well. "Good for you," he said instead.

Billy disappeared into his tiny bedroom and closed the door. Jesse wouldn't be a bit surprised if the boy fell asleep well before dark, as hard as he'd worked that day.

"Have a seat—if you'd like—or if you prefer to leave, that's fine too. I mean…"

He smiled at her and couldn't stop himself from reaching up and cupping her cheek. He would've preferred to kiss it, but he refrained. "I think I'll sit. I'll try not to outstay my welcome."

He sat in one of the rockers Newell had made, glad that Anna had found a spot for both of them, one in her room and the other in Billy's. He looked around the small room and was impressed at how homey she'd made it.

He set to rocking in slow motion. Anna lowered herself to the edge of her bed. She gave a little yawn, and he thought how tired she must be. "I won't stay long," he told her. "I know you put in long days at Blackthorn's."

"I do, but…well, it is rather nice to carry on a conversation with someone other than Rex—and Billy when he's there. He's not lying when he says he's bored with this whole situation."

"I can imagine he is. He's an active kid. What boy who's used to working outside all day wants to suddenly be stuck with a list of inside house chores?"

She giggled and thumbed at Billy's closed door. "Certainly not that one."

Rex rose from his comfortable position and set his head on her lap, gazing up with wishful eyes. "Don't tell me you want to go outside."

"Want me to take him to the alley?"

"I'll go with you," she said. She opened Billy's door to tell him they were going to take Rex out, but quietly closed it again. "He's sleeping," she whispered.

"I'm not at all surprised."

⌣

It was a lovely evening, not terribly hot and muggy like many a summer night could be. Jesse and Anna sat down on the back stoop while Rex roamed around in the alley, sniffing bits of garbage and looking for the exact spot to relieve himself. The alley had its own distinct smells—spoiled food, horse dung, and general mustiness—but over time, one grew accustomed to the odor. As they sat and mulled their own thoughts, Anna pondered how very comfortable she'd become in Jesse's presence. A gentle breeze whirred through the trees and cooled her skin. Besides the sounds of chirping birds and the occasional back-and-forth squirrel chatter, there were the clip-clop of horses' hooves and the squeak of wagon wheels on the main streets going through town. Even at the close of day, folks were still milling about, finishing up last-minute errands and making their way toward home. Her little farm came to mind, not to mention her garden, probably dry, neglected, and filling up with weeds that were crowding out her vegetable plants. She would not allow a wave of sadness to come over her, however. Although she didn't have all the things she wanted in life, she had what she needed to get by, and she trusted God would continue to provide.

"What are you thinking about?" Jesse asked.

"Me? Oh, I don't know. Counting my blessings, I suppose."

"Really? You were forced out of your home, reduced to living in a two-bedroom space, lost a good deal of your possessions, and yet you're counting your blessings?"

She smiled then looked down at her skirt and brushed off a fallen twig. "Billy and I have each other, we have our health, there is a roof over our heads, and we never go to bed hungry. Some don't have that much, so I'm grateful. Besides that, I've gained a new friend in you."

Jesse added a slanted smile to his slow nod. "You have a great outlook, and for the record, I'm grateful to have gained a new friend myself. I don't know exactly where things went wrong with us back in early spring, but I've come to know you a lot better over the last few weeks, and what I know I like." He bumped his side against her in a playful gesture, and she gave a little giggle. His words warmed her, but they also set off a bit of a warning signal in her heart. Best not grow too fond of him lest Blackthorn grow suspicious and then follow through with his threats. She felt at times as if she were walking a tightrope, trying to find a good balance without falling off.

"Why that worried expression?" he asked, his head dipping close to hers.

"Do I look worried?"

"You're thinking about Blackthorn again."

She folded her arms and swiveled to look him square on. "Since when did you start reading minds?"

He chuckled. "I'm pretty good at it, aren't I?"

Rather than immediately reply, she unfolded her arms and picked up a stray dandelion, its blossom turned to a little white globe of fuzz. She blew at it and watched its tiny seeds scatter through the air. She tossed the stem to the ground. "It's best, I think, that we keep things between us friendly—and nothing beyond that."

"Ah. Blackthorn's orders?"

She hesitated, then answered, "Yes."

"What right does he have to dictate who you mingle with?"

"Let's not talk about it."

"You always say that."

"And you always want more answers than I'm at liberty to give."

"It's only natural that I'm curious."

She sighed because she knew he was right.

Rex meandered back to them and sat down facing her, his eyes seeming to delve deep, as if he held some particle of wisdom. She smiled and petted his head. The spot where Blackthorn had hit him had scabbed over. After parting his shaggy black fur to look at it, she let go another jagged sigh. "All right, I'm going to tell you something, but you mustn't get angry and think about retaliating."

She almost felt the stiffness run through his spine. "I'll try my best. What is it?"

She knew she oughtn't to tell him, but if she didn't disclose at least a portion of her worry, he might never stop asking. "See this dried scab on Rex's head?"

He leaned forward and looked. His brow crinkled. "Yeah, what about it? How did it get there?"

"Blackthorn hit him and knocked him out."

"What?" he shrieked.

"Shhh. Please try not to overreact. It was a warning to me that if I married you, he would do more than hurt my dog, he would hurt Billy Ray. He was desperate to own my farm." There. She'd finally confessed it!

Jesse's eyes went round as moons. "Why that no-good, vomit-spewing—roach!"

"Shhh. Someone from one of the other upstairs rooms will hear you and come down here."

"So he *did* come to your house that same night you agreed to marry me. He came over after I left."

She could do little but nod her head. He jumped up, took off his hat, and started running his fingers through his thick brown hair. "He had no right." He turned a full circle, then looked down at her. "This is ridiculous. You have to go to the sheriff with this, Anna."

"No, no, I can't! He threatened me. And now that I've told you, he will go after Billy Ray. I don't trust him. Please, don't tell the sheriff. I'm afraid Blackthorn has connections. Somehow he'll find out if I go to the sheriff. I can't take that chance with Billy Ray." Fresh tears formed in her eyes, and she started to tremble.

He turned a couple of circles, tossed his hat to the step, and started holding his head in both hands, as if squeezing it would give him some new revelation.

After a few seconds, he sat down next to her, reached for her hand, and clasped it between his two. "All right, here's what we're going to do."

"What?" she asked, finding comfort in his closeness, yet almost fearing what he might have up his sleeve.

"We're going to pray."

"Oh!" Relief whistled through her veins. "I like that idea. Prayer is always best."

"And we're going to ask God to lead us and give us wisdom. James one, verse five says, *'If any of you lack wisdom, let him ask of God, that giveth to all men liberally, and upbraideth not; and it shall be given him.'* So, that's what we're going to do."

They bowed their heads, and for the next few minutes, he prayed the most soothing words, thanking God first for His love and goodness, then asking Him for guidance and wisdom. He asked the Lord to guard him against acting too hastily and interfering with the law. He also asked the Lord to keep Anna and Billy Ray safe while they considered their next steps, and that whatever those next steps were, they'd take them under God's shield of protection and with His supervision. He concluded his prayer with the words, "Grant us divine wisdom, Lord, so that nothing is said or done that would be contrary to Thy plan. In the name of Jesus, I pray. Amen."

When Anna opened her eyes, they were wet around the edges, but she didn't mind. Let the tears fall for all she cared. A sweet peace had come over her during Jesse's prayer, and she had an overwhelming sense of God's protection and care. Perhaps He would even open doors to a whole new job so she no longer had to depend on Blackthorn. She smiled up at Jesse. "Thank you for those lovely, reassuring words."

"You're welcome." He lifted one hand and dabbed at her tears with his fingertips. "No more tears, Anna. All shall be well. But tell me, has Blackthorn said anything out of the ordinary to you since you started working for him? Anything that gave you pause, that might make you suspicious of him or curious?"

"Suspicious?" She thought a moment. "No, not really. If he has anything at all to say to me, it's in the form of an order. He wrote a list of daily chores for me on my first day of work, so I follow that. Some days, he might add an item or two. But as for any conversation, we don't engage, and in fact, I never even saw him at suppertime last week. He did arrive home tonight just before supper, but we didn't talk. Rex scares him." She laughed. "He's a good boy, my Rex." She petted the dog's head again. "He doesn't like Blackthorn."

"Very smart dog. Perceptive I'd say. I bet he remembers Horace from the time he clonked him on the head. Anyway, the less you and Billy see of Blackthorn, the better. Don't do anything to ruffle his feathers."

"Well, that would mean not spending any time with you then." She gave him a playful smile. And didn't even cover it this time.

"Wrong. That would mean not letting him *see* you spending time with me." He gave her a gentle nudge in the side. Then grew serious. "We are going to approach this thing in a practical way, Anna, and for now, as long as Blackthorn remains cool and aloof, we'll hold off on things, but...at the first sign of trouble, or if anything suspicious takes place, you'll let me know. Is that a deal?"

She hesitated only briefly before answering him with a quiet nod.

"Good. Now that you've told me about Blackthorn's threats to you, I am going to treat this matter with all new respect. I understand the gravity of the situation, and I'll be extra cautious going forward."

More relief flooded her chest. "I feel better having told you.'

"And I'm thankful you finally trusted me enough to do so."

He still held her hand, except now their clasped hands rested on top of one of his spread knees. They sat quietly, listening to the chittering birds preparing to settle in for another summer evening. She relished the simple strength and comfort she drew from just sitting next to Jesse, her hand in his, her side tucked up next to his firm frame. A stray thought scrambled past her brain. She sat up a little straighter. "I just thought of something, I'm sure it's nothing, but—I don't know. It was something Blackthorn asked me tonight while he was having supper."

A fleck of interest sparked in his eyes. "What was it?"

"It was silly. As I was walking back to the kitchen, he said, 'You wouldn't happen to know anything about the location of a Wish Bone Tree on your old land, would you?'"

"A Wish Bone Tree," Jesse repeated, brow creased.

"Yes. I told him I didn't have any idea what he was talking about and I had never heard of such a tree. He seemed satisfied with that and waved me off, so I left. I cleaned the kitchen, walked out the back door, and came directly home." She studied his curious expression. "See? I told you it was nothing."

He didn't respond right away, just scratched his head, and then rubbed the underside of his nose as if pondering something.

"Have you ever heard of a Wish Bone Tree?" she asked.

He hemmed a bit. "Hm. I—have no idea what one is."

"Me either."

"What are you two doing?"

From behind, Billy Ray's quiet voice surprised them both. He was wiping both eyes with the knuckles of his index fingers.

"We're just sitting here talking. Rex needed to take care of his night-time business."

"Oh. Yeah, me too," Billy said rather groggily. Rex jumped up and walked beside him as he made his way to the outhouse on the other side of the alley and down a short path.

"I should go back upstairs when Billy comes back."

"Yes, and I should be getting home after a long day. I'll pick him up again on Wednesday morning."

They studied each other in the quiet until it became apparent that Jesse wanted to end the evening with a kiss.

"Well." She quickly stood, and due to habit, brushed off her skirt. He stood as well, facing her, searching her eyes. "Thank you for everything," she softly murmured.

He lowered his face and kissed her cheek. But he let the kiss linger. "Nothing more for now, but don't get too comfortable," he whispered in her ear.

A chill scampered up her spine. He withdrew just as Billy let the outhouse door slam shut behind him, and he and Rex started making their way back.

"I'll pick you up again Wednesday morning, friend, same place, same time."

Billy grinned. "I'll be waiting. Can Rex come too?"

In unison, Anna said, "Yes," while Jesse said, "No." They looked briefly at each other before Jesse turned his attention to Billy.

"I mean, since you are spending the day at the farm, I think it's best that Rex stay with your sister. You know, so she has someone to keep her company."

Anna realized what he was inferring. Rex provided a measure of protection for her. When she thought about it that way, it made sense.

The boy shrugged. "Okay." He patted the dog's head. "Maybe another time, boy."

They said their goodbyes there in the alley, and when they turned toward the apartment staircase, Jesse gave her arm the gentlest touch when she passed by.

29

*J*esse pawed through his top bureau drawer, reaching into the back till his hand landed on the metal box he'd promised to keep safe for Billy Ray. He pulled it out, carried it to his bed, and sat down to open it. He swallowed hard, then lifted the lid. Carefully, he removed each paper, along with the pewter-colored key, and laid them one at a time on the bed to examine them. He cautiously unfolded each creased and fragile paper. When he'd first laid eyes on the mysterious box and its contents, it had indeed captured his interest, but after some thought, he'd decided it must've played a role in an old legend of some sort. Maybe someone had created it for sheer entertainment, a game of sorts between the Blackthorns and Hansens. Perhaps, though, someone in the family saw it as more than just a game—*Horace* for one.

He picked up the box and turned it over to study the printed words on the bottom. "Property of Charles Hansen from Wilbur Blackthorn ~ 1835." Something innately told him these mysterious clues held a certain importance to Horace, so important that it had made him desperate to buy the Hansen farm. *How desperate was desperate though?* Had Horace been desperate enough to end Newell's life? No, Jesse dared not let his mind go there again. He needed more proof. Still, the physical harm Horace had done to the Hansens' beloved farm collie, as well as his threat to Anna about doing something equally bad to Billy Ray if she didn't turn the farm over to him, filled Jesse with a great deal of apprehension. He was at the point of not putting much past Horace Blackthorn. The man was evil.

His recollection of the words "Wish Bone Tree" on the map had prompted Jesse to take matters more seriously. He quickly scanned the two clues, then compared them to the map. Apparently, Horace had located the vase containing the third clue, which would indicate his need to find this particular tree so he could continue his search. Evidently, Horace had not been privy to this map as Newell had been. Did Horace suspect that Newell possessed a map? Did he even know one existed? Did Horace have a different map? More questions than he could count thrashed around in Jesse's head. *Lord, give me wisdom. Grant me insight.*

With all-new purpose, he gave the map another close inspection. Obviously, someone—a Blackthorn no doubt—had instructed another Blackthorn where to go to find the first clue. According to the map, that clue had been located on the northernmost part of the property, where the warmest waters flowed through the creek. Someone had placed an "X" with the words "Clue #1" to mark the spot. And perhaps that first clue, once found, had been placed right inside this very same metal box. Clue number two, if its words were to be taken seriously, had been buried in a vase slightly off center of the southwest quarter of the property, an "X" with the words "Clue #2" marking that location as well. And if Horace had indeed located the vase, apparently that particular clue made some mention about finding the third clue somewhere in the vicinity of a Wish Bone Tree. That would explain Horace's question to Anna about whether she knew of such a tree on her land. Another quick study of the map indicated the location of said tree. At the southernmost piece of Hansen land, there was an "X" and the words "Clue #3" next to a tree with some very small, faded letters that read "Wish Bone Tree."

Jesse's heart gave an extra thump. Giving the map a final examination, he easily spotted the location of the remaining clues. He shook his head in wonder. The map, now that he'd finally taken it more seriously, started provoking him into even more sober mulling. Should he take this to the sheriff? Was it enough to further their investigation, or was it a stretch to think Charles Berry would consider it important? Part of him still thought the whole idea of a buried treasure was a hoax. Would the sheriff laugh at him for bringing him something that could prove to be nothing more than a big waste of time? Further, this was something Newell had intended to give to his son at some point. And Jesse had as much as promised he would keep it a secret—even from Anna. Should he talk to Billy Ray, or would mentioning it force Jesse to have to explain more than Billy needed to know? The poor boy had no idea the real cause of his father's death.

A rap came to his door that so spooked him that his body jolted.

"Ma! You startled me!"

"Well, I'm sorry, I didn't mean to." Laura stood in his doorway, her graying brown hair flowing down her back, her long brocade housecoat wrapped securely around her. "I was just on my way to bed and saw your lamps still lit and your door wide open. What has you so absorbed?"

He carefully, but hurriedly, folded each paper and put them back in the brown metal box. "Nothing much, Ma."

"What is that old box anyway? Where did it come from?"

"It's—something Billy Ray asked me to put in a safe place for him. I was just looking inside it. Being a little nosy I guess."

She stepped inside his room. "Was it anything important? I mean, if he asked you to put it in a safe place, I guess it must hold quite a lot of value."

"Yes, I suppose it does. It's something Newell was going to give him at some point—when he reached the age of twelve, Billy thought."

His mother placed a hand on her heart. "Oh, well, then it *is* special. You take good care of it for him. Poor boy, having to stay cooped up in that upstairs apartment in town when he's so used to roaming the countryside and staying so active on the farm. That was nice of you to bring him here for the day. I hope you'll do it again."

"Yes, he'll be spending the day on Wednesday again."

"Oh, good. He's a polite young man. He kept telling me how delicious everything was and thanking me several times for feeding him. His sister has done very well by him."

"Yes, she has, and yeah, he is a very good kid."

"And speaking of Anna, when will you be bringing her back for dinner?"

"Next Sunday, Ma."

She smiled broadly. "Well, then, it seems my youngest son is starting to form a—hm—bond with Anna Hansen."

He gave a little chortle. "Could be."

Her smile grew. "I'm delighted. Good night, Son." She turned and disappeared down the hall, loudly humming the familiar tune to "Here Comes the Bride."

⌒

At 10 p.m., someone knocked at Horace's door. He left his library, tied the belt around his smoking jacket a little tighter, walked down the hallway, and then peered past the curtain onto the porch. Of all people, Sheriff Berry and one of his deputies stood on the other side of the door. A rock-like knot balled up in his gut. What in tarnation were they doing here? It was his bedtime, for crying out loud. Didn't they have any sense of propriety?

Even though they were the last people to whom he wished to show any pleasantries, he did don a half smile and opened the door.

"Good evening, Horace," Berry said. "Sorry to barge in on you at this late hour. Deputy Lawford and I were in the area, so I thought we'd stop in to see you."

To hide his anger at their intrusion, Horace opened his door a bit wider—but not wide enough for them to step inside. "No problem at all, Sheriff. Good to see you," he lied. "What can I do for you?"

"Well," the sheriff said, batting at a couple of mosquitoes, "might we come in—seeing as these bugs are going to suck the blood right out of us if we stand out here? It'll only be a minute."

"Uh, well, it is a little late, but"—he opened the door and gave a wave of his hand to usher them in—"come in then."

He led them into his parlor room just off the entryway. "Would you care to sit?"

The sheriff looked around the room a bit before taking him up on his invitation. He and his deputy each took a chair, so Horace sat in the divan across from them. Darned fool kept looking around at his paintings and knickknacks like he grew up in a barn.

"This sure is a nice place you got here," Berry said. "So neat and tidy. You must have a housekeeper, eh?"

"Yeah. I used to employ Florence Hardy, but she wasn't very reliable. She couldn't cook worth an empty milk can, so I had to fire her. Recently hired someone new."

"Oh, anyone I know?"

Horace scratched the back of his head, wondering why Berry would ask such a thing, but since he had nothing to hide, he decided to be truthful. "I hired Anna Hansen."

"Anna Hansen," the sheriff repeated. He studied the ceiling momentarily, then gave a couple of quick nods and centered his eyes back on Horace. "Ah, yes, her father, God rest his soul, was Newell Hansen. She works for you now, huh?" Berry brushed at the corners of his bushy mustache in a most irritating manner.

"That's right. She brings her little brother with her to work. I got no complaints about them, unless you count the fact that she brings that mutt of a dog with her too. Blamed thing growls at me every time it sees me. Anyway, the girl can cook fair, so that's a benefit."

"I think I heard something about you buying up Newell's farm."

"You heard right. It was in foreclosure, so I worked with Cyrus Daly to pay off the bank. I was happy to take it off her hands. Out of the goodness of my heart, I offered her and her little brother free housing over Henry's Hardware. You might know I own that building, and Henry leases from me."

"No, I didn't know that. That's mighty generous, you letting her and her brother live up there free of charge."

Horace started to relax. If the sheriff had come to grill him about Newell, he didn't let on. Matter of fact, he couldn't figure out why he'd come, especially due to the late hour. "Either of you care for a drink?" he asked, thinking it important to stay in the sheriff's good graces.

The sheriff looked at his deputy. "Naw. Like I said, we were just in the area, and we're technically still working. Thought we'd stop by since we saw your lamps still burning."

"I was getting ready to turn them down. You sure I can't get you a nightcap?"

"No, but that's mighty hospitable of you."

Horace wanted to make one for himself, but decided he'd best wait till after the lawmen left. No sense giving them the idea he was a drunkard. "Say, how's your investigation going?"

"Investigation?" the sheriff asked, his face crimped.

"Concerning Newell Hansen."

"Oh, that. It's somewhat of a puzzle. We're missing a few pieces."

"That's a downright shame. Might be the case will go cold, eh?"

"Yes, yes, these things happen from time to time. You know, you don't gather enough evidence, and before you know it, you have to close the book." Berry looked at his deputy and started to push himself up.

"Aren't you goin' to ask Mr. Blackthorn about them rats in the neighborhood? That is why we stopped by, after all," his deputy said.

Berry snapped his fingers. "Oh!" He looked at Horace and shook his head. "If it weren't for Tom here, I swear some days I'd leave my own head back at the office! I knew there was some reason we stopped by. A few folks around town been complaining about a rodent problem. They want the city to take care of it, so we been checking various neighborhoods to get this whole thing nailed down. You found any rats scurrying about, or you managed to kill any lately?"

Horace deliberated a bit, thinking this was a strange question. "I haven't seen a rodent, certainly not a rat, around here in a couple of years, although I might have seen a mouse or two. Far as I know, everybody's pretty good about locking away their garbage, particularly in this neighborhood. Don't know who's been complainin', but it ain't been me. Now there might be some problems up closer to town—in the back alleys and whatnot. You might better check the liveries around town too."

"You got no problems at Henry's Hardware? I only ask 'cause you say you own that building, and it's in town."

"Nope, Henry ain't complained to me about a problem, and if he had, I sure as shootin' would've handled it. I hate rats about as much as I hate dogs."

"Humph. Well, you answered our question then." Berry and his deputy rose to their feet and Horace did likewise. The sheriff stuck out his hand and they shook. "Mighty nice you invitin' us in at this late hour, Horace. Deputy Lawford and I will be getting out of your hair now. You have a pleasant evening."

"Indeed, and you as well, Sheriff—and Deputy. I'll walk you to the door."

"Like I said, mighty fine house," Berry said as they made their way through the parlor and back to the entryway.

"Thank you. It's been my home for many years." He reached the door and opened it to the comfortable evening air.

"Yes, yes, I know it has. Your daddy, he wanted you to go into blacksmithing with him, didn't he? He ran a successful operation, too, built it from the ground up if I remember, but then he sold it to Sam Hayslit."

"Yeah, blacksmithing never interested me much. I was happy when he sold it."

"Must have been a disappointment to your pa, no?"

This made Horace a trifle uncomfortable. He opened the door a little wider. "No, not at all. He understood my passion for investing in land and farming it out."

The sheriff nodded but didn't move, even though his deputy had already stepped over the threshold. Horace tried to hold his impatience in check. He wished he could shove the sheriff out the door.

Slowly, as if he were an old man, the sheriff walked through the door, but on Horace's porch, he turned, then raised an index finger. "There's only one little thing that troubles me, Horace." He sniffed. "It's nothing, I'm sure."

"Yeah? What's that?"

Berry played with his mustache some more. "Back in early April, you walked into Colbert's Apothecary and told Elmer Colbert you needed to buy some arsenic because you had a rat problem in your cellar."

Horace felt red-hot terror scamper up his spine, but he took great care to remain stoic and unaffected. He stalled only a few seconds. "Oh, that. Huh. I don't know how that slipped my mind. Yes, I did go into Colbert's a few months back." He scratched his forehead. "I happened to see a couple of varmints going through my garbage last spring. It was dark, so I couldn't see real clearly. In the end, I decided they must've been raccoons, not rats. I did put out the arsenic, but never caught anything."

"Where do you keep your garbage?"

"In a barrel next to my barn."

"I thought you told Colbert you saw rats in your cellar."

"My cellar? Uh, he must've misheard me, and I don't think I mentioned rats. No, I'm quite sure I told him I saw some varmints out by my barn. He must have presumed I meant rats. At any rate, I burn everything same night I take it out now."

"Ah. Good idea. What about that arsenic? You still got that container stored somewhere?"

"Uh. Yeah, out on a shelf in my barn. Why do you ask?"

The sheriff shrugged. "Just curious. Never can tell. You might need it again—in case them raccoons decide to come back." He chuckled at his own words.

"Yeah, that's why I keep it on hand. Lots of folks keep arsenic on hand. I'm no different."

Berry nodded. "Well, I think that's about all. Oh…you know, I just happened to think of one more thing." He and his deputy exchanged a look.

Something was up—and Horace didn't like it. No, not one bit. "What's that, Sheriff?" His irritation was growing by the second.

Rather than answer, however, Berry simply eased himself back into the house. He certainly was a quirky, aggravating man. People always raved about what a smart man Berry was when it came to the law, but in Horace's eyes, he was nothing short of a big dope.

"You don't mind that I just walked back inside, do you? This should only take a minute." Berry turned to his deputy. "Hey, Tom, I forgot to bring in that item. It's in my saddlebag. Would you mind retrieving it for me?"

"No, not at all, Sheriff." The man turned and jogged down the sidewalk to where the men had tied their horses.

Horace stood in the doorway as he watched the deputy dig something out of Berry's saddlebag. Once he had it in hand, he trotted back to the house. Vexed, Horace allowed for Tom Lawford's re-entry and then closed the door with a click.

"Here you go, Sheriff."

Horace turned and immediately recognized the small plate he'd left in Newell's cornfield. He made sure not to react, however. "What's you got there?" he casually asked.

The sheriff took the small plate. "Oh, it's nothing much, just a plate we found next to a stump at Newell Hansen's place, not far from his barn. I was just curious if you might have ever seen a plate such as this one."

Horace folded his arms and leaned in, pretending indifference, then studied the dish. After a few seconds, he shook his head. "Nope, can't say I have. Why are you asking me?"

Without answering his question, the sheriff thumbed behind him, pointing at the kitchen. "You wouldn't mind if we took a quick look inside your kitchen, would you?"

"My kitchen?" He raised his eyebrows then shrugged, keeping his arms crossed. "'Course not. Help yourself. Don't know why you'd have any desire, but go right ahead."

Berry walked down the hallway, his deputy close behind. Once in the kitchen, he stood there and took a hasty look around. "My, my, very nice kitchen you have here. You got all the modern conveniences, don't you." He stepped closer to Horace's cookstove. "You got one of them C. J. Woolson Stoves, I see. He's a fine inventor. My wife would swoon if she walked in here. Better not let her near it." The sheriff laughed as if he were the funniest fellow in all of Lebanon. It took all of Horace's self-control to prevent him from hauling off and punching the guy, his last nerve getting ready to explode.

Deputy Lawford opened both doors to his tall wooden cupboard and took a gander inside. All his dishes were neatly stacked. Horace wasn't stupid; he knew they hoped to find dishes to match the one the sheriff held in his hand. A wave of relief ran through him for having had the wits about him to pack those blasted things away in his backyard shed. No one would ever think to look out there.

"You don't mind if we take a look around a bit more, do you?"

He unfolded his arms and waved them about. "I don't have a single thing to hide, Sheriff."

Berry nodded at his deputy. "How about that buffet in the dining room?"

Both men entered his dining room for a look in the long bureau, but all the drawers contained nothing but linen tablecloths, napkins, a set of silverware, and a few other odds and ends. Certainly no dishes.

Horace almost laughed out loud just watching them.

In another minute or two, the sheriff looked at Lawford. "Well, I think we're done here, Tom." Then to Horace, he said, "I thank you for your time, Horace. Did I tell you, you have a fine house?"

"Yes, you did, Sheriff, several times, in fact. Now, if that's all, I really must be going to bed. I rise mighty early."

"Yes, yes, it's gettin' near that time for us as well, although Lawford here has night duty. I'm sure my wife is waiting on me."

Berry and his deputy left the dining room and made their way to the door. This time, Horace did not walk them to the door; instead he stood at the other end of the entryway. The deputy opened the door and let the sheriff go on ahead of him.

"Good night now, Horace," Berry said. "You have yourself a good night's sleep."

"Oh, I plan on it. And you as well."

After the door shut, he walked up to it and threw the latch down to lock it tight. He peeked past the curtain, glad to see them preparing to mount their horses. *Finally.* He dropped the curtain in a huff and let a loud curse blow past his lips.

He needed more than a nightcap now. Might be he'd take a whole bottle of whiskey upstairs to his room.

30

June rolled into July, and as the calendar ticked away, the temperatures soared. On July 7, 1865, four convicted conspirators—including boarding house owner Mary E. Surratt—were hanged for their roles in the assassination of President Lincoln. After months of drama, the culmination came in the form of the gallows. The remaining conspirators received various extended sentences. Some around the country considered it to be a day of celebration and good cheer. Many men viewed the day as an opportunity to drink their cares away, while others saw it more as a time of gratitude, so they went to their houses of worship, sang songs of praise, and thanked their Maker that justice had been served. In certain areas of the south, where many still flew their Confederate flags, the enthusiasm was quite lacking, many viewing the hangings as anything but just.

Jesse had continued to take Billy Ray to the Fuller farm every Monday and Wednesday, which turned out to be the highlights of Billy's weeks. Any time he didn't have to traipse over to Blackthorn's house for a day of household chores, he woke up in a cheery mood.

Anna's friendship with Jesse continued to blossom, and there'd even been a couple of shared kisses, but for the most part, she avoided all shows of affection, for it did not seem wise to allow a romantic relationship. She didn't need her idealistic emotions spinning out of control when so much else was at stake. She'd lost her farm, her life and Billy's were in a state of change, and the future was uncertain. And if she did decide to give her heart to Jesse Fuller, what was to prevent him from stomping on it later? Romance could be so fleeting—or so she'd heard. But she'd never experienced real love other than God's, so what did she know about it anyway? And lately, Jesse had been more thoughtful and reserved, as if he were always thinking about something but wasn't ready to talk about it. This made things between them more complicated. Besides, even if they had wanted to experience a private moment, her tiny upstairs, two-bedroom quarters didn't allow for it, nor did Billy Ray, who always seemed underfoot. Still, she didn't mind too much.

On Monday and Wednesday evenings, after Jesse brought Billy Ray home, the three of them played various card games as well as a silly little game she'd learned from her mother called "Hide the Thimble," in which one person would hide a sewing thimble in some remote spot and the others would go in search of it. Billy Ray got such a kick out of the game, especially when it was Jesse's turn to hide it. They played other games as well, acting out certain people or events and trying to get the others to guess their actions. Some nights, Jesse and Billy threw a ball back and forth in the alley, and she'd sit on the back stoop to watch and relax, batting at flies and mosquitoes, but not minding it a bit because of the laughter Jesse was able to stir up in her little brother. After watching him interact with Billy Ray, she could understand why Jesse was a favorite among his nieces and nephews. In times when she dared let her mind wander, she imagined him being a father someday, which in turn prompted her to dream about being the mother of his children.

She had accepted an invitation to Jesse's mother's home once more, but had told Jesse she didn't wish to make a habit of it lest folks—and his family in particular—think that something was going on between them. He'd playfully said, "Well, maybe something *is* going on," but she'd laughed off his comment and changed the subject.

Ever since she'd told him about Horace Blackthorn's threats, he had been true to his word about taking the situation more seriously, and she appreciated it. It made her wonder why she hadn't told him sooner. And yet that had taken a certain level of trust on her part, so she supposed in the end, the timing had never been quite right till that night.

It was Wednesday, July 26, and right on schedule, Billy Ray left at 8:50 a.m. to walk to the post office to meet Jesse for his workday at the Fuller farm. As usual, Blackthorn had left fifty minutes prior. She was always glad to see him walk out the door. Today, he had not given her any additional jobs for a change, which pleased her immensely. She had a hard enough time as it was finishing everything on his list.

Over the past month, Blackthorn had grown increasingly grouchier, snapping at her over the smallest things—she had left a wrinkle on his bedspread when making up his bed the day before; she had forgotten to put his mail on his desk; she hadn't folded his laundered and pressed shirts to his liking; and yesterday, he'd found a tiny dab of dried egg on his otherwise clean fork. She had apologized profusely and promised to do better, but he merely groused at her that it better not happen again. It seemed his constant complaints mounted—almost to a point of rage some days. Still, he hadn't touched her, and for that, she gave thanks. She believed that Rex's warning growls when Blackthorn raised his voice at her often served as a great deterrent. The man was a regular beast, but apparently, he viewed Rex as a dangerous threat. It seemed Rex sensed that fear too and played into it, which actually suited her fine. Several times, Blackthorn had insisted she leave her "stupid" dog at home, but she had told him she was happy to abide by all his orders except that one.

One particularly hot day, tired and irritated after he complained yet again about Rex after she'd cooked a fine evening meal, Anna snapped. "If Rex can't come with me, then you will have to make your own meals and clean your own house."

"And you'll have to find another means for housing," he argued back.

"So be it, Mr. Blackthorn," she told him. "God will take care of us. I'll find a different job."

To that, he grumbled something about her useless faith in a God who didn't exist. Anna attempted to talk to him about the Lord, but he immediately changed the subject, which meant he also dropped the matter of her faithful companion.

At the mid-morning hour, just after she changed his bedding and opened the windows to let in a nice cross breeze, a knock came to the door downstairs. Rex gave several loud barks to alert her to their visitor and ran across the wooden floor to the door, his nails tapping.

Anna laid her dusting cloth on Blackthorn's dresser, planning to return to it later, and wiped at her sweaty face with the back of her sleeve. She took a hasty glance at herself in the mirror over Blackthorn's chest of drawers, rolled her eyes at her unkempt appearance, and scooted down the stairs. Once in the hallway, she said, "Rex, that's quite enough barking. Let's see who it is." The dog quieted and plopped down on the floor, facing the door. Anna pulled back the curtain to peek at the caller. At first glance, she didn't think she recognized the rather stout woman standing on the other side of the door, a large tote on her arm, but upon further study, Anna realized she did look familiar.

She wiped her hand on her apron and opened the door, putting on a pleasant face. "Good morning. May I help you?" Rex moved up beside Anna, and she put a reassuring hand on his head.

"I'm sorry for the intrusion, dear. My name is Florence Hardy."

"Florence Hardy. Oh, yes, you used to work for Mr. Blackthorn! Forgive me. Won't you come inside, Mrs. Hardy?"

"Oh, call me Florence, dear." She advanced a tiny step, poked her head in, and looked from one side to the next. "The old coot isn't about, is he?" she whispered.

Anna gave a quiet giggle. "No, thank goodness."

Florence let out breathy sigh. "Good! I can't bear to look at his face. I saw him walking on the other side of the street last Thursday and nearly retched right there."

Anna covered her mouth and let go a louder snicker. "Oh, my!"

Florence gave Rex a cautious once-over. "Is he fine with me entering?"

"Oh, yes. As long as he knows I'm safe, he fully approves." Then to Rex, Anna said, "Go lie down, boy." The dog instinctively turned and walked to one of his favorite spots under the parlor window.

Florence entered the house, carrying a large brown satchel. "I'm ever so sorry about the loss of your father, dear. And then to lose your farm as well. It's a shame all around. And I'm even sorrier that it was Horace who bought it from the bank. Everyone knows him to be a greedy louse."

"Thank you for your sympathetic words," Anna said. She didn't really wish to fill her time with this woman discussing her boss, however, so she hoped Florence had another purpose in visiting.

Florence smiled kindly at her. "I hope Old Thorny Face treats you better than he did me. Most times, he didn't even pay me for my week's worth of work—or he'd pay me three or four days later than was acceptable. I finally had enough of him. One night, I begged him for my wage, and instead of paying what he truly owed me, he handed me a half-dollar. Imagine! Well, I simply never returned after that."

"He didn't fire you?"

"Oh, good heavens, no. He would've kept me indefinitely had I settled for his monkeyshines. He's a cheapskate and a cheat. Don't ever trust him any further than you can pitch him. He's a mean lout."

Anna didn't wish to enter into the woman's angry blabber, but she did have to agree with her. "I've threatened to quit a time or two myself if he didn't pay me on time. So far, he's mostly been prompt." Feeling a bit cheerful—because after all, here was someone who knew what she was going through—she leaned forward and whispered conspiratorially, "He is afraid of my dog. I do believe if it weren't for Rex, he would treat me much worse."

At that, Florence laughed heartily. "Well, ain't that the best news of the day? The ol' swine's afraid of y'r dog." Her eyes trailed to a now sleeping Rex. "Look at him lying there, sweet as a kitten. That tells me one thing about your pooch. He knows a cheat when he sees one."

"He is pretty perceptive. Fortunately, I don't have to deal too much with Blackthorn, as he leaves straight after breakfast and doesn't return most days till suppertime. He generally either tells me to make him a boxed meal for noon, or he eats at a local diner. At any rate, he's rarely here." She gave a sweep of her hand toward the parlor room. "Would you like to come in for a cup of tea or coffee?"

"Oh no, dear, but thank you. I've been working at Washington Hall, tending to cleaning chores there. Today, I'm on the upper floor, washing down the benches where the students at the National Normal University convene for their chapel services. I must get back though, as I told my boss I'd only be gone about a half hour."

"I see."

"The reason for my visit is that while I was still working here, I often took home extra food that the old tightwad didn't eat."

"Oh, I do the same! I refuse to throw away perfectly good food."

"Exactly. Well, I took to straightening out my kitchen bureau this past weekend, and ran across one of the dishes on which I had carried home some food one night. Apparently, I had washed it at my house, and accidentally put it with my own dishes rather than return it the following day."

"Oh, well, I'm certain he wouldn't have missed it."

Florence placed her satchel on the floor and began to rummage through it. "No, I'm certain he wouldn't miss it, but just the same, I could not keep it in good conscience." She continued looking past several items, until at last, she pulled out a plate and extended it to Anna.

Anna's jaw instantly dropped at the sight of it, and she dared not even take it. It perfectly matched the one that Sheriff Berry's deputy had found in her cornfield just north of the barn on the evening of Papa's passing. She had never seen any dishes like it in Blackthorn's tall cabinet or on his shelves, and she had combed his whole kitchen while looking for various pots and utensils.

"Is something wrong, dear? Your face has suddenly gone pale. Is there anything I can do for you?"

"I—no, I—don't think that dish belongs to Mr. Blackthorn." She tried to gather her composure. "I've never seen one like that in his kitchen."

"Oh, it's his all right. He bought new dishes and packed the old ones away," Florence said matter-of-factly. She straightened then and looked at the dish she still held in her hand. "He told me once that these dishes had been passed down to him from a great-aunt who'd purchased them in London."

Anna's throat went dry as beach sand. "Where—did he put the—the old set?"

"Oh, he boxed them up and stuck them in his shed out back, next to the barn. I saw them out there one day when I had to put away some yard implements for doing a bit of outdoor spring cleanup. 'Course, I didn't tell him I'd found them or he would've accused me of snooping. He's a grumpy old nitwit."

Anna swallowed hard and tried to remain calm. "Why do you suppose he stopped using them?"

Florence shrugged. "No idea, really, other than he said he'd grown tired of the pattern."

"I see." Anna had one more important question. "Do—you happen to know just when he made the switch to the newer dishes?"

"Hm, not right off." She put a hand to her chin. "Well, wait, I believe it was right around the middle of April. It had been a lovely spring day, so instead of driving my wagon to his house that morning, I decided to walk. I recall entering through the kitchen door and finding the new set stacked on the butcher block table. He walked into the kitchen upon my arrival and in his usual gruff manner, he said, 'Bought me some new dishes. I'll let you arrange them in the cabinet however you choose.' I asked him what he'd done with the old set and all he said was he put them in storage. Knowing him as I do, he'll wait till the old dishes gain in value and then sell them at auction. They're worth a nice penny, I'm sure, being as they're one of a kind and all. I sincerely doubt anyone else in town has this pattern, since they came specially shipped from

London. I think I—goodness, are you all right, dear?" Florence drew in extra close to peer into Anna's eyes. "You look terribly peaked. Come, let's go into the parlor where you can sit."

Anna allowed the woman to take her by the arm and lead her to the divan. "Something just came over me, Florence. I'm sure I'll be just fine."

"Well, it's no wonder the way I've been blathering. Sit down, dear." Gratefully, Anna did as she was told. "Wait here, and I'll be right back with a glass of water for you." Florence placed the plate next to her on the divan and disappeared around the corner and down the hall toward the kitchen, her shoes click-clacking.

While she was gone, Anna studied the dish to make sure it was the same pattern as the one the sheriff had found. Indeed it was. No doubt about it. What had Horace been doing in her father's cornfield? Her father had planted seeds just days before his passing. Surely he would have seen the dish while he was out there and brought it into the house, but he had not. It made her wonder things about Horace Blackthorn. Had he offered her father something to eat that had been on a plate identical to this one? Something containing a lethal amount of arsenic? She and Billy Ray had gone back in the house to comfort each other while the doctor examined her father and the sheriff and his deputies walked around the property. Within the first half-hour, Sheriff Berry had knocked on her door to show her the plate, but she'd told him she didn't recognize it.

Now, here she sat, staring at an exact replica. Her stomach roiled at the possibilities, and she could feel pools of sweat forming on her forehead, neck, and back. She lifted the corner of her apron to dab at her face. One thing was now more than clear to her: she had to tell Jesse tonight when he returned with Billy Ray. In fact, she would take the plate with her when she left tonight. Perhaps it *was* time to go to the sheriff—but *that* thought made her reel all the more.

Florence returned with the glass of water. "Here, dear, drink this."

"Thank you, Florence. You're more than kind."

"Are you going to be all right?"

"Yes, yes, I'm feeling much better already. I believe the heat overtook me." It wasn't a complete untruth, as the sun coming through the windows had hiked up the temperatures, rendering the morning breezes quite useless.

"It's been dreadfully hot of late, I'll give you that." Florence gave Anna a quick study. "Well, if you're sure you're fine, then I'll be on my way."

"One more thing—before you go. Might you show me where the dishes are that Blackthorn is storing, so I can put this dish with the rest of them?"

"Oh, of course, dear, follow me."

As soon as they headed toward the back door, Rex jumped up and followed after them.

31

On the drive back to town, Billy Ray talked nonstop about his day and how good it was to see Carlotta, rub her nose, and speak into her ear. "She recognizes me, you know,"

"I'm certain she does," Jesse assured him, his elbows resting on his spread knees as they bumped along on the road, his wagon wheel squealing with every pitch and turn. "Sounds like that axel needs oiling again."

"Sounds like it." Billy Ray took a fifteen-second break from talking, then started in again. "That was fun swinging from the hayloft with Isaac, Frankie, and Elias. That was mighty smart of you puttin' that rope swing up there. I sailed right through the barn door!"

"That's the idea. I'm glad you're getting along well with my nephews. They're good boys."

"Yeah, they're loads of fun, even though Isaac can get a little bossy."

That brought a chuckle. "He's always been a bit headstrong, but he's also the oldest, so I guess he thinks he has the right to order the lot of you around. You let me know if you ever have a problem with him, hear?"

"No, it ain't like that. He's real nice. He just wants us to know he's in charge."

Jesse shook his head as he drove his team, a lingering smile on his face, as he recalled the "former" Isaac—before Faith entered the picture. Joey had married her basically because he needed a full-time nanny who wouldn't drop everything and run when his kids got to be too much to handle. If he remembered right, Joey had gone through at least five nannies during his stint in the Army because his kids were so unruly. Fortunately, they couldn't scare off Faith, and it didn't take long for Isaac, the ringleader of the siblings, to figure out she was no pushover. He still had a bit of highhandedness about him, but he was worlds better these days. Jesse was proud of the way his nephew was growing up.

When there came a bit of a longer lull between topics, Jesse cut in. "You know, Billy Ray, I've been thinking about something."

"Yeah? Does it have something to do with my sister?"

"Your sister?"

"You were gonna marry her, remember?"

"Oh, that. Well, what I wanted to talk about with you doesn't concern the topic of marriage, at least not yet. But I will tell you that I'm very fond of her. Do you mind?"

"Mind? 'Course not! I'd be happy to have you as a big brother."

Jesse smiled the more. He angled a glance at the boy. "You're a fine lad, you know that? I'd be honored if it ever came to that. I have a lot of respect for you."

"Respect? For me? But I'm just a kid."

"Doesn't matter. You're mature for your age."

"Thanks."

Jesse decided now was as good a time as any to bring up the subject of the mysterious box that Newell had kept in the barn. "Anyway, I wanted to talk to you about something. You remember that brown metal box you asked me to keep stored in a safe place?"

Billy Ray went silent. "The one with the map and the clues? What about it? Did you lose it?"

"No, friend, I didn't lose it. It's as safe as can be. In fact, I brought it with me today. Not so long ago, I took a closer look at the items inside it, and there are a few things that make me think we ought to share it with your sister."

"Okay."

He turned his head toward the boy. "Just like that? You don't mind?"

"No. I s'pose she has just as much a right to see it as I do, and if there was a treasure, I'd share it with her."

"That's really kind of you, but it's not so much about any treasure as it is about Horace Blackthorn."

"What about him?"

"Well, let's just say I don't trust the man and leave it at that for now."

"What does he have to do with the metal box though and the clues and map?"

Jesse exhaled and thought about his next words. "He asked your sister if she'd ever heard of a Wish Bone Tree on the property. On that map, at the very bottom, there's an 'X' next to the words 'Wish Bone Tree'. Why would Blackthorn ask her if she'd ever heard of that tree unless he is searching for a clue?"

"So, you think he's out on our farm looking for clues?"

"I can't guarantee it, but I wouldn't be surprised."

Billy Ray scratched his head. "There were two clues in that box and the second one said something about a vase. So that must mean he found the vase and there might have been a clue inside that told him to look for this Wish Bone Tree."

"Exactly."

Billy frowned. "So if he can't find this tree, then he either doesn't have a map or he has a different one and he needs the Wish Bone Tree in order to get to the next clue."

Jesse patted Billy on the knee. "You are one smart boy, you know that?"

Billy pulled himself up straight on the buckboard and gazed off. "He's stuck."

"He's stuck all right."

"You should go out there some night when you know he's back at his house sleeping and see if you can see where he's dug so far."

Jesse's mouth gaped as he studied the young man's lightly freckled face. "Did you just read my mind?"

Billy smirked. "Maybe. I'm smart like that."

They rode the rest of the way into town, Billy Ray asking more questions about the supposed treasure, and Jesse's mind spinning with questions of his own.

⌣

Anna sat on a bench in front of Henry's Hardware keeping an eye out for Billy Ray and Jesse, Rex sitting next to her on the wooden walkway, his ears and eyes alert as folks rode their horses past or maneuvered their buggies up the street, most likely heading in the direction of their homes. She was anxious to tell Jesse about the plate Florence had shown her that morning and then the remaining matching ones they'd found in the backyard shed. Before Blackthorn arrived home that day, she had carefully tucked the dish into the satchel that she always carried back and forth to work. It held her essentials, such as yarn and needles should she have a moment to sit and work on the sweater she was making for Billy Ray for colder weather, the book she'd borrowed from Blackthorn's library, *The House of the Seven Gables* by Nathanial Hawthorn, and any leftover food from the supper she'd prepared for Blackthorn that day. She carefully watched the traffic, making sure that he wasn't about. However, she didn't worry much about seeing him because when he'd arrived home that day, he quickly ate his supper then retreated to his upstairs bedroom, telling her to leave two lamps glowing downstairs on the chance that he didn't awaken before dark. He had eaten little and was as filthy as a pig when he went upstairs, so she didn't expect him to have a reason to ride into town.

The church bell chimed the sixth hour when she spotted Jesse's wagon coming down Broadway, Billy Ray sitting high on the seat next to Jesse looking proud as a prince. It pleased her the way Jesse took such a keen interest in Billy, giving him a purpose and something to look forward to throughout the week. Most nights before bed, Billy nearly talked her ear off after Jesse left, telling all about his day's adventures, whether out in the fields working side-by-side with the others or doing assigned barn chores. When Jesse gave them permission, the boys all set off for the creek to fish or swim—or swing from that dangerous rope swing she'd heard so much about. She had told Jesse she didn't think the swing sounded safe, but he only grinned and said if it could hold him, it would surely hold the children. "You have swung from it?" she'd asked.

"I sure have. Had to test it before allowing my nieces and nephews to ride it," he said with a wink. "Do you want to try it?"

"Certainly not!" But even as she'd given him her curt reply, she thought about the excitement of taking such a risk. She'd never been much for gambling with the odds. Goodness, she'd barely even taken time out of her busy life for any sort of fun. Even when Papa had been living, their days were mostly filled with work and little play. Looking back, she regretted she hadn't done a better job of fulfilling Billy Ray's need for childhood fun and games.

As the wagon grew nearer, she rose from the bench and put on a smile. Rex dutifully stayed close to her side and gave a little bark at his first sight of Billy Ray, his fluffy tail wagging with excitement. Just how to broach the subject of the plate that Florence had given to her hadn't quite formed in her mind, but she would definitely tell him. The very thought that Blackthorn might've had something to do with her father's death put a terrible lump in her chest. How could she face him tomorrow and in the days to come knowing she carried these secret thoughts? She needed God's strength and wisdom, and that was a fact.

Jesse parked his rig and jumped down, then Billy Ray did likewise. Normally, he would park in the alley, but perhaps he didn't plan to stay as long tonight, although she hoped that wasn't the case. Her feelings for him had grown, yet it was hard to admit that to herself. Whether it could be the start of love, she had no idea. How was one even to know such things?

"Hi, Sis! We're home!"

She laughed. "I see that! Shall we go upstairs?"

"We got somethin' to show you," Billy said.

"Is that so?" She wondered if he'd found a pretty rock in the creek or perhaps even made something.

Jesse turned around and scooped up something from under the wagon seat. It was some sort of box. "What's that?" she asked.

"You'll see in a minute. It's a nice night," said Jesse. "It shouldn't be too hot if we go up to your apartment."

"All right then."

They climbed the stairs, Billy leading the way and Rex taking up the rear, as if it were his job to ensure everyone made it safely to the landing.

Once inside the small upstairs quarters, Billy Ray sprawled out on Anna's bed, and Jesse and Anna both sat in Papa's rocking chairs. Jesse held the strange brown box with particular care, as if its contents were irreplaceable. A curious level of excitement built inside her as did her desire to show Jesse the plate she'd lain on top of the chest of drawers under her Nathanial Hawthorn book.

"Open it, Jesse," Billy said.

Jesse lifted the hinged lid, and when Anna couldn't see inside it, she found herself stretching across the distance between them and craning her neck. "What is it?"

He withdrew a few pieces of paper along with a key.

"These are clues leading to some sort of treasure that may or may not be authentic. I guess we will never know for sure—unless someone finds the actual treasure. It is supposedly buried on your farm."

"What in the world?" She felt her jaw drop.

"Do you have any recollection of your father mentioning anything about a buried treasure?"

"Not that I recall…except…" She paused a moment to think hard, calling up a strange memory of a conversation she'd once overheard between her father and grandfather. "There was one time I remember Grandfather talking to Papa about a stagecoach robbery and some of the loot buried in a box. Grandfather and Papa argued a bit, which was so unlike them, but when I entered the room, the topic quickly changed directions. But that reminds me of something else." Her brow wrinkled with thought as even more memories flitted around in her head.

"What is it?"

"Several weeks ago, when I was thumbing through our family Bible, I came upon a newspaper article about a stagecoach robbery. I didn't read the article in full, just sort of skimmed through it. I have no idea why or how it landed in the family Bible, but there it was."

"Is this family Bible here or back at my place in one of the storage crates?"

Anna jumped up, went down on her knees, and reached under her cot to pull out the big book that she'd wrapped in a large piece of cloth for safekeeping. "It's right here."

Billy Ray quickly sat up. "This is gettin' interestin', Sis. How come you never told me about that newspaper article?"

"I didn't think it was important, and I still don't know if it is. Maybe we'll let Jesse decide." She sat back down and set the large Bible on her lap, then started to turn the pages, looking for the article she'd rather haphazardly placed inside. This time, it was Jesse who hovered close, his breath on her cheek as he waited for her eyes to land on the article. When at last she found it, she handed it over to him, and he quickly set to reading it. Within seconds, Billy leaped off the bed and went to stand behind Jesse to look over his shoulder and silently read along. Since Anna had already skimmed it, she slowly rocked and waited for Jesse's reaction.

When he finished, he gave her a quizzical look. "This doesn't shed any light on a possible hidden treasure anywhere on your farm, but it does say authorities recovered most of the stolen goods."

"*Most*," said Billy Ray. "That means they couldn't find it all." He looked off. "What if…" He let the sentence hang there between them.

"Yes, *what if* is right," Jesse said.

Billy Ray returned to Anna's cot and sat on the edge of it, his face a picture of intrigue.

"There is something else," Anna said.

"What?" Jesse and Billy Ray asked in unison.

She stood and walked to the bureau, then lifted the book and retrieved the plate. Turning, she held it up for Jesse's eyes, knowing Billy looked on.

Jesse gave her a blank stare. "It's a plate."

"Yes," she said.

"Where did you get that?" asked Billy Ray.

"Florence Hardy, the woman who used to work for Blackthorn, stopped by today to drop it off."

"Yes?" Jesse's questioning tone told her he had not yet made sense of what she was trying to explain. "She had one of his dishes?"

"She did indeed."

She stared at Jesse, tilting her face at him and waiting for realization to strike, but it didn't. While she didn't really wish to drag Billy Ray in on the whole sordid story, she made up her mind right then that it would be impossible to keep it from him any longer. "This is the exact same pattern that was on the plate that was found in our cornfield the evening I found Papa on the floor in the barn."

Jesse jolted. "What? That's Blackthorn's dish?" He leaped up from the chair and took the plate from her to give it a close perusal. "You never noticed these dishes at his house before?"

"No—because he packed them all up in crates and stuck them in the back of his shed. Florence told me he replaced all his dishes sometime in mid-April."

"All right, that settles it. We have to go to the sheriff."

"I know. That's already occurred to me."

Billy Ray's eyes went wide, the afternoon sun glancing off them so that they sparkled with confusion. "The sheriff? Why? What's so important about that plate? What's going on?"

Jesse and Anna exchanged looks, then Jesse placed a hand on Billy Ray's shoulder. "You know how I was telling you earlier how mature I think you are?"

"Yeah."

"Well, we're about to tell you something that you'll have to keep entirely to yourself. You cannot speak a word about it to anyone, not even my nephews."

Billy Ray pulled his shoulders back so that his spine went as straight as a pine. "You can trust me."

"I believe I can," said Jesse. "Here's the short of it, and then your sister and I will fill you in on the rest of the details." He sucked in a deep breath before continuing. "There is a strong possibility Horace Blackthorn murdered your papa."

32

That bratty brother of yours go back to the Fuller farm again today?" Horace asked Anna at the breakfast table. "Seems like he's been goin' there a lot lately."

Anna set his plate of eggs, toast, ham, and fried potatoes in front of him then stood next to him. "Yes, Jesse Fuller has hired him for the remainder of the summer. Is there anything else I can get you?"

He forked up a big helping of potatoes. "Fuller hired him, eh?" he asked before stuffing the forkful of food into his mouth. "You been keepin' y'r distance from Fuller like I told you to?" He chewed and swallowed.

She hemmed a bit. "We are just friends."

"You didn't answer my question, girlie. You ain't been spewing tales to him about me, have you?"

"I haven't told him any tales, no."

"Seems like you're evading my question. You haven't told him anything about how I'm gonna hurt your brother if you blab, have you?"

"I have not told him anything I was not supposed to tell him, Mr. Blackthorn, so stop worrying."

Without forethought, he reached up and grabbed hold of her wrist. He squeezed until she winced. "You best not, or you can kiss that little brother of yours goodbye. You think I'm fooling with you?"

"Stop, you're hurting me."

Quick as lightning, her mutt of a dog came out of nowhere and snagged Horace's arm between its razor-like teeth, its strong jaws gripping firm. Fear like he'd not known since he'd been bitten as a child came out of him in the form of a howl. "Get him off me!" He shrieked like one trapped in a grave. In that instant, he lost all sense of bravery as terror took a front seat, and all he could think about was getting this monster off him.

"Rex, get off," Anna commanded.

The dog didn't readily obey. Instead, its growl intensified, and Horace trembled like a frightened baby.

"Rex, get off him!" she repeated.

Horace let go of Anna's wrist and she stepped back, pulling the dog by the scruff of its neck.

At last, the dog released its hold, but its low growl stuck deep in its throat. The creature's eyes pierced Horace's like daggers as it stood like a trained soldier at Anna's side.

That's when the pain in his arm took hold, and when he looked down, a splotch of red penetrated his sleeve.

"Oh, dear, he drew blood. Wait there, I'll get some strips of cloth to bandage it up."

She left the room, but rather than follow her, the monster stayed put, apparently assuming its duty as guard over him. Horace lifted his upper lip at the mutt, wanting in that moment to kill the thing, but knowing he dared not move. In fact, he said not a word, fearing the dog would advance on him again. He wanted to look at his bite wound, but that would mean moving, so like a tin soldier, he sat still and waited, hating his spinelessness about as much as he despised the dog. Flashbacks of his childhood when that large black dog had knocked him over in the street and started mauling him played in his head, and new shudders of fear rushed over him, causing beads of sweat to form on his forehead. Fortunately, someone had come along and shot the dog attacking him, which was exactly what he wanted to do to this crazy canine just as soon as the opportunity presented itself.

Anna returned none too soon. "I'm sorry about that, Mr. Blackthorn, but you should not have grabbed my wrist as you did. Rex is very protective of me."

"I'll kill him, I swear," he muttered under his breath.

"Don't say such a thing."

"I don't want to see that mutt in my house again, you understand? Or at least keep him tied outside while I'm here."

"As long as you don't touch me, Rex will treat you with utmost respect. He doesn't trust you because of what you did to him back at the farm."

"Yeah, well, I should have killed him then."

"Roll up your sleeve," she ordered, ignoring his comment. With his free arm, he did as told. Fortunately, the bleeding had started to let up.

"Look, he didn't even bite down all that hard. It was more a warning bite than anything."

Horace felt like an utter fool for the way he'd carried on in front of her, and now more than ever, he wanted the beast out of his house and life forever.

"This bite hadn't better interfere with my digging today."

She paused a bit in wrapping the bandage. "What are you digging?"

"A hole. Not that it's any of your business."

"On my farm?"

"It ain't your farm, girlie."

"I know that. Are you digging a foundation for a new structure?"

"No, I'm digging a grave for that mutt right there." He nodded at the dog, which had yet to lift its vicious gaze from him.

"Don't say such things. Rex will leave you alone as long as you don't pose a threat to me."

"I'll pose a threat to him if he ever comes near me again. I don't want you ever bringing that long-snout brute back here, understand?"

She finished wrapping the bandage, then tied it off. He sat up a little straighter and unrolled his sleeve so that it dropped over the bandage. She put both hands to her waist, elbows extended. "I won't come to work without him, but you needn't fear him as long as you mind your manners."

"Pfff. I'll fire you then—and you'll be without a job and a place to stay."

"And you'll be without a hot breakfast and a tasty supper and a clean house and a—"

"Yeah, yeah, blah, blah… Just keep that dog out of my face. I swear, next time he—"

"There won't be a next time, Mr. Blackthorn—as long as you…"

"Mind my manners. I heard you the first time."

"About that hole you're digging…"

"I ain't talking to you about no stinkin' hole. I shouldn't have mentioned it in the first place, and wouldn't have if your ding-blasted dog hadn't bitten me. Now leave me be so I can finish my breakfast and be out o' here. I got work to do."

"You mean a hole to dig."

He sneered at her. "Get."

She turned on her heel, and her dog followed on her heels. At the door to the kitchen, she turned. "You ever figure out where that Wish Bone Tree was you asked about?"

He paused with his forkful of food midway to his mouth. "Yeah, yeah, I found it. Finally."

"Where was it?"

"At the south end of the property. Why do you ask?"

She shrugged. "Same reason you asked me if I ever heard of it, I s'pose. Why is it called a Wish Bone Tree, and why did you need to find it?"

"Stop askin' me questions," he told her, although keeping his voice down lest her hairy brute come after him again. "Now, get on with you. Like I said, I got work to do—and so do you. See to it you complete my list of chores."

She sniffed. "I always do."

"You better." He waved his wrist at her, shooing her out.

She left without another word.

⌒

"So you went to the sheriff, did you?" Jack asked after taking a bite out of his apple, one of the items Cristina had packed in his lunch. The brothers sat perched on the wagon bed partaking of their noon meals, consisting of fried chicken, thick slices of bread, apples, and whatever else the women had thought to pack. Laura always made a decent meal for Jesse, and his brothers often compared their packed lunches to his so they could ramble on about her spoiling him. Jesse took it in stride, and if there was anything left over, he shared.

It was threshing season, one of the busiest times of the year. In years past, Jesse had considered it his favorite, but this year, his mind was too cluttered with more pressing concerns, such as Anna and Billy Ray's safety. "Yeah, I think there'll be an arrest within a few days. Sheriff said he has to gather a bit more dirt on Blackthorn, although if you ask me, he's got plenty of evidence."

"Enough to stand up in court?" asked Joey.

Jesse shrugged. "What more does he need? He's got motive for murder. I told you I combed the land two nights ago after midnight and found two areas where Horace has been digging, one already covered back up, and the other partially dug at the south end of the property, out where those woods take over."

"So it's true he wanted the land for that supposed treasure," said Joey.

"It's absolutely true. And it's my belief he'd do anything to get it—even if it meant killing Newell."

Both his brothers shook their heads.

"It's a crying shame, Newell dying over that blasted man's greed," Jack said. "It's no wonder the Bible warns us about the dangers of greed in the book of First Timothy when it talks about the love of money being the root of all evil. Money can do terrible things to people. I'd like to get my hands on Horace, much as I know vengeance belongs to the Lord—and the law. He'll get his comeuppance."

"He better," said Jesse. "As far as I know, he's got enough on him to warrant an arrest, but I'm not the law, and I don't know what all is required before Sheriff Berry can make the arrest. He refused to go into much detail, but he did slip up and give me a few bits of pertinent information, something about Horace buying arsenic at Colbert's Apothecary back in April and also mentioning that he's caught him in more than one lie. 'Course, Anna and I took him an exact replica of the very plate his deputy had found out in Newell's field the day of the murder. If there was arsenic in whatever he served up on that plate, that would explain Newell's demise. I'm sure the sheriff knows more than he shared with me, but that's fine. I'll let him do his job as long as it doesn't drag on much longer. I don't like the fact that Anna's still working for that old coot."

Jack nodded. "Yeah, seems a bit dangerous—if he's a suspect in her father's murder. What's to say he won't do something stupid if he finds out she went to the sheriff?"

A knot twisted in Jesse's gut at his brother's mere words. "He won't find out, but I understand your worry. It's the only thing I can think about. I suggested that she quit working for him, but Anna's concerned if she suddenly quits, Horace'll grow suspicious. If he thinks the law is onto him, he might skip town."

"Or do her harm," Joey said. "You ever think about bringing up the matter of marriage with her again? I know the land is no longer available, but seems to me marrying her would get her out of that situation she's in with Blackthorn."

"She's too used to her independence, and she'd accuse me of just trying to be charitable."

"Then tell her you're in love with her, little brother."

Jesse gave a sudden jerk of his head and looked Joey square on. "What?"

Jack laughed, drawing Jesse's gaze away from Joey. "What's so funny?"

"You!" they said in unison.

"You don't even realize it, do you?" Jack asked, a big grin on his face.

"Realize what?"

"Give up the argument, Jesse Fuller. You're in love with Anna Hansen."

"I—am?" He sat there, stunned for a moment, while he allowed the truth to settle in. A tiny grin formed around the edges of his mouth. "I guess—I might be—a little."

"A little?" asked Jack. "We see it in your eyes, brother. That twinkle has been there for some time now."

"Do you think I've given it enough time?"

"You've known her all your life," Jack said. "You just didn't start viewing her in a romantic sense until recently. Take it from me, it doesn't take that long to fall in love when it's the right woman."

Jesse wiped the sweat from his brow with a cloth napkin, stuffed it into his wooden lunch box, and clamped the lid down. "I couldn't ask her to marry me. We don't even have a place to live."

"What are you talking about? Ma would welcome her with wide open arms. It's threshing season, remember? Everyone's extra busy, including the women. Ma would appreciate an extra pair of hands when it comes to putting up vegetables, cleaning out the lean-to, and drying the meat, not to mention preparing meals for all the extra hands.

Jesse gave his head several fast shakes, as if to rid his mind of all the crazy thoughts racing around. Was it possible? Had he truly fallen in love? What would she say if he told her? Perhaps he'd let the notion settle in his own head before he expressed it aloud. Yes, that's what he'd do. The last thing he wanted was to scare her off, especially now that times were so critical with Blackthorn.

"Well, what do you think? Are you going to ask her, or do you want me to do it for you?" Jack asked.

"What?" Jesse screeched.

Both brothers laughed. Next thing Jesse knew, things started flying between them—straw, sticks, an apple core, the heel of a loaf of bread, an empty tin cup, a balled up napkin, and even a plate or two. For the briefest moment, it almost felt like everything was right with the world, and they were mere boys again.

33

Anna sat on the cool wooden floor, her long nightgown covering her crossed bare legs, her toes peeking out under the hem. Billy was asleep in the other room, and two overhead oil lamps shed sufficient light to allow for reading the paperwork she'd decided to wade through now that she had some spare time and wasn't quite as tired as she was on some nights. Her hair hung down her back, but wisps of it sometimes fell off past her shoulders, so she had to keep flicking it back. Tonight, Jesse hadn't overstayed his visit, which perhaps led to her wide-awake state. He'd certainly acted like he'd had things to say, and she'd secretly wanted him to stay longer. Lately, she'd grown used to his presence, and she couldn't tell what to do with her feelings. Oh, feathers! She would just let them sit there unattended and see how long it took them to grow—if indeed they did.

Newell Hansen had organized his papers in a neat fashion inside a large oak box with a hinged lid. Old bills were stacked in one large, handmade envelope, paid ones and unpaid ones separated by a tab. Another envelope held neatly folded old letters from Grandfather Charles that dated back to when he'd first moved to Tennessee after his back injury. Yet another envelope contained a set of papers featuring notations scribbled in ink in the columns. Anna wondered if she even felt like wading through all of the paperwork right now, so deep was the pile. And that was only one box. Oh, she'd already skimmed through some of the farm papers after her father's passing, hoping to find an indication of some hidden money somewhere that would save the farm. Eventually, she'd rendered that a useless hunt and put the boxes away for another day. Perhaps now was as good a day as any for taking up the task again. It wasn't like she had anything else to do, except sleep, since she'd finished Hawthorn's book. Besides reading her beloved Bible, it seemed that Blackthorn's library was the only thing that gave her something to do to pass the time.

She'd finished the woolen sweater she'd knitted for Billy Ray, but this heat did not encourage handling yarn and made wearing a warm sweater seem a far-off necessity. Actually, living in this tiny two-bedroom dwelling did not allow for much indoor activity. If she were back at the farm, she'd be tending her garden, hanging out the clothes, putting up vegetables, hanging out flowers for drying, polishing her father's cherished set of tin cups till they shone, and baking bread. She did a lot of that for Blackthorn, but it wasn't the same carrying out those chores in someone else's house. In the other room, Rex gave a whimpering snore that made her smile. Lately, he'd taken to jumping on the bed and curling up around Billy Ray's feet. As long as her brother didn't object, neither did she. Imagine Blackthorn expecting her to keep Rex locked up in this dreadful two-room dwelling! Why, he'd melt. If the man would simply mind his manners, Rex would leave the beast alone. Out the open window, she heard some downtown disturbance, saloon patrons no doubt, and with the off-key piano music to match. She gave a long, slow sigh and went back to the task at hand, knowing that two more oak boxes lay under her bed along with the big family Bible.

She'd skimmed over several of Grandfather Charles's old letters, and finding nothing of great interest in them, refolded them for packing. She'd missed one though, so she picked it up and set to reading. In it, he talked about the Tennessee weather, how he hoped the farm was doing well, how much he missed his grandchildren, and how he'd longed to see them once more—if even for a short time. "*Seeing you again put an awful longing in my heart to see those youngsters. Perhaps next time you come, you can bring them along,*" he'd written in a rather shaky hand. She paused in her reading, wishing he'd written a date at the top but guessing it had to be shortly before his passing. He spoke a bit about his back pain and a few other aches, but passed over them quickly, talking instead about his dear departed brother Bill, whom he missed, and then mentioning Bill's son, Orville, with whom he'd been living after Uncle Bill's passing. After a bit more rambling, he signed off, but then left a lengthy postscript. It read:

> *It wouldn't hurt for you to look for that treasure on your land— long as you think it's safe. I know Horace Blackthorn is eager to get his hands on it, but don't let that happen. My father bought that land fair and square from Herbert, and don't let Horace make you think otherwise. How much of a treasure is actually there remains a mystery since it happened so long ago. I first learnt about it from my Grandfather Edward shortly after news spread about a robbery Nolan Blackthorn took part in. I was a mere boy, though, so the details didn't stick with me. I knew these men spent some time on the run before authorities finally caught up with them, so there would've been time to bury some of the loot. Once caught though, those fellows never saw the light of day again. Rumor has it that old Nolan wrote a letter to his son Herbert informing him he'd buried a box of jewels on Blackthorn land. Tales even flew that he'd dug several holes and strewn various clues throughout the property—just to make a game of it.*
>
> *Anyway, I should think after all this time, the law would have an awful time trying to figure out where the stolen goods came from in the first place. There were some reports it may have been passed from one stagecoach to another, so tracking down original ownership would be impossible, especially since so much time has passed. I mostly never pursued it because Wilbur and I were such good friends, and we didn't want anything coming between us, least of all*

that blasted treasure. I know I told you to let it go as well, but you don't owe Horace anything. Perhaps there'd be enough in there to help out your youngsters. If for no one's sake but Billy's and Anna's, you might consider trying to locate it. Obviously, don't let Horace find out, or there'll be lawsuits aplenty. Wilbur once told me Horace would do anything to get that land—might even resort to killing. If the risk is too much, then best leave that box of jewels right there in the ground.

    My best to you, Son, and never forget that God is your true source of riches, your only treasure truly worth seeking.

Father

Anna reread the letter, then skimmed over additional parts until she was satisfied she'd grasped the full of it. Oh, my! Why had Papa never told her about the treasure? Did he intend to keep it a secret for the remainder of their lives? A part of her resented him for it, yet another understood why he'd done it. He didn't want any part of greed in his family, nor did he wish for any animosity or ill will among his neighbors. Surely, had he started digging for said treasure, Horace would have found out and there'd have been blood to pay. As it was, Papa had shed blood for the sake of it, and it broke her heart to think of it. His life in exchange for what? A treasure that no one had even found yet—and perhaps never would? If ever she'd been convinced that Horace Blackthorn had murdered her father, it was now. She just knew it. Even Grandfather Charles recognized him for the murderous scoundrel he was, and now all she wanted to do was go wring that fellow's thick neck. Perhaps it wasn't very Christian of her to carry such hateful thoughts toward Blackthorn, especially since he hadn't yet been proven guilty in a court of law, hadn't even been arrested, but neither could she continue giving him the benefit of the doubt.

Oh, Lord, how can I continue working for that disgusting man, knowing that he murdered Papa? Is there enough love in the world for me to find forgiveness in my heart?

⌒

"What's y' diggin' there, Horace? You look hard at work."

Horace startled at the sound. He looked up from the hole he was standing in only to find that blasted Sheriff Berry and his deputy sitting atop their horses and staring down at him. Since he'd nailed the "No Trespassing" sign to a tree at the beginning of the driveway, no one had bothered him, but he didn't know how appropriate, or even legal, it was to tell the sheriff to get off his land. He would have liked to throw a curse word or two at Berry and send him packing. With reluctance, he ceased work, jammed the tip of the shovel into the dirt, and leaned on the old rusty handle. "What can I do for you, Sheriff?" he asked, putting on the pretense of pleasantries. "Sure is a hot day to be out and about."

"Ain't it though? I should think you'd find something less laborious yourself. Good Gussie, you tryin' to reach China?" Of course, as usual, the sheriff laughed at his own wit. Darned fool!

Horace laughed too, although not out of good cheer. "Well, I suppose it would appear that way. I'm—uh—I'm looking to put in a well back here."

"Clear at the south end of your property? Why'd you want to put one way out here for?"

"Well, I'm thinkin' about future grazing land and my need for a water line back here."

"Don't you have a creek out there behind them trees? Seems like you could draw water from that."

"Well, now that's a fine idea, but I'm thinking I'll need a well for future purposes, you know, in case I expand."

"Expand, eh? Aren't you surrounded by Fuller land on all sides?"

Horace had no idea what in tarnation was happening here, other than the sheriff was trying to corner him. "I'm hoping to talk them into selling off some of their parcels. At any rate, I'm sure you didn't come out here to watch me dig—or to discuss my neighbors."

"No, actually I didn't." Berry scratched his temple and squinted at the sun. "Well, I did and I didn't." There he went hemming and hawing again, fiddling with his crazy mustache. The man drove Horace clear to the nutty barn and back. "You know we had that nice little visit some time ago back at your place. My deputy and I dropped in on you."

"Yes, I recall."

"Well, since then, I got a few more questions."

"About what?"

"Well, namely, that plate you said you hadn't never seen before."

"What plate is that?"

"Oh, I didn't bring it with me, but that plate we found."

Horace nodded. "You mean that dish you found in Hansen's cornfield?"

"Yes, that's the one."

"I recall it, but why bring it up to me again?"

"Well, I got a wee bit of a problem, Horace."

"Oh? Something I can help you with?" Irritation danced up and down his nerves. Why did he feel like Berry was toying with him?

"It's probably nothing, you see, but I recently learned that you got a whole new set of dishes. Heard tell you picked them up at Weaver's General Store. I inquired the other day. I asked Gus Weaver if he kept any records of purchases, and what do you know? He does. Ain't that a coincidence? That's good recordkeeping there. Anyway, do you happen to remember when you bought them new dishes?"

"I can't say that I do, Sheriff, but I'm sure you'll tell me."

"Well, let's see. I wrote it down right here." Still mounted, Berry reached behind, flipped open his saddlebag, and withdrew a leather notebook. He opened it and turned to a page. "Yes, yes, here it is. You bought them dishes on April 15, same day Mr. Lincoln passed away, God rest his soul."

Horace nervously shifted his weight. "Okay, why should the date I purchased those dishes matter to you? I wanted new ones, so I went to Weaver's and bought some. Is there a law against that?"

The sheriff laughed, removed his hat, and ran his hand through his dark brown hair, which seemed to go every which way, just like his crazy mustache. Then he plopped the hat back in place. "O' course, it's all right. It's just, well, your timing is a little odd, that's all."

"How so?"

"Well, it was also just two days after Newell Hansen passed away."

"And what is your point, Sheriff? Or wasn't there a point to this line of reasoning?"

"Oh, yes, I'm gettin' to that. Do you happen to remember why you wanted new dishes in the first place, Horace?"

Horace wiped his dripping brow while fishing for the right answer. "I believe I simply wanted a new pattern."

"Hm, I see. You didn't want to replace them because they matched the one my deputy found on Hansen land?"

"'Course not. That's ridiculous."

"Well, why did you buy a new set then? Were the old ones broken— or scratched up—or might you have just been tired of them?"

"I believe I was just tired of them."

"Oh, hm." The sheriff scratched behind his ear. "That's odd. You told Mr. Weaver several pieces had broken. Now, why would you tell him *that* if they were in perfectly good shape?"

"I don't know. I suppose there were some broken dishes in the lot. I don't recall exactly. I still don't know where you're going with this, Sheriff. Would you mind filling me in—and making it quick since I have work to do?"

"Yes, yes, you have a well to dig, don't you." He gave Horace's hole a disparaging glance. "I'm sure you wouldn't mind if I took a look at those dishes now, would you?"

"My dishes? You already did take a look at them."

"No, no, I mean the former ones, the ones you replaced."

A knot turned over in Horace's gut. "I got no idea what I did with them. Good grief, I may have tossed them."

"Is that right? You didn't put them in storage—a nice set of dishes like that—given to you by a long lost great-aunt and shipped to you from England?"

Horace gave a little jolt, and his head started spinning with all manner of confusion. "Who told you that?"

Sheriff Berry flicked his wrist. "Oh, it ain't important who told me, only that you let me have a look at them. I mean, if you got nothin' to hide, then what's the problem?"

"There's no problem," he lied. "It's just that you'll have to wait till tomorrow."

"Tomorrow?" The sheriff and his deputy exchanged looks. "I guess that should be fine. I'm sure your old dishes won't be a match to that one we found anyway, right? It was just a silly notion on my part. You know, we law enforcement folk have to make sure we don't forget any important details."

"That's understandable."

"Well, then, I s'pose we'll come a'knockin' at your door first thing in the mornin'. How's seven-thirty?"

"That should be fine. My housekeeper will let you in. I'll have to go in search of those dishes, mind you. I don't rightly recall where I put them."

"We won't mind waitin'. Perchance we'll sit and enjoy a cup of coffee while we wait."

"Sure thing."

"Well, we thank you for your time, Horace. I hope we didn't waste too much of it."

"It's no inconvenience," he answered, taking up his shovel again.

The deputy turned his horse around first, but the sheriff hesitated. "You know, there is just one minor thing that bothers me."

Horace gave an audible sigh. "What is it, Sheriff?" He couldn't help the annoyance in his voice.

His deputy paused to allow Berry to continue. "Well, like I said, it's probably minor, but it concerns something you said when we first got here today."

Another sigh slipped out. "What did I say?"

"Well, when I first mentioned that dish we found, you said, 'You mean that dish you found in Hansen's cornfield?' You see, I never did tell you we found a dish in the cornfield. I simply told you we found a dish by a stump. Funny thing. How would you know there was a stump in Hansen's cornfield?"

Horace scratched his eyebrow and sniffed, trying to put on a nonchalant air. "I'm sure you told me you found that dish in a cornfield that first time you came to my house—or on any number of other visits you paid me over the past few months."

Berry shook his head. "Nope. Nope. I would've remembered a detail of that nature." He turned to his deputy. "Isn't that right, Tom?"

Deputy Lawford nodded. "That's absolutely correct, Sheriff Berry. No one puts much past you."

Berry whistled through his teeth and shook his head, then grinned. "Ain't that the truth?"

Horace held his breath for a full five-second count, waiting for what he thought was the inevitable—an arrest.

Instead, Berry tipped his hat at him. "Well, we'll see you first thing in the mornin', Horace. You have yourself a good night's rest now. Don't go diggin' to China, ya hear?" Of course, he laughed at his own joke again. The man was so irritating!

Horace could feel sweat drops beading up on every inch of his body as he watched the two turn their steeds around and ride off. What had just happened? If he could devote the next one hundred years to studying the many quirks of Sheriff Berry, it wouldn't be enough. He'd thought surely he was a goner, but apparently not. Either Berry was the cleverest sheriff this side of the state line—or the dumbest. There was no in between with that peculiar fellow. Oh, well, didn't matter. He had one thing on his mind right now, and that was getting back home and getting rid of those stupid dishes he'd stored at the back of his shed. He would haul them out of town and dump them into some deserted ditch somewhere where no wagons ever traversed. And he would instruct Anna to leave his supper on the table and go home. He didn't need her hanging around asking a bunch of questions.

He climbed out of the hole he'd dug and brushed off his filthy pants. Time to forget about that hidden treasure for now. At the moment, he had more pressing matters on his mind.

34

Anna had just put Blackthorn's supper on the table when he entered through the front door and gave it a little slam. Rex leaped up from his station on the floor nearby and started for the door. "Stay away from me, you mutt," were the man's first uttered words.

"Rex! Leave Mr. Blackthorn alone." Blackthorn eyed the dog with care, his body backed up firmly against the door until Rex returned to Anna's side. "You're just in time for your supper," she said. "You should sit down and eat it while it's hot."

"And you and your dog should head on out of here. I don't wish to talk to anybody."

"I don't especially wish to talk to you either, but I have a few things I need to finish doing."

"Such as?"

"Some items remaining on the list."

"You had all day!" he said in a booming voice. Rex sat at careful attention, noting the man's every move.

"Keep your voice down. You go eat and leave me to finish my chores. I'll try to stay out of your hair."

"Yeah, yeah, you see to it."

She really wished she could tell the ornery old snort *he* was the one who'd soon be out of *her* hair, but some things were best left unsaid, particularly when it involved a surprise element. Jesse and Sheriff Berry had stopped by earlier—while Blackthorn was out at the farm—to tell her an arrest was soon to come, perhaps as early as tonight or tomorrow, after the sheriff had settled a few more things. All day, she had hung her hopes on those words.

Blackthorn gave an angry huff and walked to the dining room, then pulled back a chair and sat. "Bring me my bottle of brew." He thumbed at the cabinet only a short distance behind him. He could easily have reached it himself, but, no, he wanted her to fetch it. She hefted a big breath of her own, but thinking it best to appease him, did his bidding. He held up his glass. "Pour." She obeyed. He gulped down the stinking stuff then held up his empty glass to her. "More." His breath reeked, but she poured. He took a few more sips then set it down with a clunk and took up his fork, scooping up his first mouthful. He chewed and swallowed without another word.

He was about as dirty as she'd ever seen him and she figured he'd spent another long day digging for that third clue. It was strange to realize that she was finally onto him. She moved away from him, but kept a vigilant eye on him as she picked up the dusting cloth she'd lain on the bureau, then left him behind to finish her dusting chore in the library, Rex following at her heels.

From a coffee table, she picked up the book she'd returned that morning, Nathanial Hawthorn's *The House of the Seven Gables*, and slipped it into the same spot from which she'd taken it some ten or so days ago. In doing so, *The Scarlet Letter*, another of Hawthorne's books, caught her attention. Rather than standing on its side, though, this book lay flat with a gold-embossed trinket box atop it. She lifted the little trinket box, then flipped open the lid. Setting it aside, she picked up the book to thumb through it. In lifting it from its place, a few pieces of paper slid out from under it and flitted to the floor. She bent to pick them up and give them closer scrutiny. To her great surprise, they were a replica of the set of clues Jesse and Billy had shown her from the brown metal box, but these were more weathered and worn, a result of excessive handling and not as careful preservation. The map too showed signs of great wear and lacked the same detail as the one Jesse held in his possession, many of the words faded almost to the point of being indecipherable. Her heart thudded hard. If she had any doubts before, they had all but vanished now. Blackthorn had wanted her property for one purpose: to find that treasure. And he had murdered Papa in an effort to obtain it. She had never personally hated anyone before, but the feelings she carried for Horace Blackthorn came close. *Lord, help me.*

"What's you doin' in here, girlie?" came the gruff voice from behind.

She whirled at the sound. Blackthorn stood propped against the doorframe, the rifle that usually hung on two hooks over the brick fireplace now in hand, not pointed at anything in particular, just loosely held, no doubt to wield his authority. His filthy face revealed bloodshot eyes, whether from fatigue or too much booze, she didn't know. She put the papers back on the shelf and laid the book on top of them, almost glad that he'd caught her. "Nothing," she said. "Just dusting."

"Is that right? When did I tell you to dust the library?"

"You didn't, but I was putting away a book, and then taking down another one, and I noticed the dust."

"I don't recall giving you permission to take down any of my books."

Her brow furrowed. "I don't recall you ever telling me the library was off-limits."

He approached, and a growl built in Rex, starting from someplace deep. She set her hand on the flat part of his head to calm him.

"Your dog best mind his manners, or I'll blow his head off. I'm sick and tired of that rotten mongrel taking over my house, and for a change, I'm at an advantage." He held up the rifle.

"Rex, hush," she whispered, willing her own self to stay calm.

"What did you see on those papers, little girl?"

"Some clues and a map of some sort."

He narrowed his beady eyes on her and rubbed his whiskered face. "Looked like you was studyin' 'em pretty close. You got any idea what they might lead to?"

She felt unusually brave, if not slightly defiant. "Looks to be some sort of map that leads to a treasure. You should know since you put them there yourself."

"Heh, ain't you gettin' a slight bit sassy?"

He pressed a little closer, and her nerves jumped. *Lord, help me stay strong.* "The words are quite faded, so it was hard to tell."

"Humph. You ever hear of any treasure in these parts?"

"You mean on my farm? Papa never told me about any such thing if that's what you're getting at, but I presume you've been digging for additional clues seeing as you come home filthy every day. I imagine that's why you wanted my farm so badly."

He lifted his lip in a smirk. "You think you're pretty smart, don't you."

"It doesn't take a genius to figure out what you're doing, Mr. Blackthorn. It's obvious you've been operating on the sly, being evasive about what you're doing, spending all your days on my old farm."

"How do you know where I spend my days? You been spying on me?"

"Not at all, but those clues you keep hidden under that book are proof enough of what you've been doing."

"Oh yeah?" He scratched the top of his head, and she swore she saw dirt fall from his scalp. "I s'pose you and Jesse Fuller been talking about it, eh?"

"Might be."

His face went red. "You've disregarded my order to stay clear of him."

"You don't own me, Mr. Blackthorn."

"No, no, that's true, I don't, even though I've provided you with income and free housing—purely out of the goodness of my heart. I told you if you ratted on me, I'd make you pay; rather, I'd make your brother pay. I s'pose you told Fuller that as well. I'm not an idiot. I see you've purposely kept your brother clear of me, worried I'll make good on my promise."

"I don't put anything past you."

He stared her down in silence until his gaze made her squirm with discomfort. "What exactly have you told the sheriff?"

Anna narrowed her eyes and stared back at him. "What makes you think I've told him anything?"

"He's been comin' around askin' me all sorts of questions. I see the suspicion in his eyes."

She sucked in a silent breath for courage. "Mr. Blackthorn, if Sheriff Berry is coming around asking you questions, it's only because you've done something to cause suspicion. Don't try to put that on me."

He gave an ice cold, emotionless smile. "You are a feisty one, ain't y'."

She ignored his statement.

"Are you suspicious of me too?"

"I'm always suspicious of you," she said.

He tossed back his head and laughed, but it was not a pleasant chortle. Quite out of character for him, he reached up and lifted her chin. She instinctively stiffened but stayed her ground, eyes glued on him with intentness. "What exactly are you suspicious of, little miss? You think I did something to your pa?"

A chill raced up her back at his blatantly forthright question, even though he had played directly into her hand. "I am certain you did." As hard as it was, she kept her voice staid and unfeeling. "It was the only way you could be assured of getting possession of the property because you knew as long as my father had air to breathe, he would prevent you from taking over the farm."

"Humph, you are pretty smart, ain't y'. You figure that all out on your own? I ain't sayin' you're right or anything, but you're pretty conniving just the same."

"Oh, I'm right. My papa had good cause for not wanting anything to do with you. He was always careful not to say unkind things about you, but I could tell your presence made him uneasy. You should be ashamed of yourself for killing so kind a man."

He lifted his eyebrows at her and went back on his heels. "I don't know where you come off so sure of yourself."

Rex did not appreciate something in Blackthorn's tone, for he let out a snarling growl.

"Tell your dog to sit down and stay. We're stepping out of here—and away from his ugly face."

"He won't like that one bit."

"Would you rather I blow his head off right here in front of you? I'll make you clean up the mess just to remind you who's in charge here."

She shivered at his callousness. "Sit, Rex." At first, the dog resisted. "Sit," she repeated, a little more firmly this time. He obeyed.

"Good. Now back out of here slowly, little missy. Easy does it."

Out in the hall, he reached across her and pulled the heavy oak pocket door closed, then latched it. Instantly unhappy, Rex began to frantically bark and jump against the door. "He doesn't like being separated from me."

"Too bad for him. In time, he'll get used to it."

In time? That frightened her, for she didn't understand what he inferred. "He'll scratch up your door."

Blackthorn pushed her toward the kitchen. "He can scratch all he wants. I'd rather replace my door than have to replace a bloodied-up rug. It's imported, you know. Most all of my possessions are."

"Including those dishes you got from your great-aunt?"

She should have known better than to make such a barefaced statement, for with his free hand, he snagged hold of her arm and yanked her around, squeezing so hard that she felt sure he'd leave a bruise. She winced in pain.

"Who told you about those dishes?"

"No one you need to know about."

"Old Florence Hardy no doubt. That big-mouthed ninny. What else did she say?"

"Ouch. Let go of me."

Instead, he gave her a couple additional pushes down the hall to the kitchen, then while holding tight to her arm with one hand, he used his rifle arm to pull back the curtain covering the drainpipes under the sink and withdrew a wooden box containing several tools and other small items. He brought out a ball of twine and a knife, and at the sight of them, a sinking feeling settled in her gut. What exactly did he have in mind?

"Turn around and put your arms behind your back," he instructed.

The idea of being tied up didn't set well. In fact, the very notion gave her instant panic. "Why? What are you going to do?"

"Just do what I say!" he bellowed. "I told you not to go tattling to Jesse Fuller or I'd hurt your brother. Well, since your brother's not here, I'm gonna have to punish you."

"What? That's ridiculous. Haven't you already done enough damage to my family? You killed my father, you stole my farm out from under me, and you've torn my world apart."

"Shut up, you little she-weasel." He yanked her around so she faced out, set down his gun on the butcher block, and snagged hold of both her arms and dragged them painfully behind her back. Next, he took up the twine and started weaving it around her wrists, so tight that it felt as if the blood had stopped flowing. She tried to kick him, but he whipped her around after tying off her hands, and pushed her down on a kitchen chair, making her land with an awkward thud. He took up the twine again, and this time, he clasped her ankles and began fastening them together as well, binding them tight so that she had no ability to move them except to kick them upward. At one point she managed to wallop him good under the chin, to which he gave a loud curse. To her great surprise, he did not return a punch to her jaw. In the other room, Rex made such a racket she was sure he would tear a hole through the door.

Once he finished tying her ankles, he fastened them to the chair leg, making her completely immobile, then at last stood up and assessed his work. "Comfortable?" he asked, taking up the rifle from the butcher block and laying it across the table in front of her. She eyed the weapon, wishing she could somehow free her hands and turn the thing on him. She convinced herself that if she could get her finger in the trigger, she wouldn't even think twice about putting a bullet through his stomach. But just as quickly as the thought occurred, she wanted to take it back because of the vile feelings it stirred, feelings quite foreign to her. She'd never personally hated anyone before.

"Now then, back to my original question. What exactly did that ol' biddy Florence Hardy tell you about those dishes?"

Anna tried to wiggle free from the scratchy twine bindings, but her movements only increased the pain. Would answering his question backfire on her? And what exactly had he meant by saying he planned to punish her? *Lord, give me wisdom. Tell me what to say to him that will lead to the best possible end.*

He sat across the table from her, eyes affixed on her.

"She returned a plate that she had once borrowed. I told her I didn't recognize the plate as belonging to you, but she told me that you used to use the pattern before you packed it away last spring and bought a new set."

"And that's all?"

"Yes...except that the sheriff—"

He leaned forward. "Out with it!"

"First, tell me why you've tied me up."

"You'll find out soon enough."

"Are you going to take me somewhere?"

He growled low in his throat. "I might. You never know, I just may need you as barter for getting out of town."

"Barter?"

"I might have to. Finish what you were saying about the sheriff."

She closed her eyes and heaved a sigh. "I know you murdered my papa because you used one of your old plates on which to deliver him some sort of food laced with arsenic. The sheriff found the plate not far from the barn and showed it to me that night, and after Florence returned that plate belonging to you, I immediately recognized it as matching the one the sheriff showed me."

"Ah, but no one can prove I still have those dishes. I'm about to dispose of them."

"You're too late."

He frowned. "What do you mean?"

"I saw them—out in the backyard shed—and so did the sheriff. Your secret is out, Mr. Blackthorn."

His face went as red as beet juice, and his bloodshot eyes shimmered with something like fear.

"You look like you need a glass of water, Mr. Blackthorn. Are you going to keel over?"

Just like that, Blackthorn rose from his chair, picked up his gun, and disappeared into the dining room. She realized after a bit of racket that he was pouring himself some more whiskey.

Oh, Lord, bring me through this awful ordeal. May it come to a peaceful ending. By the sounds of it, Rex wanted it over as well, his frantic barking and clawing at the door not slowing in the least.

35

his was wrong, all wrong. How could everything have fallen apart so quickly? He hadn't even finished digging the third hole that would lead him to the next clue, even though he knew he was close. After days of searching the property, he'd finally found the tree with the letter B carved into it, and when looking up the massive trunk, could even see why someone had nicknamed it the Wish Bone Tree. At the midway point in height, its trunk was split like a wishbone. After locating it, he'd done just what the clue had instructed, walked ten paces north and begun digging shovelfuls to reach the blown glass jar that contained the next clue. Surely, it was only a shovelful or two further. Had he really come this close only to be stopped short so suddenly? He was so furious, he could spit.

He poured his glass to the rim, gulped it down, then filled another and stood there pondering and drinking before returning to the kitchen. What to do with Anna now that he'd tied her to the chair? He'd told her he planned to use her as a decoy to get out of town, but, really, what was the point? She'd likely just slow him down. Should he just leave her there, confined to the chair, and make a run for it? At least if he did that, she couldn't run straight to the sheriff's office—or even straight back to her quarters above the hardware. In time, when she didn't return, her brother would come looking for her, but by then, he'd have skipped town. He took yet another long gulp of brew. If that blasted dog didn't shut up, one of the neighbors would soon come knocking. He cursed at himself for his lack of smarts when it came to thoroughly thinking this thing through. Now he was in a grand mess. If the sheriff truly had pinned the murder on him, he was going to prison, and how was he going to survive that? And what was to become of all his properties? Was everything he'd ever done in life for naught?

Horace headed back toward the kitchen, weaving a bit as he walked, his vision blurred and his thoughts a trifle fuzzy. The girl sat there looking helpless and distraught. It occurred to him that his life wasn't worth much more than a pile of dirt.

He sat back down and tried to gather his faculties. Why had everything gone so strangely uncertain?

"Why don't you just untie me?" Anna said.

"Shut up. You're bound for a reason. I just need to think."

"You could always consider turning yourself in."

"Shut up!"

"Things will go better for you if you do."

"And how do you figure that? I killed a man. You think they're going to go easy on me in a court of law? No, they'll either hang me for my crime or put me behind bars where I'll live out my remaining days." There. He'd at long last finally admitted it. He'd killed Newell Hansen. He fingered the trigger on his gun, wondering what it would feel like to turn the barrel on himself and let the bullet penetrate the muscle and enter his heart.

"I should hate you, you know," she said in a tone so soft, he barely heard it.

He dared to look her full on. "Yeah, well, you and everyone else."

"But I don't."

He raised his head now. She had him curious. "Yeah? Why not?"

"I can't. God won't allow it. I mean, I could just as easily defy His plan for me, but I know I couldn't live with myself. You hated my father, but I don't have to let your hate rub off onto me. Hate eventually kills a person's spirit. Just look what it's done to yours—made you an overbearing, spiteful, bitter, and friendless individual. It doesn't have to be that way though, Mr. Blackthorn. You could turn yourself over to the law, and then begin the work of turning your *life* over to the *Lord*."

"Pfff, that's nothing but a bunch of fluffy talk. I'm about as interested in listening to your lies about God as He is about looking at the likes of me."

"Oh, but He *is* interested. He created you to serve and honor Him—and to share His love with others."

"Stop talking to me about your God nonsense. It's too late for me." Without another word, he turned the rifle on himself, pointing the tip of it at his chest, tough as it was to manipulate it around.

"No! Don't do it, Mr. Blackthorn. Don't!" she screamed.

⌒

In that brief timeframe, the kitchen door slid quietly open and in stepped the sheriff, as graceful and lithe as a preying cat. Anna wanted to say, "It's about time," but of course she kept her mouth zipped shut and took care not to move, watching him with eagle eyes over Blackthorn's shoulder as he tiptoed up behind him. Earlier that day, he and his deputy had plotted their moves, even while not knowing exactly what Blackthorn's would be, but knowing they couldn't make an arrest without a full confession. Somewhere outside, Jesse lurked, though she knew not where. She only knew she wanted this whole ordeal to be behind her, but she also didn't want Horace Blackthorn to kill himself.

Quietly, with a calmness that only came from God, she said, "Put the gun down, Mr. Blackthorn. You don't even have to untie me. Just lay down the gun."

"Shut up." His voice was anything but calm. If anything, it wobbled, as did the hand that held his rifle at the ready.

Not to be frightened into silence, she continued. "You have already killed one man. Don't make it two by ending your own life. If you allow yourself to live, there'll be time to make things right with God—and before you say it's too late, let me tell you that when Jesus hung on the cross, there were two other men hanging on either side of him. One clearly rejected Him, but the other, a convicted thief, asked for forgiveness. In that very instant, Jesus said to him, *'Verily I say unto thee, Today shalt thou be with me in paradise.'* It's right in the Bible, Luke twenty-three, forty-three. Mr. Blackthorn, receiving Christ isn't something you have to fret over. Forgiveness is yours for the asking. You already have *my* forgiveness. Now all that is necessary is that you ask it of Jesus. Just like the thief on the cross, forgiveness can be yours."

Blackthorn stood there pondering...even as the sheriff moved silently and stealthily behind him. He was completely unaware that the sheriff was closing in on him. Just as he started to lower his rifle, the sheriff reached up and grabbed his wrist, causing the rifle to fall. Startled, Blackthorn tried to bolt, but just as quickly, two deputies rushed in, tackled him to the ground, and whipped him onto his stomach. One put a knee on his back and then put handcuffs on his wrists while the other shackled his ankles.

Sheriff Berry gave a sharp whistle, and Jesse flew into the room and ran to Anna. Going down on both knees, he gathered her to his chest. Only then did it occur to her that her prayers had been answered and the long ordeal was over—all praise to God. Tears rolled down her cheeks, and then the racking sobs started, sobs that took her by surprise because she hadn't realized until that very moment just how much Blackthorn had rattled her nerves. Jesse quickly untied the twine binding her wrists and feet. Once free of them, she collapsed like a sopping towel into his arms, her mind and body numb.

In the library, poor Rex's bark had started to go hoarse. A couple more deputies appeared out of nowhere. "Pl-please, go let my dog out," she said.

"Sure thing, miss," one of them said.

Soon, Rex came flying down the hall and into the kitchen, barking and whining. She put her arms around the dog's body, and the three of them, Rex, Jesse, and Anna, all huddled close like friends who'd not seen each other in decades.

～

July rolled into August and August into September. To Anna's great pleasure, a judge had ruled that the sale of her farm had been mishandled. It went back into her hands, and as previously planned, the Fuller brothers assumed the debt, but they worked out an arrangement whereby she could maintain ownership of the farmhouse and a small parcel of the surrounding land, allowing her to enjoy her farmyard and, best of all, bring her garden back to life. Thankfully, there had been adequate rains to keep most of the flowers and vegetables in healthy condition despite the overgrowth of weeds that threatened to choke them out. Rex and Billy Ray settled right back into farm life; Jesse even brought the horses, goats, chickens, and Carlotta the cow back to the barn. It appeared from all outward appearances that everything had returned to normal. In many ways, it had; yet in other ways, everything was different.

Anna obtained a job at Flossie's Tailoring Shop on Silver Street to make ends meet, working at the shop two days a week—Mondays and Wednesdays, when Billy was at the Fuller farm—and working from home the remaining days. She was so grateful to Miss Flossie for hiring her and suspected she'd done so out of the goodness of her heart. Anyone who read the *Lebanon Western Star* knew of her misfortunes, her father's murder, and then the loss of her farm. Thus, when she walked into Flossie's Tailoring Shop, the woman hired her on the spot, even accommodating her wish to work from home as much as possible. On the days she worked in town, Billy Ray stayed busy doing barn chores as well as continuing to help at the Fuller farm. She didn't want to be beholden to Jesse, but he was adamant about it not being a burden, and besides, he and his nephews enjoyed the boy's company.

Now that all the legalities of farm ownership were behind them, she found her reasons for seeing Jesse had all but ceased. Billy rode one of their horses over to the Fullers' or even walked if he felt like it, so there was no need for Jesse to give him a ride. And with their father's murder solved, they had no cause to investigate the case further or worry that Blackthorn would cause any additional trouble. That was all good, and it pleased her to know that he could never hurt anyone else. Yet at the same time, learning the truth about him and what he had done opened a wound in her that she'd formerly patched up. Now she found herself walking an all-new path of grief. At times, rivers of heartache threatened to drown her; at other times, she simply felt numb, unable even to shed a tear. In all her life, she'd never been so confused. Some days, she felt strong and capable, but on other days, she wanted to crawl into a hole and stay there forever. So when Jesse said he wanted to continue to see her, she could not bend to his wishes. Her inability to get a handle on her emotions made furthering a relationship with him impossible. At least for now.

"But I've grown accustomed to looking after you," he had said with a tiny wink.

"And I don't need looking after, especially not now," she'd countered. "The Lord looks after me just fine."

"So what you're saying is you have no need for me?"

"I didn't say that." She knew she'd hurt him.

"You're withdrawing, Anna. Can't you see it? You haven't even been coming to church."

That much was true, and she felt guilty for it, especially since her refusal to go to church affected Billy Ray. "I can't face anyone right now. They'll ask questions and I don't feel like talking."

"Not if I'm there to keep them from it. I can help you through this."

"The Lord and I will work through it."

"Pushing me and everyone else away isn't the answer, Anna. You have experienced a great loss, and it'll help you to talk about it."

"But I don't even understand what's going on inside me, so how can I explain it to you or anyone else?"

"You have to give it a try," he had said with pleading in his tone. "I'm a good listener."

She had heaved a big sigh. "At the moment, all I need from you is lots of time and space. If you could give me that, I'd appreciate it."

That is where they had left matters. She'd kept rocking on her farmhouse porch and he'd eventually ridden off, with no promise of returning and no real resolution. And that had been a month ago. Oh, she knew he was hard at work on the farm. Billy Ray kept her informed of that. It was harvesttime, after all, and everyone was working from dawn till dusk. But still, one month? She had to admit she missed him immensely, but what if they did start dating, no holds barred, and he decided she wasn't what he was looking for after all? Could she withstand another major heartbreak? And since he'd gone an entire month without attempting to see her, had he already concluded she wasn't the one he wanted?

News spread fast about Cyrus Daly's unethical banking practices, after which he voluntarily left his position as bank president, hastily sold his house, packed up his family, and left Lebanon. Whether Anna or others in the town would have had legal grounds for suing him was unclear, but if they had, no one pursued it, seeming more content that he'd merely pulled up stakes and vanished.

As for Horace Blackthorn, he sat in jail awaiting the judge's final sentencing—death by hanging or life in prison. At his attorney's suggestion, he pleaded guilty and waived his right to a trial, a great relief to Anna, for now, she would not have to appear in court to testify against him. Not that she was afraid of him, but she simply wanted nothing more to do with him other than to ask the judge to consider leniency, to keep him locked up until the end of his days. Life behind bars seemed an adequate sentence, particularly since he'd waived his right to a jury trial. Besides, she wanted him to have plenty of time to consider giving his heart to the Lord.

Before their falling out, Jesse had said they ought to talk about the buried treasure and whether to pursue digging for it, but she'd said she was too overwrought to discuss it. "Do what you want," she'd told him, but that had not satisfied him.

"It's not mine to do with as I choose," he'd said. "It belongs to you and Billy Ray."

She had merely shrugged. Clearly frustrated, he had dropped the matter.

She and Billy Ray had finally returned to church last Sunday, but to Billy Ray's dismay, they'd sat in the back row, then promptly left after the service. She had seen Jesse sitting five rows from the front with his family but didn't want to dally afterward for fear of running into him. There was too much explaining to do on her part, and she simply wasn't up for it. Besides, after a whole month of not seeing him, she had no idea what sort of thoughts even ran through his mind. Had he given up on her? It wouldn't surprise her considering their last conversation. Billy Ray had given her the silent treatment all the way home and throughout lunch. Once finished, he had vanished to the barn, and she had used that opportunity to retreat to her bedroom for a good cry. What on earth was wrong with her?

It was Friday morning. Anna had a sewing project to finish for Miss Flossie, but she would make time for some gardening before it got too hot. She grabbed a bucket out from under the sink with which to hold some fresh vegetables and headed out the door. Billy had ridden one of the horses over to Frankie Fuller's house. They were going to spend the first half of the day working in the fields and the afternoon fishing and playing ball, so she had the house and yard to herself. Even Rex had tagged along with Billy today, his loyalties somehow switching from her to the boy since returning to the farm. She'd thought more than once that perhaps her gloomy demeanor hadn't set well with the dog. Even Rex had grown weary of her!

Heaving a sigh, she trudged down the path to the garden, her seven-foot-tall sunflowers poking their faces skyward, and her tomato plants standing proud, their juicy red fruit ready for picking. When she should have taken joy in their winsome beauty, she could not muster up the emotion. *Lord, help me to appreciate the bounty You have provided, the many blessings of life—my farmhouse and garden and barn—all these good things. Help me accept that Papa's life was wrongfully taken, and that a horrid man's selfish actions caused it. May my heart and soul be lifted above these ugly circumstances so that I can set a fine Christian example for my brother. And Lord, if Jesse and I are to ever be a couple, please restore and heal me. Do whatever it takes to bring me full circle so I can feel whole again. I pray this in Thy holy name. Amen.*

36

You certainly have turned into a big ol' sourpuss," Laura told Jesse at breakfast that cool September morning.

"You sound like my brothers." They'd been commenting about his grouchy mood for weeks.

"I suspect it has everything to do with Anna Hansen's rejection of you. I'm sorry she doesn't appear interested. There must be some reason for it."

"Yeah, there is," Jesse said while pushing his eggs around on the plate. "She said she needs time and space. Away from me. That just tells me one thing. She's not attracted to me."

"Time and space could also mean just that and nothing more. She has much to process, Son."

The windows were open to the dawn, and outside, the birds' wakeful chatter was more of an annoyance to him than anything. Why should everything be going perfectly fine for them but mournfully wrong for him? He was in love with a woman who no longer showed a shred of interest in him. Here he thought he'd been making progress with her, even stealing a few kisses when she'd been living in that upstairs apartment. He was sure he'd started winning her over—even come dangerously close to expressing his love to her before running out of courage. And then at long last, Sheriff Berry made the all-important arrest of Horace Blackthorn—followed ten days later by the judge's ruling that the farm had not gone through the proper foreclosure channels and should go back into Anna Hansen's hands until such time as she came up with the proper funds for paying off the debt or another arrangement for resale could be made.

She'd been thrilled at the opportunity to move back into her farmhouse and regain the farmyard, along with the barn and what few farm animals she had, with the stipulation that the Fuller brothers would purchase the majority of the land. However, upon her moving back into her comfortable little house and Jesse's suggestion that they begin a serious courtship, she'd started backing away from him. What exactly had he done to make her turn tail? At times, he felt his very presence made her squeamish. Community Methodist Church seemed a most likely place for recapturing a level of friendship, but, alas, she'd decided to quit going, probably afraid of running into him.

"What do you think is really going on—under the surface I mean?" Laura took up her steaming coffee cup and sipped, her hazel eyes grilling him over the rim. To her credit, until this moment, she had completely respected his need for privacy concerning his relationship with Anna, but he supposed he couldn't expect her to resist forever.

He shrugged. "I have no real explanation other than she's not interested. I asked her out a couple of times after Blackthorn went to jail, even told her Billy Ray could come, but she declined my invitations. I told her I really cared for her, but she said she just couldn't think about a relationship with me or something along those lines. She said she couldn't really explain what she was feeling, and the best thing I could do for her would be to give her time and space. So that's what I did."

"All right, that's good. At least, she was honest with you about that. What was she like throughout the whole investigation process?"

He cast his eyes upward while thinking back. "Amazing is a good word to describe her—and fearless. She willingly cooperated with

Sheriff Berry, even when she knew the dangers involved by staying in Blackthorn's employ. He was a murderer, for cryin' in a sink, and yet she continued her responsibilities until Sheriff Berry could move in and make the arrest. Ma, seeing her wrists and ankles bound in twine that day, and her tied to that kitchen chair as she was, scared me so much. I have thanked God numerous times for the way everything turned out. No one was hurt, and justice was served. Ma, Blackthorn's windows were open that day, and I hunkered down under one of them and listened to her tell him how much God loved him."

Laura shook her head in wonder. "She's a remarkable woman."

"She certainly is."

Laura looked off, as if in deep thought. "She's been through so much in the span of her twenty-one years, losing her mother first and having to assume the role of parent as a young child. Then losing her grandfather when Charles moved to Kentucky, and then her father's passing away and the notion that he died at the hands of a murderous villain. Think of it!

"For her brother's sake, it was essential that she hold everything together when Newell first died. She had to wear a brave front for him because if she fell apart, why, Billy Ray would have no one. Imagine what went on in her head.

"She has lived her life trying to be a mother to Billy, playing the role of housekeeper, gardener, farmer, cook, laundress, seamstress, and everything else that goes along with keeping a house in order. Having to drop out of school as a young girl to help raise her brother, helping Newell operate the farm, and then finding out after his death that she would lose it. Remaining strong even in the face of foreclosure, and then finding out her new employer was her father's murderer. Even helping Sheriff Berry crack open the case must have drained her of any reserve energy. Is it any wonder she's having a difficult time? Her emotions must be wound up tighter than a ball of yarn." Her brows drew together in a thoughtful frown. "Good heavens, Jesse, that girl has suffered mightily!"

He grimaced. "You're right, Ma. And she's reached the end of a very frayed rope and needs rescuing but won't admit it."

"Perhaps it's time you convinced her."

"And how do you expect me to do that when she very clearly stated she didn't need me?"

"I'm of the opinion she's too overcome to know what she needs. Goodness, who knows, but maybe she's just now starting the true grieving process? Delayed, yes, but sometimes, that's how grief works."

"So, should I continue giving her time and space?"

"No, no, goodness, you've already given her a month. It's time you start wooing her."

"Wooing her? Isn't that what I tried to do earlier only to be rejected?"

Laura laid a hand on Jesse's arm. "Don't let your bruised ego rob you of an opportunity, Jesse. She's had enough time to think things over. I cannot guarantee your success, but you will never know if you don't at least try. Woo her with kindness, patience, and understanding, just as our Lord does with us when He's trying to gain our attention. Lovingly wait for her to come to her senses. If things go as I suspect they will, I think she'll realize you were just what she needed all along."

Jesse sat there letting her words digest. He pushed his plate forward and folded his hands in front of him. "Woo her, eh?"

She smiled at him, picked up her coffee cup, and took another sip. Her eyes twinkled as she studied him over the rim. "Do you think you can do it?"

"If I can't, what good am I?" He stared out the window. "Hm. I don't know the last time she actually had fun. I am going to make every effort to make her laugh."

"Make it your mission," Laura said with enthusiasm.

"I intend to. I'll tell my brothers I'm taking the afternoon off. I don't care if it is harvesttime."

"Doesn't she have a job now?"

"Today's Friday. She works from home on Tuesday, Thursday, and Friday. I'll talk her into taking some time off from her seamstress job this afternoon and plan something fun for us. Maybe I'll pack us a lunch and take her on a picnic."

"Oh, I can pack you a tasty meal."

"No, I'll come home around eleven and pack it myself. It might impress her if she knows I actually went to the trouble to put together a picnic myself."

Laura clapped her hands. "Oh, my stars in glory, I can hardly wait to hear—"

He put up his palm. "Ma, don't expect me to give you a detailed story later. Shoot, I don't even know if she'll accept my invitation. I have no reason to believe she will, but I'm going to give it all I have."

"All right, I won't ask. But I will be praying. You can't keep me from doing that."

"I always welcome your prayers, Ma. Always."

Anna finished the cuff of the second sleeve on a dress she was making for a Mrs. Jean Crowder—who must be a very stout woman, she thought. There were times that Anna wondered if Miss Flossie had given her enough fabric for the project. Thank goodness, with some clever finagling, moving pattern pieces around and taking care to use up every spare inch of fabric, she managed to eke out just enough. Now she had but to finish up on a few details, such as sewing on the buttons, stitching the hem, and snipping any hanging threads. It would be complete and ready for Mrs. Crowder to pick up on Monday morning. Anna stretched, rolled her aching shoulders, and glanced at the clock. Eleven-thirty. Time to think about what to make for lunch.

She rose from her sewing table and walked to the kitchen. From the windowsill over the sink, she picked up a tomato and then scrounged around in a shallow wooden box for a sharp knife with which to slice it. A tomato sandwich would suit her just fine, she decided. Just as she positioned the tomato for its first slice, the sound of a neighing horse had her setting down the knife and walking to the window overlooking the front yard. Her chest jolted at the first sight of Jesse coming up the drive, sitting high on the buckboard, dressed in a neat pair of dark gray trousers from what she could tell, a white shirt, and wearing his black hat and suspenders. What in the world? She hadn't seen him in a month, and he picked now to show up—when she least expected him? Her heart skipped a beat, and then another, which confounded her to no end. The last time they'd talked, she'd told him she needed time and space. Well, he'd given it—but had it been enough? The way her nerves jumped at the sight of him made her think perhaps it had. He brought his horse to a halt and jumped down from the buckboard, tossing the reins over her hitching post. Gathering courage, she walked to the front door and opened it. "Good morning, Jesse," she said as coolly as possible.

He grinned up at her, and she almost floated off the porch. If she could ever get a firm grip on her emotions, it would be a miracle. "Good morning, Anna. I've come to fetch you away."

He walked up the steps and stopped just one foot away from her. She straightened herself and lifted her chin. "Fetch me away? For what purpose?"

"To take you on a picnic. It's plenty warm today, so you won't need a wrap."

"What?"

"You heard me. Whatever you're doing can wait. It's time you had a little fun."

"Fun?" Good gracious, granny! When was the last time she'd actually had fun? She couldn't recall it. She'd barely even smiled lately, not even at Billy Ray.

She thumbed behind her—at nothing in particular. "But—"

"But nothing. Where's Rex? He can come along."

"He followed Billy Ray to your place today."

He glanced down at her bare feet. "You might want to put on some shoes."

Embarrassed at her shoddy appearance, she started to shake her head. "No, no, I'm much too shabby looking to go anywhere."

"You're as beautiful as a flower." He bent at the waist, bringing his face close to hers. "I'm only here as a friend, and you need a friend."

"I do?"

"More than anything." He lowered his chin a tad. "Shoes?"

She could hardly believe her eyes or ears. Here he was, standing right in front of her—after a month-long absence.

With only a trifle bit of reluctance, she turned on her heel and went inside to search out her white stockings and her one and only pair of tie-up shoes, her nerves jangling all the while.

37

Their first stop was on the banks of Turtle Creek, the waterway just on the outskirts of town. On their way, they had passed citizens out shopping for wares, businessmen on their way home for a bite of lunch or heading to some eatery, and farmers loading up their wagons with supplies. Jesse knew several passersby, and as he directed his horse down Broadway through town, Anna at his side, many had waved and shouted their greetings. He waved from his perch, a smile on his face that hadn't left him since he'd pulled onto Drake Road. He'd done most of the talking on the drive, not caring one tittle that her responses were sparse. She was sitting next to him, and that's all he cared about.

He reined his horse to a stop in the shade of an old tree and jumped down, then immediately came around and helped Anna to the ground as well. "Thank you," she said as formally as if they'd just met. She brushed the wrinkles out of the front of her skirt, then removed her bonnet to get a better view of their surroundings. "This is lovely."

Looking at her out of the corner of his eye, he said, "Yes, it certainly is." He wondered if she knew his answer held a double meaning. Turning his back to her, he brought down the basket containing their lunch and set it on the ground. Then he snagged hold of the blanket his mother had handed him that morning. As for the checkers game, that remained under the seat. He had a number of ideas stirring around in his head for how they would spend their afternoon together, and he planned to use as many of them as he could to get her to enjoy herself.

He spread out the blanket while she stood off to the side and watched. He wanted her to open up to him, but if today wasn't the day, then so be it. He remembered his mother's words—something about being understanding, kind, patient—just as our Lord is with us when He's trying to gain our attention. He opened up the basket and began bringing out the food items, humming to himself. He'd brought a basket of apples, washed and shined, a fresh loaf of bread, some butter and jam, a couple of perfect tomatoes, dried beef, some thinly sliced cheese, and a jug of cold water. He'd also packed napkins, plates and cups, and all the necessary utensils. Laura had baked oatmeal cookies just that morning and insisted he take a plateful. "I think I've packed plenty, Ma."

"You can never have too many cookies," she'd answered with a sly wink. "Besides, every good meal must end with dessert." And so he'd brought her famous cookies.

"You went out of your way," Anna said, one of her first initiated statements.

He sat down on the blanket and put out a hand to her in invitation. "Nothing but the best, my lady."

"Oh!" To his surprise, she smiled, took his hand, and sat down on the blanket, spreading her wide skirt around her.

"Good thing you don't wear those big metal hoops. I've said it before, I don't know how women can abide those things."

"I never will understand it myself. I'm not in fashion, but I don't much care."

"You look quite fashionable to my eye."

"Ha! You don't have much of an eye for fashion then, but I thank you for your kindness."

There was a slight pause as he quietly studied her. "Well, may I say a prayer for our meal?"

"Yes, please."

He did not take her hand, although it would've been so natural. He offered a prayer of thanks for the food, for the sunshine, for family, and for friendship. Then he asked that God would be present in their day and quickly closed with a hearty amen. He brushed his hands together and smiled. "Did you bring your appetite?"

"I was just thinking about how hungry I was getting before you showed up. I was going to make myself a tomato sandwich."

"You still can, if you like. As you can see I brought a couple of tomatoes and a fresh loaf of sliced bread. By the way, I packed this lunch myself, I'll have you know, but I didn't bake the bread."

To that she gave a little giggle. It was a start, and his heart sang at the tingling sound of her laughter.

She entered more into the conversation as their lunch progressed. They talked about Billy Ray readjusting to farm life and how happy he seemed. "Kids are so easygoing. They take things as they come and live in the moment," he said. "He certainly does have a grand time with my nephews."

"Yes, he enjoys their company. He always comes home and tells me about their adventures. Sometimes, I worry something will happen to him. I know it's silly of me, but…my mother died, my father died. Something could happen to him as well."

"Hm." He didn't want to say too much for fear of erecting a barrier. *Kindness, patience, understanding…* "Would you say you worry more about him now than you ever did before?"

She gazed off, as if to ponder his question, then gave a shrug. "I don't know. Perhaps."

He wiped his mouth with his napkin then took a couple swallows of water. "Why do you think that is?"

"I have no idea. He's eleven now. I suppose the older he gets and the more independent, the more I contemplate what could happen."

Jesse nodded, wanting to weigh his words before speaking them. "It's almost as if you expect something else to go wrong."

"Yes, I suppose."

"I can understand why you'd feel that way."

"You can?"

"Most of your life has been centered around losses, so it's no wonder. But then we have to remember that we don't serve a God of fear."

"Yes, that is true. I've been practicing giving my fears to God. Whenever one crops up, I give it to Him."

He smiled. "That's the right attitude."

They chatted and munched, chatted and munched, covering a host of topics: from the farm, to harvest, to the children starting back to school in late fall, and right down to Laura Fuller's cookies. Because his neck and back had grown achy from sitting, Jesse flopped backwards on the soft blanket and looked skyward at the puffy clouds. "I see an elephant." He pointed above him. "See it?"

To his wonder, she too lay down, albeit a good six inches away from him, but next to him nonetheless. "I see a lamb."

In comfortable silence, they continued studying. "There's a horse's head."

"A dog over there."

"A man with a big nose!"

"And a beard!" he tagged on, looking at the same shape she'd pointed out.

"Now it's changed to an old woman with long, straggly hair!"

Soon they were both laughing, and he couldn't help the joy welling up.

After a bit, he rose and walked to the wagon to retrieve the checkerboard game.

"What have you there?" Anna asked.

"Ever play checkers?"

"Well, of course, but not for some time. Papa used to enjoy playing checkers with me after a long day out in the fields." A strange look came over her, and he immediately regretted bringing out the game.

He paused midway back to her. "We don't have to play it."

"No, I—I'll play. In fact, I'll beat you, I'm sure."

"Is that a challenge?"

"No, it's a promise."

He chuckled and walked back to the blanket. Sitting down, he crossed his legs as he unrolled the cloth board and placed it between them. He then opened the cloth pouch and dumped the wooden pieces out, half of them white oak circles, and the other half dark. He set them on the proper squares and, once they were in place, he nodded at her to begin. She moved the first white piece, and then it was his move. They continued until, much to his dismay, she made the first jump. "Ugh, you got me. How did that happen?"

"You weren't paying attention."

"Ah, but I was," he countered. "You snuck up on me."

She gave a tiny giggle, and it was his turn again, and then hers; each of them was playing as tactically as possible when she cornered him and jumped another of his pieces, getting closer to the front line where he would have to "king" her. A bit of a competitive spirit rose up in him as he determined to get the next jump, at which he succeeded—not just once, but twice, and then a third time. There were moans and groans from both sides, and then she got a definite edge on him with three kings to his two. The game went on until, with a lack of solid strategy on his part, she won the match and gave a loud whoop. He laughed at her enthusiasm, challenged her to a second game, and soundly beat her that time. But on the tie-breaking game, she took the clear lead halfway through. From that point forward, he could not regain his momentum.

"Agh!" he groaned, falling backward, feet planted on the blanket, knees up, and both hands covering his face. "You were not kidding when you said you would beat me. You're good at this game, girl. You didn't even give me fair warning."

She gave a light slap on his shoulder. "Yes, I did. I told you I would beat you. Papa taught me how to think strategically. I've tried to interest Billy Ray in the game, but he's too much of a wiggle worm to want to take the time."

Jesse swabbed at his wet brow, feeling the effects of the sun even though the large tree under which they lay provided plenty of shade. He looked up at her from his prone position. "Want to go get our feet wet?"

"Yes!" she said without hesitation. "I might even splash my face."

He sat back up. "Me too."

They removed their shoes, and he stood first, then took her hand to help her up. She willingly took it, but then he quickly released it so she wouldn't shy away from him. So far, she'd been having a good time, and he wasn't about to ruin things.

They walked down the bank to the flowing stream. He stepped in first and wiggled his toes in the cold, refreshing waters, then lowered himself to the bank, spreading his broad knees. She followed suit, gingerly poking her toes in and then lifting her skirts a bit to protect the hem of her gingham dress. Soon, she was sitting next to him—not too close, but close enough that their elbows touched. The tenderest of feelings floated through him, and he knew afresh that he loved her. He couldn't risk telling her just yet. Too much was at stake.

"Did you get enough to eat?" he asked her, picking up a smooth stone and sending it sailing across the water.

"More than enough." She held her stomach. "I shouldn't have had that second cookie, but it was so scrumptious. Please thank your mother for me."

"I'll do that." He picked up another stone, this one a bit flatter and perfect for skipping. He gripped it just so between his fingers and slung his arm sideways, releasing the rock at just the precise right time.

"Good job. That was about five skips."

"I think I counted six."

"Oh yeah?" Her tone carried a wee bit of challenge, which encouraged him to seek out another flat rock. He repeated his technique, and this time, the stone went a little farther and he counted eight skips.

"That was maybe seven," she said.

"No, it was eight."

"Papa tried to teach me the technique for skipping rocks once, but I wasn't nearly as interested in learning that as I was in learning checkers."

"So, that means you can't beat me in a rock-skipping contest."

"I don't know. It's been a while since I tried." She dug around in the ground next to her until she found a rock. But rather than remain seated, she stood and positioned herself, feet apart, fingers situated on the rock so as to get a comfortable grip. She pulled back her arm, and then with precision, sent the stone flying across the top of the water, the thing clearly skipping at least eight, maybe nine, times.

His jaw fell. "Well, bully for you! How did you do that?" He gawked up at her.

She shrugged, as serious as a grave marker. "I could probably do better if I practiced."

"If you practiced? What other tricks do you have up that gingham sleeve, young lady? I'm learning all kinds of things about you today."

She smiled and sat back down. "I'm a regular mystery, aren't I?"

A mystery all right. Finished with the rock skipping, he pulled at a few blades of grass. "Can you whistle through a blade of grass?"

"Now there's something I can't do. Show me."

"Ha! I can't do it either, but I figured it was just another of your many hidden talents. Growing up, there was a Hubie Gardener that could do it. He tried to teach me, but I never caught on. Might be he could do it 'cause he'd knocked out his front tooth when climbing a tree."

That garnered a genuine laugh out of her, and his insides almost melted. "I love when you do that," he said.

"What?"

"Laugh."

"Oh." She covered her mouth and grew serious.

He couldn't help it. He took her hand and pulled it away from her mouth. "You have a beautiful smile too—when you dare to reveal it."

"Lately, I haven't had much occasion."

"The past few months have been pretty rotten, but there are blessings behind every battle, and you must admit it's a relief to know Blackthorn is behind bars."

She gave a quiet nod. He touched her chin and gave it a tiny lift. "Right?"

"Yes. If I could just get beyond the sadness that seems to have engulfed me."

"Can you describe your sadness?"

"It's like a dark canvas has been draped over the sun."

He thought about that for a moment, glad that he'd started to crack open a window into her soul, but not wanting her to slam it shut on him. He had to tread carefully. He not only tried to remember what his mother had said that very morning, but he also prayed for God to give him just the right words to speak.

"Have you ever considered all that you've been through in your short lifetime?" She stared at him as if she hadn't a clue what he meant. "Think about it. You lost your mother at a very young age. Besides your father and Billy, the only other close relative you had was your grandfather, who had to move away to a warmer climate. Your schooling was stolen from you because you had to basically take over the role of mother for Billy's sake. You had to maintain your household while your father kept up the farm. A trusted hired hand stole almost all of your father's hard-earned cash, and then before Newell could save the farm, Horace Blackthorn took his life. Then—you lost the farm. That's a great deal for a twenty-one-year-old woman to bear."

He saw the tears building in the corners of her eyes, and he prayed he hadn't overstepped some boundary. "I suppose I have had a bit harder life than some."

"Some? How about most?"

She gave a quiet laugh and swiped at her damp eyes. "I've turned twenty-two, by the way. My birthday was three weeks ago. Both Billy and I had recent birthdays, but neither of us felt much like celebrating. Well, *he* may have wanted to celebrate, but I'm afraid his sister has been quite the sourpuss of late."

He smiled and nodded. "There is always next year."

"Yes, next year." She stared off for a lingering moment, then released a soft sigh. "All in all, God has been faithful to me. What I'm experiencing now is just a little black spot in an otherwise sun-filled day. I'll be fine in time. I'm convinced of it."

"And you'll stop worrying about Billy Ray?"

"Probably not. Ha! But I'll try to be more diligent about remembering God's in control."

"And isn't that a comforting thought, that God *is* in control? No matter what hardship comes our way, we can depend on God for strength and courage."

She nodded. "It's funny. I know all that with my head, but sometimes I have to wait for my heart to catch up. Does that make sense?"

"Absolutely. It's human, actually. As humans, we'd much rather survive on good feelings than on faith. Good feelings are warm and comfortable. Faith is hard work."

"You are so right." She sobered, and he noted her brow furrowing in thought.

"What is it?" he asked.

"Oh, nothing, really. I just wanted to thank you for being a good friend to me."

He wanted to ask her if that was all she considered him to be—a friend. He wanted to ask her how she'd felt about that month-long separation they'd both endured. Had she missed him, or had she discovered she truly didn't need him in the way he wanted her to need him?

They sat momentarily, allowing the birds' chatter and the whistling wind to lull them. Then, throwing caution aside, he stood and extended a hand down to her, and to his surprise, she took it. "Let's go for a walk."

"To where?"

"I don't know. Wherever the restful winds take us."

38

In the end, it had turned out to be the loveliest of days with Jesse—relaxing and thoroughly enjoyable. He'd made every effort to give her a good time, packing a picnic lunch and requiring nothing of her, bringing a blanket and even a checkers game, challenging her to that and a rock-skipping contest, both of which she'd won. She smiled now when recalling his shocked expression at her expertise.

She hadn't even felt any pressure to begin a romantic relationship with him, nor had he attempted to kiss her, although she had to admit to being slightly surprised by that, if not disappointed. He hadn't even suggested they ride together to church today—only asked that she at least acknowledge him from across the sanctuary if he should happen to wave at her. A very small part of her wondered if she might be starting to feel somewhat normal again, if maybe, just maybe, she was beginning to climb out of the dark hole in which she'd found herself. She thought about all the things Jesse had said to her about walking in faith and trusting God and believing that He's in control, no matter what comes along, whether hardship or heartache or pain.

"You ready, Sis, or are you goin' to just keep standing there fixing your hair in front of that mirror?"

She jumped at Billy Ray's voice. "Oh! Was I doing that?"

He looked her over a bit. "Yeah, and you finished that bun in your hair about five minutes ago." He tipped his head to the side. "Is that a new dress?"

Anna glanced down at herself. "Why, yes it is. Miss Flossie had some extra pieces of cloth that she told me I could have, and I found I had enough to stitch myself a new dress whilst taking breaks from working on our clients' orders." She held out the fabric on either side of her skirt in both hands. "Do you like it?"

He wrinkled up his nose. "I guess. It's a good color for you."

It was one of the closest things to a compliment she'd gotten from him in a long while, and it was enough to warrant a warm tingle in her heart. "Well, thank you very much. I've been looking over the extra fabrics Miss Flossie lays out in hopes of making you a new pair of knickers and a shirt."

"Don't worry yourself over it. I don't really care about getting new knickers. I make do with my old stuff 'cause that way I don't have t' be extra careful."

"Well, these would be for school when it starts up in November."

"Aargh. Don't go talkin' 'bout school just yet. We still gotta finish harvest."

She gave herself one last glance in the mirror, then headed for the door. The skies threatened of rain, which was not a bad thing. Her garden was thirsty for a good drenching. "Come. We don't want to be late for Sunday school. You want to drive the wagon for a change?"

"Can I?"

"You hitched her up, didn't you? You might as well drive the team."

They climbed aboard, he ahead of her so he could turn and assist her up. Soon they were heading north on Drake, passing the Fuller family farm, then turning left on Miller, and at the next intersection turning left on Broadway and heading south toward the center of town and Lebanon Community Methodist Church.

The reverend's message that Sunday morning was about the Sermon on the Mount when Jesus challenged His disciples to live wholeheartedly for God through faith, not simply through keeping God's laws, but by serving as a member of God's kingdom, honoring Him, but also loving and serving others just as Christ would do. He spoke about glorifying God and being a shining light to the world. His sermon made Anna question her own level of faith and rehash in her mind all the things she and Jesse had talked about on their picnic two days ago.

How much did she truly trust God? Was there a glow about her that folks noticed when they passed her on the street? Yes, she had reasons to grieve, but so did a wealth of others. Goodness, they'd just come through four years of a horrendous war where brother fought against brother, cousin against cousin, and even father against son, depending on which side you hailed from. It was a bloody fight, although a righteous one, but so many lives were lost and so many families affected, it made her own sense of loss seem almost to pale in comparison. In those quiet moments, while listening to the pastor wrap up his sermon, she confessed her sin of selfishness and asked for forgiveness. No great feelings of relief or freedom came over her, but she knew in her heart that the Lord had heard her prayer and had even then begun a work of renewal in her life.

After the sermon, the closing hymn, and prayer of dismissal, Billy Ray stepped out into the center aisle ahead of her. Spotting one of the Fuller boys, he said, "There's Frankie. I'm goin' out to the churchyard with him, Sis." She didn't even have a chance to respond before he disappeared in the melee of worshippers. She watched him hurry to the back of the church and then follow Frankie and some other boys out the door, their voices raising like shouts of liberation as soon as they got their first breath of outside air. Thankfully, it hadn't rained yet, but the skies certainly threatened when she peered through the open windows, and the trees were bending in the wind.

She scanned the church and put on a smile for no one in particular, glad that she'd not felt compelled to sit in the back row that morning.

She *was* feeling better. She felt it in her heart even as a splash of joy washed over her spirit.

"Good morning, Anna." She recognized Laura Fuller's friendly voice and turned full around to greet her. "How are you, dear?"

"Hello, ma'am. I'm doing quite well, thank you."

"I'm happy to hear it."

She hadn't seen Jesse that morning but didn't want to ask about him for fear of sounding forward.

"I believe Jesse already went outside."

"Oh!" She hadn't asked, but Laura had offered the information anyway. Now she found herself curious to know why he hadn't even made a point to greet her that morning. Hadn't he said to her on Friday that she must be sure to smile at him should he wave at her from across the sanctuary? Here she'd primped for too long in front of the mirror, worn a newly stitched dress, taken extra care with her hair that morning, even stringing a ribbon through the braid, and rubbed some lovely lilac oil onto her throat and wrists. But all for naught. *Oh, Lord, but I'm a confused woman when it comes to Jesse Fuller.* She had never experienced feelings of love and wasn't sure she'd recognize the emotion even if it slapped her in the face, but—but was this the beginning? Could it be?

"It's been awhile since I've seen you, dear. How have you been since the whole ordeal with that wretched man Horace Blackthorn?"

Suddenly, the notion of talking to a woman about the matter strongly appealed to her. "I—I suppose I've been feeling somewhat down for some odd reason, but the sermon this morning truly helped me take my eyes off myself. There are so many in the world much worse off than I, and I am so thankful to have my farmhouse back."

Laura smiled. "Yes, I'm thrilled everything worked out."

Anna glanced down a little shyly and then lifted her eyes to Laura. "It wouldn't have had it not been for your sons' generosity. And I wouldn't be surprised but what you had something to do with the negotiations, so I must thank you as well."

"You're most welcome. After everything you've been through, you deserve to have some bit of happiness."

"That's kind of you."

Laura studied her for a moment as if contemplating something. "You know, it is all right to grieve your losses. You've had many."

"That is what Jesse told me on our picnic. I do think I've still been grieving my father's passing, even more so after learning that Horace Blackthorn caused his death. He could be with us today if it weren't for that hideous act of greed. And all because of some treasure that no one really knows for certain is buried somewhere on the farm."

They walked slowly to the back of the church, moving with the other parishioners, Laura looping her arm through Anna's in a motherly sort of way. Anna found comfort in her touch.

Near the exit door, Laura pulled Anna to the side to allow for others to go ahead of them. "You know, after my beloved Martin passed away in fifty-eight, I thought my whole world would come to an end. I know your situation is different in that you lost your father, not a husband, but grief is grief, no matter what level or circumstance. I think I understand a bit of what you feel. At least my boys were fully grown when Martin died, but you have a young brother to care for, and I'm sure at times that must seem quite overwhelming to you. You've had to play the part of mother to him rather than sister. Children are not quick to show their gratitude, but you must know he loves and appreciates all you've done for him."

Laura's words nearly coaxed the tears to fall, but Anna blinked to hold them back. "Your words are so encouraging to me. Losing your husband must have been dreadful."

"It was, but you know, throughout that eight-month stretch in which he was so ill and then at long last, dying, I did learn a great deal about trusting the Lord through difficult circumstances. I found that even when I can't sense God's presence every minute of the day, He is there nonetheless. In His Word, we find promise after promise that

He'll never leave or forsake us. We are always on God's mind. Isn't that a marvelous thought?"

Anna had never thought of it in quite that way—always on God's mind. "Yes, it's almost more than a person can comprehend."

"That it is, but it's true. No matter what may be happening to someone on the other side of the world, or just on the other side of town, everyone—each living, breathing soul alive today—is on God's mind, and He is calling them to trust Him with their whole hearts. That's how it is with you, dear. Although you are wrought with grief and perhaps a bit of confusion and most definitely sadness, you will get through this. You will get to the other side because God is with you, and He brings strength, healing, and courage."

Anna smiled at the revelation. "I feel as though I've just heard two wonderful sermons this morning, the reverend's and now yours."

Laura tossed her head back and laughed. "Oh, I'm no preacher, dear. I'll leave the preaching to Reverend Fisher. I merely wanted to tell you a little about my own personal experience."

"And I appreciate it so much. You have helped me more than you know."

Laura nodded and lay a hand to her arm. "I hope you'll return for Sunday dinner again soon."

"I would like that."

"How about today?"

"Oh! I—I, well, it's nice of you to invite me, but—I wouldn't want to impose."

"Nonsense!"

"Yes, nonsense," came a male voice. Jesse! Anna's cheeks went hot. How long had he been standing there unseen?

"I meant to invite you myself, but I see my mother beat me to it."

Unexpected excitement welled up within her, first at seeing him and then at the prospect of spending Sunday afternoon with him. Had he really meant to invite her—no expectations? Or had he just gone along with his mother's premature suggestion because he felt obliged?

"You must come, dear," Laura insisted. "We're celebrating Frankie's birthday, and I know that Frankie and Billy Ray have become good friends."

Anna hesitated to give an answer. "I do have some pressing things that need doing at home."

"On the Sabbath?" Jesse asked, teasing her with a crooked grin and a single arched eyebrow.

"Well, I suppose—if you're sure it's no bother."

"Miss Anna Hansen, it is no bother at all. In fact, it would be my pleasure if you'd join us," Jesse said with a partial bow.

She placed her palm to her upturned mouth. "Goodness. How could I possibly say no to that?"

Jesse smiled and turned to his mother. "I'll arrange for Isaac to drive you home, Ma, so I can drive Anna's wagon."

"Well, all right then, it's settled. I'll see you at the house."

While Anna might have been a bit thrown off by the sudden change in her Sunday plans, her heart thumped with enthusiasm. What was that tingly feeling flooding her chest, that gentle urging that challenged her to take a risk? She and Jesse were both so different, yet so compatible. He was strong, so sure of himself, schooled, and intelligent. She was more quiet and timid, uneducated, and inexperienced. What did he see in her? She knew in an instant what she saw in him, but what could possibly attract him to her? That was the mystery, for it seemed too good to be true.

Lord, grant me wisdom to know Your will—and the boldness to obey.

39

Well, that went better than planned. That morning before church, Laura had said she was going to look for an opportunity to talk to Anna. She said she wanted to encourage her and asked that Jesse give them a few minutes of privacy after church. "Don't try to push me on her, Ma. She won't go for that."

"I'll do my best not to even mention you."

"Well, that would be the day," he'd joked.

He forgot to tell her to leave the invitation to Sunday dinner to him, but in the end, it may have worked out better this way. At least Anna had come.

They had celebrated Frankie's birthday that day, and it felt so natural having Anna at his side to join in the family festivities. In the midst of the excitement, Jesse announced that both Anna and Billy Ray had recently also turned a year older, so the entire Fuller gang shouted out belated birthday greetings, thereby triggering streaks of pink to splash across both of their faces. There had been laughter, happy conversation, and Laura's delicious chocolate cake to top off the celebrating, after which all of the children disappeared outside, with the exception of ten-month-old Martin Jack. The baby happily crawled among the adults

315

gathered in the living room, where the lively talk ranged from Reverend Fisher's fine sermon to how the new president, Andrew Johnson, was faring to the building of new railroads across the country. About the time the conversation shifted to women's fashions and the latest recipes, the men grew restless.

"Well, who wants to try that new rope swing Jesse put up for the kids a couple of months ago?" Jack asked.

"You're not serious, I hope," Laura said.

"I wish I could," said a very pregnant Faith, due in early November.

"You won't catch me on it," Cristina said. "That thing looks treacherous."

"Treacherous? Nah," said Jesse. He had placed his arm along the back of the divan behind Anna, his fingertips grazing her shoulder, and to his delight, she hadn't moved away. He wondered what she would do when he told her he loved her. He would do it today if the timing felt right. "Come on out to the barn, and I'll demonstrate."

"This I must see," said Joey.

All seven adults rose.

"I'll just watch," said Laura. "I'd give it a try, mind you, but this is the Sabbath, and I'd be afraid the Lord might strike me down for my lack of observance."

"I'm convinced the Lord doesn't mind a bit of family fun on the Sabbath," Jesse said.

"Hmph, just the same, I'm content to stand back and watch."

"And we're content to let you," put in Jack. "When you broke your leg last year, the whole family suffered with you out of commission. We're not taking any chances on any more broken bones."

"Oh, pooh." She flicked her wrist. "You all survived just fine, but don't worry, I know my limits, and that swing surpasses them."

They all advanced to the front door.

"Um…just what is involved in staying put on this so-called swing?" Anna asked in a quiet tone. Slowly but surely, she had started crawling out of her shell, joining in on the family's conversations and laughing at the children's antics.

Jesse grinned down at her. "Sitting on the giant knot and wrapping your legs tight at the ankles. That's it. Oh, and hanging on for dear life." He touched her at the middle of her back to encourage her to go ahead of him. She did, and out the door all the adults went, heading down the porch steps and toward the barn. The children were over in the side yard, the boys playing catch with a couple of balls, and the girls sitting on the ground under a tree playing some sort of game in the grass. When the kids spotted the adults walking toward the barn, they all jumped up.

"Hey, where're y'all goin'?" asked Isaac.

"Yeah, what's goin' on?" Elias asked.

"Jesse's going to demonstrate how to use his swing," said Joey.

"I'll show you," offered Frankie.

"Me too!" said Elias.

"Hold up," said Jack. "You can all demonstrate your amazing skills later, but first, we want to watch your Uncle Jesse."

Jesse grinned. "You know, kids," he said to his nieces, nephews, and Billy Ray, while pointing his thumb at the adults, "I don't think they have any faith in me."

"Oh, he can do it," said Billy Ray. "He's the one who hung it."

Inside the barn, Laura craned her neck upward. "How in the world did you manage to sling that rope over that beam?"

"Ma, some things are better left a mystery."

"Oh, good gracious! I should have known better than to ask. And what sort of skill is required to get on that contrivance?"

"I'll show you."

He winked down at Anna, then walked to the center of the barn, snagged hold of the thick knotted rope, then carried it with him up the tall ladder leading to the hayloft. Once he reached the top, he looked down at the adults who all peered up at him. He especially sought out

Anna and noted her wide-eyed expression. Did she, along with the rest of the adults, think him a crazy loon?

"Jesse Fuller, I can't believe I didn't come out here sooner to inspect that awful contraption. Are my grandchildren really swinging on that thing?"

"They certainly are, Ma. Well, I haven't allowed Miriam to try it yet."

"I don't want to either. It looks pernickety," the six-year-old said, her eyes dancing as she used her favorite newly discovered word.

"And I won't allow it yet anyway," said Faith, handing her wiggling nephew back to Cristina, her own round belly looking ready to burst with child. "Maybe when you're about ten."

"Are y'all ready to be astonished?" Jesse asked his onlookers.

"We are holding our breath," said Joey in a dull voice.

"Make way because I'm going to sail right through the doors."

"Oh, my stars and garters," Laura exclaimed. "Is that safe? What if you miss the doors?"

"Ma, have a little faith in your wisest son," Jesse said with a grin.

"Wisest?" his brothers said in unison.

"More like the most lunkheaded," said Jack.

Jesse laughed them off, got a good grip on the thick rope, stuck the bottom knot between his legs and positioned himself on it, and then crossed his legs at the ankles. Looking down one last time, he gave a giant leap and loud whoop and flew through the air, out the door, back in, not quite reaching the hayloft that time, then sailed toward the door again, not quite making it outside, then back again—until he let go and jumped to the ground. "Exhilarating!"

"My turn!" the boys shouted all at once.

"Wait!" Jesse held a hand up to the kids and looked from one adult to the next. "Any of you want to try?"

After a short pause, Anna said, "I'll go."

He couldn't believe his ears.

"Nooo!" Cristina squealed. "Seriously?"

Without so much as a moment's hesitation, Anna took the rope and proceeded to climb the ladder, lifting her long skirts at every rung. How exactly was she going to wrap her legs around that knot? Jesse's heart pumped with excitement at her daring spirit.

She got to the top and looked down. "I may be having second thoughts," she said with a little giggle. If ever Jesse loved her, it was in this very moment.

"You can do it, Sis!" Billy Ray yelled.

"Yeah, you can do it!" squealed the other kids.

"It's really fun," said Elias. "Just hang on tight."

"You're braver than I," said Cristina.

"And me!" said Faith.

"And me!" said Jack, although Jesse knew better. Both of his brothers had tested the swing before allowing their children to ride it—although neither of them would admit that truth now.

"Wish me luck," she shouted down, positioning herself, her skirts wrapped carefully around herself so they wouldn't flare.

"Luck? I'm praying!" said Laura.

"Go, go, go!" the children chanted.

Soon, she made the giant leap, and down she flew, her shrill scream rising to the rafters, followed immediately by rousing laughter. "It's so fun!" she shouted, letting go of one hand and dipping it down as she sailed back and forth, back and forth. "I must do it again!"

"She is really something," whispered Laura to Jesse.

His heart swelled with happiness. "I must agree."

～

Anna could not believe she'd let go of her doubts and insecurities and flown like the wind out the barn door on that crazy, frightening swing. She didn't consider herself to be a fearless individual, but taking that one tiny risk had freed her up for taking more. Perhaps love would be her next big leap. Only time would tell.

After everyone moseyed out of the barn, Jesse announced he was taking Anna for a walk down to the creek.

"Can we come too?" asked Miriam.

"No!" every adult declared in unison.

"Just go back to playing, kids," said Jack.

Something was up. Anna felt it. And yet, her heart was too afraid to think about it. Did Jesse have something other than a simple walk in mind? Did Jesse's family members sense it too? Was she ready to receive it—whatever it was?

He boldly took her hand and pulled her along while the children ran off in the opposite direction and the adults walked back toward the big house. Jesse and Anna made their way down the sloping path toward the creek at the edge of the property. Her pulse kept jumping, and she was certain that when she looked down, she could see the bodice of her dress popping in and out with every heartbeat. *Lord, prepare me for whatever lies ahead. If it's nothing, then so be it, but if it's something—though I dare not hope for it—then give me wisdom and discernment as to how to respond.*

They reached the creek bank. "Shall we wade?" he asked.

"Yes, that's a wonderful idea." The rain had so far held off, but the air was hot and sticky and the sky overcast. They both bent to remove their shoes and stockings. Jesse rolled his pant legs up to his kneecaps. She in turn lifted her skirts as she dipped her toes into the refreshing waters.

"I know I told you on the ride home that I like your new dress, but let me tell you again. That shade becomes you." He bent forward to see into her eyes. "It matches your blue eyes."

"Thank you."

He took her hand again, and she was glad for it. The rocky bottom made for uneven walking, and her hand in his helped to steady her.

"I'm glad you came for dinner."

"Thank you for having me. Your family is so much fun to be around."

"You fit right in."

"I do?" She sneaked a peek at him. "I'm just a plain farm girl, and your family is so refined."

He laughed and bumped against her. "I don't see a single plain thing about you, and I happen to like farm girls—you in particular. And in case you hadn't noticed, my dear, we're farmers too."

She couldn't help the nervous giggle that came out of her.

On seeming impulse, he pulled her out of the stream and up to a weeping willow planted on the bank, its branches bending low. He reached into his pocket and withdrew a small pocketknife. He commenced with carving something into the bark of the giant trunk. "What are you doing?" she asked.

"You'll see. Don't look yet."

She turned her body away and watched the lazy stream float by. It took a few minutes, but at last he invited her to turn. There, carved into the tree, was a perfectly etched heart and inside it were the words, "Jesse Loves Anna." She stared at it for several seconds, the actual words not quite registering—until they did. *What?* Could it be?

He placed his hands on her shoulders and situated her so that they faced full on. Although he stood a head taller, their eyes were perfectly trained on each other. Her heart had now taken to doing little flips, and she almost forgot to breathe.

"I've known for some time," he whispered, his eyes warm as a stove on a winter's eve. "And that month apart from you cemented it even more in my head and heart. I can't live without you, Anna. I really can't."

"Oh, my!" she gasped. "But I—"

He put two fingers to her lips to shush her. "I love you, Anna Hansen, and that's all there is to it. I have wanted you to be my bride for three long months. I may not have loved you right from the start, but it didn't take long for my heart to tell me that I need you and I want to share my life with you."

Tears formed in her eyes. "I'm feeling—*something*, but...I've never been in love before, so—how do I know?"

Jesse chuckled. "Nor have I, my sweet lady. I have been in strong *like* before—when I was about twelve—with Iris Fortune. But it didn't last long. I found out she was in strong like with Charlie Spingle, so I stopped chasing her around the schoolyard."

She couldn't help it. A spurt of giggles rolled out of her. "And then there was Martha Weaver. You mustn't forget about her. Surely you were in strong like with her as well."

"Nope, that was only *mild* like. I'm afraid my experience with love is quite limited. Matter of fact, I'd have to say you're the only one for whom my heart has ever truly fallen. What do you say to that?"

She thought a moment, her insides tingling with utter excitement. "So, do you suppose I'm feeling the same things you're feeling?"

"Perhaps we should throw caution to the wind and see if a kiss will clarify matters."

More giggles, but these the nervous kind. "Perhaps so."

He tenderly cupped her cheeks in both hands and slowly lowered his face until their lips met. Instantly, an eager affection came rushing out of her. This must be love, she told herself. What else could it be? Glory goodness, this was it! "Jesse," she whispered between kisses. Kisses that were gentle, but urgent, soft and slow, but searing. "I love you. I really and truly do!"

He gave a quiet chuckle and kissed the tip of her nose. And then her forehead, and then both cheeks. "I know you do. I've known for some time. It was just a matter of you giving your fears to the Lord, and swinging open the doors of your guarded heart."

They relished in more kisses, his lips warm and sweet on hers.

And overhead, two squirrels flitted from one willow branch to another, and the sun, long hidden from the day, finally poked its head out, and it was as if the day had just begun.

EPILOGUE

I see it, I see it!" came Billy Ray's shouts. "It's a box! There's an old cloth wrapped around it. Jesse, look!"

"I see it, too, buddy. Isn't that something? At last."

After two long weeks of everyone pitching in to finish the search for the hidden treasure, it had at long last come to fruition—or so it would seem. Everyone, both children and adults, even Laura Fuller, stood with mouths agape around the four-foot-deep hole, awaiting the results of their efforts. Jesse and Billy Ray stood inside the pit, shovels propped against the side. Jesse went down on his knees, then looked up at Billy Ray. "Well, come on, Billy, this is what you've been waiting for."

"All of us been waitin' for it," said Frankie eagerly, his eyes round as platters as he peered over the edge.

With the help of the map, they had finished the digging that Horace Blackthorn had started. He'd been off the mark by a foot or two down by the Wish Bone Tree, so they'd had to expand the hole before locating the blown glass jar that contained clue number four. Anna had been the official "keeper of the clues" and after reading them aloud several times to whomever the designated diggers were for that day to get the big picture, she'd pretty much memorized them. Clue number four read, "At dawn or dusk, in constant view, find you the lucky final clue. Where creek runs deep and horses graze, where once there blew a fiery blaze. Dig next to the stump of the Sweetgum tree and find a box containing a key. Though weary, you, the end is near. Go to the biggest boulder and find it here; four feet under, in a cloth unfurled, a small, locked chest with coins and jewels."

Once they had located that clue, everyone knew they were getting closer, so no digging was allowed unless witnesses were present—not because the family was worried someone would cheat, but because no one wanted to miss the excitement.

It had taken a bit of figuring to determine just which boulder was the biggest, as there were a few located on the property, but using a measuring tape, they finally came to a consensus and the digging commenced. As for the buried key, it was identical to the one Newell had stored in his box in the barn. They were of the opinion that Newell's was a spare in case the buried one could not be found or had become badly corroded.

Now, here they all were, gathered around the massive hole and gazing over it, impatient to get their first glimpse of this so-called, long-awaited treasure. Even Rex, who'd been sniffing the ground and meandering his way in and out of the Fuller assembly, seemed particularly interested in the giant hole in the ground.

Billy Ray crouched down next to Jesse and put his hand on the box. "My hand is shakin'," he said.

"Open it, Billy Ray!" Isaac said. "I can't wait no longer."

"Yeah, but first, I got somethin' to say."

Everyone held his or her breath, Anna most of all. Like everyone else, she wanted him to get on with it. For weeks after she and Jesse had proclaimed their love for one another, she'd continued to drag her feet with regard to this treasure, and Jesse had been patient with her, declaring it her decision to make. It had been Newell Hansen's long-kept secret, and a big part of her believed it should remain so. But then one night before going to bed, Billy Ray had convinced her that keeping the secret made no real sense.

"I s'pose Papa didn't want no one losin' their minds whilst lookin' for it," he reasoned. "Or maybe he thought the whole idea was greedy or sinful 'cause the property was stolen. But the judge even told you they got no account of that robbery in Cincinnati sixty years ago 'cause the records were destroyed in a fire. He said whatever we find is ours to keep."

Her eleven-year-old brother had made a lot of sense, and so Anna had finally given him and the Fullers her blessing to proceed with the treasure hunt. It had been the judge's suggestion that since the clues had been handed down to Newell, the proper thing to do would be to hand them down to Billy Ray, which Anna had been fully in favor of doing. Even though the property belonged to the Fullers now, all three brothers agreed with the judge.

"What did you want to say?" Jesse asked.

"Well." Billy cleared his throat and looked from one adult to the other—and then to each of the children. "I been thinking. You all did your part to help find this treasure, either just givin' your support or takin' a turn at digging, so I really don't want to keep this treasure to myself. Since my sister is marrying Jesse next week, that'll make me your kin, too. So I want to divide it up between all us kids."

There were gasps all around, mostly from the adults.

"Well, that's mighty generous of you, Billy Ray, but entirely unnecessary," said Jack.

"Yeah, it's really your treasure to keep," offered Isaac.

Pride for Billy Ray's level of maturity welled up in Anna. When had he turned into this levelheaded, kindhearted young man?

"Nope," he insisted. "I made up my mind already. I was thinkin' about it and prayin' about it last night in bed. God told me I should share it, and so I want to obey Him."

"Well, we can hardly argue with that if it's something God instructed you to do," said Joey. "Why don't we find out if there's even anything in there worth sharing? If there is and it amounts to anything of great value, then the parents and your sister can decide how to go about distributing it and whether each child's share should go into some sort of savings account."

"Okay then," said Billy Ray, grinning up at everyone while he brushed his hands together before grasping hold of the box partially wrapped in cloth. He reached down and started to lift it, but stopped. "It's heavy," he said to Jesse.

"Let me help you then." With his hands, Jesse dug around the edge of the box, peeling away the tattered cloth, and finally lifting it out. He grunted as he handed it up to Jack, who carried it to a blanket laid out on the ground on the other side of the boulder. Everyone gathered around the somewhat ornate metal box with some sort of finely etched carvings on it. It appeared to be bronze if Anna judged correctly, although it was badly corroded from years of resting in the earth untouched.

Jesse climbed out of the hole and lent a hand down to help Billy out. Soon, everyone stood in a circle, the box at the hub. Jesse reached into his pocket and handed Newell's key to Billy Ray.

Even baby Martin, while easily distracted by the gathering of people, seemed especially interested in the box, as he crawled to it and tried to lay his hands on it. Joey soon scooped him up into his arms.

"Hurry up and open it," said Frankie, going down on his knees next to Billy Ray. Rex gave a single bark as if to urge him on.

Billy fumbled with the keyhole, trying to get the key to work, but with no success. Soon, Jesse took over, and with a bit of time and effort, finally managed to turn the key. "It's all yours, Billy," Jesse said with a sweep of his hand. "Open it up." Jesse took a quick moment to look up at Anna and give a warm wink.

Slowly but surely, Billy Ray lifted the lid—and squealed.

Frankie, kneeling next to him, let out a whoop. "Look at that!"

Everyone leaned in for a close look. The box did indeed contain a treasure—uncut gems, jewels, and gold rings, bracelets, and necklaces, along with a mountain of gold coins.

"What on earth?" exclaimed Anna. "That's top rail! We can't possibly keep that—it's too much. Someone lost a fortune in that robbery." She plastered her hand over her mouth. She felt faint.

Soon others were making murmuring sounds and chattering about the treasure. Billy Ray sat quietly, eyes rapt, mouth gaping. Finally, he found his voice. "What are we supposed to do with this?"

"Since we will soon be kinsmen, you should share it," said Miriam. "I want a new doll."

That brought a sudden burst of laughter from everyone. Soon, Laura cleared her throat and raised her hands. "Here's what I think."

Everyone, including the children, gave her their full attention. Even baby Martin quieted.

"Jesse, you and your brothers should take the box and its contents to the bank tomorrow and see if you can find someone to appraise its value," Laura said.

She directed her next words to Billy Ray. "You mentioned that when you prayed last night, you sensed that you were supposed to share the bounty with your new cousins. God has blessed us so mightily by bringing you and your sister into our family. Have you considered that you ought to tithe ten percent to the church?"

Cristina stepped close to Anna and put an arm around her shoulder. Anna smiled and leaned into her embrace. Her breaths stalled while she waited for Billy Ray's response.

"That's exactly what I want to do, give a tithe," he said. "That's what the Bible says to do and I want to obey it 'cause it's God's Word."

Laura dropped down beside Billy to give him a hug. "That's wonderful," she said. "Reverend Fisher mentioned just a few Sundays ago that the church needs a new roof. Your tithe will certainly help with that."

"That's a grand idea," said Jesse.

"Thank you for reminding us about the privilege of sharing our blessings," said Anna, as more pride for her little brother welled up inside. She cast a quick glance at Jesse, and when their eyes connected, he gave her a wink and mouthed, "I love you."

Laura was right. God had blessed all of them, far more than anyone could imagine. Just the very notion that she was about to become a Fuller was a blessing in itself. The fears of her past had lifted, and God had filled her with a fresh awareness of His presence. Yes, the loss of Papa still stung deeply, and the manner of his death would always strike her as cruel and heartless. But she did not hate Horace Blackthorn for his sinful, selfish act. As she continued to pray daily for him, she knew that one day, he would read the Bible that she had sent to him and take God's Word into his heart. Nothing was impossible with God. Nothing. She was marrying Jesse, after all, and what bigger miracle could there be than that?

After their wedding, Jesse planned to move into her little farmhouse with the intention of enlarging it over the next year. They wished to add to their family soon, so they'd need another bedroom—or two. And he wanted to give her a larger kitchen and a sewing room so she could continue to work for Miss Flossie. Oh, she didn't *have* to work, but she enjoyed sewing for other folks around Lebanon and the opportunity to socialize, swap recipes, and share the joy of the Lord.

"Well, shall we go back to the house to celebrate?" asked Laura. "I have fresh blackberry pies sitting on the pie shelf."

"Yes!" came several shouts of enthusiasm, Rex adding two barks to the vote.

"Who's going to fill up this big hole?" asked Jesse.

"Us boys will all come back after pie," Isaac offered.

"It'll be a lot easier filling it back up than digging it," said Jesse. "Take care not to bury anybody."

"Jesse Fuller, don't give those boys any ideas," Laura scolded.

"Ma's right," said Jack. "There'll be a headcount before bedtime tonight."

Everyone had a good laugh, including the boys.

"I'll put that treasure box under my wagon seat," said Jack.

"Good idea since it's heavy," said Jesse.

Jack hefted it up. "Anybody want to hitch a ride on the wagon with my pregnant wife and me?"

"I do!" several said, hurrying ahead to climb aboard.

"My soon-to-be-bride and I will walk, thank you," Joey said, taking Anna's hand. Rex came up beside them, sniffing the air and following their lead.

It was late October. There'd been cool, rainy days off and on, and most of the leaves on the trees had turned various shades of red, orange, purple, and yellow, but today, the sun shone bright and it was warm enough to be outside without a wrap. Those who chose to walk moved along at a good clip, but Jesse and Anna lagged back, clasped hands swinging between them.

Anna's heart and mind were full with all manner of good thoughts and feelings. No matter how many times she mulled the idea of becoming Mrs. Jesse Fuller, she could not quite accustom herself to it. She gave his hand a little extra squeeze. "Thank you for everything," she said.

"What have I done to deserve thanks?"

"You took Billy Ray and me into your heart, loved us unconditionally, and accepted me just the way I am, plain and simple."

"Hm." He stopped her right there on the edge of the plowed cornfield and turned her to face him. "There is nothing plain and simple about you, my lovely almost-wife."

What could she say to that? He would have none of her arguing, that was for certain. All she could do was tilt her chin up and silently invite him to kiss her. He obliged, of course, and right there on the edge of that cornfield, with God watching on, he made her senses spin.

In the distance, a crow cawed. Rex barked at it, trotting ahead when he caught sight of a rabbit.

Could life get much better than this? Anna seriously doubted it. One last kiss sang through her veins, and then they resumed their steps toward the big house, two hearts entwined, a lifetime ahead of them, and more blessings than they could count.

ABOUT THE AUTHOR

*B*orn and raised in west Michigan, Sharlene MacLaren attended Spring Arbor University. Upon graduating with an education degree in 1971, she taught second grade for two years, then accepted an invitation to travel internationally for a year with a singing ensemble. Afterward, she returned to her teaching job, then in 1975, she reunited with her childhood sweetheart, and they married that very December. They have raised two lovely daughters, both of whom are now happily married and enjoying their own families. Retired in 2003 after thirty-one years of teaching, Shar loves to read, sing, travel, and spend time with her family—in particular, her adorable grandchildren!

Shar has always enjoyed writing, and her high school classmates eagerly read and passed around her short stories. In the early 2000s, Shar felt God's call upon her heart to take her writing pleasures a step further, so she began to pursue publishing one of the many manuscripts she'd written. In 2006, her dreams of publication became a reality when she signed a contract with Whitaker House for her first faith-based novel, *Through Every Storm*, thereby launching her professional writing career. With almost two dozen published novels now gracing store shelves and being sold online, Shar gives God all the glory.

Over the years, Shar's books have reaped awards and nominations in several categories such as the American Christian Fiction Writers Book-of-the-Year, Road to Romance Reviewer's Choice Award, Inspirational Readers' Choice Award, and the Retailers' Choice Awards, to name a few. *Their Daring Hearts* was named a 2018 Top Pick by *Romantic Times*, and *A Love to Behold* was voted "Book of the Year" in 2019 by *Interviews & Reviews*.

Her latest series, "Hearts of Honor," centers on the three Fuller brothers and includes *Her Rebel Heart*, *Her Steadfast Heart*, and *Her Guarded Heart*.

Shar has done numerous countrywide book signings and has participated in several interviews on television and radio. She loves to speak for community organizations, libraries, church groups, and women's conferences. In her church, she is active in women's ministries, regularly facilitating Bible studies and other events. Shar and her husband Cecil live in Spring Lake, Michigan, with their beloved collie, Cody.

Shar loves to hear from her readers. If you wish to contact her as a potential speaker or would simply like to chat with her, please send her an e-mail at SharleneMacLaren@Yahoo.com. She will do her best to answer in a timely manner.

Additional resources:

www.SharleneMacLaren.com

www.instagram.com/sharlenemaclaren

twitter.com/sharzy_lu?lang=en

www.facebook.com/groups/43124814557
(Sharlene MacLaren & Friends)

www.whitakerhouse.com/book-authors/sharlene-maclaren

QUESTIONS FOR GROUP DISCUSSION

How did you like the story as a whole?

What did you like best (or least) about this book?

Since this was a faith-based novel, did you find the message too "preachy" or just the opposite, not enough of a clear gospel message?

What character(s) seemed most believable to you? Why?

Did the plot keep you engaged?

Did this storyline or the writing style remind you of any other books or authors you've read?

Share a favorite quote from the book—something that truly resonated with you.

What emotions did this story evoke in you?

What do you think is the primary message the author wants to convey?

Would you recommend this book to others?

Welcome to Our House!

We Have a Special Gift for You ...

It is our privilege and pleasure to share in your love of Christian fiction by publishing books that enrich your life and encourage your faith.

To show our appreciation, we invite you to sign up to receive a specially selected **Reader Appreciation Gift**, with our compliments. Just go to the Web address at the bottom of this page.

God bless you as you seek a deeper walk with Him!

WE HAVE A GIFT FOR YOU. VISIT:

whpub.me/fictionthx

WHITAKER HOUSE